R.L. STINE'S
DANGEROUS GIRLS

including

Dangerous

Girls

and

Dangerous

Girls

The Taste of Night

Table of Contents

Dangerous Girls

A novel by
R.L. STINE

HARPER
TEEN
An Imprint of HarperCollins*Publishers*
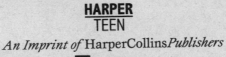 Parachute

*For Robert O. Warren,
who always asks the right questions,
even if I don't always have the right answers!*

Contents

Part Three

Part One

Chapter One

The Most Dangerous Day

*S*ummer *can't* be over already. Do I really have to leave Camp Blue Moon?

That's what Destiny Weller was thinking on the day she started to become a vampire.

She watched the yellow bus rumble away, carrying the last of the campers with it. The bus bounced over the narrow dirt road, then turned and disappeared into the trees.

"Hey, we're free!" someone yelled. "The little animals are gone!"

"Party time!"

"Who has car keys? Can we get a keg? Can we at least get some six-packs?"

A red afternoon sun was sinking behind the trees. The air suddenly carried a chill, a hint that summer was nearly over.

Destiny turned and searched for her sister, Livvy. The counselors gathered around the grassy hill that overlooked the road, laughing and joking, hugging each other, celebrating the end of the camp season.

She spotted Livvy in a circle of girls clustered around Renz. He was flirting with them, hugging them one by one. All the girls adored Renz, and why not?

He was so good-looking, tall and tanned, with that wavy, black hair, those dark, bedroom eyes—devilish eyes—that irresistible smile. So charming and funny and . . . grown-up.

Not like the other guys in camp, Destiny thought. Not like the counselors and junior counselors whose idea of a good time was going skinny-dipping in the lake after lights-out, or putting snakes in each other's beds.

Renz was too sophisticated for that.

Destiny didn't really know much about him. She knew that his real name was Lorenzo Angelini, and he had just a hint of an Italian accent, which made him even sexier. He had been hired as head waterfront counselor. But when Uncle Bob, the owner of Camp Blue Moon, suddenly took sick just before the kids arrived, Renz became head counselor.

"I see who you're staring at." Nakeisha Johnson came up behind Destiny and grabbed her shoulders, startling her.

Destiny laughed. "He's looking good in those tennis whites, isn't he!"

"Summer's too short," Nakeisha said. "Think I could follow him home? Maybe he'll adopt me."

"Actually, I'm watching my sister," Destiny said. "Do you believe those short shorts? You can see half her butt."

Nakeisha gazed at the crowd of girls around Renz. "Well don't turn green or anything. You know you're jealous. Renz spent so much time with Livvy."

"*All* the guys spent time with Livvy," Destiny replied. She watched Renz give Livvy a farewell hug, holding her close, his hands all over her bare back.

"Stop shaking your head," Nakeisha said. "How can identical twins be so different?"

"I told you. We're fraternal. Not identical," Destiny said.

"Oh. Right. Well, that explains it," Nakeisha replied, rolling her eyes.

"I'm fifteen minutes older," Destiny said. "See. I've got to act like the older sister."

A yellow jacket buzzed around them.

Destiny swatted it away. High in the darkening sky, a flock of honking geese flew in perfect V-formation, making its way from Canada. On the road below, the camp station wagon sped past, tires spinning up dust, jammed with counselors heading to town to buy beer.

"Everyone's acting happy, but this is so sad," Nakeisha said. "Tomorrow we'll all go our separate ways. I won't see you anymore." She turned and wrapped Destiny in a hug.

Destiny hugged her back. "You've been such a good friend. I really am going to miss you."

Both girls had tears in their eyes.

"At least you're going home to New York," Destiny said, letting go. She ran a hand through her short, straight blond hair. "Not boring little Dark Springs, Mass."

Nakeisha wiped tear stains off her cheeks. "I just got something in my eye, that's all. It's not like I hate saying good-bye or anything. You've got my e-mail address, right? And my cell number?"

Destiny nodded. "We can Instant Message each other."

"Maybe you can come to New York for Thanksgiving?"

Destiny laughed. "Yeah, if I win the lottery or something."

"Hey, know what? I'll be doing college visits in September and October. I know I'll be in Boston. Maybe I can come through Dark Springs."

"Excellent!" Destiny said. Over Nakeisha's shoulder, she saw Livvy, cigarette in hand, lip-locked with Cory Field, one of her many admirers. His arm around her shoulders, Cory began to lead Livvy toward the trees by the lake.

"Livvy—wait!" Destiny shouted. She took off running. "Hey, Liv—stop!"

Her sister turned and took a long drag on the cigarette. Cory kept his arm around her. "Hi, Dee. What's up?" Livvy asked.

"How's it going?" Cory said. "Pretty quiet without the kids, huh?"

Destiny nodded. "Liv, you haven't started packing," she said.

"Yeah, I know."

Destiny stared at her sister. Livvy did everything she could to look different from her twin. Destiny wore her hair short, so Livvy kept hers long, letting it flow down over her shoulders. Destiny hardly ever wore makeup, just a little blush and lip gloss from time to time. Livvy liked purple or dark red lipstick, and her biggest suitcase this summer had been filled with eye makeup.

Livvy had one nostril pierced, usually wore three different earrings in each ear, and loved to wear rings on every finger. She wanted to get a butterfly tattoo on her shoulder, but held off, knowing her dad would give her all kinds of grief.

Destiny would never admit it to anyone, but she secretly admired her sister for having so much style.

Livvy was always trying to give her a makeover. One night last year when they were juniors, she allowed Livvy to work on her—lipstick, mascara, even streaks in her hair.

When she had finished, Livvy started to smile. "I don't think so," she said, holding her hand over her mouth. "I don't think so."

She turned the mirror to Destiny, and they both started to laugh. They collapsed to the floor, knocking over Livvy's makeup mirror, laughing until tears rolled down their cheeks.

Destiny thought about that night often. It was just a few weeks before their mother died, a few weeks before tragedy turned their lives upside down. And it was a night she felt so close to her sister, a night their closeness overcame their many differences.

Now Livvy tossed her cigarette down and stamped it out with the toe of her sandal. "You're already packed?" she asked Destiny.

Destiny nodded. "Well, yeah. Dad and Mikey will be here at the crack of dawn tomorrow. You should get started. Your stuff was spread all over your cabin."

Livvy grinned. "I know. I'm a slob." She and Cory exchanged glances.

"I'll help you, if you want," Destiny offered.

"Thanks. I'll do it later. We're all going to meet by the lake. Did someone tell you? The counselors and the J.C.s. We're going to stay up all night and get totally trashed."

Cory flashed Destiny a thumbs-up and a toothy grin. "Last chance to party."

Destiny sighed. "Well, can't you just pack up first?"

Livvy snapped at her. "I said later, *Mom*!" Her expression immediately softened. "Oh. Sorry."

But the word hung in the air between them.

And they shared the same thought: *We don't have a mom.*

Our mom killed herself last year.

Livvy squeezed Destiny's hand. "Sorry, Dee. I'll be there in a few minutes. Promise," she said. Then she tugged Cory toward the woods.

Destiny turned and made her way up the hill to the cabins. The sun had dipped behind the trees. Crickets began to chirp. Renz's circle of girls had dwindled to two admirers. He raised his eyes to Destiny as she passed, and waved at her.

Destiny waved back. She saw him watching her as she reached the main lodge at the top of the hill. He's been watching me all summer, she thought. But he's never invited me for one of his late-night walks by the lake. I had to hear about them from the other junior counselors.

And Livvy. Yes, Livvy fell under his spell too. And it's no secret he spent a lot of time with her.

Is Nakeisha right? Am I jealous?

Well, yes.

She saw a group of counselors building a fire in the campfire circle. Ronnie Herbert, a J.C. Destiny had hung out with—just a friend— came running up, a blue-and-white Camp Blue Moon T-shirt pulled down over his baggy khaki shorts. Ronnie took a scrap of paper from his shorts pocket. "Can I have your e-mail, Destiny? Can we keep in touch?"

"Of course," she said. "You know, Providence isn't *that* far from Dark Springs. We could meet sometime."

"Cool." Ronnie scribbled down her e-mail address. Then he hugged her. "This is so hard, saying good-bye to everybody." He turned and saw Nakeisha walking toward the campfire circle. "Hey, Keish, wait up!" He took off after her, waving his slip of paper in the air.

Destiny made her way past the campers' cabins, empty and forlorn looking, some of the doors hanging open, revealing the bare bunk beds with their flat, gray mattresses. At the end of the row, she pulled open the door to Iroquois, the cabin she had shared with her campers.

She spotted a red hair scrunchy on the floor, the only sign that six eight-year-old girls had once lived here. Destiny's bags were lined up neatly in front of her bunk.

She sighed. Should I go across to Arapaho and start to pack up Livvy's stuff? I know Livvy will wait till morning and keep Dad, Mikey, and me waiting.

She considered it for a second, then decided, *No way.* That's *her* problem. I really *am* starting to think like a mom.

It's my last night at Camp Blue Moon, my last night before I have to go back to the real world—and I'm going to have FUN.

Destiny changed into jeans and a camp sweatshirt. Then she hurried back outside to help build the fire, unaware of the horror that awaited her.

Chapter Two

A Romantic Walk

By eleven o'clock, the campfire had burned down to a pile of crackling red and purple embers. The beer had run out—a mountain of empty cans poked up over the rim of a metal trash can—and bottles of red wine were being passed around a circle of six or seven counselors.

Destiny joined a group of junior counselors who had their own circle around their own small fire and were singing the familiar camp songs they had been forced to sing all summer, but adding crude and extremely gross new lyrics. They laughed and hugged each other and sang under the full moon, their faces reflecting the dying firelight.

Several couples had wandered away from the big campfire to make their way through the trees to the lake. Destiny saw Livvy disappear into the woods again with Cory Field.

"Good night. I'm outta here. Gonna get my

beauty sleep." Nakeisha crushed a Coke can in her hand and tossed it onto the pile of cans in the trash. "Catch you in the morning, Dee. Don't leave without saying good-bye, okay?"

Destiny laughed. "We've already said good-bye twelve times!" She watched her friend climb the hill to the cabins.

I'm going to catch some sleep too, Destiny decided. I know Dad and Mikey will be here at six A.M. on the dot.

She waved good night to her friends, climbed to her feet, and began to walk to her cabin. She was halfway up the hill when a figure stepped out of the shadows and blocked her path.

"Renz. Hi," Destiny said, nearly walking into him.

"I've been looking for you," he said softly.

"Really? Me?" She could feel her cheeks growing hot. *Don't sound like such a jerk.*

His smile was dazzling, even in the darkness. She could feel his eyes burn into hers. "It's still early. You're not checking out, are you?"

"Well . . ."

He took her hand. "Want to take a walk? Down by the lake? We haven't had a chance to talk for a long time."

"Yes. Okay," she heard herself say.

Renz squeezed her hand. "Good," he whispered.

He slid his arm around Destiny's shoulders and guided her down the hill. He pointed at some counselors dancing around the dying fire. "Have you ever seen such bad dancing? It's a good thing it's dark and they can't really see each other."

Destiny frowned. "They've had too many beers to care."

He stared hard at her. "You don't like to drink?"

She shook her head. "One beer and I start giggling like a ten-year-old."

Why am I telling him this?

She followed him down the grassy hill to the narrow dirt path that led through the trees. "Isn't it a beautiful night?" He pulled her close as they walked. "But also a sad night. No one wants to go home."

"It was an awesome summer," she replied. "Livvy and I . . . we had a very bad year. Camp was the perfect escape."

Renz lowered his hand from her shoulders and slid it around her waist. "You want to escape from your home?"

He helped her over a fallen log. They followed the path past a row of low pine shrubs. "No. Of course not," she said. "I'm looking forward to going back. You know. Senior year and everything."

"It's so nice down here," he said softly, bringing his face close to hers. "The pine needles smell so fresh, and I love the way the lake glows under the moonlight. Let's pretend we're not going home tomorrow, Destiny. Let's pretend we're going to stay here in the woods forever."

She laughed.

Is he for real?

He led her to a broad tree stump near the water, and they sat down. The lake shimmered like silver under the light of the pale full moon. He wrapped his hands around hers and held them in her lap.

My hands are ice cold. Can he tell how nervous I am?

"The lake looks beautiful without a hundred screaming kids splashing around in it," she said.

He flashed her his dazzling smile. "I've been watching you all summer," he whispered.

She raised her eyes to his. "You have?"

"I hoped we would be able to spend time getting to know one another."

Destiny rolled her eyes. "It's the last night of camp, Renz. What makes me think I was the last girl on your list?"

He didn't answer. Instead, he placed a hand gently under her chin, brought her face to his, and kissed her.

A short kiss, but sweet.

Destiny blinked. "You're very nice," she said. "But I know you've brought every female counselor and J.C. down here this summer."

"They weren't like you," he whispered.

"Oh, right," she said.

"But I'm telling the truth," he insisted. "They weren't like you, Destiny. *Believe me. They weren't like you.*"

Chapter Three

"It Won't Hurt for Long"

Renz kissed her again, longer this time, holding his hands on the sides of her face. He saw her eyes close. He felt her body relax.

She's enjoying it. She's beginning to feel what I feel.

But when she finally pulled away, Destiny laughed. "You're much too old for me, Renz." She squinted at him. "How old are you, anyway? Nineteen? Twenty?"

He grinned. "I turned two hundred last month. You're right. Much too old for you."

"Well, I know one thing. You're not like the guys in my high school. Where did you grow up? In Italy?"

Renz nodded. *I don't want to talk. I didn't bring you down here to talk.*

"I grew up in the north, in the hills where there is poverty—and strangeness."

He squeezed her hands. The pale moonlight

sparkled in her blond hair.

"Strangeness? Like what?"

"The people in my village had many superstitions and many fears," he told her, speaking softly, holding her close. "They were most terrified of the ancient vampires who lived in the caves that circled our village. The vampires were said to fly out at night in the shapes of blackbirds and bats. They would attack the villagers—men, women, and children—and empty their veins of blood."

Destiny gave him a playful shove. "You're trying to scare me, right?"

Renz nodded. "Yes. Actually, I was born in Philadelphia."

She laughed at his joke.

Pulling her closer, Renz's skin tingled with excitement. His mouth, his throat—they suddenly felt so dry. . . . He felt alert. Alive. Ready.

He held her by her arms and lowered his face to hers. He whispered, "Do you believe in vampires, Laura?"

With a short gasp, Destiny jerked her head back. "Excuse me? Vampires? And who's Laura?"

He stared at her, licking his lips. His whole

body tingled. He knew his hands would tremble if he let go of her. "Laura? Well . . . you remind me of someone, that's all."

He pulled her close again. Her expression softened. "I've thought about you, too, this summer," she said, avoiding his eyes.

She's shy like Laura, he thought. Not like her twin.

"And did you notice me watching you?" he asked eagerly.

She hesitated. "Well . . ."

He kissed her again. Lightly. He was so afraid to move too fast. He had waited so long to bring her here, to bring her to this moment.

But now the moment was here.

"I'm so happy I found you again, Laura," he whispered, gazing into her eyes. "I've been searching for you for so many years. I knew I'd find you again."

Those words made her struggle to pull free. But he grasped her arms tightly and held her in front of him. "Don't pull away, Laura. Tonight we are reunited."

"Renz—what the hell are you talking about? Let go of me! Now you're really scaring me."

"Don't be scared, darling. I know you have

waited for this moment as I have. It won't hurt for long. I promise it won't hurt for long. And then we will be together once more, together forever."

She squirmed, struggled to swing her arms, to lash out at him with both fists. "Let go. Let go, you creep! Are you crazy?"

Staring into her eyes, he let her struggle. Staring deeply . . . penetrating her mind.

She uttered a long sigh and settled back, limp in his arms.

"That's better, Laura. You feel calm now. You don't want to resist me. Tonight under the full moon I shall drink your blood, and you shall drink mine. Two long drinks, that's all it will take, darling. And then you will be Laura again. Then you will be immortal like me. And we will live together forever."

Destiny made a weak attempt to squirm free.

"Shh," he whispered. "Don't try to move. Don't try to think, darling. Keep staring into my eyes. That's right. See? Your mind is emptying. You remember nothing. You are floating in a cloud."

Bleating sounds escaped her lips, like a tiny, frightened animal caught in a trap. Her head fell back, her throat pale in the moonlight.

Pale and soft. And delicious.

"I have fogged your mind, and you won't remember a word I've said. You won't even remember *me* until I want you to. Until I am ready to fly with you, to spend every night—for eternity—with you."

Renz leaned forward, lowering his face to her throat. "You feel nice, don't you, Laura? You feel dizzy and happy, and the stars are spinning so gracefully, aren't they? It's all so beautiful and soft, isn't it, darling? So romantic. You always were so romantic."

Her soft cries stopped. Destiny stared up at him open-mouthed, her eyes glassy, her chest moving rapidly up and down.

Renz gently pulled down the neck of her sweatshirt. His curved fangs made a wet *slick* sound as they slid down from his gums. He worked his tongue over the fangs, trying to wet them. But his mouth was dry as sand.

Finally, he could resist no longer. He lowered his head, pushed out his bristled tongue, and licked her neck. Licked it, his rough tongue scraping over the soft skin. Licked it hungrily.

Then he opened his mouth wide and with a

groan from deep in his gut, brought the fangs down. Pierced the pale skin. Sank the sharp fangs deep into her throat.

And began to drink.

Chapter Four
"What Does He Want With Me?"

Destiny gazed up at the purple night sky. White dots of light shimmered and danced. The full moon, surrounded by glimmering stars, grew brighter, brighter . . . until she had to lower her eyes.

She felt Renz's hot forehead against her chin. His thick black hair tickled her flesh. She heard a lapping sound, like water running. No. Like a dog drinking noisily from a bowl.

Destiny felt a gentle pain at her throat, softer than the bite of a mosquito. With a sigh, Renz raised his head.

What was that dark liquid spilling down his chin?

Destiny struggled to think. But the moon shone so brightly—like a harsh spotlight—and the stars danced so giddily, she felt dizzy, sleepy. She couldn't focus.

She liked Renz's smile, his wide eyes, his

forehead gleaming with jewels of sweat. But why were his teeth curling over his chin? And what was that dark liquid that smelled so sharp and metallic?

Focus. Focus.

She blinked hard. But it all seemed fuzzy, far away.

She gazed into Renz's eyes, glowing black, staring down at her. And as she stared, she realized to her amazement that she shared his thoughts.

She saw a young, black-haired boy, six or seven, bare chested, in ragged, stained trousers that came down just below his knees. The boy, dirty faced, ribs poking out, carried a fishing pole much too long for him. He dragged it along a dusty road.

Destiny knew it was Renz—Renz as a young boy. Renz in the northern Italian village where he grew up in poverty.

It's as if he is showing me his life, she realized. He's sharing his story with me.

She saw the boy return home slump-shouldered, tears running down his cheeks. No fish on the line. Destiny recoiled as she saw the grizzled, weary-looking man—Renz's father—give the boy a backhanded slap that sent him reeling into the wall.

Ouch. She could feel the slap, feel the pain spread over her cheek.

She tried to blink the pain away. And when she opened her eyes again, the boy was on a ship, ocean waves tossing against its gray sides. Frothy water washed over the swaying deck where the boy—young Renz—stood so uncertainly at the rail, frightened, one little face in a crowd of older, frightened faces.

Destiny could see the pictures clearly in her mind.

She saw the boy covering his tattered clothes with a heavy, gray overcoat that was much too big for him. Saw him arriving in New York City, then trudging through the streets, dodging horse-drawn carts and carriages, everyone dressed in black, the street a sea of black hats, all the men wearing hats.

How long ago this must have been.

She closed her eyes, and now the boy had grown into a young man. She recognized Renz—his proud way of standing, his loping walk, the black hair bouncing on his head as he strode down the street.

She watched as Renz suddenly turned into a narrow alley crammed with trash and stacks of old newspapers. And then she saw another man, lanky and pale, with straight white hair pulled back in a loose-flowing ponytail. The man had silver-gray eyes, a stubble of white beard. He wore a navy-blue suit and had a navy cape draped over one shoulder.

Destiny watched the two shake hands. She understood. Renz recognized the man from his ship, the ship that carried him to America. Yes, the man was from Renz's village.

Destiny cried out as the happy reunion suddenly turned violent.

The white-haired man pushed Renz against the building wall. Destiny watched the yellowed fangs curl down. Watched the man sink his teeth into Renz's throat and drink, blood running down the front of his dark suit.

Then Renz bit hard into the old man's neck and began to lap up his blood. They were drinking each other's blood! She couldn't bear to watch.

She closed her eyes, but the images continued to flood her mind. She saw Renz prowling the streets once again, but this time at night, only at night. She watched him attack birds and squirrels in the park, sink his teeth into their bellies, and drink.

And she felt his thirst, felt the overpowering need that forced him to seek out victims—human victims—and drink, drink until the thirst was momentarily quenched.

She saw him struggling to keep his secret. And then she felt his fear as he realized his secret had been uncovered. Men were collecting weapons, preparing to hunt him down. She felt his terror, and then she watched him flee.

She saw a blur of towns and villages cloaked by the dark of night. And she watched him settle far away from the city, far away from those who meant to destroy him. A small New England town where the winters were long and the days were short.

Another blink. She saw Renz in the moonlight with a beautiful young woman. The woman dressed in a simple blue gown, her blond hair flowing down the back of her dress.

She looks like me, Destiny realized. And at once, she knew the young woman's name: Laura. The high cheekbones, the green eyes, the fine blond hair . . . Laura resembles me so much.

Except for the sadness in her eyes.

Such sad eyes.

Destiny saw how much Renz loved Laura. He adored her. And then in another blink of her eyes, she saw Laura's open casket. The sad eyes shut forever. It happened so quickly.

She saw Renz's angry tears. And heard his angry, desperate vow to find Laura again. To be reunited with her no matter how many decades or centuries it took.

Destiny saw it all as the stars swirled above her and the sky continued to spin.

But I'm not Laura, she told herself, the world so distant now as if she saw it through a curtain of gauze.

I'm not Laura.

So what does he want with me?

Chapter Five

"I'll Follow You Home"

Renz gazed down at her, breathing deeply, feeling the cool night air brush against his hot face. He licked his lips, the rich, iron-tasting liquid so sweet on his tongue.

The lake lapped gently against the grassy shore. Trees whispered and shook. Somewhere a night dove cooed. Renz felt alive again; alive and strong.

He felt happy, almost giddy. Reunited with his lost love.

He wanted to shout it into the wind. He wanted to fly over the lake, crying her name.

"Laura . . . Laura . . . !"

But first we must finish, he told himself. I have drunk deeply. And now it is her turn.

I'm here, darling. I know you have waited as long and impatiently as I have.

He had searched for Destiny at the last full moon. But to his dismay, she had left camp on a canoeing overnight. He had to wait four long weeks for the full moon to rise again.

And now finally, here she was in his arms, ready to take the final step.

"Oh." He raised his head abruptly, hearing the snap of a twig on the ground.

No. No. No.

He pulled himself up. Tilted Destiny's head up. Slid his arm around her shoulders.

He could smell someone approaching. A girl. He could hear the blood pumping through her veins before she even appeared.

He turned as Nakeisha stepped into view.

"Destiny? I was looking for you. I forgot—" Nakeisha saw Renz with his arm around Destiny. "Oh. Sorry. I didn't know. I mean . . . catch you later."

Nakeisha spun around and darted into the thicket of trees.

Had the spell been broken?

Renz turned back to his love, his prize.

Destiny sat up, shaking her head. "Wow. I feel so dizzy."

"Don't move," Renz whispered. "You're okay." He reached to hold her, but Destiny jumped up and stepped away from him. "Come back, Destiny. Just for a few moments."

She blinked at him. "No. Sorry. It's late. And I feel so . . . weird."

She waved to him, blinking in confusion. Then she took off, running through the tall wet grass, moonlight reflecting off her hair.

He watched until she vanished behind tall pines. Then he opened his mouth in a cry of fury.

So close. So close, my darling Laura. But you didn't finish.

His skin tingled. The hair on the back of his neck prickled. He could still taste her blood on his tongue.

We *will* be together for eternity, Laura.

I will follow you. I will follow you home.

You won't know me. You won't remember me. So it will be easy.

Our blood will mingle. I promise.

I will come. I will come for you.

I won't let you get away this time.

Part Two

Chapter Six

"Did She Stay Out of Trouble This Summer?"

$\mathcal{D}$estiny watched her dad's SUV rumble up the hill toward the cabins. "Crack of dawn," she muttered, shivering in the damp morning air. *I knew he'd be the first to arrive.*

"Hey, Livvy!" She cupped her hands and shouted into Arapaho. "Wake up! Dad and Mikey are here."

"Give me a break. I'm packing," her sister shouted back.

Destiny yawned and hugged herself, wrapping the sleeves of her camp sweatshirt around her shoulders. *Why am I so tired this morning?*

I see Dad didn't get the front fender fixed. And the car is covered with dust. He probably didn't wash it all summer.

Destiny's mom had always taken care of the practical matters, allowing her husband to spend all his thoughts on his veterinary practice and his research.

With Mom gone, the car will just disappear under a mountain of dirt, Destiny thought. "Hey, Liv—do you need any help?"

No answer.

Destiny turned and saw Chris Harvey, the lanky, blond-haired arts-and-crafts counselor, bent over, throwing up noisily against the side of his cabin.

"Late night, Harvey?" someone shouted from one of the cabins.

"How about a beer, Harvey?"

Harvey was in no position to reply. Destiny watched him stumble into his cabin, wiping his face with his T-shirt.

Car doors slammed. She turned and saw Mikey come bursting from the car. Slipping in the dewy grass, she ran down to meet him.

"Hey, you're tall!" she said, wrapping him in a hug. She brushed her hands through his thick, coppery hair.

"Dad got me a new game," he said, holding up his Game Boy. "See? It's like a NASCAR race."

"I haven't seen you all summer, and you just want to show me a game?" She hugged him again.

"Yuck. Stop doing that." He pulled back.

"It's a really awesome game. I'll show you how to play on the way back." He glanced around. "Where's Livvy?"

"Packing. Go help her." She gave him a shove toward their sister's cabin.

He took off toward Arapaho. "Hey, Liv, we're here! Check out my new game!"

Destiny turned to see her dad come striding up the hill, arms outstretched, a smile on his face. His glasses glinted red in the early-morning sunlight. The thick tuft of gray hair bobbing on top of his head was unbrushed as usual. His heavy gray eyebrows moved up and down like two fat caterpillars above the glasses.

"I believe I know you from somewhere," he said.

Destiny hugged him hard. She pressed her cheek against his. "Ouch. You didn't shave."

He rubbed his chin. "Guess I forgot."

His beard has turned white, Destiny observed. And he looks so tired.

She squinted at him. "Have you been putting in more long nights in your lab?"

He nodded. "Pretty much." His smile was sad. "With everyone gone and the house empty, what else should I do?"

Destiny swallowed hard. "Well, we'll all be home now. It won't be so quiet anymore."

"That's what I'm afraid of!" he said. Behind the glasses, his pale blue eyes flashed.

They both laughed.

Livvy emerged from her cabin in shorts and a sleeveless T-shirt, dragging a suitcase, a backpack, and three other canvas bags, clothes spilling over the tops. "I couldn't fit it all in," she said.

She dropped everything and ran to hug her dad. "Hey, I missed you!"

He stepped back to study her. "You look positively healthy."

Livvy frowned. "Is that a compliment?"

He continued to stare. "No tattoos?"

"Of course not, Daddy. I promised, remember?"

He turned to Destiny. "Did she stay out of trouble this summer?"

"No way," Livvy said before Destiny could reply. "Why would I want to stay out of trouble?"

Dr. Weller chuckled. He raised his eyes to Livvy's cabin. "We're missing one family member. Where's Mikey?"

Livvy rolled her eyes. "He found some new

kind of worm he's never seen before under my bed. He was following it around the cabin, studying it. He's just like you, Dad, fascinated by animals and insects."

"Our cabins are a great place to study mutant insect life," Destiny said. "He could be in there for hours."

"Mikey is definitely growing up," Livvy said. "He used to *eat* the worms. Now he just follows them."

"Let's start packing up the car," Dr. Weller said, massaging the back of his neck. He sighed. "We've got a long drive home."

"Dad looks so much older," Livvy said. She whispered even though they were upstairs in their room.

"It's just because his whiskers turned white," Destiny said.

Livvy shook her head. "He looks really tired. He's kinda stooped over. And didn't you notice how he keeps sighing all the time? His whole face is different. It's like sunken or something."

Destiny peered down the stairs to make sure the door was closed. The twins shared a long, low room above the garage. It had been empty storage space when the Wellers moved in and the girls were little. But their father built walls, painted, set down carpet, and turned it into a big room with lots of privacy that they could share.

Destiny loved the room because it was like having her own apartment. When her friends came over, they always hung out there.

"I think Dad's been working too hard," Destiny said, stuffing dirty camp clothes into a white laundry bag. "He didn't take any vacation at all this summer."

Livvy, sprawled on her bed, watched Destiny unpack. "He's been strange ever since Mom died, like a zombie or something."

"We all miss Mom," Destiny said softly. "It's just weird being back in this house without her. I keep expecting her to come up here and help us unpack."

"Me too," Livvy whispered.

They both fell silent. Destiny checked the bottom of her suitcase. Empty. She had finished unpacking. Her sister's bags sat against the wall, untouched.

"And what is Mikey's problem?" Livvy asked. "He played that dumb Game Boy game all the way home and barely spoke to us."

Destiny shrugged. "I'm worried about him. I asked him how he liked his day camp, and he said it was totally boring. He said he didn't make any new friends because he didn't want to. And he didn't learn to dive because there was too much chlorine in the pool."

"Oh, wow," Livvy said, shaking her head. "Is it shrink time for Mikey?"

Destiny sighed. "You know how close he was to Mom. And he's only eight years old, the poor kid."

She crossed the room and dropped down on the edge of her sister's bed. "It isn't going to be easy, Liv. We're really going to have to help out a lot more here at home."

Livvy leaned back against the headboard of her bed, crossing her legs in front of her. "Tell me something I don't know. I already quit the cheerleading squad so I could be home with Mikey afternoons, didn't I?"

She sighed. "This is our senior year. It's supposed to be totally awesome. You know. Fun? Exciting?"

"We'll have fun," Destiny said, reaching out and squeezing her sister's arm. "Don't worry.

We can still have fun."

She turned when she heard heavy footsteps on the stairs. "Hey—who's there?" she called.

"It's me!" a deep voice boomed in a heavy foreign accent. "I've come to drink your blood!"

Chapter Seven

She Can't Stop Screaming

Destiny jumped up and ran to the stairwell. Peering down, she saw their friend Ari Stark halfway up the stairs. Ari, short and stocky, his serious face topped by curly black hair, wore baggy khaki cargo shorts and a T-shirt with a grinning mummy across the front.

"Hey, what's up?" he called. "Check this out." He held up a DVD. Destiny read the title: *Curse of the Vampire's Daughter*.

Livvy came over to greet Ari. She groaned when she saw the DVD. "I am *so* not in the mood for another one of your gross vampire movies."

"But it's Part Three," Ari protested. His gums showed when he smiled. "It's the best one. The special effects are awesome."

Livvy tossed back her hair. "I'm, like, sick of awesome effects. What's so great about awesome effects?"

Ari looked hurt. Horror movies were his life.

"We haven't seen you all summer," Destiny said, "and you just want to sit and stare at a movie?"

"Yeah," Ari replied. "Well, hey. How was camp? Did they show any movies?"

"We didn't have time for movies," Livvy told him. "We were too busy having sex every night."

Ari's cheeks turned red.

Destiny and Livvy shared a smile. *He believes us.*

"And what did *you* do all summer?" Livvy asked him. "You have a paper route or something?"

"Ha ha." Ari's face was still red. "I just hung out. You know. I helped my dad a little at the restaurant. It's been kinda scary here in town."

Destiny's eyes went wide. "Scary?"

Livvy's cell phone rang. She ran to her desk and picked it up. "Yeah. Hi. Where are you? *Our* front yard? Well, yeah. Come up. We haven't seen you in months." She clicked off the phone.

"Who was that?" Destiny asked.

"Everybody."

* * *

"I missed you so much." Ana-Li May wrapped her arms around Destiny. "I kept trying your cell for weeks, but you never answered."

"The camp was deep in the woods," Destiny said. "My phone was useless. I missed you too. . . . What's different about you?" She stepped back to study her friend.

Ana-Li was tiny and thin, like a delicate bird. For such a little girl, she had a surprisingly deep, womanly voice. She also had a warm, winning smile, and enough energy for five people.

She gave Destiny a playful shove. "There's nothing different about me. You just forgot what I look like. You know. Out of sight, out of mind."

"I tried to e-mail you," Destiny said, "but my laptop—"

"So how was camp? Meet any great guys?"

"Not really. I made some good friends, though."

"Too bad," Ana-Li said. She waved to Livvy across the room. "I struck out too. That physics workshop I went to at M.I.T.? Geek City."

"Let's talk later. Just you and me," Destiny said. "I love what you did with your hair. Wish I could have such perfectly straight black hair."

"That's so funny," Ana-Li said. "I always wanted to be a blond."

Destiny tugged her friend's hair. "Maybe we should trade."

They both laughed.

Destiny turned to say hi to her other friends. They were all talking at once, their voices ringing off the low ceilings of the room above the garage. They sprawled on the cream-colored carpet, sat on the long, cushiony couch that divided the room between Destiny's territory and her sister's half, and perched on the edges of the beds.

Destiny felt a wave of happiness sweep over her. The house had felt cold and gloomy last spring when her mother . . . when her mother killed herself. So many tears. So many long silences.

And after it had happened, their friends suddenly treated the twins differently. No one made jokes. Everyone acted tense and awkward. The girls felt kids were watching them whenever they walked down the hall at school.

We weren't us anymore. We were the girls whose mother committed suicide.

Eight weeks of working at Camp Blue Moon

had helped Destiny get away from all that. And now her friends' voices warmed her, made her feel safe and comfortable in her house again.

Standing by the door, Destiny gazed around the room at everyone.

On one end of the couch, Ari was talking with Courtney DeWitt, gesturing wildly with his hands, as usual, telling her about a horror convention his cousin had taken him to.

Courtney hadn't changed a bit over the summer, Destiny saw. She was still skinny but round-faced, with her straight brown hair pulled back in a high ponytail, the kind everyone had in fourth grade.

"I hate this round face," she once complained to Destiny. "Every time my dad calls me Babyface, I just want to slug him!" Now she kept tugging at a hole in the knee of her jeans as she listened to Ari.

Destiny turned to Ross Starr on the other end of the couch. Ross had shaved his blond hair short over the summer, and everyone had to comment on it.

"What did *you* do this summer?" Destiny called to him.

Ross lowered the Mountain Dew can he'd

been chugging from. He flashed Destiny his winning smile. "I was a lifeguard. What a blast. Check out this tan."

"A lifeguard? For real? Where?"

"Jersey shore. My aunt has a house there."

"Did you rescue anyone?" Ari asked.

Ross's eyes flashed. "Well, no. But I had to give mouth-to-mouth a few times."

Everyone laughed. Destiny studied Ross. She'd been thinking about him all summer. "You've been working out?"

He grinned and flexed his biceps. "Check out this new bod. I think I want to live forever!"

"Why?" Ari asked.

"Think of all the girls I could have!" Ross smiled.

Livvy slid next to Ross on the couch arm. "You're bad," she said. She tugged playfully on the tiny silver hoop in his ear. "Did you miss me this summer?"

Ross squinted at her. "Which one are you?" More laughter.

Destiny groaned. Is Livvy going to come on to Ross now? Does she have to have *every* guy?

Livvy and Ross were laughing about something. Livvy had her arm loosely draped around his shoulder.

I can't believe she's doing this in front of Courtney, Destiny thought. Livvy knows that Courtney is crazy about Ross. And she knows I have a crush on him too.

Fletch Green sat on the floor at the other end of the couch, his long legs crossed in front of him. He was talking into a cell phone.

When Fletch turned off his phone, Destiny made her way over to him. "You and Ross had summer basketball practice?"

He scratched his wavy, carrot-colored hair. "Didn't you hear? Coach Bauer called off summer practice. He's still messed up about his wife."

"Oh. Right."

Coach Bauer's wife died suddenly near the end of the school year. Marjory Bauer wasn't that old, forty-eight or forty-nine, like the coach.

Bauer took a leave from school. Destiny remembered the rumors about him. That he went berserk or something. That neighbors could hear him talking loudly to himself late at night. That he had lost all interest in coaching the team.

"So are you guys gonna be any good this

year?" Destiny asked.

Fletch shrugged. "Ross and I are the only seniors. We'll have to step it up."

"Any more Coke?" Bree Daniel called from across the room. Sitting on the floor across from Ari and Courtney, Bree waved her empty soda can in the air.

Destiny really couldn't stand Bree, with her screechy mouse voice and her piles of streaky blond hair that fell over her face, and her pierced eyebrows that always made Destiny cringe. Bree had recently become Livvy's best friend. Or, as Destiny put it, Livvy's Bad Influence. Bree was the one urging Livvy to get a tattoo. And Livvy had never smoked a cigarette until she started hanging out with Bree.

"There's a kind of bug that spits out juice that makes human skin dissolve," Ari was telling Courtney. "I saw a show about it on the Discovery Channel."

"Ari, get a life," Fletch said. His cell phone rang. He raised it to his ear.

"I'll go downstairs and bring up some more drinks," Destiny said, making her way to the stairs. "And I think we have some bags of nacho chips." She raised her eyes to Livvy, who was practically in Ross's lap. "Hey, Liv, where's Dad? Have you seen him?"

Livvy shrugged in reply. She didn't take her eyes off Ross.

Weird, Destiny thought. Dad usually likes to come up and hang out with my friends. She started down the stairs.

"Do you have any cookies or anything?" Bree called after her. "I'm really starving."

Destiny pushed open the door and stepped into the kitchen. It took her eyes a moment to adjust to the single, dim ceiling light over the kitchen table.

"Oh. Hi," she said when she realized her dad was sitting at the table. Across from him sat Coach Bauer, his face solemn, hands clasped on the table. Destiny saw a deck of cards in front of her dad, but they appeared untouched.

"Hi, Coach," Destiny said. "How are you?"

He nodded. "Not bad." The orange light glared off his bald head.

Destiny turned to her father. "It's kind of dark in here, isn't it?"

"It's okay," he answered softly. "My eyes have been bothering me. Too much time in the lab, I guess." He removed his glasses and rubbed his temples.

Destiny pulled open the fridge. "Don't you two want to come upstairs? You know. Say hi."

They looked at each other. "Maybe later," Dr. Weller said. He picked up the deck of cards, but he made no attempt to deal them out.

Destiny grabbed a couple of six-packs of soda and balanced two bags of tortilla chips on top of them. She stopped at the doorway and turned back to the two men. "Come on up if you want. I think we're going to watch one of Ari's disgusting movies."

Her dad gave her a short wave. "Have fun."

When Destiny returned, her friends were in a heated discussion. Ari paced in front of the others, talking animatedly. "There were two of them," he was saying. "I'm not making this up."

"Two what?" Destiny asked, tossing a soda to Bree.

"Two deer," Ari said. "In Millerton Woods."

Destiny turned and stared at him. "What are you talking about? There are *hundreds* of deer in those woods."

"You've been away. You don't know what's

going on here," Ari said. "The two deer were dead. Their blood was drained. For real. Totally drained."

Livvy rolled her eyes. "And how many horror movies did you watch this summer?"

"It's not a movie," Ari insisted. "It's for real. I saw it on the news."

"Ari gets all his news on the Sci-Fi Channel," Ross said.

Ari didn't laugh. "There were other animals too. Raccoons and some squirrels. They were dead and their veins were empty, totally dry."

"Cute little squirrels and raccoons? You are *so* making me sick," Livvy said, holding her stomach.

Fletch shook his head. "Courtney, you'd better hide your cats if Ari comes over!"

Courtney let out a gasp. "Yuck. Who would suck cat's blood?"

"Feeling thirsty, Ari?" Bree asked. "I hear a dog barking next door. Yum!"

"It's not a joke," Ari insisted. "I . . . I know what it is. It's vampires. There are vampires out there who are doing this."

Ross and Fletch exchanged skeptical glances. Bree choked on her soda.

"Remember in third grade when Ari thought Mr. Hubner was a werewolf?" Ross said. "And it turned out he just didn't shave that day?"

Grinning, Fletch climbed to his feet and put his arm around Ari's shoulder. "Didn't you write a paper for Mrs. Klein about real vampires in history—and she flunked your ass?"

"Mrs. Klein is very narrow-minded," Ari said, pushing Fletch away. "Maybe if you would tear yourself away from your PlayStation and watch the news once in a while—"

"I saw it on TV," Ana-Li interrupted. "There was a scientific explanation for the whole thing. They said it was a virus. Some kind of mutant virus that was killing the animals."

"How can you believe that crap?" Ari demanded. "Of course they're going to say it's a virus. They're not going to tell you the truth."

"I think a virus that dries up all your blood is a lot scarier than vampires," Destiny said. "I mean, anyone can catch a virus—right?"

Courtney shivered. "Can we stop talking about this?"

Destiny tossed a bag of chips at Ari. "Are we going to watch your movie or what? Come on. We don't want to think about deer-eating viruses. Put in the movie."

Everyone moved to the couch or the floor to watch the TV. Ari slid the DVD into the player. Destiny dimmed the lights.

"Ari likes these vampire films because they're like his home videos," she heard someone whisper.

"I'm buying him a Silly Straw for his birthday," Livvy whispered. She made loud slurping noises.

"Everybody shut up," Ari said, squeezing into the center of the couch between Courtney and Ross. "These Vampire's Daughter movies are the *best*." He turned to Courtney, the most squeamish one there. "If it gets too scary, just close your eyes."

"I'm shutting them right now," Courtney said. She shut her eyes and grabbed onto Ari's arm.

The movie started with dripping, blood-red credits and booming organ music. The opening scene showed a black-caped female vampire creeping across a sleeping teenage boy's darkened bedroom. The boy woke up—just in time to scream—as the vampire sank her fangs into his throat.

"Hey, I think I know that guy!" Ross shouted.

"I'd like to know *her*," Fletch chimed in. "Is she hot or what?"

"She's got a definite dental problem," Bree added.

"She probably went to your father!" Livvy joked.

Bree's dad was a dentist. When they were in fourth or fifth grade, he did the braces for just about every one of Destiny's friends.

Destiny usually enjoyed the kidding around during Ari's dreadful horror movies. But as the film started, she suddenly felt strange—a fluttery feeling that began in her stomach and rose up to tighten her throat.

She took a long drink of soda, but it didn't seem to help. Sitting on the floor, she pressed her back against the front of the couch. She watched three vampires transform from bats into human form. They forced open the window of a girl's house and slipped inside.

Destiny's chest tightened. A cold sweat made her hands clammy. She swallowed hard.

Am I coming down with something? Why do I feel so strange?

On the screen, a tall, thin vampire, who reminded her a little of Fletch, crept up behind a couch where a teenage girl was reading a magazine. He lowered his head, sank his fangs into the startled girl's neck—

—and Destiny began to scream.

She opened her mouth in a high, shrill wail from somewhere deep inside her. She saw her friends turn to face her. Saw their shocked expressions.

She heard Ari's shouts. "What's wrong? What's wrong with her?"

She saw Ana-Li drop down beside her and throw her arms around her. "Dee, it's okay."

But no. It wasn't okay.

It wasn't okay because she couldn't stop screaming.

Chapter Eight

"You Won't Get Away From Me"

Cloaked in darkness, Renz stood in the street, staring up at the Wellers' house. A black mist encircled him, hiding him from sight as he moved across the front lawn to the house.

A silver scooter lay on its side at the edge of the driveway. Two cars were parked next to each other in front of the garage.

Destiny, you and your sister have visitors, I see.

He could hear their voices, their laughter. He raised his eyes and saw light in the window of the room at the top of the garage. The mist swirled around him as he moved up the driveway to the back of the house. Now he could hear the heartbeats in that room, hear the pulsing of blood through veins.

He gazed up at the window and listened for one heartbeat. One special heartbeat.

Laura, I am here for you. Laura, I can feel

your heart quicken for me.

You know I'm out here. You know I have followed you.

Yes, we must wait. We have weeks until the next full moon.

That will seem like an eternity to me, darling. But at least I can be nearby while I wait.

I will be watching you. I promise to stay near you all the time. I won't let you out of my sight.

You won't get away from me. Not this time.

And as you begin to change, to gain your powers, you will be ready for me. Ready to start your immortal life at my side.

Can you hear my thoughts, Laura?

Can you sense that I'm here? Can you feel my nearness?

He stood so still now, like a dark statue inside the circling dense fog. Listening . . . listening . . .

And then he heard the shrill scream from the room above.

Destiny's scream.

A smile spread over his lips. "Yes . . . yes!"

Chapter Nine

Such a Powerful Craving

How long did she scream? Destiny had no idea. When she finally stopped, it was like waking from a dream. Ana-Li held her tightly. Livvy stood above Ana-Li, pale, her mouth open in shock and concern.

Destiny blinked, then gazed at her friends. Her throat ached and her heart throbbed in her chest.

"Are you okay? What was *that* about?" Livvy asked, smoothing back Destiny's hair.

Ana-Li stepped back. "You—you frightened us."

Destiny shook her head, clearing it. "Sorry."

Livvy helped Destiny onto the couch. "Should I call Dad? Do you need a doc or something?"

"No, I'm fine," Destiny said, swallowing, her mouth still dry.

Livvy let out a long sigh. "Jeez, Dee. You

really freaked me out."

Ari shook his head. "You never used to scare so easy. Next time I'll bring an Olsen twins movie."

"That's not funny," Livvy said sharply. She held onto Destiny's hand. "What frightened you, Dee?"

Destiny rubbed her head, still feeling dazed. Her friends' faces kept going in and out of focus. "I don't know. I . . . can't explain it, Liv. But I feel okay now. Really."

Ana-Li handed her a Coke. Destiny took a long sip. The others were all on their feet, staring at her.

"I guess we're not going to finish the movie," Ari said. "Anyone want to come to my place and watch it?"

There were no takers.

Bree glanced around uncomfortably. "Maybe we should go."

A short while later, Destiny saw her friends heading to the stairs. "Whoa, wait." She struggled to her feet. "It's early. Come on. You don't have to leave."

"Catch you tomorrow," Courtney said. "You should get some rest, Dee. You're just totally stressed, I guess." She and Bree, Fletch, and Ari disappeared down the stairs.

"Call me later, okay?" Ana-Li said with concern as she followed the others to the stairs.

Ross approached Destiny, rubbing his close-shaved head, his green eyes studying her. "Glad you're all right. That was kinda freaky."

Destiny forced a smile. "I was just trying to rescue us from that awful movie."

"You could be an actress in one of those vampire films. That was awesome screaming."

"Glad you liked it."

Why did I scream like that? Why?

Livvy quickly stepped between them. "You heading out?" she asked Ross. "I'll go with you."

He shrugged his broad shoulders. "Yeah. Sure."

"I'll help clean up later," Livvy said.

Destiny stood in front of the couch, surveying the clutter of paper cups, empty soda cans, tortilla chip bags. She listened to Ross and Livvy clump down the stairs. The back door slammed.

I told her this summer I had a major crush on Ross. How could she do this to me? A burst of anger burned her chest. It slowly faded as she continued to think about Livvy. She had worried about Livvy all summer.

No. Actually, she started worrying before the summer began. She wondered why her sister suddenly started hanging out with Bree Daniel. Bree was wild and kind of slutty and didn't care about school or much of anything else except partying. Bree's parents had divorced last year, and it turned out neither of them wanted custody of her. She went back and forth from one parent to the other, but she was pretty much on her own.

Why did Livvy want to copy her?

And why did Livvy go after *every* guy in camp this summer? What was she trying to prove?

Destiny spent so many nights lying on her cot in the small camp cabin after lights out, staring up at the shadowy ceiling, worrying about her twin.

Mom didn't love us enough to stay with us. Is that why Livvy is so desperate to find love everywhere else?

Whoa. *You're* the one who freaked out tonight, Dee. You'd better not try to be Livvy's shrink.

With a sigh, she started to collect the trash.

This is so typical. Livvy runs out and leaves me here to clean up.

She carried the litter down to the kitchen. "Dad—hi."

He hadn't moved from the kitchen table. Alone now, bathed in the dim, orange light from above, he had a veterinary journal spread out in front of him. He stood, pushing his glasses up on his nose.

"Poor Coach. I don't know how to cheer the man up," he said, moving to the sink and rinsing out a mug.

"You both looked pretty grim to me," Destiny said. She leaned her head against his shoulder. "You okay, Daddy?"

"Define *okay*."

She gave him a shove. "*You* define it."

He shrugged. "I'm enjoying my work a little."

"Yeah?"

"Well, taking care of the puppies with diarrhea and cockatoos with seeds stuck in their beaks isn't too exciting. But my research work is keeping me on my toes."

He looks so much older up close, Destiny thought. *I've only been away a couple of* months. His skin didn't used to look so drawn and powdery. And his eyes used to be bright and alive. All the color seems to have faded away.

"What are you doing in the lab?"

"It's hard to explain. It's a kind of stem-cell research. Only with animal tissue. You know, animals get a lot of illnesses that could be genetic. If I can alter the genetic makeup, maybe I can eradicate some of the illnesses."

"Sounds like a lot of laughs, Dad. And what do you do for fun?"

"I stand here and let you make fun of me."

They both laughed. He hugged her. "I'm glad to have you girls back. It was awfully quiet around here all summer. And it was nice to have your friends in the house tonight. Great to hear all that laughing and screaming."

Mainly screaming, Destiny thought.

She said good night and hurried back upstairs to her room.

Hours later, Destiny awoke bathed in sweat, silvery-cold moonlight washing over her from the open window. She sat up in bed, feeling shaky, her skin tingling.

What time is it? She squinted at the clock

radio on the nightstand beside her. One forty-five?

Mopping her forehead with her nightshirt sleeve, Destiny sat up, wide awake now. And thirsty. She kicked off the covers and stood up.

I'm wide awake. And I need to do something about this thirst.

No. It was more than thirst. Her stomach growled. Hungry . . .

Starving.

I feel empty, completely empty. I have such a powerful craving.

Craving . . . for what?

In the rectangle of moonlight, she pulled on a pair of jeans and a T-shirt. Then she crept barefoot to the stairway. Down the stairs, so lightly the floorboards didn't squeak once. To the kitchen door and out into the cool, clear night.

Crickets chirped loudly—pounding in her ears—as if the volume had been cranked up. All of her senses alive and alert now.

Heart pounding, Destiny followed her hunger—around the side of the house, past the garden hose left tangled on the ground, past a clump of tall weeds, past Mikey's silver scooter beside the driveway.

Such a strange, powerful craving. Her mouth watering now. The back of her neck prickly and cold.

She began to jog, bare feet slapping the dew-wet grass.

She stopped when she saw the rabbit hunched at the side of the driveway. Its ears perked up. It stiffened, then froze in place.

Destiny dropped to her hands and knees in the grass.

She swallowed hard. She tried to force down her hunger. But her whole body ached with it.

Slowly, slowly, she began crawling over the grass.

I'm hunting . . . hunting like an animal.

Why am I doing this? I *love* little bunnies. I want to learn to take care of little bunnies—like Dad.

I love them. Yes, I love them.

Love them.

Love them.

She pounced.

The rabbit let out a weak squeal as Destiny grabbed it around its middle. As she tightened her hands around it, she could feel its heart thudding, feel its warmth in her cold hands, feel its chest heaving up and down.

I love bunnies.

I love bunnies.

I'm so hungry.

She stretched the rabbit out, baring the pink skin of its belly. She raised the soft belly to her mouth—

—and *someone else's hands* grabbed at the head. *Someone else's hands* tugged the rabbit away from her.

"NO!" Destiny whispered. She pulled the wheezing rabbit back with a hard, desperate tug—and raised her eyes. . . .

"Livvy—no!"

"Give . . . it . . . back." Livvy grabbed its ears and pulled.

The rabbit let out a final squeal.

Destiny had it by the middle. She lowered her head and sank her teeth into the soft, warm flesh.

The rabbit jerked, then went limp.

And both girls buried their faces in the warm body, and fed . . . fed so hungrily on the warm blood . . . satisfied the craving, the new craving, their frightening new hunger.

Destiny heard a rustling in the trees.

Was someone there?

She didn't care. She had to drink. She couldn't stop.

Finally, the rabbit corpse lay like a crumpled bag in their hands. Destiny heaved it into the hedges. She felt the thick, warm blood rolling down her cheeks, her chin.

Still on all fours, she stared at her sister. Panting hard. The sweet metallic taste on her tongue, on her lips.

Like an animal, she thought. Like a wild beast.

A hoarse groan escaped from Destiny's lips. And then finally, she found her voice. "Livvy," she whispered. "Livvy, what has happened to us?"

Part Three

Chapter Ten

"We'll Get Back to Normal"

A short while later, Destiny and Livvy were in the long T-shirts they slept in, standing awkwardly across from each other in their room. Destiny had turned on all the lights—the lamps, the ceiling lights, even the desk lamp—frightened that the darkness might swallow them up or turn them into creatures again.

"I . . . don't know what to say," she whispered.

"Oh, Destiny!" Livvy cried, and flung her arms around her sister. She pressed her face against Destiny's cheek and let her tears fall with her sister's.

"I'm so scared," Livvy said, when they finally let go of each other. "That was so . . . horrible."

Destiny pulled Livvy over to her bed. They sat down together. Livvy clasped her hands tightly in her lap. Destiny kept rubbing her face. She had taken a long, hot shower. Had she washed all the blood away?

"I'm not sure what happened out there," she said. "I just suddenly felt so hungry."

"Me too," Livvy whispered. "It was like . . . I couldn't help myself. I couldn't stop myself."

Destiny nodded. She bit her lip to keep more tears from coming.

"We killed that little rabbit," Livvy said, tugging at her long, wet hair. "We ripped it apart, Dee, and we—we drank . . ." Her voice faded.

Destiny didn't reply. She stared hard at a spot on her sister's neck. "Let me see that." She scooted closer and brushed a tangle of Livvy's hair out of the way.

"Dee, what is it?"

"A little red mark." Destiny rubbed her finger over it. "A tiny scab."

"Oh my God!" Livvy whispered. "Dee, you've got one too."

Destiny uttered a soft cry. They stared at each other, the two sisters suddenly so close, yet each lost in their own horrifying thoughts.

Tiny throat wounds . . . the overwhelming urge to feed on animal blood . . . Ari's story about vampires loose in the woods . . . animals drained of their blood . . .

The terrifying word—*vampire*—hung silently between them. Destiny refused to say it.

"It's the virus," Destiny said, breaking the silence. She coiled her hair around her finger, tangling it and untangling it. "That's it."

"Virus? What are you talking about? You mean the virus Ana-Li was talking about?"

Destiny nodded. "We caught it."

"I guess that's possible," Livvy said, shaking her head. "But I don't feel sick. Do you?"

"No," Destiny whispered. "But these marks on our necks . . . maybe we should talk to Ari," she said, thinking out loud. "We could swear him to secrecy, and—"

"Are you crazy?" Livvy jumped to her feet. "We can't tell *anyone* what we did. It's so . . . sick. It has to be a secret. We can't let anyone know."

"But Ari knows about these things," Destiny argued. "You heard him tonight, talking about the deer in the woods. He's a total expert on everything strange happening in the world."

"Dee, Ari lives in a total fantasy world. He spends all his time at the movies and on *Star Trek* websites. He is a sci-fi geek. He thinks half the teachers in school are werewolves and zombies!"

"Okay, okay." Destiny motioned for Livvy to lower her voice. "Sit down. I'm just saying he knows a lot of stuff. I don't know who else could help us—do you?"

"Well . . ." Livvy lowered her head, thinking. "Maybe Dr. Curtis? If it *is* a virus, he would—"

"No way," Destiny interrupted. "We can't go to our family doctor. He'd tell Dad."

"Oh. You're right."

"And we can't tell Dad," Destiny whispered, glancing to the stairs. "We can't let him and Mikey know. Dad is still messed up over Mom. It's been six months, and he's not getting any better. He seems really depressed. It scares me. He doesn't need any more bad news. I think it would just put him over the edge. And Mikey . . ."

"Mikey has changed too," Livvy said. "He never used to be so skittish. This afternoon, a cat wandered into the yard, and Mikey ran into the house. He never was afraid of cats or dogs. It was sad to see him run away like that."

"He never used to spend so much time in his room," Destiny said. "Mikey is definitely very troubled. We have to be careful, Liv. We can't let Mikey know about us. We don't want to scare him."

"Scare *him*?" Livvy whispered. "*I'm* scared, Dee. I'm really, really scared." Her body seemed to crumple, her shoulders shook, and she began to sob.

Destiny wrapped her in a tight hug. "We'll get back to normal, Liv," she whispered. "We won't let it happen again. We'll find a way. I know we will."

But a terrifying thought lingered in her mind:

What if we don't?

What if we don't?

Chapter Eleven
Ari's Frightening News

As the morning sun began to rise, Destiny turned away from the light. My eyes, they're burning. My eyelids feel like they're on fire! Did the sun always shine so harshly into the room?

"Livvy, are you awake?" Destiny called in a low whisper. "Do you feel the sunlight? Do your eyes hurt?"

"Yes. What's with the light? Ow."

"I don't know." Destiny hurried to the window and shut the blinds. She squinted at the clock radio: six forty-five. "We have to hurry outside, Liv. Before Dad and Mikey wake up."

"Huh? What for?"

"The rabbit. I tossed it somewhere in the front yard. We have to find it and hide it where they won't find it."

Livvy scrambled to her feet, pushing the long tangles of hair off her face. Her nightshirt clung to her body, wet with sweat. "What a horrible night."

"Shhh. Just get dressed," Destiny ordered. "We'll hide the rabbit, then get back into bed."

They pulled on shorts and T-shirts, then tip-toed barefoot down the stairs and through the house to the front door.

Careful not to make a sound, Destiny pulled open the front door. The morning air smelled fresh and sweet.

Livvy stepped out first and Destiny followed, squinting up at the bright orange sun rising over the trees. "Ow. The sun is so bright."

Shielding their eyes, they crossed to the side of the yard and began to search along the hedge. "There it is." Destiny saw it first—the dead rabbit, curled like a limp glove on the grass.

She glanced around frantically. "Let's take it to the woods behind the backyard. No one ever goes there."

They made their way across the lawn to the hedge. The rabbit's eyes had sunken into its head. Its belly was ripped open. Dark, dried blood caked the gray fur.

"We did this," Livvy murmured.

Destiny felt her stomach tighten into a knot. "Don't talk. Let's just get rid of it." She took a deep breath. Then she bent down, swatted away a swarm of flies, and picked up the dead rabbit. "It's stiff."

Destiny turned and, holding the rabbit corpse in both hands, started to the back of the house.

"Good morning," a voice called.

Destiny looked up to see her dad jogging toward them, perspiration drenching the front of his gray sweatshirt. She whipped the rabbit behind her back.

"I had a nice run this morning," he said, mopping his forehead with his hand. "Hey, you two are up awfully early."

"Uh . . . I guess we got used to camp time," Destiny said.

"Yeah. Up at the crack of dawn," Livvy added.

"It'll take a while to get back to our old lazy routine," Destiny said. "You know. Staying out till two, sleeping till noon."

He continued to squint at them. "Maybe you should come running with me in the morning. It really gives me energy for the whole day."

"Maybe," Destiny said, gripping the rabbit corpse behind her.

"Hey, can you help me?" a voice called from the house.

They all turned to see Mikey, in his blue-and-white striped pajamas, standing at the front door. "Eddy escaped again," he shouted.

As Mikey ran across the lawn, Destiny let the rabbit fall to the grass behind her.

"That dumb hamster?" Livvy said. "How does he get out of his cage?"

Mikey shrugged. "I don't know. I was playing with him last night. Maybe I left the door open. I— hey, what's that?" Mikey pushed Destiny out of the way and stared down at the dead rabbit. "Oh, gross. What happened to it?"

Destiny spun around and pretended to be surprised. "Oh, my—what is it? A rabbit?"

"Looks like someone ran it over or something," Livvy said.

Their dad strode over and squatted beside Mikey. He scratched his graying hair as he studied the rabbit corpse. Then he grabbed it and turned it onto its back. "Nasty," he said. "Very nasty."

Destiny gazed at her father's face. *Does he suspect what really happened?*

Dr. Weller turned the rabbit over again.

"Maybe a fox did this. Hmmmm. Or maybe it's that virus everyone is talking about."

Destiny bent down, pretending to be concerned. "Virus?"

Her dad nodded.

Mikey gave Dr. Weller a shove that almost toppled him over. "The stupid rabbit's dead. What about Eddy?"

"Oh. Eddy." Dr. Weller jumped to his feet. "Come on. Let's go find the escaped convict!" He and Mikey went running into the house.

Destiny turned to Livvy. "Dad believes in that virus, but we know how the rabbit died. I . . . I'm so confused. I don't know what to think. We've got to talk to someone. You know. Find out more about what's been going on around here."

Livvy crossed her arms in front of her. "There's no way we're going to tell Ari what we did."

"Of course not," Destiny said. "But he knows so much about what's been happening in Dark Springs. Maybe he could help us. Maybe—"

"I promised Bree I'd hang out with her today," Livvy said. "Besides, I feel perfectly fine this morning. I think it was a virus, and now

I'm almost back to normal."

Destiny sighed. "Well, I don't feel normal. Every time I think about that rabbit—"

"Okay, okay. *You* go see Ari. He has a big crush on you anyway. So go talk to him. And listen to all his crazy ideas. But don't tell him anything about us, Dee. Don't even hint. You know what a total gossip he is. If you tell him anything, the whole school will know!"

Destiny stared at her twin. "Don't worry. We'll keep our secret—no matter what."

Ari's house was a ten-minute drive from Destiny's. She took the old banged-up Honda Civic Dad had driven to near-death, then passed down for the girls to share.

Ari lived in a long, rambling ranch-style house in the better section of Dark Springs. The street was blanketed in shade from the towering trees that lined both sides. Destiny pulled up the asphalt drive, passing two gardeners who were clipping the hedge that ran across the front of the yard.

She found Ari in his cluttered bedroom at the end of the long, carpeted hall. The walls were covered with framed horror movie posters.

DRACULA RISES ONCE AGAIN! proclaimed the poster over Ari's bed. Mounted on the wall above the poster, a fur-covered werewolf mask stared down at her.

Ari's bookshelves were jammed with books and magazines. A six-foot-tall plastic *Star Wars* Jedi Knight stood beside the bookcase, light saber raised, as if protecting them. The new Anne Rice novel lay facedown on Ari's unmade bed.

Ari had his back to her. He was hunched over his keyboard, clicking furiously, headphones over his ears. Destiny crossed the room and tapped him on the shoulder.

"Hey!" He jumped up, jerking the headphones off. "Destiny—whoa! You scared me."

"Sorry. You couldn't hear me." She raised her eyes to the monitor. "What's up?"

He set the headphones down on the desk and minimized the window he had been viewing. "Nothing really. These *Star Trek* chat rooms . . . they're so boring. I think it's all horny twelve-year-olds looking to hook up. No one wants to talk about anything serious."

Ari glanced back at his computer monitor. "It's strange. I'm still into *Babylon 5*, but no one else is anymore. It's like no one is loyal to anything. They're all into Yu-Gi-Oh and all this stuff that's for babies."

"It's tragic," Destiny said, trying to keep a straight face. But she couldn't. She burst out laughing.

Ari laughed too. "Okay, say it. I'm weird. Everyone thinks I'm weird. Whatever."

"I don't think you're weird, Ari." Destiny dropped down on the edge of the bed and picked up the Anne Rice book. "I think it's cool that you're into . . . stuff."

He looked at her. "You do?"

She nodded and gazed at the spread-winged bat on the book cover. The image sent a chill down the back of her neck.

"Well, what's up with you, Dee? What was that about last night? You totally freaked."

She shrugged. "I don't know. I think you scared me, Ari. You know. Talking about those deer in the woods and everything."

"Everyone was making jokes." Ari wheeled his desk chair up to her and sat down on it backward, resting his arms on the chair back. "But it isn't funny. It's for real."

"What's for real?"

"The dead animals in the woods with their blood drained. That's not any kind of virus." He shook his head. "Virus . . . that's what they put in the newspaper so people won't get scared. But I know I'm right. I know it has to be vampires."

"But, Ari—"

"And here's why I know I'm right. Do you know the latest? Know what I heard? I heard there are vampire hunters in Dark Springs."

"Vampire hunters? Ari, what are you talking about? That is *so* not possible."

"I read it online from two different people."

Destiny set the book down and clasped her hands in her lap. "You mean hunters like on *Buffy*?"

"Real vampire hunters, Dee. I heard they were training, getting ready."

"What does that mean? Getting ready for what?"

"It's a no-brainer. It means I'm not the only one who thinks there are vampires in Dark Springs. The hunters believe it too. And they are going to go after them and kill them all."

Chapter Twelve

"There's No Cure"

Destiny stared at Ari, thinking hard. She realized he was waiting for her to react, but she didn't know what to say. The silence hung heavily between them.

"One of the hunters was sitting in your kitchen last night," Ari said finally.

"Excuse me? You mean Coach Bauer?"

Ari nodded. "It's just a rumor," he said, lowering his voice.

The housekeeper entered the room, carrying laundered towels to Ari's bathroom. He waited for her to leave.

"I mean, I don't know it for sure. But some people in a chat room said Bauer had joined the hunters. One guy said Bauer was the leader, but I think that's crap."

Destiny swallowed. She pictured the coach and her dad sitting at the kitchen table so glumly, barely speaking, the light so low. "Coach

Bauer? A vampire hunter? It sounds crazy."

Ari shrugged. "Not that crazy. People talk about him. How he got weird after his wife died last spring. You remember. He had to take a leave from school."

"Give him a break," Destiny said. "The poor man's wife died. So he needed time off for a while. Ari, this kind of gossip is just ugly. My dad hasn't been the same since my mom died. Do you want to start rumors about him too? I don't think you can blame Coach Bauer for being upset."

"But the whole thing was strange. My family and I went to the funeral. It was a closed-casket funeral. My mom said that was very odd. Mrs. Bauer died of a heart attack. So why wasn't the casket open?"

Destiny shook her head. "I'm sorry. This is too dumb. Maybe it's a family tradition to keep the caskets closed. There could be a hundred reasons, Ari."

"But there's more," Ari insisted. "People said that after his wife died, they saw Bauer trapping rabbits and squirrels behind his house. He set out these traps all over his backyard, and he caught animals in them."

Destiny squinted at him. "For what? Why would he do that?"

Ari shrugged again. "Beats me. I'm just telling you what I heard. Maybe he was going to use the animals to lure and trap vampires. I don't know."

"That's crazy," Destiny insisted. "The whole thing is ridiculous."

"But cool," Ari said, grinning. "I mean, wouldn't that be *amazing* to see a real vampire? I'd join the hunters. Really. If they would take me, I'd join. I'd do anything to see a real, live vampire—wouldn't you?"

"No way. I think it would be terrifying." Destiny shuddered. She stared hard at Ari. "You really would join them?"

He nodded.

"It's totally outrageous," she said. "We live in a tiny, quiet town. How would someone in Dark Springs ever become a vampire?"

"It's easy, Dee. It could happen to anyone, I guess. Even people in Dark Springs. You just have to be bitten by a vampire."

"That's it? What happens after you're bitten? You become a vampire? That's all there is to it?"

He scratched his head. "Well, some of the books I've read say there's a little bit more. There has to be a full moon at its peak in the sky. And a vampire has to drink your blood under the light of the moon, and you have to drink the vampire's blood."

Destiny scrunched up her face. "Yuck. All that blood drinking is so gross." She suddenly realized she had her hand on the mark on her throat.

"I'm just telling you what I've read," Ari said.

"Well, is there a cure?" Destiny blurted out. "I mean, people who are bitten. Can they be cured?"

Ari thought for a moment. "I don't think so."

"You can't ever become normal again?" Destiny realized her voice had risen several octaves.

"No. There's no cure. I've never read about a cure. Maybe if the person is only a neophyte . . ."

"A what? A neophyte?"

Ari climbed to his feet. "I could give you some books to read, Dee, if you're interested." He started to his bookshelves.

"No. Just tell me what a neophyte is," she insisted.

"It's kinda like being a half-vampire. If a

102

vampire drinks your blood, but you don't drink theirs, you're only a neophyte."

"And—?"

"You'll be a neophyte until the next full moon. Then the vampire can finish you—exchange blood with you—and make the transformation complete."

Destiny could feel her heart pounding. "And what if he doesn't finish you? What happens to you?"

"You go crazy or something. Some books say you become like an undead creature, half-human, half-vampire. You spend all your time trying to satisfy your hunger for blood."

This is crazy, Destiny thought. This can't have anything to do with Livvy and me.

But the memory of last night—of the powerful craving, of hungrily devouring the rabbit's blood—made her tremble. Her mind spun with ugly, terrifying thoughts.

Destiny realized she had shut her eyes. She opened them to find Ari staring hard at her. "What's wrong, Dee?" he asked, his eyes penetrating hers as if searching for answers in them. "What's up with you? How come you're suddenly interested in vampires?"

She took a deep breath.

Ari dropped back into his chair and brought his face close to hers. "What's up, Dee? Come on. Tell me."

"Oh. Wow. Sorry," Destiny said, smoothing back her short hair. "I just remembered something. I promised Dad I'd go to the supermarket. And what am I doing? I'm sitting here listening to your disturbing vampire stories."

She started for the door. He remained sitting backward on his desk chair. "Hey, it's great that you came over, Dee. Glad you don't think I'm weird because I'm interested in vampires and stuff."

"It was interesting. Really."

He jumped to his feet. "Where are you going? The Stop and Shop on Sweetwater?"

"Well, yeah."

"I'll go with you. Mom and Dad are at the club, playing seventy-two holes or something. There's nothing in the house to eat."

Destiny had her shopping list in one hand and pushed the cart with the other. Ari tagged along beside her, muttering about how he couldn't decide what to buy.

"My dad is really losing it," Destiny said, shaking her head. "There's no food in the house. I don't think he's gone shopping in a month! His mind, it's just . . ." Her voice trailed off.

It was a little after two in the afternoon, and the long supermarket aisles were nearly empty. In the vegetable section, a white-uniformed boy was spraying water on the lettuces. In the middle of one aisle, Destiny saw an old woman, leaning heavily on the handle of her shopping cart, reaching for a box of cereal on a shelf high above her head.

"Where *is* everyone?" Ari asked. "It's so deserted. Do you think an alien invasion has taken place, and you and I are the last few people on earth?"

"That explanation wouldn't be first on my list," Destiny said.

"Did you see that *Twilight Zone* where a man wishes everyone would go away—and they do? That was a classic."

He continued to talk, but his voice faded from Destiny's mind. Instead, she heard a loud rush, like the roar of the ocean. She covered her ears, but she couldn't shut out the sound.

Blinking hard, she could see Ari talking, but

she couldn't hear him over the deafening roar. She stopped in front of the meat counter. Her mouth began to water. She swallowed hard.

The roaring sound faded as her hunger rose.

I'm not imagining this. I'm *so hungry*.

Supermarket music jangled in her ears. Her senses were suddenly alive. The tangy-sour aroma of the meat in the refrigerated shelves filled her nostrils.

Hungry . . .

Ari stood beside her, one hand on the side of her cart. She could hear the tinny supermarket music and she could hear the steady pulsing of the blood through her veins.

Her heart raced as the craving swept over her.

Ari was bobbing his head in time to the music. His pale throat suddenly gleamed in Destiny's eyes.

Her stomach growled with a gnawing emptiness. She could feel saliva dripping down her chin.

I can't help it. I can't stop it.

She grabbed Ari by the shoulder and lowered her mouth to his throat.

Chapter Thirteen
"I Need To Feed"

"Ouch!" Ari gave a startled cry and pulled away. "Hey, supermarkets turn you on?"

Destiny wiped her chin. Her eyes stayed on his neck. She could see the blue vein pulsing down from his jawline.

"Dee, I didn't think you *liked* me." He leaned forward and kissed her. He glanced around to see if anyone was watching. Then he lowered his head to kiss her again.

I'm so hungry. I need to feed.

Yes. Yes. She wrapped her hands around his shoulders, preparing to pull him close and sink her teeth into his throat.

But no.

I can't. I can't do it to Ari.

It took all her strength to push him away.

He grinned at her, excited by her kisses.

He doesn't understand. I'm so hungry, I'd do anything . . .

"Ari, would you do me a favor?" Her voice came out tight, shrill through her clenched teeth. "My dad needs pipe tobacco. It's called Old Farmer, I think. Could you find it for me?"

He nodded, his eyes still wide. "No problem."

She watched Ari take off down the long aisle. When he was out of sight, she turned to the meat display. Her chest heaved and she began to pant. Her hands shook as she reached down for a package of meat.

A package of liver. A wet-looking slab of purple meat, dripping with blood.

Dripping . . .

Oh yes. Oh yes.

She lifted it off the shelf and brought it close to her face. The rich aroma of the meat, of the red blood, made her dizzy.

Oh yes.

With a loud grunt, she ripped away the shrink-wrapping. Then she raised the package to her face and began to drink. She sucked up the blood noisily, her tongue lapping the bottom of the package. Then she grabbed the slippery liver in one hand, held it over her head, and squeezed it, squeezed all the good juice from it, squeezed it into her mouth. Every drop. Every last drop.

It tastes so rich, so delicious. So . . . satisfying.

She shoved the slippery red meat into her mouth and chewed. She could feel blood running down her chin.

Lowering her eyes, she saw Ari returning, jogging up the aisle. "Oh, no." She pulled the raw liver from her mouth. A frantic moment. Where to hide it?

She opened her bag. Stuffed the liver into it and shut it.

Heart thudding, still dizzy with pleasure, Destiny wiped the blood off her chin with the back of her hand. She turned to greet Ari—but her eyes stopped at the nearest aisle.

A white-uniformed store clerk came running toward her, eyes wide, motioning to her, shouting, "Miss! Miss!"

He saw me. He watched the whole thing.

He saw me.

Chapter Fourteen

A Snack at the Pool

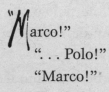"Marco!"

"... Polo!"

"Marco!"

"... Polo!"

Destiny watched the group of kids playing in the shallow end of the pool. Two boys were having a splashing war. Water tossed up over her sneakers. The lifeguard, a tall, skinny guy with a fabulous tan, blew his whistle and pointed at them.

Destiny pushed her sunglasses up on her nose. The afternoon sun beamed brightly down from a clear blue sky. Eyes burning, she searched the crowded pool for her sister.

Some guys from school were hanging out near the volleyball net. She saw Ana-Li, racket in hand, heading to the tennis courts with a girl Destiny didn't recognize.

And who was that good-looking guy with

the wavy black hair standing in the shade by the fence? Despite the bright sun, he wore a black, long-sleeved shirt and black shorts.

Why is he smiling at me?

Do I *know* him?

"Hey, Dee—where's your bathing suit?" Courtney called from the snack stand. She and Bree had on string bikinis. They both held ice cream pops and waved them at Destiny.

Destiny hurried over to them, nearly colliding with two little girls running with pool floats toward the lawn chairs at the side.

"Gotta soak up these last rays," Bree said. "The pool closes on Friday."

"Boo hoo. I hate it when summer ends," Courtney said. "I can't believe I'm already thinking about what to wear the first day of school."

"I'm wearing this!" Bree declared, motioning to her bikini. "How about you, Dee?"

"Have you seen Livvy?" Destiny asked breathlessly, ignoring her question. "She left me a note at home. Said she was coming here."

Bree licked her ice cream. "She's right over there." She pointed. "She brought Mikey and his friend. See?"

Destiny saw Livvy in the pool. She turned and took off running, her sneakers thudding on the wet concrete.

"Hey, is anything wrong?" Courtney called after her.

Livvy saw Destiny and waved. She was pushing Mikey and his friend on a small, red plastic raft. "Where is your bathing suit?" Livvy shouted.

"I didn't come to swim. I . . . need to talk to you," Destiny said.

"Hey, Dee—" Mikey called. He slid off the raft. "Watch. I learned this stroke at day camp." He came splashing across the pool.

"Very nice," Destiny called.

"It was hot. I brought Mikey and Chris," Livvy said. "What's up?"

Destiny squatted down so she could talk quietly. She leaned over the pool. "Something bad happened, Liv. At the supermarket. I was almost caught. I—"

"I thought we were going to race," Mikey interrupted, holding on to the side of the pool.

"Not now. Dee and I are talking," Livvy said.

"You promised!" Mikey cried. He made a grab for Livvy's arm, missed. His hand bumped off her sunglasses, and they sank quickly to the bottom.

"Oops—!" Mikey started to laugh.

Destiny saw Livvy's eyes go wide. Her mouth dropped open. She grabbed at her eyes and started to moan.

"Nooooo! They're burning! Burning!"

Mikey gave her a shove. He laughed again. He always loved Livvy's dumb jokes.

But Destiny could see that her sister's pain was real.

Livvy pressed her hands tightly over her eyes. "Help me! Dee! My eyes! They're burning up!"

Destiny gripped Mikey's shoulders. "Dive down. Get her glasses."

Mikey dove down, his feet momentarily poking up over the surface. He came up with the sunglasses and shoved them into Livvy's hand.

Gasping loudly, her shoulders trembling, Livvy slid the glasses onto her face.

"Ha ha. Very funny," Mikey declared. He splashed a wave of water onto Livvy. "Your jokes are so stupid." He turned and floated back to his friend Chris.

Livvy gazed up at Destiny. "It . . . it's okay now. But . . . what happened?"

A feeling of dread swept over Destiny. "Livvy, our eyes—they can't stand the bright sun." She gasped. "And look at your skin. Did you put on sunscreen? You're totally sunburned."

Livvy gazed down at her arms and legs. "Oh, wow. I haven't been here more than half an hour! Dee, what does this mean?"

"We have to go," Destiny said. She climbed to her feet and called, "Mikey, Chris, out of the water now. Let's go."

"Aw, please—ten more minutes," Mikey whined.

"No. We have to go," Livvy said. She grabbed both his hands and tugged him to the steps. "You guys had a good swim."

Mikey splashed her again. "You're stupid. It was too short."

"Maybe I'll bring you back tomorrow," Destiny said. "Would you like that?"

"No."

Destiny found Mikey's beach towel and wrapped him up in it.

"Stop being such a grump," Livvy said.

"Make me."

Livvy turned and saw Chris come running toward them, his baggy swimsuit dripping water. "Do we really have to go?" Chris called. And then he slipped on the wet walkway and toppled heavily to the concrete.

"Ow!" He let out a cry and didn't move.

"Are you okay?" Livvy called. She ran to him. She dropped down beside him. "Chris?"

He sat up slowly. "My knee."

"You scraped it," Livvy said.

Destiny and Mikey hurried over to them.

"It's bleeding," Chris said, holding his leg.

Destiny stared at the blood, bright red even through her sunglasses. It glistened wetly on the bent knee.

Livvy leaned over, grabbed the boy's leg with both hands, and lowered her face to the knee.

"Livvy—don't," Destiny said softly.

But Livvy leaned lower and started to lick up the blood.

"Livvy—" Destiny called. "No—"

Livvy's tongue made rapid lapping sounds as her head bobbed over Chris's knee.

"What is she doing?" Mikey cried. "Why is she doing that?"

Chapter Fifteen

What Does Coach Bauer Know?

Livvy let go of Chris's knee and raised her head. Destiny could see the dazed expression on her sister's face.

"Why did you do that?" Mikey grabbed Livvy's shoulder. "What's your problem?"

Livvy stared up at him.

"It's a first-aid trick we learned at camp," Destiny told him, trying to keep her voice steady. "That's the fastest way to stop the bleeding." She turned to Chris. "How does it feel?"

"Okay."

Livvy helped Chris to his feet. "See? The bleeding's almost stopped. We'll put a bandage on it when we get home."

Destiny studied her brother. Did he believe her first-aid story? He was still watching Livvy warily.

Destiny turned and waved good-bye to Bree and Courtney. As the four of them made their way to the parking lot, Destiny saw the young man in black still standing in the shade. Still smiling.

Still watching her.

She looked away quickly.

What is *his* problem?

Up in their room, the door closed, Livvy grabbed Destiny's hand. "I couldn't stop myself. I suddenly felt so hungry. I saw the blood on Chris's knee, and—"

"Shhh." Destiny squeezed her sister's hand. "It's okay. I think they believed my first-aid story."

"But it's *not* okay. We're not okay. We . . . maybe we . . ." her voice trailed off.

"Maybe we were bitten by a vampire." Destiny finished the sentence for her. She felt a chill go down her back. "I've been thinking and thinking. Maybe at camp. It's the only place it could have happened."

Livvy let go of Destiny's hand and dropped onto her bed. "Dee, we've got to find someone to help us."

"Yes, we do," Destiny said. "And we may not have much time." She told Livvy what she had learned from Ari, about vampire hunters in

Dark Springs, about full-fledged vampires and neophytes.

"But isn't there an antidote?" Livvy whispered. "If we were bitten, isn't there something we can do to get back to normal? What did Ari say?"

Destiny shook her head. "Ari didn't know."

She told her sister about the supermarket incident, about the clerk running toward her, pointing and shouting. "I knew I'd been caught. I was in a total panic. He saw me drop the liver in my bag. I told him it slipped out of my hand. I said the package had come open. I said someone did a bad wrapping job and I got blood all over me."

"And did he believe you?"

Destiny nodded. "Yes. He started to apologize." She swallowed. "I was so scared, Liv. It was such a close call."

A heavy silence fell over them.

Livvy fingered the mark on her neck. "Maybe we *were* bitten. Maybe we're becoming vampires. I . . . I can't believe it. But maybe it's true."

She buried her face in her hands. "Do you really think there are hunters, Dee? Would they hunt us down and kill us if they found out about us?"

"Maybe," Destiny whispered. "I don't know."

"But we haven't done anything wrong," Livvy said with a sob. "It isn't our fault."

Destiny had the feeling that Livvy wanted to say more. She waited for her sister to continue, but Livvy sat in silence.

As Destiny reached to hug her sister, she had an idea. "Coach Bauer," she said aloud.

Livvy glanced up at her. "What about him?"

"Ari said Coach might be one of the vampire hunters. He might even be the leader. Maybe he knows about vampires, Liv. Maybe he could tell us what to do."

Livvy pulled away from Destiny. "Are you crazy? If Coach is one of the hunters, *no way* we can tell him what happened to us. He'll shove stakes through our hearts or something."

"Of course he won't," Destiny said softly. "Coach has known us since we were babies. He and Mrs. Bauer were at our house all the time. He's like family. He would never hurt us, Liv. And he might know something that would help us. I think we should go see him right away."

Livvy hesitated. "I'd be afraid, Dee. Really."

"Well, maybe we could tell him we're worried about a friend from camp. We just need information. He might know exactly what we should do."

"But, Dee, that's so lame."

"We're desperate, right? We have to try *something—*"

The phone rang. Destiny picked it up.

"Hi, Dee. It's Dad. How's it going?"

How's it going? Not exactly great, Dad.

"Everything's fine."

"Listen, dear, I won't be home till late. Two dogs got into a fight behind the playground. One of them had its eye clawed out. I think maybe if I'm lucky, I can put it back in."

"Yuck, Dad. That's really gross."

"Destiny, you're the animal lover in the family. If you want to be a doctor or a vet, you can't say things are gross."

"I guess."

"Anyway, can you feed yourselves? And take care of Mikey till I get back?"

"No problem, Dad."

"Thanks, kid. I love you. See you later."

Would you love me if you knew I suck down liver blood in the supermarket?

"Love you too, Dad. Bye." She turned to Livvy. "Dad won't be home till late."

"No problem," Livvy said. "I'll make my specialty for dinner."

"Your specialty? What's that?"

"Frozen pizza."

"Take off the crust for me," Mikey said.

"Can you wait? It isn't even out of the oven yet," Livvy replied. "And what's wrong with the crust?"

"Mom always cut off the crust for me," he said. And then his eyes went wide and his cheeks reddened. "Just cut it off, okay?"

Destiny stared at her little brother. "Mom cut off the crusts for you because she liked to eat them herself. She thought the crusts were the best part. You know, one night I caught her down here late at night eating a whole plate of pizza crusts."

She bent down and whispered in Mikey's ear, "It's okay to talk about Mom. You can talk about her any time you want to."

He looked at her. "Shut up," he snapped.

"Excuse me?"

"Just shut up." He stamped out of the kitchen.

Livvy peered into the oven window. "Almost ready."

Destiny pulled three dinner plates from the cabinet and carried them to the kitchen table. As she set out the plates, something on the bench against the window caught her eye. "Hey, what's that?"

She picked it up. A fat notebook, the cover scratched and worn, pages practically bursting out. She hoisted it onto one knee to flip through it. "Livvy, look—it's Coach Bauer's playbook. He must have left it here last night."

Livvy was lifting the pizza from the oven. "He'll come back for it."

"No. Don't you see? This is our excuse."

"You mean—"

"Our excuse to go see him tonight. We'll tell him we came to return the playbook. Then we'll tell him we've been hearing all these rumors about vampires, and maybe he'll tell us something to help us."

Livvy stared at the playbook. Destiny could see the fear on her sister's face.

"I'm frightened too," Destiny said. "I'm terrified. But we have to talk to someone. Coach Bauer might be our last hope."

Chapter Sixteen

Anyone Home?

Destiny's sneakers crunched over the gravel driveway. She clutched the playbook against the front of her sweatshirt. The wind, suddenly cold—a hint of fall days to come—gusted and swirled, shivering the old trees around the house, making them creak and groan.

"It's completely dark," Livvy whispered, a few steps behind Destiny. "I don't think he's home."

"He might be in back. We'll give it a try."

Destiny gazed up at the two-story shingle house. A loose shutter dangled from an upstairs window. Clumps of tall weeds poked over the front stoop. Beside the front window, a rhododendron bush lay withered on its side, flattened as if trampled.

"What a dump. The house used to look so nice when Mrs. Bauer was alive," Livvy whispered. "Remember? She was always bragging about her garden."

Destiny climbed onto the concrete stoop. She heard a dog barking, probably from the house across the street. A strong gust of wind nearly sent her tumbling off the stoop. No porch light. Her hand fumbled for the doorbell, finally found it, and pressed it.

"He's not home," Livvy whispered. She hugged herself. She wore a thin T-shirt.

"It's freezing out. How did it get so cold? We were just at the swimming pool. What crazy weather! Put on your coat right now." Destiny could hear her mother's voice.

She could picture Livvy stamping her feet, refusing to put on anything warm. It was the main thing Livvy and Mom argued about. It went on for years—the jacket war—and Mom never won once. Livvy was so stubborn, she'd walk to school through snow in just a T-shirt and jeans, just to win the battle.

She glimpsed her sister, shivering, hair blowing in the gusting wind.

At least *some* things never change.

No answer. Destiny pushed the bell again and held it down. She could hear the metallic ring on the other side of the door.

"He isn't here," Livvy said. "Let's go. I'm freezing."

Destiny put her ear to the door. No sounds inside the house. "We can't leave Coach's playbook out here on the stoop. Come on. The back door is probably open." Just about everyone in Dark Springs left their back doors unlocked. "We'll leave it for him in the kitchen."

Destiny led the way to the side of the house. She stepped around two bags of mulch stacked against the wall. One of the bags had come open, spilling its contents onto the grass. The bedroom windows were dark.

She turned the knob, and the kitchen door swung open easily. The girls stepped into the dark kitchen. Destiny closed the door behind them.

Livvy hugged herself. "It's nice and warm in here." She made a disgusted face. "Yuck. Smells like fish."

"Yes, it does," Destiny whispered. Then she called out, "Anyone home? Coach Bauer? Are you home?"

Silence. Destiny heard the clink of the ice maker inside the refrigerator.

She held the fat notebook in both hands.

"I'll leave it on the table," she whispered. "We'll have to come back, Liv. If he knows anything about vampires . . ."

She set the playbook down—and froze when she heard a groan nearby. "Did you hear that?" she whispered.

"Yes."

A creaking floorboard. Another groan.

Destiny gazed around the dark kitchen. Where's the light switch?

"Coach Bauer?" Her voice came out tight and shrill. "Coach? Is that you?"

A scraping sound. Loud breathing.

Someone is here. Someone is very close.

It has to be Coach Bauer. Why doesn't he answer?

"Coach? It's us—Destiny and Livvy."

Another muffled groan. From behind the door to the basement?

Destiny jumped as a hand grabbed her shoulder from behind. She cried out.

"Sorry," Livvy whispered. "I didn't mean to scare you. I . . . I don't like this. Let's get out of here."

"Okay."

But before she could move, Destiny heard

the creak of a door. She turned and watched with growing panic as the basement door slowly, slowly swung open.

"Coach? Is that you?"

Livvy tugged her arm. "Let's go!"

Destiny moved to the wall. She found the light switch and flicked on the kitchen lights.

"No! Oh, no!" She uttered a moan of horror as the pale, hollow-eyed figure stepped out from the basement. Clamping her hands to the sides of her face, Livvy opened her mouth in a high scream of terror.

Clinging to each other, the girls stared wide-eyed as the ghastly figure loomed closer.

"Mrs. Bauer!" Destiny shrieked. "It can't be. You're dead!"

"I'm not dead," Mrs. Bauer said in a hoarse whisper. "I am *undead*."

Chapter Seventeen

"He Won't Let Me Die"

Livvy gripped Destiny's arm so hard it hurt. Destiny gasped in horror as the woman moved toward them. Her bloodless face, the gray skin sagging over her jaw, the eyes sunken deep into the dark, round sockets, her skin peeling off, a patch of yellow bone visible beneath a hole in one cheek.

She used to be so beautiful. Mom always talked about how she wished she could look like Marjory Bauer.

"He . . . won't . . . let . . . me . . . die." The hoarse rasp rattled from deep in her throat. Every word seemed a struggle.

"Mrs. Bauer? Is it really you?" Livvy, hiding behind Destiny, finally found her voice.

"The poor man—he won't . . . let me die. He . . . can't . . . bear . . . to . . . part with me." Deep in their sockets, the gray eyes rolled up till only white was showing.

"He doesn't know how . . . selfish . . . he's being. I . . . want . . . to . . . *die!*"

"Mrs. Bauer—please—" Destiny staggered back, stumbling over Livvy.

"I . . . want . . . to . . . die, but he won't . . . let me!"

"Dee, look—look what she has in her hand," Livvy whispered.

Destiny lowered her gaze. Mrs. Bauer gripped a wooden stake in her hand, shaved to a point at one end.

"The poor man," Marjory Bauer continued. When she shook her hair, Destiny could see the skin tear at the back of her neck, a wide hole revealing gray tendons and yellow bone. "He keeps me here. But I want to die. Please? Please?" She raised the stake. She held it out to Destiny.

Destiny took another step back, into the kitchen counter. "Mrs. Bauer, what are you saying? How did this happen to you?"

"He keeps me in . . . the . . . basement," she continued, ignoring Destiny's questions. "He still wants me near him. But . . . I . . . can't . . . stand this life. Asleep all day . . . no light . . . never seeing the light. Forced to prowl . . . and to feed."

Again she raised the stake to Destiny. "Please? Please end it for me?"

"No!" Destiny cried. Her back pressed against the counter. She couldn't escape. "No, I can't, Mrs. Bauer."

Destiny glanced at her sister. Her eyes were wide with terror. She had backed up to the kitchen door and was fumbling for the knob.

"I'm sorry. I can't do it," Destiny told the woman. "I—I just came to return Coach's playbook. Livvy and I—we won't tell anyone about you. I promise. We'll keep your secret. We—"

Mrs. Bauer floated closer. She had Destiny trapped against the kitchen counter. She raised the stake one more time, and Destiny saw that the skin had fallen off her fingers, leaving only bone.

"You . . . won't help me . . . escape . . . this nightmare?"

"I'm sorry. No. I can't. Let me go. Please."

The sunken eyes rolled up in her head again. "Jenny took my dolly when I was five. Did you know that?"

Destiny swallowed. "I—I don't understand what you're saying."

Livvy motioned frantically for Destiny to

escape with her out the door. But Mrs. Bauer had Destiny pinned against the counter.

"Jenny took my dolly, so I had to buy a new one. I was only five. I cried and cried. I didn't want to play with Jenny anymore."

Oh my God. She's completely lost her mind.

Mrs. Bauer's eyes rolled down and locked on Destiny. "So hungry," she murmured through her blackened lips. "Always so hungry. I must feed now. That's why I awoke. I must . . . feed."

She loomed over Destiny . . . so close now, Destiny could smell her rotting skin. "Thank you . . . for coming, dear." Mrs. Bauer let the wooden stake drop from her hand.

"Mrs. Bauer, please. We won't tell anyone. I swear. I—"

"Thank you for coming. I'm hungry . . . so hungry. I must have blood. Now."

Her bony hands shot out fast. She caught Destiny by surprise. Destiny tried to squirm free, but the hands were strong, inhumanly strong. They wrapped around her head and tightened.

Destiny saw Mrs. Bauer's sunken eyes go wide with excitement. She saw the curled, yellow fangs slide down from the woman's blackened gums.

She tried to scream. She tried to pull free. But the bony hands held her in place.

Mrs. Bauer's sunken belly made a wet, gurgling sound. Destiny felt a wave of sour breath wash over her face as the woman dipped her head—and lowered her fangs to Destiny's throat.

Chapter Eighteen

Who Is the Restorer?

Destiny gave a final cry of protest and waited for the pain to shoot through her body. She felt Mrs. Bauer's dry tongue scrape against her skin. And then she heard the woman let out a startled gasp.

Mrs. Bauer pulled back her head. Her eyes, sunk so deep in the hollow cavities, stared at Destiny. "You too," she whispered.

Livvy grabbed Mrs. Bauer by the shoulders. "Let go! Let go of my sister!"

Mrs. Bauer drew back, stumbling over Livvy. She spun around and ran a bony finger along Livvy's throat. "You too," she whispered again. "You too. You too."

Livvy jumped away. Feeling the spot on her throat where Mrs. Bauer had touched her, Livvy edged beside her sister. "Let's go, Dee. Come on. Let's get out of here."

"You were bitten too," Mrs. Bauer

whispered. "I see the marks. And . . . I can . . . see it . . . in your eyes."

Trembling, still feeling the scrape of the woman's dry tongue on her skin, Destiny threw an arm around her sister's waist. "Wait. Don't run away," she whispered. "She won't harm us. Maybe she can help us."

"You have until . . . the next full moon," the woman rasped. "Not much time. Only a few weeks. Save yourselves. Save yourselves."

"But—how?" Destiny cried. "What do we do?"

"Only a few weeks," Mrs. Bauer repeated. She scratched her cheek and a chunk of skin fell off. "But . . . be careful. The hunters are out. The hunters . . . will find you."

"So it's true?" Destiny asked. "There *are* vampire hunters in Dark Springs?"

"Jenny took my dolly," Mrs. Bauer said, her eyes rolling up into her head. "Jenny took my dolly, so I pushed her in the mud. Her Sunday School dress was ruined. Ha ha."

"Mrs. Bauer, please," Destiny said. "Are there really hunters?"

"Jenny gave me a lollipop, but I hit her in the face with it."

"Can you help us?" Livvy cried. "Can you help us get back to normal?"

Mrs. Bauer moved quickly again. She lurched forward, grabbed Livvy's hand, and pinched the skin hard. "You're a lovely one. You don't want to be like me. Undead. Ha ha. What rhymes with undead?"

Livvy winced from the pain. She swung her arm, but the woman kept the tight grip on her hand. "Well, can you help us?" Livvy choked out.

"Have you seen . . . the Restorer?" Mrs. Bauer asked. She let go of Livvy's hand and turned to Destiny. "The Restorer is the one. He can . . . restore your life. Too late for me. He couldn't help me. But you . . . may have a little time."

Destiny's heart began to race. Was there really someone who could save them? Someone who could keep them from becoming like Marjory Bauer?

Her heart thudded in her chest. "Who is the Restorer? How can we find him?" she asked.

"Too late for Jenny," Mrs. Bauer said, shaking her head. "She fell off a horse and cracked her skull open. Good-bye, Jenny. I'm sorry I was so mean to you. I didn't know you would fall off your horse, did I?"

Destiny grabbed the woman's tattered sleeve. "Please. Tell us. How can we find the Restorer?"

"You need parental guidance. Guidance."

"Huh? Guidance? I don't understand," Destiny said.

"The hunters are coming," Mrs. Bauer replied. "They know who's been naughty and nice. They know. They're going to kill the naughty ones. But . . . they won't kill me. My husband . . . won't let them kill me. Please—kill me."

"Mrs. Bauer—the Restorer? Tell us."

"So hungry."

"Please?"

"So hungry. I must feed. You too. You too. You're one of them. You're one of us."

"Yes, but who is the Restorer?"

"So hungry." Mrs. Bauer spun away from them. Destiny could see the torn skin, the gaping hole in the back of her neck. The woman pulled open the door and disappeared into the night.

Destiny held on to her sister. A heavy

silence enveloped them, the only sound their rapid breathing.

"Is this really happening?" Livvy said finally.

"Let's go." Destiny pulled Livvy out the door. "Can you drive? I feel shaky."

"I guess."

Inside the car, Livvy dropped the key on the floor. She fumbled for it, then struggled to jam it into the ignition.

"Oh my God. That poor woman," Livvy said, shuddering. "Did you see what she looked like?"

"I'll never forget it. I'm going to have nightmares forever." Destiny grabbed Livvy's arm. "Look at me. I can't stop shaking. We can't let that happen to us, Liv. We can't! We have to find the Restorer. There isn't much time."

Destiny fiddled with the dashboard dials. "Can't we turn the heat up? I can't stop shivering."

"Destiny, there is no such thing as a Restorer. It was just crazy talk—like Jenny and the lollipop."

They drove home in silence. Dr. Weller's SUV was parked in the driveway. Through the windows, Destiny could see all the lights on in the house. Still shivering, she jogged to the back door.

Their dad greeted them at the door. In the harsh light on the porch, he looked tired, old. "I just got home a few minutes ago," he said softly. "There are some people here to see you."

Destiny and Livvy stared at each other. They both had the same thought.

The hunters!

Chapter Nineteen
Ari Strikes Out

Destiny gasped when she stepped into the living room and saw the visitors. Courtney, Fletch, and Ross sat on the floor, cheering Mikey on as he played a PlayStation racing game.

Courtney climbed to her feet. "Dee, hi. Why do you look so shocked?"

Destiny and Livvy exchanged glances. "We . . . uh . . . just didn't expect you," Destiny said.

"Where were you?" their dad asked. "I was surprised to find Mikey with Mrs. Mitchell next door."

"Uh . . . just doing some things," Destiny answered. Pretty lame. Could everyone see how upset and frazzled she was?

"Yeah. Things," Livvy echoed. Not helpful at all.

"Well, it's Mikey's bedtime," Dr. Weller said, scratching his graying hair. "How about it, Mikey?"

"How about *no way*?" Mikey replied, his fingers moving rapidly over the controller, his car rounding a turn on the video speedway.

Fletch used Mikey's shoulder to help push himself up from the floor. "Pretty cool game." He stretched his long arms over his head. "You guys want to go out or something?"

"I don't think so," Destiny said. "I'm . . . really tired."

Ross stood up. "It's only a few days till school starts. We've got to make the most of it. Who wants to go down to Donohue's, get some burgers, see if anyone else from school is hanging there?"

"I don't have any money," Courtney complained. "Someone has to treat me."

Fletch turned to her. "Hey, Court, we're always treating you. How come you never have any money?"

"Maybe it's because I'm poor?"

"Nice move, Fletch." Ross slapped his friend a low-five. "Got any other questions for her?"

"Give me a break." Fletch grabbed Ross and started wrestling around.

"Hey, cut it out, guys," Destiny said.

Please leave, everyone. Please. I'm so frightened, I can't think straight. I keep seeing that hideous woman . . . keep hearing her warnings rasping in my ears.

Ross held up a fifty-dollar bill. "Look— birthday money from my grandmother. I'll treat everyone at Donohue's."

Fletch put an arm around Ross's broad shoulders. "You the man!" He turned to Livvy. "You coming?"

Livvy crossed the room to Destiny. "Maybe we should go," she whispered. "You know. Help take our minds off . . . everything."

Destiny shook her head. "Not me. But if you think it will help you . . ."

Livvy had her eyes on Ross. "Yes. Maybe it will. . . ."

"Come on, you two," Courtney called from the front door. "Before Ross changes his mind."

Livvy turned and hurried after the others. She pulled her cell phone to her ear. "I'm calling Bree, guys. Maybe she'll want to meet us."

The door closed behind her. Destiny shut her eyes, enjoying the silence. But as soon as she closed them, she pictured Mrs. Bauer, her skin torn and decayed, her eyes tiny marbles sunk deep in her skull.

Destiny started to the stairs. Her dad stood

at the stove, waiting for the kettle to boil. He turned when he heard her enter. "Not going out with your friends?"

Destiny shook her head. "No. I'm kinda tired."

He narrowed his eyes at her, studying her.

Should I tell him what's happening to Livvy and me? Should I?

The teakettle on the stove whistled. He turned back to it.

Destiny hurried up the stairs to her room. She dropped down at her desk and clicked on the lamp. Then, elbows on the desktop, she buried her face in her hands.

This is a nightmare. I feel so helpless, so all alone.

I almost told Dad just now. But I can't do that. He looks so terrible, so old and sad. Besides, what could he do?

Destiny stepped to the mirror. She smoothed her fingers gently over the tiny puncture mark on her throat. Why doesn't it heal? She brought her face close to the glass.

What did Mrs. Bauer see in my eyes?

Yes. My eyes do look strange. My pupils are so tiny.

She picked up the phone and punched in Ari's number. He picked up after the third ring.

"Ari, hey. It's me. What are you doing?"

"Dee—hi. I'm watching *Night of the Living Dead*. The 1990 version. I'm comparing it to the 1968 version. You know. The original."

"Which is better?" Destiny asked, trying to sound interested.

"The original, of course. The grainy black-and-white photography is so much more terrifying."

"Ari, can I ask you something? Remember what we were talking about this afternoon?"

"You mean vampires?"

"Yeah. Well, I have one more question. Have you—"

"How come you're so interested in vampires all of a sudden, Dee?" hc asked.

He sounds suspicious, she realized. She felt her throat tighten.

"Hey—I know why!" he said. "I knew it! I knew it!"

Destiny nearly dropped the phone. I should never have gone to see him. He's figured it out.

"It's because you agree with me!" Ari

declared. "You agree that it's not a virus that killed those animals. It's vampires."

"Well . . . yeah." Destiny let out a long breath of air. "Right. And I . . . uh . . . want to learn as much as I can."

Whew.

"Cool," Ari said. "What were you going to ask me?"

"Well, have you ever heard of someone called the Restorer?"

Silence at the other end.

Then, "The Restorer? You sure you don't mean *The Regurgitator*? I remember a low-budget, independent film—totally gross—called *The Regurgitator*. This giant creature kept throwing up on Tokyo."

"No. It's not a movie," Destiny said impatiently. "I think it's supposed to be a real person."

"The Restorer?"

Come on, Ari. Please know who it is. Please come through for me.

"Is the Restorer a teacher?" Ari asked.

"Huh? Why do you say that?"

"I kinda remember some book I read on vampire lore. A long time ago. There was a teacher in it who claimed he could cure vampires. Is that what you mean?"

"Yeah. I guess. A teacher. . . . Can't you remember anything else?"

"No. Not really. I guess I struck out, Dee. You stumped me. You win the prize."

She sighed. "What's the prize?"

"Uh . . . you and me go to a movie tomorrow night?"

"What's *second* prize? No. I'm kidding. We'll have to see about tomorrow. Hey, I've got another call. Catch you later."

She clicked off the phone. She didn't have another call.

But she had to think. A teacher . . .

Mrs. Bauer had said *parental guidance*. And Ari had said a *teacher*.

Who else could help her? Who else might know about the Restorer?

Coach Bauer?

An image from her childhood flashed into her mind. She saw Coach Bauer looking much younger. Destiny remembered him tossing a football to Livvy and her. How old were they then? Seven or eight? Dad stood in the drive-way, grinning, hands in his pockets. Barking out plays at the top of his lungs, Coach made the two girls run across the front yard, across the neighbor's yard, and heaved the ball high in the air at them.

Livvy always ducked. But sometimes Destiny would leap up and—miraculously—catch the ball. That made Coach cheer and jump up and down. When they went to toss it back, Bauer would warn them: "Don't throw like girls. Pull your arm back. Don't throw like girls."

Destiny loved Coach Bauer because he was the only adult who didn't treat her like a delicate little princess.

Thinking about those football games in the front yard, Destiny sobbed. Poor Coach. Hiding his undead wife in the basement, refusing to let her die. Forced to go out and hunt the vampires who ruined her life—and his.

The frightening thoughts circled her brain. Destiny slid over to her desktop computer. She pressed the power button and waited for it to go through its startup humming and beeping. Then she went online and called up Google.com.

She typed in *The Restorer* and *vampires*, and waited to see what the search engine found.

It took only a few seconds. Surprisingly, there was only one result.

But one will be enough if it's the right one!

Her hand trembling, Destiny clicked on the link. The website came up slowly. Destiny groaned when she read the large, blue headline at the top of the screen:

99% EFFECTIVE!

AMAZING HAIR RESTORER

GUARANTEED BY DOCTORS!

Disgusted, Destiny spun away from the computer.

Where else can I look?

She turned back to the screen—and discovered that she had an Instant Message:

Nak123: Hey, Dee. Izzat you?

Destiny leaned over the keyboard and typed.

Destiny1W: Nakeisha? What's up? i miss you!

Nak123: I miss you too, girl. And I miss camp. I think camp should

be 10 months and school 2 months
in the summer.

Destiny1W: You got that right.
School start yet?

Nak123: Next week. Just hanging
out with friends. Baby-sitting
and stuff. You?

Destiny1W: Same. Hear from anyone
at camp?

Nak123: Not really. Planning my
college visits. You?

Destiny1W: Not yet.

Destiny hesitated. Did the vampire bite
Livvy and me at camp? Is that where it hap-
pened? Could anyone else have been bitten?
She took a deep breath and then typed.

Destiny1W: Hey, Nak—you been
feeling weird or anything since u
left camp?

Nak123: What kinda weird?

Destiny1W: Not normal-type weird.
I mean really STRANGE.

Holding her breath, Destiny waited for the answer. When it finally appeared, her mouth dropped open in shock.

Nak123: Yes. How did u know? i
change into a bat every night and
go flying around looking for
victims.

Chapter Twenty
Murdered

Whoa. Destiny stared at the words on the screen.

Is Nakeisha serious? Is she making a joke? I've got to know. . . .

```
Destiny1W: Me too. I capture
animals and drink their blood.


Nak123: That's what 8 weeks at
Camp Blue Moon will do to you. I
grew hair on my face and i howl
at the moon.


Destiny1W: lol
```

Nakeisha was joking. Destiny let out a sigh.

The girls chatted online for a few more minutes. Nakeisha wrote that she'd be traveling with her mom this fall, looking at colleges, and they might drive through Dark Springs. Destiny replied that she couldn't wait to see her.

When she got offline, Destiny's eyelids felt heavy and her muscles ached. What a long, dreadful day, she thought, yawning.

Stretching, she walked to the open window and peered down on the front yard. Snakes of black cloud rolled over the pale half moon. The yard lay in deep shadow. A car rolled past slowly, one taillight out. Destiny could hear the music on its car radio.

Destiny squinted hard and saw a gray squirrel with a nut in its mouth, darting across the grass.

I can hear it. I can hear the squirrel's footsteps.

Destiny clapped her hand to her mouth. She suddenly felt sick. Her stomach lurched. She fought to keep her dinner down.

I'm changing. My body is changing. My hearing is becoming . . . inhuman. Oh my God. I can hear a squirrel's footsteps.

She shut her eyes and listened hard. Concentrated.

She could hear breathing. Mikey, asleep, breathing slowly, steadily, in his room downstairs.

And she could hear her dad, humming softly to himself, probably reading a book in bed. His stomach growled. She could hear his stomach growl all the way up in her garage room!

Where is Livvy?

Livvy and I have *got* to talk. We don't have time to waste.

She picked up the phone and punched in Livvy's cell number. Livvy answered on the second ring. "Where are you?" Destiny asked.

"You know. Donohue's."

"Well, come home now. We've got to talk."

"But it's still early, Dee."

"No. Come home, Liv. Right now. There's no time for hanging out with friends. We've got to make a plan."

Livvy hesitated. Destiny could hear the crowd at the restaurant, the steady thump of the reggae music on the stereo there. "Okay. Be right home. Promise."

Destiny clicked off the phone. She won't come for another hour or two. I know her. I'd better go get her.

She pulled on her denim jacket, brushed her hair, found her sneakers. Then she crept out of the house.

She stepped out into a cool, cloudy night. The wind gusted, sending dead leaves swirling off the ground in wide circles. Donohue's was just five or six blocks toward town. Destiny zipped her jacket and started to jog.

Three blocks from home, she saw a figure walking toward her on the sidewalk. "Livvy!"

"Hi," her sister called. "What are you doing out here?"

"Coming for you," Destiny answered, breathing hard from her run.

Livvy frowned. "I told you I'd be right home."

Destiny shrugged. "I just wanted to get some air."

"I'm a little worried about Bree," Livvy said. "How come?"

"Well, she said she was coming to meet us. But then she never showed. I tried her cell, but . . . no luck."

"Weird," Destiny muttered.

They turned and started walking toward home. The moon kept sliding behind clouds, then reappearing, making it seem as if the pale light over the lawns and houses kept turning on and off.

"Can you hear it?" Destiny asked. "Can you hear every leaf rustling? Can you hear bugs crawling in the trees?"

Livvy's mouth dropped open. "Yes. Yes, I can, Dee. It's . . . terrifying. Every sound so clear. As if the whole world is closing in on us or something."

As if we're some kind of animals, Destiny thought. Some kind of night creatures.

Destiny pointed. "Hey, what's that?"

They had reached the vacant lot just cleared next to the corner house. Destiny squinted at something on the ground beside a large backhoe. Was it a pile of rags the workmen had left behind?

No. The clouds parted. Moonlight washed over the lot, revealing a pale, white leg.

No. Two legs, gleaming so brightly against the darkness of the ground.

Destiny's eyes focused on the pile of blond hair, silvery in the pale light from above. And then the whole scene faded like a dream, and the sprawled, still figure appeared to sink into the ground as clouds covered the moon and darkness spread again.

"Oh, no. Bree!" Livvy let out a choked whisper and took off running, her sneakers thudding the ground, hair bouncing behind her. Destiny took a deep breath and hurried after her.

Please, no.

But, yes. It was Bree.

She wore a short skirt and a brown leather jacket. She lay on her back, legs spread, one arm bent beneath her body. Her thick hair covered her face.

"Bree? Bree?" Livvy shouted her name in a high, shrill voice. "Bree? It's me." She dropped down beside Bree and began smoothing the hair off her friend's face.

"Bree? Bree? It's Livvy. Bree?"

Breathing hard, Destiny stood behind Livvy, staring down at the unmoving girl. Bree's eyes were open. They gazed up blankly, wide with horror. Her lipsticked mouth was open, as if frozen in a scream.

"Bree? Please move. Please!" A sob escaped Livvy's throat. "She's . . . dead. She's dead, Dee. Oh my God, she's dead."

Chapter Twenty-One
Destiny's New Neighbor

Moonlight washed over them again. Destiny blinked as Bree went out of focus, pale skin glowing in the light. And then Destiny's eyes stopped at the dark stain on Bree's gleaming throat.

Oh, no.

Destiny stooped beside her sister and narrowed her eyes at the spot. She reached out a trembling hand and smoothed her finger over Bree's throat. The skin felt so cool and soft.

Two tiny puncture wounds. Dark droplets of blood clinging to the holes.

Someone drank her blood.

Someone drank all her blood and killed her.

Livvy raised her head and stared through her tears at Destiny. "Dee, how long have you been out here?"

Destiny's mouth dropped open. The question stunned her. "Huh? What do you mean?"

"Did you get the hunger again?" Livvy demanded, holding Bree's lifeless hand. "Did you, Dee? Did it happen again?"

Destiny gasped and staggered back. "Are you accusing me? Livvy, are you accusing me? Have you gone crazy?"

Livvy stared up at her, tears rolling down her face. She let Bree's hand fall to the grass. She jumped to her feet, sobbing loudly.

"I—I'm sorry," Livvy said through her tears. "I'm sorry, Dee. I didn't mean it." She threw her arms around Destiny and held her tight, pressing her hot, wet cheek against her sister's.

"I'm sorry. I'm sorry."

"It's okay," Destiny whispered. "I understand. It's okay."

But it wasn't okay.

My own sister, accusing me of murder.

What next?

Destiny stepped out of the house, pumping her legs high, trying to stretch her muscles. A light rain was falling, but she didn't care. She had to get out.

She jogged down the driveway and turned right, heading to Drake Park three blocks down.

157

She turned her Red Sox cap around to let the rain hit her face. The cold raindrops felt soothing on her hot forehead.

Three days of pounding rain, and so much sadness.

Bree's funeral, with the wind tearing at the black umbrellas. The gravesite—the deep, rectangular hole—half filled with brown mud. Rain pattering the dark wood coffin. Like tears. Like tears raining down from the charcoal sky.

Was Bree really inside that coffin? It seemed so impossible.

I'll never forget Livvy's sobs. Dad's grim face. His head bent so low on his shoulders as if it was broken. His hand on my shoulder. I'll never forget how light it felt, the warmth filtering through my dark blouse.

And Coach Bauer so pale and tight-lipped, head bowed, sitting by himself in the last row of the church. I watched him during the service. He never looked up. Was he thinking about Marjory, his wife? Was he thinking that in her hunger she had murdered Bree?

And Bree's mother, her cries echoing off the church walls. "Why? Why did this happen? Somebody tell me!" she screamed. She collapsed beside the casket and had to be helped away.

And as the minister spoke, the sobs in the room drowned out the organ music. . . .

The rain stopped, but drops still fell from the trees. Destiny crossed the street and, running hard, made her way into the park. Her shoes splashed up waves of water from the puddled ground. Behind her, a car horn honked, but she didn't turn around.

I want to run till I'm exhausted. I want to run till I can't think anymore.

But the cool wet air made her more alert, made her thoughts clearer, sharper. The soft thuds of her steps rang in her ears. But she could also hear the scamper of rabbits and squirrels under the trees. She could hear the trickle of water in Drake Creek, the shallow bed of brown water on the far side of the park. She heard a chipmunk's light footsteps as it burrowed through the wet grass.

Destiny pressed her hands over her ears.

I can't stand this. I have to get my life back.

"Hello." A young man stepped out from behind a tree.

"Oh!" Destiny cried out.

He had a warm smile. "I'm so sorry. I didn't

mean to startle you."

Destiny squinted at him. *I've seen him before. Where have I seen him?*

He wore a long black trench coat open over a tan sweater and tan slacks. His wavy black hair was slicked straight back.

"I love walking here," he said. "It's so peaceful." He had a slight foreign accent.

Destiny nodded. "Yeah. No one uses this park much."

He came closer. He stared into her eyes without blinking. "Do you live nearby?"

Destiny motioned with her head. "A few blocks."

Is he nearsighted? Why the intense stare?

"I'm new here," he said. "I just moved a few weeks ago."

Destiny shoved her hands into the pockets of her rain slicker. "Do you like it here?"

A smile spread over his handsome face. "Oh, yes. Very much. And I'm going to like it a lot more in just a few weeks."

Destiny blinked. "A few weeks?"

He nodded. He kept his intense gaze on her as he stepped closer.

He's starting to creep me out, she decided.

He's really good-looking, but there's something about him . . .

"I've gotta go," she said.

But he grabbed her by the shoulders and held her in place. "Don't go, Laura. I don't want you to leave." His eyes burned into hers.

Destiny gazed into them, unable to look away.

"Waiting is so hard for me," he said. "I watch the moon every night, and I think about you. I think about us and how happy we'll be in a few weeks."

Destiny heard the trickle of the creek and the rustle of the leaves in the trees. But she couldn't hear his words. What was he saying to her?

He pulled her to him and pressed his face against hers. "Having you so close to me, Laura . . . I can hardly bear it."

His face felt cold against her cheek. She struggled to hear what he was saying. But it was lost in a steady rush of wind.

"I'm going to stay close to you," he whispered, his dry lips brushing her ear. "I'll be where I can see you every day. And when the time comes . . . when the time comes, my love, *you* will come to me. You will come to me and drink my blood. Then you will be mine forever."

The trees with their fading leaves tilted and swayed above Destiny's head. She felt so dizzy, so weak.

"I'm sorry. I can't resist any longer," he whispered. He pulled back his head, his black eyes glowing.

Destiny struggled to look away. But she couldn't turn. She couldn't move. His eyes were black tunnels, endless, leading nowhere.

He pulled open her rain slicker. He tugged down the neck of her sweatshirt. His mouth opened to reveal curled, yellowed fangs.

"Can't wait any longer . . . can't wait." He lowered his head.

Destiny felt a pinprick of pain at her throat.

She couldn't move, couldn't breathe. Her eyes were as clouded as the sky. But she could see his dark, curly hair beneath her chin . . . see his head bob up and down at her throat as he drank . . . drank . . . drank.

Chapter Twenty-Two

"You Didn't Like Bree"

"What's up?" Livvy turned away from the makeup mirror on her dressing table as Destiny entered their room. "Where've you been?"

"Drake Park," Destiny said. She pulled off the yellow rain slicker and tossed it onto her bed. Her arms and legs ached. She felt so weary. "I went for a run."

Livvy squinted at her. "In the rain?"

Destiny sat down on the bed and pulled off her wet, muddy sneakers. "I just had to get some fresh air. How are you doing?"

Livvy shoved tubes and jars of makeup away. "Not great. I can't stop thinking about Bree. I just can't get my mind off her."

Destiny crossed the room and put her hands on her sister's shoulders. "It's hard. I think about her too. I guess it will just take time."

Livvy's expression turned cold. "You never liked her."

"Huh?"

"I know you didn't. You thought she was a bad influence. Because she was so . . . different. She always did what she wanted to. She didn't care what people thought of her."

Livvy's eyes locked on Destiny. "You thought she was slutty. You thought she was cheap—didn't you! You hated it because I started spending more time with her."

"Livvy, listen. I didn't—" The words caught in Destiny's throat.

"It was so obvious how much you resented Bree."

"Listen to me," Destiny shouted. "Being angry at me isn't going to help. I know you're angry that your friend is dead. But taking it out on me isn't going to bring her back. You and I, we have to—"

"What's that?" Livvy interrupted. She raised a finger to Destiny's throat. "You're bleeding."

"What?" Destiny leaned into the mirror. "Oh, no." Her heart started to pound as she stared at the two red droplets of blood on her throat. Livvy handed her a tissue, and she wiped the blood away.

And now Destiny stared at the two red marks, the tiny cuts in her skin. Fresh red cuts.

Livvy jumped to her feet and angrily shook Destiny. "I knew you've been keeping secrets from me. You didn't go for a run. Where have you been? Tell me the truth. What were you doing?"

"I . . . don't know," Destiny stammered.

"Tell me how this happened," Livvy demanded.

Destiny stared in horror at her reflection. "I can't. I can't explain it, Liv. I did go for a run and—"

"It's not true!" Livvy cried. "You're doing something. You're doing something and not telling me!"

"Livvy, listen to me. Please!"

Livvy's hands were balled into tight fists. "No! You listen to me. I believe what you said, that you didn't kill Bree. But you were there, Dee. You were right there where she was murdered, and you had no reason to be. And now . . . you come home with bite marks on your throat. And you won't tell me the truth about it."

"I don't *know* the truth!" Destiny cried.

"Yes, you do! What are you doing? *What are you doing?*"

Destiny reached to hug her sister, but Livvy pulled away. "You're hysterical. You're not thinking clearly!" Destiny cried. "You have to believe me. I'm not doing anything behind your back, Liv. I'm in the same mess you're in and—"

"*You* didn't lose your best friend," Livvy said through clenched teeth. She slammed her fist on the dressing table, sending tubes and bottles flying. Then she spun away and stomped down the stairs, slamming the front door behind her.

Destiny leaned close to the mirror and studied the fresh marks on her neck. Her hand trembled as she rubbed a finger over them. Her whole body shook.

"Livvy, don't leave me now," she whispered. "I need you more than ever."

The doorbell rang.

Chapter Twenty-Three
A Death in the Family

Destiny hurried down to the front door and pulled it open. "Ross—hi!"

She realized she had her hand over the fresh red wounds. She lowered it slowly, adjusting the top of her sweatshirt.

Ross stepped into the house. He wore a blue-and-red Red Sox jacket over faded jeans. "How's it going, Dee?"

"Not great. How about you?"

"About the same. Hold still." Ross reached out and pulled something from her hair. He showed it to her—a curled, wet leaf.

"I was running. In the park," she said, smoothing back her hair. "You know. To get some fresh air. Time to think."

He nodded. "Fletch and I got a basketball game together at the playground this morning just to take our minds off things. We played in the rain. We didn't care."

She led him into the kitchen. "What's up?"

He pulled up a kitchen stool. "I was over at Courtney's. She had to leave for her tennis lesson."

She poured out two glasses of orange juice and handed him one. "I talked to Courtney this morning. You know how scared she gets at Ari's movies. Now she says she's terrified to leave her house at night."

"Yeah. I tried to cheer her up." He took a long drink.

"Courtney has always been such a scaredy-cat. Remember when we were little and a bunch of us went behind her garage and made scary noises and howls, and we convinced her that her garage was haunted? And for weeks, she was too terrified to go in it and get her bike?"

"That was before I moved here," Ross said. "How come you were all so mean to Courtney?"

Destiny shrugged. "Kids are mean, I guess. And Courtney was always such a good victim."

The word *victim* hung in the air between them. Destiny wished she hadn't said it. She sighed. "School starts on Monday. It's our big-deal senior year. No one feels like going."

"Did you see the paper this morning?

They're calling the guy who murdered Bree the Vampire Killer. Because her blood was totally drained. The police say it's some kind of sick maniac."

Destiny blinked. *Sick maniac.* She rubbed a finger over the tiny wound on her throat. *Sick maniac.*

Did the same sick maniac bite me? Does he plan to kill me too? Why can't I remember? Why?

"So they don't think it's a virus anymore?" Destiny asked, struggling to clear her head.

"No," Ross replied. "They dropped the virus story. They think it's some twisted sicko who started with animals and now has moved on to people."

Destiny nodded, trying not to reveal her fear.

"I heard there might be a curfew in town," Ross continued. "Everyone has to be inside by ten o'clock."

"Maybe they'll catch the guy," Destiny said softly.

"Maybe it's a real vampire," Ross said, spinning the glass between his hands.

She stared at him. "Now you sound like Ari."

"Ari could be right about this. No joke. But

if it's a real vampire, there are people in town ready to deal with him."

Destiny narrowed her eyes at Ross. "You mean . . . the hunters?"

His eyes widened. "You've heard of them?"

Destiny moved closer to him. "What do you know about them?"

Ross shrugged. A strange smile crossed his face. "Nothing, really. Just rumors."

"Ross, have you ever heard of the Restorer?" Destiny blurted out.

He finished his orange juice. "Restorer? You mean *paint* restorer or something?"

"No. The Restorer has something to do with vampires." She looked at him eagerly.

Please—know something.

Ross shook his head. "No. I never heard of that." He studied her. "How come you're asking about that?"

She could feel herself blushing. "It's just something Ari was talking about."

Ross raised his eyes to the hallway. "Is your dad home? I actually came to see him."

"Dad?" Destiny couldn't keep the surprise from her voice. "Dad's at his office. He's been working six days a week. But he said he'd be home early today. If you want to wait."

"Well . . ."

"Why'd you want to see Dad?"

Ross scratched his short hair. "My dog is sick. I wanted to ask him about it."

"Sparky? What's wrong with him?"

Ross hesitated. "I don't know really. He's throwing up and stuff."

Destiny studied him. He seemed so uncomfortable, not like Ross at all. She had a strong feeling he was lying about the dog. But why would he lie?

"Think he'll be home soon?" he asked.

Destiny nodded. "You can help me with a project while you wait."

"Project?"

"I convinced Dad the garage needs to be painted. He's been in such a daze, the whole house is falling apart. I'm trying to snap him out of it. So, he said he'd paint the garage if I drag everything out and pile it on the side of the house. You can help me."

Ross rolled his eyes. "Sounds awesome."

"Oh, come on. It won't take long." She pulled him out to the garage.

They started with the bikes and gardening

equipment. Then Ross dragged out heavy bags of peat moss and planting soil. They talked about friends and school starting and the summer, and carefully avoided mentioning Bree.

He's such a great guy, Destiny thought. I like him so much. She pictured him with his arms around her . . . kissing her.

"You're so different from your sister," Ross said. His cheeks turned pink. They were carrying out Mikey's bike and a bright-yellow plastic Mercedes that he pedaled around in when he was three.

"Different? How do you mean?" Destiny asked.

Before Ross could answer, a voice called from the garage door. "Hey, you two, what's up?"

Ross's eyes went wide. "Livvy, hi."

Livvy wore a blue vest and a tight, cropped pink-and-blue T-shirt and a pair of low-slung jeans. She ignored Destiny. Her eyes were on Ross. "Why are you cleaning out the garage? You moving in?"

He set down the carton he'd been carrying. "Destiny asked me to help."

"I think Dad asked *you* to help too," Destiny said to Livvy. She didn't mean to sound so shrill, but she was unhappy that Livvy had barged in just when she and Ross were starting to really talk.

Livvy walked over to Ross and pulled a clump of dust off his shoulder. She gave him a sexy smile. "Want to take a little break?"

Ross turned back to Destiny. "We got a pretty good start."

Destiny nodded. "Yeah, thanks. It was really nice of you to help out."

Livvy pulled him out the door and to the side of the garage. Destiny heard them giggling about something. She decided to take a break too. Brushing off the front of her jeans, she started toward the house.

She pretended she didn't see Livvy and Ross. Livvy had him backed against the garage wall. His arms were around her waist. Her hands were pressed against his cheeks, her head was tilted to one side, and she was kissing him, a long, passionate kiss.

Destiny turned away and ran into the house.

Livvy and Ross remained at the side of the garage for about half an hour. From the kitchen window Destiny watched Ross leave. Then she grabbed Livvy as she entered the kitchen. "You and I have to talk."

Livvy glared at her. "Can I get something to drink first?"

Livvy grabbed a can of iced tea from the fridge, popped the top, took a long drink, then followed Destiny up the stairs to their room.

"I don't understand why you're not helping," Destiny said. She couldn't keep her voice from trembling.

Livvy stared at her. "Helping with the garage?"

"No. You know what I'm talking about. Helping to find a way to save us. Helping to find the Restorer. You just pretend that we've got all the time in the world."

Livvy sighed. "What are we supposed to do? Look him up in the phone book?"

"We have to do everything we can," Destiny replied. "We have so little time. I've been through every book in the library about vampires and the supernatural. I've gone through website after website. I called someone in the science department at the junior college. I had another long talk with Ari, but he's starting to get suspicious. I'm so desperate, I even called a supernatural-phenomenon hotline I saw advertised in a magazine."

"And?" Livvy asked.

Destiny frowned. "Nothing. No mention anywhere. No one has heard of anything called the Restorer. No clue. Livvy, I'm so terrified."

"Think I'm not?" Livvy replied.

"But you're not helping me," Destiny said. "You're pretending it's all going to be okay. But it isn't. We have maybe a week or two at the most. We can't let the days go by like this. You've been acting strange, Liv. Ever since Bree died, you've been so angry at me."

Livvy lowered her head. Her hair fell over her face, but she made no attempt to push it away. "Okay, okay. What do you want me to do?"

"The first thing is, we have to stick together. We can't let things drive us apart." Destiny thought of Ross. She forced him from her mind.

"We can't give up, Liv," she continued. "We have to do whatever we can to find this Restorer. We'll go back to Mrs. Bauer. She knows more than she told us. We'll go back there. We'll find out what we need to know, and we'll save ourselves."

A sob escaped Livvy's throat. She tore at the sides of her hair. "How can there be any hope? I lost my best friend. And I'm thirsty. I'm thirsty all the time. I'm not getting enough blood, Dee. I'm not!"

Destiny put an arm around her sister's shoulders. "We'll find the Restorer in time. I know we will. I know—"

A high, shrill scream made Destiny jump.

"Help me!"

Mikey's cry from downstairs.

Both sisters scrambled to the stairway.

"Eddy's dead!" They heard Mikey scream. "Eddy's dead! Help me! My hamster is dead!"

Destiny turned and stared at Livvy.

Livvy spun away. "I couldn't help it," she whispered. "I was thirsty."

Chapter Twenty-Four
The Hunters Are Here!

Their dad called while they were still calming Mikey down. Destiny picked it up.

"I've got to work late. I've got two cats here that need stomach operations. Can you girls take care of Mikey tonight?"

"Sure, Dad. No problem. But I'm worried about you. You're working late every night. When are you going to take a break?"

Destiny heard her father sigh. "Beats me. When animals stop getting sick, I guess. See you later, Dee." He clicked off.

Destiny stared at the phone. Mom could always force Dad to come home. I know he cares about us. But why does he want to spend all of his time in his lab now?

She turned to Livvy. "Dad's going to be late. He wants us to watch Mikey."

"But what about Mrs. Bauer?"

"I have an idea." She punched in Ana-Li's

number. "Hey, Ana-Li. It's Destiny. Can you stay with Mikey for an hour or two?"

"Sure," Ana-Li replied. "What's up? Why can't you and Livvy watch him?"

"Uh . . . Dad wanted us to run some errands. You know. Supplies he needs. He can't get away from the office."

Pretty lame. Will she buy it?

"No prob. I'll be right over."

Destiny turned back to Mikey. "You feeling any better?"

"No," he grumbled. He gazed from Livvy to Destiny. "Will you die too?"

Stunned by the question, Livvy gasped. "What on earth?"

Destiny understood. The poor kid. He lost his mom and then his pet. He knew about Bree. So much death this year.

"Livvy and I aren't going to die," she said softly. "We're going to stay with you, Mikey. And we'll always take care of you."

He stared back at her, studying her.

I hope I'm telling him the truth.

Poor Mikey. Poor Mikey. If we don't find the Restorer, he could lose us too.

She turned away quickly to keep him from seeing the tears in her eyes.

* * *

The car headlights bounced off the fog, sending shafts of yellow light shooting in all directions. Destiny drove slowly, leaning over the steering wheel. The sky was solid black, and the fog rolled over the car as if swallowing it.

Livvy was hunched low in the passenger seat, knees on the dashboard, arms crossed tightly in front of her black sweater. "I can't believe you're dragging me back there," she whispered.

Destiny slowed for a stop sign. "Do we have a choice? I told you, I've been doing research day and night. And I haven't found any clues. Not one."

"But this woman is . . . a vampire. She's crazy. She's totally out of her head. She could be really dangerous."

Destiny lowered her foot on the gas. "She won't harm us, remember? She said we were almost vampires too. You keep forgetting that part."

Livvy touched the mark on her throat. "We're doomed, Dee. That crazy woman is not going to help us."

"She *has* to help us," Destiny insisted. "No more negative talk. She *has* to help."

She pulled the car to the foot of the driveway. Coach Bauer's house stood in darkness, half hidden by the curtain of fog. It looked unreal to Destiny, like a movie set of a haunted house.

It *is* haunted. By a woman who's not alive and not dead.

"Turn on the flashlight. I can't see a thing," Livvy whispered as they made their way up the driveway.

"No. No light till we get inside," Destiny said. "We don't want anyone to see us."

"Ow." Livvy tripped over a large rock at the side of the house and stumbled into the shingled wall.

"Careful," Destiny whispered, gripping Livvy's shoulder and helping her to stand upright. "I don't see any lights in the house. Coach isn't home."

"Probably out with his hunters, killing all the vampires in town," Livvy muttered.

"Shhh. Stop. This is freaky enough."

"What if Mrs. Bauer isn't here? What if she's out flying around, killing some of our other friends?"

Destiny stopped short and held Livvy back. "Pull yourself together," she said. "Stop whining. And stop acting like a child and forcing me to be the grownup."

Livvy opened her mouth to protest, but changed her mind.

"Just remember why we're here," Destiny said. "To find out about the Restorer." She carefully pulled open the back door. She poked her head into the dark kitchen. "Anybody home?" she called softly.

Silence.

The cold of the fog clung to her as she stepped into the warm kitchen. She rubbed the back of her neck, trying to smooth the dampness away. Then she clicked on the flashlight.

She sent the circle of light dancing over the room. Dishes were piled in the sink. An empty Hungry-Man dinner box sat on the counter beside two empty beer bottles.

She moved the light to the basement door. The door stood open a crack. Had Mrs. Bauer escaped? Was she out on the prowl?

"Come on," Destiny whispered.

Livvy hovered close behind as Destiny followed the beam of light to the basement door. Destiny pulled the door open slowly. "Anyone there?" she called down.

Silence.

Destiny could hear the hum of the refrigerator. Somewhere outside, far down the block, a car horn honked.

Keeping the light on the stairs, Destiny led the way. The wooden steps creaked and groaned as the girls made their way to the basement.

Destiny stopped at the bottom to catch her breath. If only she could slow her racing heart.

"Where is she? Is she down here?" Livvy stood so close, Destiny could feel her hot breath on the back of her neck.

Destiny moved the circle of light slowly around the cluttered basement. It swept over rows of cartons stacked three high. Past an old couch. Past a large black steamer trunk with a big lock clasped to the front.

The light stopped on a narrow bed against the far wall. First Destiny saw the dark quilt that covered the bed. Then she saw the head on the pillow. Mrs. Bauer!

"At least she doesn't sleep in a coffin," Destiny murmured.

"You've seen too many of Ari's movies," Livvy whispered.

Destiny's legs began to tremble, but she forced them to take a few steps toward the sleeping woman. Suddenly, Mrs. Bauer cringed, let out an angry cry, and shielded her eyes with the back of a bony hand.

Destiny lowered the flashlight. She hadn't even realized she had flashed it into the woman's face.

With a groan, Mrs. Bauer raised herself to a sitting position. She rubbed her sunken eyes, deep in their round sockets. Scraggly hair fell over her face.

"Who is it? Have you come for me?" Her voice came out muffled, as if from somewhere far away. Her bony hands and arms trembled in front of her. "Who are you?"

"It's . . . us again," Destiny managed to whisper. "The Weller twins."

The woman tilted her head one way, then the other. "I used to know a twin, but she died."

Destiny's throat felt dry. She realized her hands were trembling. "Mrs. Bauer, we don't want to disturb you. We just want to ask you—"

"I knew a twin, but she died . . . she died . . . she died . . ." Mrs. Bauer sang the words in a hoarse sing-song.

"We want to ask you one question. Then we'll leave," Destiny said.

"I'm so hungry," the woman rasped. She

stood up, the dark quilt tangled around her long black shift. "So hungry."

"Who is the Restorer?" Livvy asked, clinging close to Destiny. "Please—tell us. Who is the Restorer?"

The woman tilted her head from side to side again. "So close," she whispered. "So close."

"What is so close?" Destiny demanded. "The Restorer? The Restorer is so close?"

"Hungry," Mrs. Bauer murmured. She stuck a finger deep into her eye socket and pulled out a dead fly. "Hungry. So close."

"Is the Restorer close?" Destiny pleaded. "Please—tell us. We need to know who the Restorer is."

"You know, don't you?" Livvy asked. "Don't you? Can you tell us?"

"He . . . couldn't . . . restore me," the woman replied. "He tried. It was . . . too . . . late. Too late for me."

"So you know the Restorer. Where can we find him?" Destiny asked again. "*Please*—tell us."

"So close. So close."

Destiny held her breath, waiting for Mrs. Bauer to say more.

"Tell us!" Livvy pleaded. "Tell us!"

A heavy thud above their heads made all three of them jump. With a gasp, Mrs. Bauer stumbled back against the wall.

Destiny heard a door slam upstairs. Then more heavy thuds. Footsteps. Rapidly crossing the kitchen floor.

"The hunters!" Mrs. Bauer whispered, sunken eyes rolling wildly in their sockets. "They've come. They've found me."

Destiny swallowed hard. "The hunters? They've come here to—"

"To kill me," Mrs. Bauer said. She had her hands at the sides of her head, tugging at her patchy hair. "To kill me."

Livvy grabbed Destiny's arm. "Hurry. We have to get out of here. They'll wonder why we're here with her. And if they check our throats and see the marks, they'll kill us too."

The door to the basement swung open. Destiny heard men's voices, talking rapidly, excitedly. The bright beam of a flashlight swept down the stairs.

Destiny spun around, her eyes circling the basement. "There's no way out, Liv," she whispered. "No way out. We're trapped."

Chapter Twenty-Five

"Come and Get Me!"

Livvy pressed her hands against her cheeks, her features tight with fear. Destiny grabbed Mrs. Bauer's bony arm. "Is there a way out? Can we get out?"

"They've come," Mrs. Bauer replied, her eyes on the stairs. "The hunters have finally come."

Squinting into the darkness, Destiny saw a stairway along the far wall. Did it lead to a door to the outside?

Yes.

"Hurry." Destiny let go of Mrs. Bauer and broke for the stairway. She heard Livvy running close behind. Destiny scrambled up the steep stairs on all fours, then reached up and pushed the metal door open a crack.

She let out a happy cry as the night sky came into view. Using all her strength, she pushed the door open and scrambled up and onto the grass.

Then she turned and helped pull Livvy up. She could hear footsteps crossing the basement. Men's voices. Cries and shouts.

Destiny squinted through the fog. Beyond the low shrubs at the back of the yard, she could see the black silhouettes of trees. The woods. "Let's go."

She and Livvy took off, running full speed, shoes slipping over the dew-wet grass. As they neared the trees, Destiny glanced back—and saw Mrs. Bauer climbing out of the basement.

Mrs. Bauer scrambled to her feet and began to lurch toward the trees. "Come and get me!" she shouted. "Come and get me!" Her black shift flapped in the wind. Her scraggly hair flew around her skeletal face.

Destiny and Livvy reached the safety of the trees. They ducked down beside each other, hiding in the darkness. Breathing hard, they peered back to the yard.

Bright halogen lanterns sent wide circles of white light over the grass. The lanterns swept over the ground, bright as day, lighting the figures pursuing Mrs. Bauer, trapping her in harsh spotlights.

Holding on to the rough bark of a tree,

Destiny could see their hooded sweatshirts, hear their shouts.

"Livvy—that tall one—is that Coach Bauer?"

"I don't know. I think so."

"And those guys shouting to each other. Oh my God. I think I recognize their voices. Aren't those guys from the basketball team?" Destiny whispered.

Livvy stared straight ahead. "I . . . I think so. Is Ross there? Has he become a hunter? Oh no. Why didn't he tell us?"

Destiny grabbed on to her sister as the dark-hooded hunters formed a circle around Mrs. Bauer. "Come and get me! Come and get me!" Shrieking at the top of her lungs, the woman spun in the white light, arms floating above her head.

And then one of the hunters moved forward quickly. His arms shot up. And in the shifting lights, Destiny saw the wooden stake he held between his hands.

Mrs. Bauer appeared to tumble back as the man lurched forward. He hoisted the stake high over his head—and plunged it into her chest.

Like the howl of a wild animal, Mrs. Bauer's

shrill scream echoed off the trees.

Destiny let go of her sister and covered her ears with her hands. But she couldn't shut out the horrifying wail of anguish.

Then, silence as Mrs. Bauer fell to the grass.

"No! Oh, no." Livvy uttered a low cry.

Destiny gasped and clasped a hand over her sister's mouth.

"Who's that?" a boy called.

A chill of horror rushed down Destiny's back as the hooded figures turned away from the fallen woman.

"There's someone in the woods," a boy said.

"Is that Fletch?" Livvy whispered. "Yes, I think it is."

Destiny and Livvy exchanged a terrified glance.

"More vampires. In the woods. Get them!" one of the men commanded.

The white circles of light turned toward the trees.

Destiny froze as the hunters trotted toward the trees, lights held low, searching the ground.

They're going to catch us and kill us too. They're going to shove a wooden stake in my heart. My own friends. My own friends are going to kill me.

Destiny gave Livvy a shove, and the two girls took off, running side by side, ducking under low branches, dodging shrubs and upraised tree roots.

"This way," a guy shouted, close behind them.

Lights bounced off the tree trunks.

Destiny lowered her head and ran. She darted through a wide patch of tall reeds and kept going. A narrow, trickling creek ran along the other side of the reeds. She and Livvy splashed over the creek, running hard, into the tangle of trees on the other side.

Weird. I'm not breathing hard, Destiny thought. And suddenly, she also realized that she could see the trees and weeds and shrubs so clearly, as if it were daytime.

She saw Livvy shoot ahead, moving from one side to another, darting and dodging as if there were a path.

I've never run this fast, Destiny thought. I can see every tree leaf, every weed, every rock on the ground.

Where are the hunters?

Destiny glanced back. No lights. Their voices far behind.

She and Livvy picked up speed. They were practically flying over the ground now, senses alert, not growing tired, no aches in their sides, not even breathing hard.

"We're okay," Destiny whispered. "We've outrun them."

Livvy murmured, "I never ran so fast."

"Yes, we outran them easily," Destiny replied. "It . . . it's because we're not human anymore. We outran them because we're *creatures* now."

Livvy's mouth dropped open. "You're right, Dee. Something horrible has happened. I can see bats hiding in those trees. And . . . and I can smell their blood. I can hear their blood pulsing, and smell it . . . smell it. . . . Ohh, I feel so sick."

"Oh, Livvy," Destiny wailed and pulled her sister close, into a tight hug. "How much time is left? In a few weeks or a few days, we won't be ourselves anymore. We'll be disgusting night creatures, living for blood, crazy as poor Mrs. Bauer."

"I'm hungry *now*," Livvy moaned.

"We've got to find the Restorer," Destiny said. And then added in a trembling voice, "Soon."

"But how? She didn't give us a clue, Dee."

"I know. She kept saying he was close. Close."

"But that might not be a clue at all. She was out of her mind, Dee. She wasn't making any kind of sense."

"I know, but . . ."

The hunger overcame her so suddenly. A powerful gnawing in her belly, a coiling ache that made her groan.

She saw the raccoons slinking silently at the edge of the woods, gray fur glimmering, tails waving behind them. Destiny counted—six small ones led by a big, fat one.

"Yes! Yes! I'm so hungry!"

Using fallen leaves to wipe the blood from their faces, the girls stepped out of the woods. They found themselves on Steinway Street, five or six blocks from their house.

Destiny checked in all directions. "We lost the hunters," she said, striding toward the street.

"This time," Livvy added glumly. "But what if they saw our car parked there? They'll know—"

"We have to get it—fast."

Deep in thought, they didn't see the figure on the sidewalk until they nearly bumped into him.

Destiny uttered a startled cry.

He wore a dark sweatshirt, his hair flew wildly around his face, and his jeans were stained and torn.

"Ari!" Destiny cried. "What are you doing here?"

Chapter Twenty-Six

Is Ari a Hunter?

"Did you see the hunters?" Ari asked breathlessly. "I heard they were out tonight. I tried to find them."

"We . . . didn't see anyone," Destiny said.

"I'm totally disappointed," Ari said, shaking his head. "I really want to see a vampire."

Does he suspect something? Destiny wondered. How come he's staring at Livvy and me like that?

"Where are you two coming from?" he asked.

They both spoke up at the same time.

"The mall," Livvy said.

"Courtney's house," Destiny answered.

Ari narrowed his eyes at them. "You're putting me on, right?" He stepped up closer to Destiny and pointed. "Is that blood on your chin?"

"Huh?" Destiny gasped and rubbed her chin

with a finger. "Oh, yeah. I just bit my lip. It's nothing."

I don't like the way he's staring at me.

Is Ari lying? Is he actually a vampire hunter? Did he join the hunters? Was he at Coach Bauer's with the others? Did he follow Livvy and me?

I can't believe it. I went over to his house and asked him about everything. I practically *told* him I was a vampire. How could I be so stupid?

"Maybe I'll come by later," Ari said to Destiny.

Come by with your hunter friends? To kill Livvy and me?

"Not a good idea," Destiny said. "Livvy and I have to get our beauty sleep. I mean, school starts tomorrow. Remember school?"

Ari grinned. "Oh, yeah. School. I almost forgot."

"Dee and I have to figure out what we're going to wear," Livvy said. "That could take hours."

"So, Dee, maybe you'll help me with my French this semester?"

Why is he playing this game? Trying to throw us off the track?

"Yeah, sure. No problem," she said.

"Great." He flashed Destiny a smile. "See you guys tomorrow." He pulled the sweatshirt hood over his head, turned, and began to jog toward his house.

Livvy couldn't hide her fear. "Did he see us in the woods just now? Is he one of Coach Bauer's hunters, Dee?"

Destiny shook her head. "I don't know. I don't know what to think."

They returned to the car and drove home in silence. Destiny couldn't stop thinking about Marjory Bauer. Again and again, she heard the woman's shrill scream as the wooden stake came down. She saw the stake pierce the poor woman's body. And then there was such a heavy silence, such a heavy, terrifying silence.

The poor woman wanted to die. She wanted her husband to kill her. Did Coach Bauer finally do it? Was he the hooded figure who drove the stake into her chest?

The twins crept into the house through the back door. "Oh." Destiny uttered a low cry when she heard the voices in the living room. Peeking through the hallway, she saw her dad and Coach Bauer.

Bauer was even more pale than usual. He appeared very upset. He kept burying his face in his hands, then looking up and talking rapidly.

Dr. Weller kept shaking his head sadly.

Both men were speaking just above a whisper. Destiny couldn't make out their words. Frozen in fear, she held on to her sister and stared at the two men.

Is Coach Bauer telling Dad about killing his wife?

Did he see us there in the woods?

The next morning, a raw, gray day threatening rain, Destiny and Livvy gazed at Dark Springs High from across the street.

It was a three-story old-fashioned school building built of yellow bricks that had weathered to a muddy brown over the years. A thick wall of ivy grew up to the slanted, black-slate roof, darkening the front of the school even more. Two tall brick chimneys, side by side at the back of the building, coughed puffs of black smoke into the charcoal sky.

"It looks like some kind of haunted castle today," Livvy said, adjusting her backpack on her shoulders.

"It's just your mood," Destiny said. "And these sunglasses make everything look darker."

The girls' eyes had grown even more sensitive. Now they had to wear sunglasses whenever they went outside.

"How are we going to explain the shades, Dee?"

"Maybe no one will ask."

They crossed the street. Destiny felt a cold drop of rain on her forehead. She and Livvy jogged to the front entrance. They opened the door to the roar of voices and slamming lockers.

Ana-Li stopped Destiny outside the principal's office. "Hey, what's up with the shades?"

"It's some stupid eye infection," Destiny said. "Livvy and I both have it."

Ana-Li turned to look at Livvy across the hall, talking to a group of boys. "Wow. Check out Livvy's low-cut jeans. Are those sexy or what? I can't believe she wore those to school."

Destiny sighed. "Livvy is Livvy."

She caught Ana-Li examining her. "You're so thin, Dee. Are you on a diet or something?"

"Not really."

"Bell's going to ring. You know where your homeroom is?"

"I just got here, Ana-Li. I have to check out the list. Catch you later, okay?"

"Donohue's for lunch? I'll drive."

"Yeah. I guess. Maybe."

Destiny pushed her way through a group of kids to get to the bulletin board where the homeroom assignments were listed.

"He's gorgeous," she heard a girl behind her say. "Wait till you see him. I mean, movie-star gorgeous."

"Someone said he's student-teaching for McCall," another girl said. "But I heard he's the new college advisor."

"Maybe he tutors after school," the first girl joked.

Both girls laughed.

Destiny elbowed her way into the crowd around the bulletin board. She found the homeroom sheet for seniors and searched for her name.

"Dee, you're in Ms. Downs's room with me."

Destiny turned at the sound of the familiar voice. "Courtney, hi. Hey, you cut your hair."

"Last week," Courtney said, puffing up the sides of her short, bobbed hair. "That ponytail was so lame. Where've you been, Dee? I keep calling you, and—"

"Sorry. Really. Things have been weird."

"Have you been sick? You look kinda pale."

"Well—"

It shows. Everyone can see that I've changed.

"Move it. You're blocking traffic." Fletch gave Destiny a playful shove. "Hey, what's up? I like the shades. Let me see them."

He made a grab for them, but Destiny pulled away. She knew the bright hall lights would burn her eyes.

"Hey, Dee, I only wanted to look at them."

"I've got an eye infection."

"Gross." He backed away, stumbling into some other guys, waving with both hands for her to stay back.

The first bell rang. The hall began to empty out as kids made their way to their homerooms. Destiny looked for Courtney, but she had disappeared down the hall.

Destiny hurried past two boys who looked very lost, obviously freshmen. She hurried up the stairs, her backpack bouncing on her shoulders, then turned to go down the first hall—and walked right into a young man.

"Oh. Sorry."

She stared at him. At his wavy black hair slicked straight back, his broad, tanned forehead, the black, piercing eyes, the warm smile.

He wore a creamy white turtleneck over tight-fitting black slacks. He had a silver stud in one ear.

He must be the gorgeous new teacher. That girl was definitely right!

"Sorry. It was my fault," he said. "I wasn't watching where I was going." He had a slight Italian accent.

"No problem," Destiny managed, a little overcome by his dark-eyed stare, his amazing good looks.

"My name is Lorenzo Angelini," he said. He took her hand and shook it. "But everyone calls me Renz. I'm new here. I truly hope we'll get to know one another."

Part Four

Chapter Twenty-Seven
Lorenzo and Laura

As Renz watched the students hurrying to their classrooms, a familiar longing swept over him. Memories of his youth came flooding back. He pressed his back against the tiled wall, remembering. . . .

If only he could make time go backward. Back to those bright, cloudless days two centuries ago when Laura Hanover walked her father's fields in the tiny farming village of Dark Springs.

Lorenzo Angelini had lived his life in a fog of hunger and desire. For centuries, he knew only hunger—the hunger to remember, the hunger to feed, and the hunger to find the beautiful, lost Laura again.

These desires shaped his life. He had been a vampire for so long, and had consumed so much blood—it had kept him from aging. He appeared young and robust. He could walk in bright daylight without being burned up by the sun.

But daylight was no different than night to him. He lived only to survive the blackness that surrounded him day or night. He lived only to find Laura.

Laura with her creamy skin, her high, proud cheekbones, her sparkling emerald eyes, as green as the high pasture grass they walked through together.

Her voice . . . her wonderful laugh . . .

Renz could no longer hear them. Time had taken them away from him. And now he struggled to hold on to her smile, to remember the sweet gardenia aroma of her perfume. It took all his power to picture her walk, those long strides beneath the skirts that swept over the ground.

That night in the alley in New York, the vampire changed his life forever. Now he lived in eternal winter. Eternal winter . . . until he saw Laura.

A gray fall day. He had been running, fleeing one angry town after another, a stolen, beaver-fur overcoat draped over his tattered black suit.

"What town is this?" he asked the owner of the ramshackle, two-story boardinghouse. Dark

Springs, he was told. Lorenzo took a room for a half dollar a week. At the end of the week, he didn't pay it. He bit the old man's throat instead and drank him dry. The blood was sour, too old, spoiled like a wine gone bad.

That day, he saw Laura. A town market, villagers crowding the narrow Main Street and the open plaza. She was helping her father, carrying a basket of potatoes to a market stand.

Their eyes met.

He stared. She didn't lower her eyes. He felt something—an attraction. Did she feel it too? He couldn't tell by her slow, half smile.

He gathered his courage and walked over to the stand. He knew already that he was in love with her. He knew that he had to win her and keep her with him for all time.

He had to make her immortal too.

She laughed as he teased her about the potatoes. He drew a face on one and said it resembled her father. She grabbed it away from him and protested, "How can I sell it now? Go away. You will make us poor."

But he could tell by the blush on her cheek and the flash of her green eyes that she didn't want him to go away.

Lorenzo knew his charms. So many young women had fallen for him, for his Italian good looks, his wavy dark hair, the mystery in his black eyes. So many young women had fallen . . . and died.

But not Laura, he decided. Laura will live with me through the centuries.

Soon, he was taking long walks with her through the pleasant little village, laughing with her . . . kissing her, gently at first, then showing his passion. What a thrill when she showed the same passion for him!

Seeing his tattered suit and, perhaps, the wild look in his eyes, Laura's father didn't approve of Renz. The couple had to meet secretly in town or at the bubbling springs at the dark rock hills.

One warm summer night by the springs, the scent of marigolds and pine floating in the air, a full moon high in the cloudless sky, Lorenzo wrapped Laura in a tender hug, brought his face close, and whispered, "I want you to be with me always."

To his surprise, she pulled away. "Father will never allow it," she said, tugging tensely at the long sleeves of her blouse. "He is set against you, Renz. For reasons I cannot fathom. He will not allow us to marry, and as much as it tears my heart in two, I cannot go against my father. I have no choice but to follow his wishes."

Lorenzo had expected as much. Farmer Hanover was a big, strong-spirited man, quick to anger. Once, in fury, he had heaved a pitchfork at a traveling salesman and nearly killed the man. And Lorenzo had seen him lift a three-hundred-pound hog off the ground and toss it back into its pen.

The man was a lion with a lovely, gentle doe for a daughter.

Lorenzo gazed up at the yellow full moon as Laura fell back into his arms. Tears rolled down her cheeks and stained the shoulder of his shirt.

"I would wish it any other way," she sobbed, "but we must continue to meet in secret. If Father finds out, there is no telling what he would do. He could kill you, Lorenzo. If his anger got the best of him, he really could."

"I know a way we can be together for always," he whispered. "It will cause a little pain, but only for a short while. And then we will live side by side for eternity."

She gazed at him, her cheeks red and

tearstained, her lovely, green eyes wide, brimming with more tears. "Lorenzo, my darling, what are you saying? I have explained to you that Father will not allow—"

"Your father cannot stop us, Laura," he said. And then he could wait no longer, for the full moon had reached its peak. His curled fangs lowered from his gums. "Ignore the pain, my loved one. After this night, we shall know only pleasure."

He sank his fangs deep into her throat.

She uttered a startled gasp, but made no cry, no scream of protest. She did not fight him or try to squirm free.

Drinking her warm, sweet blood, he knew she was his.

That moment was the happiest of his life.

As he finished, she sank her teeth into his chest and drank his blood.

The bloods mix under a full moon at its peak, he thought. And now Laura is mine.

Blood dripping from their lips, they kissed.

Renz heard the angry, shouting voices, but he didn't want to end the embrace. Hands grabbed him roughly and pulled him away.

Renz turned to see Laura's red-faced father,

chest heaving under his black coat, hands clamped into tight fists. His entire body quivered with rage.

Two somber, bearded men in long waistcoats stood at Farmer Hanover's side. Renz lowered his gaze to the muskets with their long bayonets in their hands.

"Kill him," came Hanover's command.

The men obediently raised their bayonets.

Laura jumped in front of Renz and opened her mouth in a wail of protest. Her father shoved her aside, sent her sprawling to the grass.

Then the two men grabbed Lorenzo by the arms. They held him in place as Hanover raised his giant fist and pounded it into Lorenzo's face.

I can feel pain, Lorenzo realized with surprise.

The fist came down again, this time on Lorenzo's left ear.

He heard Laura scream again.

Another powerful swing and the fist caught him between the eyes. Pain roared through his head.

Groaning, Lorenzo climbed unsteadily to his feet. He jerked free of his two captors, ducked another swipe from her father's tight fist—and took off running into the woods.

Lowering his head into the wind, he dove through the trees. He could hear the thuds of the boots of the men pursuing him. But they could not shift shapes as he could. As he reached the trees, his body shrank into a new form, and he ran as a field mouse, low in the grass.

But his thoughts were not of escape. His thoughts were of Laura.

Her father came too late. He cannot separate us now. He cannot keep us apart. For I have drunk her blood and she has drunk mine, under the light of the full moon.

Lorenzo scampered into a deep hole in the ground. He could hear the men searching for him through the trees, cursing under their breath. He waited for their footsteps to fade.

Laura, I will come to you later tonight. I will come to you after your churlish father has fallen asleep. And I will take you away, take you far from here where you will no longer have to fear him.

He waited until the moon dropped behind the trees. Then, still a field mouse, he made his way through the tall grass of the north pasture, to the back of the low, pine farmhouse.

The field mouse stopped on the sandy

ground behind Laura's bedroom window. Its body raised up, shifted, cracking noisily, the sound of stretching bones, as Lorenzo resumed his human form.

He leaned against the rough wood wall and edged up to the sill of the window. Curtains fluttered in the gentle, warm breeze. The window stood open wide. *As if inviting him in.*

Yes. Laura would be waiting for him. Of course, she would expect him to come rescue her. To come carry her away from this dreary farm forever. To lead her to a life that would transcend the centuries.

He gripped the windowsill and pulled himself up. His boots scraped the pine wall as he let himself inside. The silky curtains tangled around him as he lowered himself to the bedroom floor.

"Laura?" His whisper came out louder than he'd planned, but he heard no reply.

Can she be sleeping so soundly after the terrible scene at the springs?

Lorenzo untangled himself from the curtains and took a step toward her bed. "Laura? I have come for you."

Still no reply.

Her bed came into view against the bare wall. Lingering moonlight cast blue shadows over the folds of the bed quilt.

"Laura?"

He could see her head, tilted slightly on the pillow, her fine, blond hair falling over her face.

Yes. Laura. Beautiful Laura. Waiting for him with her window open.

"Laura? It's me."

He reached out a hand and gently touched the shoulder of her nightdress.

And then he raised his eyes to the bed quilt and saw it . . .

. . . saw it . . .

His eyes bulged and his hand fell off her shoulder.

Howling in rage, in shock, in pain, Lorenzo staggered back, fell back against the curtains. Let them wrap themselves around him again, muffling his screams, his wails of horror and sadness.

Chapter Twenty-Eight
Laura, Again

Through the gauzy curtains, he could see it silhouetted in the faint, dying moonlight.

The stake.

A wooden stake, driven through Laura's chest. A circle of dark blood, dried now, around the stake, running onto the quilt.

Laura. Beautiful Laura, sleeping so peacefully, arms under the quilt, hair sliding over her lovely, pale face.

Laura, murdered by her own father, murdered to keep her from Lorenzo, from the eternal life he had planned for them together.

Lorenzo pulled the curtains around him as if forming a cocoon—a cocoon to hide him from the sight of his beautiful Laura, lying so peacefully in her bed, the wooden stake protruding up from her still body, tilting toward the wall.

Another sob escaped his throat. He wrapped the curtains tighter around him and shut his eyes. But that didn't stop the tears from falling.

And then his grief turned to fury. He ripped the curtains away, planted a final kiss on Laura's cold cheek. Then he made his way to her father's room.

The man was awake, sitting in a wooden rocking chair beside a dying fire. His features were twisted in anger. Large drops of sweat glistened on his forehead.

His big, powerful hands gripped something in his lap. Only his eyes moved when Lorenzo entered the room.

He's waiting for me, Lorenzo thought.

In the flickering red light from the remaining embers, he saw the object in Hanover's hands—a pointed fence post.

He plans to kill me too. But no. Laura will be avenged.

Lorenzo dove for Hanover's throat and sliced into it with his fangs. Hanover opened his mouth to protest, but only a gurgling sound escaped.

The wooden stake fell from his hands and clattered onto the floor.

Lorenzo drank his fill, drained the man,

then ripped open his throat with his hands. He wrenched Hanover's head off, and flung it into the fire.

His heart still pounding with fury, he took one last look at the goggle-eyed head lying upside down in the orange embers. Then he left, lowering himself from the window, into the darkness.

Darkness for the decades to come. How many years passed? Nearly two hundred? He couldn't remember.

He couldn't bear to venture very far from Dark Springs. He kept to himself, prowling at night for creatures on which to feed. The decades passed without hope, without pleasure of any kind, without light.

Until he saw Laura again.

Laura?

No! It couldn't be!

But she had Laura's face, her high cheek-bones, her smile, her bright green eyes. Lorenzo stared at her, frozen in disbelief. Stared at her across the high school parking lot.

She leaned against a black SUV, her eyes on the back entrance, tapping the car roof impatiently with one hand. Her fine, blond hair fell loosely to her collar. Her face . . .

Her face . . .

Laura.

She checked her watch. He saw the wedding ring on her finger. She brushed back her hair. She bit her lip fretfully.

Lorenzo's excitement, his disbelief, held him back. But he forced himself to approach her. "Have we met? I believe I know you." He flashed her his most charming smile.

Still biting her lip, she narrowed her eyes at him. "No. I don't think so."

Lorenzo scratched his head. "I'm so sorry. My mistake. I knew a woman named . . . Hanover. She resembled you so much, I—"

"Hanover?" the woman's eyes grew wide. "Really? There were some Hanovers in my family. But that was way back, generations ago."

He grinned. "I see. I must be confused. I'm Lorenzo Angelini," he told her. "Are you waiting for someone?"

She turned back to the school. "Yes, my daughters. I told them I'd pick them up now. I should go in and get them." She saw his outstretched hand. "Oh. Sorry. I'm Deborah

Weller. Nice to meet you."

The touch of her hand thrilled him. He held on to it until she pulled it away.

The back door of the high school opened. Two blond-haired girls came running out.

"Destiny! Livvy! Over here," Deborah called.

She motioned to her daughters to hurry, and pulled open the car door. "Nice to meet you, Mr. Angelini."

"Nice to meet you too."

Very nice indeed.

Chapter Twenty-Nine
The Vampire's Kiss

"Who has the cheese fries?"

Ari raised his hand and the waitress dropped the plate in front of him next to his double cheeseburger.

"You on a diet, Ari?" Ana-Li reached across the table and grabbed a cheese fry off the plate. "Ow. They're hot."

Ari grinned at her. "Take another one and I'll smack you."

Ana-Li grabbed another one.

Ari grabbed her wrist. "Drop. Drop."

Destiny saw the manager watching them. "Give it a rest, guys. How embarrassing would it be to get kicked out of Donohue's?"

"It wouldn't be the first time," Ari said. He bent Ana-Li's wrist back until she dropped the fry—into his Coke. Ana-Li burst out laughing.

Livvy appeared beside the booth. She gave

Ari a shove. "Move it over." She squeezed in next to him. "You already ordered?" She gazed at Destiny's plate. "Two hamburgers?"

Destiny nodded. "I'm starving."

"You never used to eat burgers rare like that," Ana-Li said. "Yuck. It looks like blood dripping from them."

Livvy waved the waitress over. "I'll have a hamburger too. Very, very rare, and a diet Coke." She turned to Ana-Li. "What's up?"

"Ari won't share his fries."

Ari slammed his hands on the table. "Here. Take them all." He shoved the plate toward Ana-Li.

"Thanks." Ana-Li began eating them one by one.

Livvy leaned across the table and whispered. "Hear what the girls in the next booth are talking about? That new guidance counselor. What's-his-name? Renz."

Ari grinned. "Yeah. He's always telling everyone to call him Renz. What kinda name is that? Sounds like something from a sci-fi movie. Renz the Destroyer!"

"He is definitely cute," Ana-Li said.

Destiny put down her fork. "Cute? You're

kidding, right? He's not cute. He's totally gorgeous."

Ana-Li giggled. "Dee likes the dark, mysterious types."

"Hey, I have an appointment with him after school," Destiny said. Across the table, Livvy had a scowl on her face. "Liv, what's your problem?"

Livvy shook her head and sighed. "Nothing. No big thing. Really. Well . . ."

"What is it?" Destiny asked.

Livvy played with one long, dangling earring. "Just thinking about Bree. You know. How she's missing senior year and everything."

"I miss her too," Ana-Li said in a whisper.

Ari swallowed a big chunk of cheeseburger. "On TV this morning, they said the police don't have a clue about the Vampire Killer. And the hunters don't have a clue either."

Destiny gaped at him. "The hunters? What about the hunters? They were on TV?"

Ari's cheeks burned red. "No. Some guys were talking. You know. About vampires in town and the vampire hunters. I really don't know much about it. You've heard the rumors too—right?"

He took another bite of cheeseburger,

avoiding Destiny's eyes.

So he really is one of the hunters, Destiny decided. Why did he blush like that? Because he didn't mean to mention them. It just slipped out.

Destiny gazed across the table at Ari and felt a shiver race down her back. I've known Ari since third grade. Is he really going to hunt me down and kill me? Are Livvy and I really going to be killed by our own friends?

"Bree would have loved the senior overnight trip," Livvy said. "She was really looking forward to it."

"Yes, she would have," Ari said, sighing. His expression brightened. "I'm bringing a super-sized sleeping bag. You know. In case any girls get lonely during the night." He grinned at Destiny.

"Some kids got caught last year," Ana-Li said. "Mr. Arthur walked into the tent and . . . there they were, messing around. It was so not cool."

"I heard about it," Livvy said. "They both got suspended."

"Worth it," Ari said, cheeseburger grease running down his chin. He grinned at Destiny. Destiny looked away.

Ana-Li handed him a napkin. "I heard the school is bringing a lot more chaperones this year," she said. "You know. To make sure no one messes around."

"Hey, maybe Renz will be a chaperone." Destiny tried to join the conversation.

"You've really got a thing for him," Livvy said, frowning at her sister.

Destiny shrugged. "What's your problem? I can't like older guys?"

"Anyway, the senior overnight should be cool if it doesn't rain," Ana-Li said. "I heard it's a four-mile hike to get to the camping ground."

"Can't we drive?" Ari asked. He laughed at his own joke. "Guess what? It's gonna be a full moon that night." He grinned at Ana-Li and did a werewolf howl. "Owooooo. It could get pretty freaky."

Destiny shuddered. She hadn't known it was the night of the full moon. She suddenly felt cold all over.

Livvy glanced at her watch. "Where's Ross? He said he'd meet me."

"Are you sure?" Destiny asked. "He's been at that booth behind you for half an hour. He's with Courtney." She pointed.

"Huh? You're joking." Livvy spun around.

Ross sat beside Courtney in the booth near the front. He had his arm draped around her shoulders, and their faces were close together as they talked. They both laughed and Courtney pressed her forehead against his cheek.

Livvy jumped to her feet. "I don't believe it. That creep. What's he doing with Courtney?"

She stepped away from the booth and went storming down the aisle.

"Livvy—come back," Destiny called. "Hey—just calm down. What are you going to do?"

Her hair bouncing behind her, Livvy strode past Ross's booth. She kept her eyes straight ahead. She totally ignored them. Destiny watched her bang the glass front door open and disappear outside.

"Whoa. Bad news." Ana-Li clapped a hand over her mouth.

The waitress appeared with Livvy's hamburger and drink. She stared at the empty spot in the booth. "Is she coming back?"

"I don't think so," Destiny said.

After school, Destiny made her way down the stairs, past the empty lunchroom, and found

Renz's office at the end of the hall next to a janitor's closet. She knocked on the wooden door, then pushed it open.

She saw him standing at an empty bookcase, his back to her. He turned as she entered, and a smile crossed his face.

His wavy hair glistened under the single ceiling light. His dark eyes flashed. "Welcome to my castle." He motioned around the room.

"I think it used to be a supply closet," Destiny said. The narrow room had no windows. The bookcase, a low file cabinet, a desk, a desk chair, and a folding chair in front of the desk were the only furnishings.

"You know the old joke," he said. "The room is so small, I have to go outside to change my mind."

Destiny laughed, harder than she meant to.

He motioned for her to sit down in the folding chair.

She gazed at the empty shelves. "Mr. Angelini, where's all your stuff?"

He lowered himself to the edge of the desk in front of her. She could smell his aftershave or cologne, sharp, not sweet. "Please. Renz," he said, leaning over her. "My books haven't arrived yet. They were delayed. I feel so lost without them." He smiled at her again, his black eyes locked on hers.

Destiny felt a shiver of excitement.

"I need to decorate," he said. "Put something up on the wall. Something colorful." He sighed. "I'm not good at transitions. Moving to a new town. A new job. It takes me a while to get going."

Destiny smiled up at him. "I don't know what it's like. I've lived in Dark Springs my whole life."

I feel so comfortable with him. It's strange. As if I've known him a long time. This is our first conversation, but I'm not nervous at all.

He stood up and closed the door. "We should talk about colleges. I'll get your file, Laura."

Destiny blinked. "Laura? No. I'm Destiny."

He stood close. The aroma of the cologne washed over her. She inhaled a piney smell, an outdoors smell, the smell of the woods.

"No," he whispered, "you're Laura. Don't you remember me, Laura? Aren't you happy to see me again?"

With surprising strength, he pulled her to her feet.

"Mr. Angelini, please. I don't understand. I—"

Destiny made no attempt to resist as he wrapped her in his arms, brought her face up to his, and pressed his lips to hers.

Chapter Thirty

Destiny Finds the Restorer

"Laura . . . Laura . . ." he whispered when the kiss finally ended.

Destiny gazed into his eyes. I know you. I know your thoughts. I know who you are.

The room darkened, as if a gray fog had risen over them. The piney aroma carried her to the woods. In the darkening fog, she could hear the flutter of birds' wings, the cry of night animals, and the rasping chirp of crickets.

"You remember me, don't you, Laura?" he whispered, his breath tingling her ear. The tingle continued down her neck, her back. She knew she was shivering. She couldn't stop.

He held her tightly. "You remember me. And you remember our love for each other. You remember the full moon . . . the night our love changed us, blood for blood."

His gaze didn't move from her eyes. He didn't blink.

Destiny felt powerless to look away, to move, to protest. She took a deep breath and finally found her voice. "You have powers . . ." Her words came out muffled, as if from far away.

Renz gazed at her. "What did you say?"

"You're doing something to me. You have powers, don't you?"

A smile spread slowly over his face. "Well . . ."

"Please tell me. Tell me about your powers."

A jarring sound made her jump.

A knock on the door.

Renz let go of her and moved back.

The door swung open. The fog lifted.

Blinking, Destiny stared at Ari as he poked his head into the room.

His eyes went wide. "Oh. Sorry." He didn't let go of the doorknob. "I didn't know you were busy, Renz." He squinted at Destiny. "How's it going, Dee?"

She blinked. "Fine."

"Did he get you into college yet?" Ari asked.

Renz chuckled. "In case you don't realize it, Ari, getting into college is a long process." He edged away from Destiny and stepped up to Ari. "Did you want me for something?"

"You said you had brochures. You know, from Brown and Tufts."

"Let me see." Frowning, Renz moved to his file cabinet and began sifting through the top drawer.

Destiny gazed at him, so good-looking in that black turtleneck, those tight, black jeans.

Renz handed Ari a couple of brightly colored brochures. "I'm not sure if they accept the standard application," Renz said, backing Ari to the door. "I'll check."

Destiny climbed unsteadily to her feet. "I guess we're finished for today?"

Renz turned and stared at her. He appeared to be thinking hard. "Yes, we're done." His smile made her feel so warm. "But we need to talk about school visits. Discuss it with your parents, okay? Then we'll talk again."

Destiny thanked him and made her way out of the tiny closet. Ari was waiting for her in the hall. "How'd it go, Dee?"

"Okay, I guess."

They walked together past the lunchroom, then up the stairs. "Are you in love with him like all the other girls in the senior class?"

Destiny laughed. "He's pretty damn cute."

Ari shook his head. "Aren't college advisors supposed to have all kinds of books and papers and stuff? His office is totally empty. He spends all his time out in the hall, flirting with every girl who passes by."

"Ooh, jealous, jealous," Destiny teased.

"Oh, for sure," he replied, but his cheeks turned bright pink.

"Ari, how come you're here so late after school?"

He shrugged. "I had a few things to do. You walking home?"

"No, I drove this morning. Want a lift?"

"Hey, yeah. Good deal. Thanks."

She drove him to his house. They talked about French class. He made her promise to help him. They gossiped about some kids who'd been cutting class to hang out in their cars at the springs. Ari talked about two new horror DVDs he'd rented, both of which he said were awesome.

Destiny pretended to listen, but she barely heard a word Ari said. She still felt strange, off-balance, fogged in. She couldn't stop thinking about Renz.

He was so warm, so friendly and caring. Some of their conversation drifted back to her.

Just words and phrases, floating in her mind . . .
Blood for blood . . . powers . . . full moon . . .
Laura . . .

Destiny struggled to make sense of it all.

Suddenly, she realized that Ari was staring at her. At the marks on her throat? Was he staring at the marks on her throat and figuring out what had happened to her?

"Dee, there's something I have to tell you," he said softly.

She pulled the car into his driveway. Her heart started to pound. She couldn't speak. She nodded, signaling him to go on.

"Well . . ." He hesitated. His hands fidgeted at his sides. "It's just that . . . I . . . kinda like you."

Then he lurched toward her and pressed his lips against hers.

The kiss lasted only a few seconds. Destiny was so shocked, she barely kissed him back.

He grinned at her. "Maybe I'll see you later."

"Yeah, maybe," she replied, still stunned.

He jumped out of the car.

Destiny drove home, pulled the car into the garage, and hurried straight up to her room. "Hey, Liv," she called.

Livvy sat at the computer, typing an e-mail.

She finished her note, sent it, then turned to face Destiny. "Where've you been?"

Destiny tossed her backpack onto the floor. "I told you. I had an appointment with Mr. Angelini."

"How'd it go?" Before Destiny could answer, Livvy said, "Oh, by the way, while I was online, you got an IM from Nakeisha."

Destiny walked over to her sister. "Yeah? What'd she say?"

"She's coming to Dark Springs. On Saturday. She's doing college visits in Boston. But she said her mother would drop her off here for an hour or two."

"Cool."

But Destiny wasn't thinking about Nakeisha.

"What did you and Renz talk about?" Livvy asked. "My appointment isn't until after the senior overnight."

"We . . . well, we talked about . . ." Destiny struggled to remember. Struggled to put the words together.

"He . . . he said something about blood," she said, thinking hard.

Livvy had been adjusting her nose stud. Her

features widened in shock. "He—what?"

"Oh my God," Destiny murmured. "Oh my God, Liv. He talked about blood. Yes. I can remember it now. He said something about blood for blood, about the full moon."

Destiny shook her head, as if trying to shake the words out, as if trying to tug out a clear memory.

Livvy stood up and stared at her sister, her head tilted, her expression alarmed. "Dee, are you okay? Are you cracking up?"

"Oh my God. Oh my God," Destiny repeated, still shaking her head. "It's true, Liv. I . . . I asked him if he had powers. And he said *yes*!"

"But, Dee—"

"Oh my God. Don't you see, Liv? Don't you see?"

Livvy narrowed her eyes at Destiny. "See what?"

"Renz is the one," Destiny said, her voice breaking with emotion. "He was letting me know today. Renz is the one, see? *Renz is the Restorer!*"

Chapter Thirty-One
Livvy vs. Courtney

Sunday night, the girls retreated to their room. Destiny had an essay due for French class, but she sat staring at her computer, unable to get Renz out of her mind.

Tomorrow morning, we'll see him first thing. We'll ask him to restore us, to give us back our normal lives. He can help us. I know he can. Livvy and I are going to be okay.

Across the room, Livvy talked on the phone to friends.

Loud voices interrupted them. Destiny turned to see Ross and Ari at the top of the stairs.

"What's up? Last-minute homework?" Ari asked.

"Did you hear about Charley Robbins?" Ross asked. "He was caught stealing doughnuts from the Pick 'N Pay. You believe it? He had a box of doughnuts under his sweatshirt. What a total jerk."

"He's toast. He's dead meat," Ari said. "Someone said he did it on a dare."

"I ran six miles this afternoon," Ross said. "All along the reservoir. It was great. I'm in shape for basketball, I think. Fletch was supposed to meet me, but he never showed up. I called him, and he said he has turf toe. How can you have turf toe if you've never been on turf?"

Ari rubbed his stomach. "You got anything to eat? My parents were out, and I forgot to have dinner."

Normal life, Destiny thought. After Livvy and I see Renz, we'll go back to a normal life. We won't have to worry every time the doorbell rings. We won't have to wonder if Ross and Ari are vampire hunters.

She ran down to the kitchen to make Ari a sandwich. To her surprise, he followed her. "I didn't really want a sandwich," he said. "I thought maybe we could be alone." He kissed her again, this time longer.

She pulled away. "Ari, I—don't know what to say. I mean, I'm not sure . . ."

He sighed. "Maybe I *will* have that sandwich."

She made a ham sandwich for him. Then

they returned to the room upstairs.

Destiny instantly saw that Livvy and Ross had made up. They were pressed together on the couch. Livvy had one leg over his lap, and her arms were around him. Her hair fell over his face as she kissed him.

Footsteps on the stairs. Courtney appeared.

She had a blue knit cap over her brown hair. She wore a pale blue sweater over a red T-shirt and khaki cargo pants. "Hey, what's up, Dee?"

Her smile faded when she saw Livvy and Ross across the room.

Livvy swiveled around, but she still had one leg over Ross's lap. Her red lipstick was smeared around her mouth.

"Ross, you creep!" Courtney cried through gritted teeth. She stomped over to the couch. "You said you were coming to my house!"

Ross raised both hands, signaling for a truce. He tried to disentangle himself from Livvy. But she slid an arm around his shoulders and snuggled close, staring up at Courtney, challenging her.

"Guess he forgot," Livvy said, smoothing back Ross's blond hair.

"You *bitch*!" Courtney screamed. She dove

at Livvy, grabbed her by the shoulders, struggled to pull her to her feet.

"Let go of me," Livvy said.

"Hey, let me up!" Ross pushed Livvy out of the way and stood up, dancing away from the couch. "Courtney—stop!"

Sobbing, Courtney tugged Livvy up. She gripped Livvy's hair with both hands and pulled.

Livvy let out an angry cry. She ducked her head, but couldn't free herself from Courtney's grip. "Let go! Let go of me!"

"Hey, stop it! Both of you! Stop it!" Destiny screamed.

But both girls ignored her. Courtney jerked Livvy's head from side to side. The two girls wrestled on their feet.

Livvy grabbed Courtney's arm. She snapped it hard.

Destiny heard a sickening *crack*.

Livvy let go of her and stepped back, breathing hard, eyes wide with surprise.

Courtney's arm dropped limply to her side. Screaming, she fell to her knees. "You broke it! You broke my arm!"

Livvy turned to Destiny. "I didn't mean

to. It just snapped!"

"It hurts! It hurts!" Courtney moaned. She struggled to raise her arm, and let out a cry of pain.

Destiny hurried over to her. Ross helped Courtney to stand.

"It was an accident," Livvy said, pressing her hands to the sides of her face. "Really. I hardly did anything."

Courtney cradled the broken arm in her good arm. "I can't stand it. It hurts so much."

Destiny felt her stomach lurch when she saw ragged bone poking out through the torn skin. "We've got to get her to the hospital." She turned to Ari. "Did you drive?"

"I'll take her," Ross said. He helped Courtney to the stairs.

Tears poured down Courtney's cheeks. She turned and scowled at Livvy. "You jealous bitch. You've snapped it in two! How could you do this to me? I'll kill you for this!"

Livvy opened her mouth to protest, but no sound came out.

Ross slid his arm around Courtney's shoulders and guided her down the stairs.

"Ross, don't go!" Livvy called. "Stay with

me. Let Ari take her."

Ross didn't answer. Ari hurried to the stairs. "I'd better go with them and help out."

They disappeared down the stairs. Destiny heard the kitchen door slam behind them.

Livvy hugged herself. She crossed the room to Destiny. "I hardly touched her," she said. "It was just an accident. I didn't try to break her arm. You believe me, right?"

Destiny sighed. "Yes, I believe you."

Livvy shut her eyes. "Courtney started it. She grabbed me first. What does she think she's doing? She knows I love Ross."

Destiny gasped. "Love? Did you say 'love'?"

Livvy nodded. She opened her eyes. "Yes, I did. Why are you staring at me?"

"Well . . . for one thing, Ross is probably a vampire hunter. Do you think he'd love you back if he knew—"

"He cares for me. He told me so."

"But you know Ross. He never goes with anyone for long. He always has three or four girls chasing him."

"This is different," Livvy insisted. "He and I—we've talked. He's serious about me. Courtney has been trying to break us up. But I can't let her do that. She asked for it, Dee. She really did."

Destiny shook her head. "She asked for it? She asked for a broken arm? Did you see the bone sticking out through the skin?"

"I'd like to do worse to her."

"Don't say that, Livvy. That's horrible."

A sob escaped Livvy's throat. "You don't understand me, Dee. You're just like everyone else."

"Stop talking like that," Destiny snapped. "We have more important things—"

"Nothing is more important than Ross and me!" Livvy screamed.

"Calm down. Calm down. You're not thinking clearly. Listen to me, Liv. Right now, getting to Renz is more important. We have to see him as soon as we can and tell him we need his special powers. We—"

Destiny stopped when she heard the front door slam. A few seconds later, she heard heavy, trudging footsteps in the kitchen.

Both girls went to the stairs. "Dad, is that you? Are you home?" Destiny called.

No answer.

Destiny led the way down the stairs. "Dad?"

He had his back to them. He was hunched over the sink, washing his hands.

"Dad?"

When he turned, Destiny let out a cry. His shirt was torn open and stained. Streams of dark blood had caked on his forehead. Both hands were cut and bleeding.

"Oh my God!" Destiny cried. "Dad—are you okay? What happened?"

Chapter Thirty-Two

"Her Blood Was Drained"

"I'm okay," he said. "Really."

"But, Dad—"

Both girls rushed over to him. "What happened?" Destiny repeated.

"A little car accident," he said.

Livvy caught him as his knees started to fold. "A car accident? Are you hurt? Are you okay?"

"I'm fine, really." He swung free of Livvy and stuck his hands under the rushing hot water in the sink. "My mind wandered, I guess. I hit a mailbox. No big deal."

Destiny stared at him. "Your mind wandered? Dad, you've got to get yourself together. You could have been killed."

"I know," he said, shaking his head. "But I'm fine. Really."

"You're not fine," Destiny said. "You're not yourself, and you know it."

"You've been working too hard," Livvy said. "Look what time it is."

"I know. I know," he muttered. "When you're right, you're right." He forced a smile. Then he shut off the water and went dripping across the kitchen, heading to his room.

Destiny and Livvy exchanged nervous glances. "He's all cut up," Livvy murmured.

"I'm really worried about him," Destiny said.

She looked out the kitchen window. Her dad's SUV stood in the driveway, close to the garage. Light from the kitchen washed over it.

"That's so weird," she said to Livvy. "Come here. Check this out. Dad's car . . . it looks perfectly fine."

Two days later, the phone woke her up. Destiny raised her head off the pillow and gazed out the window. The morning sky was still charcoal gray.

She fumbled for the phone and picked it up. "Hello?" Her voice was still hoarse from sleep.

She heard someone crying on the other end.

"Hello? Who is this?"

Muffled sobs. Then a choked voice she

didn't recognize. "Dee, it's me."

"Who? Please—"

"I'm sorry. I can't stop crying."

"Ana-Li? Is that you? What's wrong? Are you okay?"

"Yes, I'm okay. I mean, no. You see, Courtney . . . it's Courtney . . ."

A shock jolted Destiny wide awake. She jerked up in bed and dropped her feet to the floor. "Courtney? Yes, I know. She broke her arm the other night."

"Her arm? No. No. No. She's dead, Dee," Ana-Li said between sobs. "Her parents . . . they found her in the backyard. She's dead. Her blood . . . oh my God . . . her blood was drained, Dee. Courtney's dead."

Destiny held a hand over her mouth to keep from screaming. Ana-Li's voice sounded unreal in her ears. The words weren't making sense.

She didn't *want* the words to make sense.

Please let this be a mistake.

But no. Through her sobs, Ana-Li continued. "There's no school. School is canceled. Everyone is afraid. It's so frightening, Dee. The Vampire Killer—he . . . he struck again. Poor Courtney. I . . . can't believe it. I just saw her yesterday. First Bree and now . . ."

The Vampire Killer?

No. I don't think so.

"I . . . I'll call you back, Ana-Li. I can't talk now. Later, okay? I . . . I'm too upset." She clicked off the phone and tossed it onto the bed.

"Livvy!" she screamed.

She stared at her sister across the room, on her stomach, hair spilling over the pillow, one hand trailing over the side of the bed to the floor.

"Livvy—you killed her!"

Livvy raised her head sleepily. "What are you talking about?"

"Don't pretend. Don't play innocent with me." Destiny grabbed her twin by the shoulders and shook her awake. "You killed her. You killed Courtney."

Livvy pushed Destiny's hands away and yawned. "Oh my God! Courtney's dead?" She shut her eyes. "How? How did it happen?"

"You know how!" Destiny cried. "You did it—didn't you, Livvy! You were afraid you'd lose Ross. So you—you—" Destiny's voice broke into sobs.

Livvy turned her face away from Destiny.

"That's horrible," she murmured. "Horrible news. I really can't believe it."

Trembling, Destiny stared down at her sister. "You're not even pretending to be sorry. How *could* you, Livvy? Courtney didn't have to die—just because she and Ross—"

"Leave Ross out of it," Livvy snapped. "I didn't do it, Dee. I swear to you."

Destiny's voice broke again. "My own sister. I . . . I can't even *look* at you."

"Well, you won't have to for long."

"What does *that* mean?" Destiny cried. "What are you saying? Have you gone crazy? Are you that far gone? Have you gone nuts like Mrs. Bauer?"

"Speak for yourself, Dee." Livvy stood up and, pulling down her nightshirt, made her way to the bathroom.

Destiny strode up behind her and spun her around. "Livvy—you killed for Ross. You killed a human being. Doesn't that mean anything to you? Don't you even realize what's happened to you? Don't you think about the trouble we're both in? We have to find Renz right away. We have to be restored."

"Maybe I have my own plan," Livvy said

through gritted teeth.

"Huh? What are you saying?"

Livvy dove into the bathroom and slammed the door.

"What are you saying, Livvy?" Destiny demanded. "What kind of plan?"

Chapter Thirty-Three

A Valuable Nature Lesson

"Where's your sister?" Ana-Li asked.

Destiny shrugged. "Beats me. She left the house right after breakfast. She didn't say a word to me."

"She's just afraid," Ana-Li said. "We all are. Our friends are dying off one by one. None of us knows how to deal with it. So Livvy acts angry. That's her way. She'll calm down . . . once they catch the murderer."

Destiny spent the day at Ana-Li's house. Ari and Fletch and some other kids dropped by after lunch. No one felt much like talking. But somehow it felt safer to be together.

Destiny thought about Livvy all day. And she thought about Renz. School is closed. Livvy and I can't see him today. How much longer can we wait?

She returned home at dinnertime to find the house empty. A phone message from Dad said that he was working late and that Mikey was staying at a friend's. No sign of Livvy.

Destiny didn't feel hungry, but she shoved a frozen pizza into the oven. She forced down a slice without even tasting it, then went up to her room. She began to pace back and forth, wondering what she should do next.

She picked up Livvy's nightshirt from where it had been tossed on the floor, folded it, and placed it on Livvy's bed. Livvy's eye shadows and lipsticks were a jumble on her dressing table. Destiny began to straighten them, putting caps on the tubes and bottles.

Destiny didn't start to feel strange until just after eight o'clock. That's when her skin started to tingle, her back itched, and she felt a powerful gnawing sensation in the pit of her stomach.

She ignored it at first. But the tingling became an ache and the gnawing, tumbling feeling in her stomach nearly doubled her over.

I need some fresh air.

She opened the window and took several deep breaths. She gripped the windowsill so tightly her hands ached.

Please . . . *please* . . . make this stop.

So hungry. I'm so hungry.

She felt her hair stiffen and heard it crackle. And then her skin was crackling too. Her grip on the sill loosened, and her hands shrank quickly.

What's happening to me?

She felt herself pulling inward . . . closing in . . . changing so fast. All crackly and stiff.

Muscles tightened. Vision blurred. Banging heartbeats made her chest throb.

Am I sick? What's happening? I can't control it!

She saw her clothes in a rumpled pile below her. She felt herself floating up, floating effortlessly.

She fluttered off the windowsill. Sailed across the room, up to her dresser mirror.

"NOOOOOOOO!" Her scream escaped as a shrill whistle.

Spreading her wings, she squinted into the mirror. Her sight strange, fragmented. But she could see clearly enough.

She could see her fur-covered body attached to the thin, veined wings, her tiny, red eyes, her rodent mouth hanging open as she stared . . .

. . . stared at the bat in the mirror.

Screeching in horror, she turned, flapping

her wings frantically, and spun in midair.

Hungry. So hungry now.

She sailed through the open window, out into the night.

I'm not human anymore. I'm a bat. I . . . want to go home. I want to go back.

But the hunger drove her through the purple-gray sky, over the dark houses. The cool wind felt good, rushing under her wings. She could feel her rapid heartbeats drumming in her chest, and feel the gnawing hunger in her belly.

Her wings flapped silently as she swooped low over a wooded field—and found what she was searching for. An owl on a high tree limb, staring straight ahead, so still, feathers bristling in the wind. A fat owl, filled with delicious blood . . .

She swooped at it, opening her mouth hungrily. Screeching down, she dug her teeth into its chest.

She didn't expect it to fight back. But the owl slashed a deep cut in her left wing. Thrashing wildly, it tore at her belly with its beak.

They tumbled off the tree branch. Fell to the mossy, wet ground.

The owl thrashed and cut. Destiny flapped hard above it, keeping her long teeth clamped deep in its belly.

The owl screeched, clawing at her wings, thrusting its beak into her middle, sharp jab after jab.

Pain shot through Destiny's body, paralyzing her. She lost her grip on its belly. Blood spattered her throbbing body, and she realized it was her own blood.

I've made a horrible mistake. I didn't know . . . owls are stronger . . . stronger than bats. I didn't know . . .

Too weak to flap her wings . . . too weak to escape.

She lay on her back on the blood-wet grass, the owl perched on her tiny, gray belly. Its talons tore at her thin wings again. Its beak dug into her throat.

I didn't know . . . I didn't know . . .

Chapter Thirty-Four
A Surprise From Dad

*D*estiny opened her eyes.

I can't see. I'm blind.

But then the stars came into focus. And the nearly full moon behind wisps of gray cloud.

She saw the roof of her garage. Raised her head from the grass, turned, and saw the back of her house.

I'm lying in the grass behind my house. I'm totally naked.

She sat up. Rubbed her chest. Dried blood.

It's real. It really happened.

How did I fight off the owl? How am I still alive?

Slowly, the terrifying memory came back. As the owl attacked her, she had started to transform. Back to her human body, hands furiously shoving the bird away.

The startled owl raised its wings, turned, and flew off into the night.

Destiny shivered. Her legs were wet with dew, so cold against her skin. She pulled a brown leaf from her hair, then got up onto her knees.

She turned to the house. Mikey's yellow bike stood propped against the back wall next to his soccer ball. She could see lights on in the kitchen and in the room above the garage—her room.

She stood up slowly, testing her arms and legs. Her muscles ached, but she could walk. Keeping in the darkest shadows, she made her way to the back door and peered in.

No one in the kitchen.

Silently, she pried open the door and slipped inside. The clock over the stove read eight forty-five. She had been gone less than an hour. She listened for voices. No. No music, no TV on. No one home yet.

Still shivering, her mind spinning, Destiny crept up to her room. She took a long shower. And as the steamy hot water rushed over her, she decided.

I have to tell Dad.

I can't keep this a secret anymore. It's gone too far. I turned into a bat tonight. What if it's too late for me? What if it's too late for Renz to fix me?

I'm too scared to face it all alone. I'm no longer in control of my own body. The moon is nearly full. I have to tell Dad. I can't keep it all inside me any longer.

She pulled on a T-shirt, an oversized sweater, and jeans, grabbed the car keys, and hurried out to the garage. Dad had the SUV, but the Civic was still in its place.

Destiny's hands shook. She grabbed the steering wheel to steady them.

I have to tell Dad. After all, he is a doctor. Maybe . . . maybe . . .

She backed the car out, nearly scraping the driver's side against the garage wall.

Calm down, Dee. Concentrate on your driving.

She glanced at the dashboard clock. Nearly nine thirty and Dad was still at work. That poor man. Why is he working so hard?

The streets slid by in a blur. Before she realized it, she was pulling to the curb in front of her dad's animal clinic. Street lights washed over the square, redbrick building. The sign above the glass door was simple, stenciled in blue letters on white: WELLER VETERINARY CLINIC.

Destiny climbed out of the car. She wiped her cold, wet hands on the legs of her jeans. Her heart thudded in her chest.

I've never been so nervous to talk to Dad. What will he think when I tell him? What will he say?

The blinds were only half closed on the wide front window beside the entrance, and she could see that the lights were on in her dad's waiting room. The examining rooms and the lab were at the back.

Destiny took a deep breath and made her way to the door. But a flash of movement in the window caught her attention. She turned and stepped to the window, stooping to see inside between the blinds.

"Oh, wow."

She slid to the side so she wouldn't be seen. Her dad sat on the waiting room desk, gesturing and talking to a group of guys seated in front of him.

They had their backs to the window. Keeping out of view, Destiny squinted hard into the brightly lit room.

It's some kind of meeting. But that doesn't

make sense. Why would Dad be having a meeting this time of night?

And then she recognized Ross in the chair closest to the window. And Fletch beside him. And across the room, other guys from Dark Springs High.

Destiny slid away from the window. She pressed her back against the cold brick wall.

What are those guys doing there with my dad?

What could they be talking about?

Holding on to the brick wall, she leaned forward again and peered into the window. They were all standing up. She could hear the scrape of their chairs. Her father opened the coat closet door. He leaned inside.

A car passed behind her on the street, sending its headlights over Destiny. She stood up straight. The car slowed, then continued on its way.

Her eyes burned from the bright lights. Blinking hard, she swung back to the window. Dr. Weller stepped out of the coat closet. Destiny could see him clearly. She could see what he was holding. Wooden stakes, sharpened to a point at one end. He handed one to each boy.

"Oh, no."

She didn't want to believe what she was seeing. Staring through the window glass was like staring into a dream.

That isn't my dad. Those aren't my friends.

She didn't have long to think about it. Someone shut off the lights in the waiting room. The window went black.

They're coming out.

Chapter Thirty-Five
Is Ross Dangerous?

I don't believe it. But it's true. Dad is a hunter—Dad and my friends are vampire hunters.

Destiny spun into the street. She ducked behind her car as the front door of the building swung open.

She held her breath and peered over the front fender. The boys stepped out quickly, holding the stakes close to their sides. She saw Ross whisper something to Fletch. Fletch laughed and gave him a playful shove.

Dr. Weller backed out of the building. He locked the front door. Took several deep breaths, gazing around.

No. Please. Dad, please don't look here.

Hunched behind the car, Destiny watched them move quickly, silently up the sidewalk. She turned and saw her dad's SUV parked on the corner across the street.

Squatting low, Destiny moved to the other

side of her car. Another car passed by. Its head-lights spilled over the boys. Destiny saw them hide the wooden stakes so the driver wouldn't see.

They piled into the SUV. She watched her dad lower himself behind the wheel. He started it up. The taillights flared red. After a few seconds, the SUV pulled away from the curb.

Destiny jumped to her feet.

Where is Dad going? She fumbled for her car keys. Dropped them onto the sidewalk.

Trembling, she grabbed up the keys and hurried into the car. It felt good to sit down. Breathing hard, she started up the car and headed after them.

A few seconds later, she began to catch up. They were driving fast through North Town, the old part of Dark Springs. Small houses crowded together on tiny lots. An all-night grocery on one corner. A boarded-up movie theater.

Destiny hit the brake when she saw the SUV pull to the curb. The doors swung open, and the boys were out of the car before it even stopped.

Destiny swung the car over, her eyes on the boys. She bumped over the curb and bounced hard.

The boys were running across a narrow front lawn, leaping over the shrubs, moving silently, stakes raised high over their heads.

Whose house is this? I've been inside it. Isn't it the school librarian's house? Mrs. Lindros's?

The hunters' faces were hidden in shadow. But she could see their black silhouettes leaning forward as they ran.

Then she heard the shouts. Heard the crack of breaking glass. Heard heavy thuds as they broke the front door down.

Oh my God. Oh my God. I don't believe this. They're breaking in. My dad is breaking into a house. They're going in.

A few seconds later, she heard more shouts. And then a woman's high wail. A wail of pain, of horror.

Destiny covered her ears. But she couldn't shut out the terrifying cry.

I've got to get home. I've got to tell Livvy.

She wheeled the car around. Made a wild U-turn, nearly smashing into the side of a parked pickup truck. The squealing tires reminded her of the woman's high shriek.

My dad . . . my own dad . . .

What am I going to do?

* * *

She found Livvy lying on her bed, reading an issue of *People* magazine. "Where've you been?" Livvy asked coldly as Destiny hurried across the room to her.

"Listen to me. We—we're in trouble," Destiny cried.

Livvy rolled her eyes. "Tell me something I don't know."

Destiny dropped down on the edge of the bed. "You don't know *this*. Dad is a hunter. I saw him. I saw him tonight. Our own dad is a hunter."

The magazine fell from Livvy's hands. "Oh my God. That's impossible!"

Destiny took a deep breath. "It's true. I saw Ross and Fletch with him. And other guys from school. They broke into Mrs. Lindros's house."

"The librarian from school?"

Destiny nodded. "They killed her. I heard her scream. It was so horrible!"

Livvy pulled herself up. She shook her head hard. "Ross was there? With Dad?"

"Yes. I swear. They're both hunters."

"But Dad wouldn't hurt us. We're his daughters."

Destiny swallowed hard. "I don't know what he would do if he found out. He's been lying to us all this time. He said he was working late. But all the while, he's been a hunter."

Livvy tugged at a strand of hair. "I—I just can't believe it."

"You've got to stay away from Ross," Destiny said. "He's a hunter too."

"So what?" Livvy cried.

"So what? Have you lost your mind? If Ross found out our secret—"

"Ross would never hurt me," Livvy insisted. "Never. Ross loves me, Dee."

Destiny's voice came out in a shrill whisper. "Would he still care about you if he knew? Would he?"

"You're just jealous," Livvy said. "You're jealous that Ross is in love with me."

The words stung Destiny. "I'm not jealous. He's a hunter. And if he knew—"

"*He already knows!*" Livvy cried. "Ross already knows. I told him. He knows all about it."

"What? How could you?" Destiny screamed. "How could you put us both at risk? We swore to keep the secret. We swore to each other. How could you tell him?"

Livvy turned her face to the wall and didn't answer.

"When did you tell him? What did he say? Answer me," Destiny demanded. "Answer me, Livvy. What did he say?"

Livvy didn't move and didn't reply.

"Don't you realize what you've done?" Destiny cried. "Don't you realize the danger we're in now?"

Chapter Thirty-Six
Renz Makes a Promise

Destiny watched Renz walk down the hall. He appeared startled to see her, but a smile quickly replaced his surprise. "Good morning, Destiny. Waiting outside my office door? Hope you haven't been waiting long."

"I wanted to talk to you before school began."

He switched his briefcase to his other hand, pushed open the door, and waved her in before him. At his desk, he turned and smiled at her again, his dark eyes flashing. "You look tired. Are those lines under your eyes?"

"I didn't sleep much last night," Destiny said. "I was worried about coming here . . . about talking to you. I . . . well . . . this isn't easy."

His eyes burned into hers. "What's on your mind?"

Destiny stared back at him. "Well . . . I don't

267

really know how to say this." Her throat suddenly felt dry.

I can't do this. This is crazy. I should turn and run.

Renz leaned closer. His eyes caught the light. "Why don't you just say it? It can't be that difficult."

Yes, it is.

"Well . . ."

His eyes appeared to glow. He didn't blink. She suddenly felt as if he was reaching into her mind, reading her thoughts.

"You want to talk to me about the full moon, don't you?" he said softly.

Destiny gasped. He *did* read her mind.

She nodded.

"You're nervous about Saturday night," Renz said.

Destiny nodded again. "You know!" she whispered. "You . . . you *are* the Restorer—aren't you!"

He blinked. "The *what?*"

"The Restorer. It's you. You're the one who restores people to their normal lives after they've been bitten."

He didn't answer.

"Please, tell me, Renz." Her voice broke. "Tell me the truth. Are you the one? Are you the Restorer?"

Renz gazed at her for a long moment. He seemed to be thinking hard. Finally, a smile spread across his handsome face. He took Destiny's hand.

"Yes," he whispered. "Yes, I am."

His hand felt warm and dry on her cold hand. She let out a long sigh of relief. "Oh, thank God," she cried. "Livvy and I— we need you, Renz. We need you desperately. We don't have much time. Will you help us?"

He pressed her hand between both of his. He stood and came up close beside her. "Don't worry anymore," he whispered. "The full moon is Saturday night. I'll be there, at the senior overnight. I will come for you. And I promise I will take care of you then."

"Thank you. Oh, thank you," Destiny whispered.

Chapter Thirty-Seven
Summary Camp Memories

Destiny greeted Nakeisha at the front door, and the two girls hugged. Destiny led her friend into the living room. "You look great!"

Nakeisha spun around, modeling her outfit. She wore a white sweater vest over a silky orange top, a short brown suede skirt, and dark tights. "It's my college interview outfit. Check it out."

Destiny laughed as Nakeisha paraded back and forth like a model on a runway. "Hope you don't walk like that at your interviews. How's it going?"

Nakeisha shrugged. "Not bad. I've only seen a few schools. Mom wants me to stay in the east. She won't let me apply to any California schools."

Nakeisha's eyes narrowed on Destiny. "Have you lost weight?"

Destiny bit her bottom lip. "A little."

"Well, don't lose any more," Nakeisha said in her usual blunt way. "You look like we did after that two-day canoe trip. Wrecked."

"I . . . haven't been sleeping well," Destiny said, motioning for Nakeisha to sit on the green leather couch. "I don't know why. Senior-year-itis, I guess."

Nakeisha glanced around. "Nice house. Is Livvy home?"

Destiny dropped beside her on the couch. "No. I don't know where she is."

"Hope she comes by. I wanted to say hi to her."

"Livvy and I haven't been getting along." The words burst from Destiny's mouth. She hadn't intended to say them.

She didn't want to involve Nakeisha in her troubles. She didn't want to tell Nakeisha anything about what was going on.

"I'm not surprised," Nakeisha said. "You two are so different. It's hard to believe you're really twins."

"Well . . ." Destiny had the sudden urge to tell her friend everything. But she forced the words back.

"Hey, you know who I heard from?" Nakeisha asked. "Ronnie Herbert. Know what he's doing?"

Destiny shook her head. "I only got one e-mail from him, at the end of summer."

"You know how he was such a wizard with the camp computers? Well, he started his own computer repair business after school. You know. Doing upgrades for people, installing hardware, and stuff. He said he's making money big-time."

"Good for Ronnie," Destiny said, trying to sound enthusiastic.

"Hear from anyone else at camp? Oh, wait." Nakeisha jumped to her feet. "I forgot. Know what I brought?" She went to the front hall, rummaged in her bag, and pulled out a thin book. "Did you get this?"

"What is it?"

Nakeisha returned to the couch, holding the book up to Destiny. "It's the camp yearbook. It just came yesterday morning."

"I didn't get mine."

Nakeisha pushed it into Destiny's lap. "Well, check it out. Look. We're on the cover."

Destiny moaned. "Oh, great. That horrible day it rained like crazy. We look like drowned rats."

Destiny quickly turned the page. "There's the campfire from hell. I'll never forget those screaming little kids."

Nakeisha laughed. "Half of them wet their beds that night!"

"Hey, nice picture of Livvy," Destiny said, holding the book closer. "Who's that guy she's with?"

Nakeisha grabbed the book to study the photo. "What day was it taken? Livvy was going with a different boy every day, wasn't she? I mean, she didn't leave anyone for us."

Destiny's eyes rolled over the photos. "Oh, wow. This is great."

I wish I was back in camp. I wish I could turn the clock back . . .

"But do you know what's totally weird?" Nakeisha took the book and flipped quickly through the pages. "No photos of Renz. Not one."

Destiny's mouth dropped open. "Renz . . . ?"

"Go ahead. You look." Nakeisha shoved the book back onto Destiny's lap. "Renz was everywhere, right? He was in every activity. So how come they left him out of the yearbook?"

Destiny swallowed hard. She let the yearbook slide from her lap, onto the floor. "Renz? At camp? He's at my school. No way he was at camp."

"Huh? At your school?" Nakeisha jumped to

her feet again. She pressed her hands to her waist and frowned at Destiny. "Are you totally losing it? I'm talking about Renz. R-e-n-z. We hung out with Renz all summer. You panted after him and followed him around just like all us girls. Are you telling me you don't remember that?"

Destiny stared up at her friend. She suddenly felt dizzy. She gripped the side of the couch.

Renz at camp. Renz, the new college advisor from school, at camp. How can that be?

And suddenly, she saw herself with him. She and Renz at the lake . . . the full moon high above the shimmering water. Renz leaning over her . . . kissing her . . .

Oh my God.

Slowly, the truth began to filter into her spinning mind.

I get it. I get it now.

No pictures of Renz in the yearbook.

No memory of him at camp. But he was there. I knew him. I hung out with him. I . . . kissed him.

No pictures and no memories of him . . .

Vampires can't be photographed . . .

Renz is a vampire. Yes. It's so obvious now, thanks to Nakeisha and the yearbook. Renz is the vampire who ruined our lives.

"He's not the Restorer," she said, thinking out loud.

Nakeisha continued to stand over her. "What? You're not making any sense, Dee."

Oh, yes, I am.

Renz isn't the Restorer.

Nakeisha was talking, but Destiny couldn't hear her, her words drowned out by Destiny's terrifying realization.

Destiny pressed her hands to the sides of her face and shut her eyes. Renz isn't the Restorer. . . . My dad is a vampire hunter. . . . My closest friends are hunters too. My sister isn't speaking to me. After Saturday, I will be like Mrs. Bauer, a mad creature driven night and day by an endless craving for blood.

"Destiny? Are you freaking out or something? Are you okay?" Nakeisha's voice—far away, miles away—broke into her thoughts.

No. I'm not okay.

I'm not okay.

I have no one to turn to, no one I can trust.

Saturday night . . . Saturday night . . . Saturday night . . . my life will be over.

Part Five

Chapter Thirty-Eight
Renz Drinks Deeply

Renz sat at his desk, leaning back in his chair, eyes shut. "Destiny." He whispered her name. Thinking about Saturday night filled him with excitement. "Destiny . . . Laura. Yes, you will become Laura."

Memories flooded his mind. It was last spring . . . only last spring, but it seemed so long ago . . . when he spotted his love behind the high school, waiting for her daughters again. Yes, she called herself Deborah Weller, and she was married to a boring-looking veterinarian.

But I don't care what you call yourself. Tonight you will be Laura again, he thought, gazing up at the full moon. He let the moonlight warm him, then returned his eyes to her. He was afraid to let her out of his sight, afraid he might lose her.

Ever since that chance meeting in the school parking lot, he had been thinking about

Deborah Weller, following her, watching her. He would creep up to the kitchen window at night and watch the family eat their dinner. Through the window, he watched her and enjoyed her laugh, her smile, her bright green eyes.

Laura, do you sense that I am near?

Do you sense my love for you?

We are separated, Laura. But not for long.

And then, a few days later, Renz knew the time had come. The full moon sent silvery light over her SUV as she waited in the empty parking lot. He moved out of the shadows, toward the car, ready to claim his bride.

She had the windows closed. Her blond hair fell softly to her shoulders, caught in the light of the moon. He tapped lightly on her window and saw her jump in surprise.

She gazed out at him for a long moment, then remembered him. She rolled down the window. "Mr. Angelini? How strange. We keep meeting in this parking lot."

Her throaty voice, like velvet. Like Laura.

"Could you help me?" he asked, barely able to keep his voice from quivering. "I dropped my keys. If you open the door, the car light will help me find them."

She didn't hesitate. She opened the car door.

He reached in and grabbed her.

He held her so tightly, she couldn't scream.

At last. At last. *At last.*

The fangs slid down and he drove them deep into her throat. He drank hungrily, noisily, holding her powerless against him.

When he had drunk his fill, blood flowing over his lips and chin, he raised his head and whispered, "Now, you must drink, Laura. Now you must drink my blood."

He raised his throat to her. He could see the haze in those deep green eyes, the confusion on her face.

"Drink," he ordered. "Drink and we will be together."

She turned her head.

The doors to the school opened. The twins appeared.

No. Oh, no.

Renz loosened his grip. He backed away, then slithered into the shadows of the trees at the edge of the parking lot.

He watched the girls run to the car. Watched Laura mopping at her throat with the collar of her blouse. Covering up the wound. Greeting the girls. Confused. Dazed and unaware of what had just happened to her.

But I know what has happened, he thought. I have drunk your blood under the full moon, and now you need to drink mine. I need you. I need you.

The girls were inside the car now. He heard the click of the door locks. He waited until the car pulled away, out of the parking lot. And then he tilted back his head and uttered a long, animal howl, a howl of anger and frustration and pain.

The days went by. Renz knew he had to wait a month, until the next full moon. He watched her house. What was she doing in there? She seldom came out.

What did she tell her husband? Her daughters? That she was sick?

Evenings, he saw the husband returning from his veterinary lab. Renz saw what he brought for his wife. The husband brought animals home—rabbits, hamsters, small rodents. For his wife to feed upon?

So the husband knows, Renz decided. He brings her food. But he can do no more for her. He is powerless.

Only I can save you, Laura. Only I can return you to the life we planned so many decades ago.

The days and nights passed so slowly. The last winter storm gave way to warmer spring nights. Renz watched the moon, waiting.

At last, the full moon rose high over the trees. Laura's house stood dark except for a light in her bedroom. The twins had spring break and were away at a friend's. The little brother had gone to a sleepover a few blocks away. The husband worked late at his lab.

Renz knew all these things because he stayed close—close to the house and its inhabitants.

If I look away for a moment, she might disappear. And I might lose her again.

But no. The moon floated high and full, lighting the house like a spotlight. And Laura was in her bedroom.

Awaiting me.

He crept along the side of the house, pressing against the shingles, making his way to her room in the back. The bedroom window was open, curtains fluttering in the light breeze.

He hesitated for only a moment, pushing

back his excitement. But he could already taste her sweet blood on his tongue. And once their blood had mingled, he could picture her joy at being reunited with him.

He raised his hands to the windowsill and hoisted himself easily into her room. He pushed away the filmy curtains. A dim bed-table lamp provided the only light.

He stumbled back against the wall when he saw her, trying to blink the horrible sight away.

The sight of Deborah's body, dangling so stiffly from the ceiling light. Her bare feet floating above the floor. The thick rope around her neck. Her head tilted back, eyes staring blankly at the ceiling, her face blackened, purple tongue hanging from her open mouth.

"No!"

He spun to face the wall. He couldn't bear to see this.

Why did you do this, Laura? Why did you rob me once again of a bride?

He hunched there, facing the wall without moving for what seemed like hours. Finally, he moved to the window. "Farewell, Laura," he called softly. "Farewell. I have lost you once again."

He climbed out the window. He strode across the grass. He didn't look back. "You have escaped me. But you have two daughters. Two Lauras. You got away from me, Deborah. *But I will never let them go!*"

Chapter Thirty-Nine
Destiny Keeps Her Date With Renz

Ana-Li tossed a Frisbee to Destiny. It bounced off Destiny's outstretched hand and sailed into the side of a tent.

Ana-Li laughed. "I hope no one is in there."

Destiny loped over the grass, picked up the Frisbee, and spun it back to her friend. She gazed up at the rising full moon, already high in the purple night sky.

A shiver of fear ran down her back. *I'm trying to pretend that everything is normal. But Ana-Li must see how distracted and frightened I am.*

In the middle of the circle of tents, the campfire crackled and sent up sparks. Some kids were poking at it, trying to make it flame up. At the edge of the clearing, someone had cranked up a boombox, and several kids were dancing.

Away from the noise, a group of parents

and teachers—the chaperones—stood chatting near the lakeshore.

Ana-Li made a low toss, and the Frisbee rolled toward the fire. "We got such a beautiful night," she said. "Not a cloud in the sky."

Destiny muttered a reply. Her stomach gnawed. She fought back the hunger.

Soon I won't be able to control myself. Soon I won't be able to satisfy my craving. After tonight, Livvy and I will become creatures, creatures to be hunted down by my father and his hunters.

Destiny handed the Frisbee to Ana-Li. "I don't really feel like playing," she said. On the other side of the campfire, she saw Renz, surrounded by a group of girls, teasing them, everyone laughing, having a good time. Near the boombox, some girls were pulling Mr. Smith, the Spanish teacher, over to dance.

A sudden wind made the trees whisper. Destiny shivered again. She glimpsed her dad with the other parents at the shore.

Dad, if you only knew what was about to happen to your daughters . . .

"Everyone's trying really hard to have a good time," Ana-Li said. "I mean, it's the senior overnight and everything. But who really feels like partying that much? With two girls from our class dead . . . our two good friends . . ." Her voice trailed off.

Destiny sighed. "Senior year was supposed to be the best year of our lives. . . ."

Ana-Li glanced around the campground. "Where's your sister?"

Destiny shrugged. "We're sharing a tent, but I haven't seen her since we arrived. She's probably off in the woods with Ross. I don't see him, either."

Destiny's stomach growled. Her senses suddenly became sharp. She could hear the blood coursing through Ana-Li's veins. She could hear conversations on the other side of the campground. A babble of voices, all talking at once, all so loud in her ears.

"Think I'll get a hot dog or something," Ana-Li said. "Sure you don't want to come?"

"No, thanks." Destiny watched Ana-Li trot off to the food table. She turned and found Ari right behind her.

"Surprise!"

She jumped. "Hey, don't sneak up on me like that."

"Thought we were going to hang out tonight," he said.

Destiny had completely forgotten about him. "Yeah, I know. But—"

"There's a cool little dock on that side of the lake." He pointed. "Some kids are over there. You know. Partying."

"I don't think so," Destiny said. "I'm sorry, Ari. I . . . I'm feeling a little weird. I'm going to go lie down. In my tent."

His eyes flashed. "Can I join you?" He laughed. "Just kidding."

"Maybe I'll feel better later and I'll catch up to you," Destiny said. She could see the disappointment on his face.

"Okay. Catch you later," he said.

Maybe.

Maybe you'll see me and maybe you won't.

Maybe if you see me, you won't recognize me, Ari.

I did everything I could to find the Restorer. I worked so hard for Livvy and me. But I failed.

And now the moon is rising in the sky. Everyone thinks it's beautiful, the autumn full moon, so golden and big.

To me, it looks like death.

Her stomach gnawing, her throat aching with thirst, Destiny tried to bury herself inside her sleeping bag. But the tent walls were so thin and transparent that she could see the flickering light of the campfire through them. And the voices outside were loud. They seemed to be in the tent with her.

What time is it?

Will Renz really come for me when the moon is high?

She closed her eyes, but opened them when she heard the scrape of the tent flap.

She sat up slowly.

The tent flap opened, revealing the full moon high in the black sky.

And then, Renz poked his head in, blocking the moon, his eyes wide with excitement.

"Laura, it is time," he whispered. "I have come for you. Are you ready?"

"Yes," Destiny whispered. "I'm ready."

Chapter Forty
"At Last"

Leaning into the tent, Renz reached out his hand. Destiny grabbed it and allowed him to pull her to her feet.

"At last," he whispered, a smile spreading over his handsome face.

He led her out of the tent.

Destiny saw the orange embers of the dying campfire. They sent up red and yellow sparks like jewels into the night sky.

Renz held her in his arms. He pressed his mouth to her ear. "I've waited so long for this night."

Destiny's skin tingled. Her muscles tensed.

He lowered his face to hers. His fangs curled down from his gums. "Are you ready, Laura? Are you ready?"

"Yes," Destiny whispered. "Yes, yes . . ."

Then she grabbed the wooden tent pole she had placed beside the tent. Raised it high. And with a groan, shoved it deep into Renz's chest.

His eyes went wide and he uttered a startled hiss. He staggered back—

—and Destiny shoved the stake deeper.

"Oh, no. Oh, no," Renz whispered, arms flailing. He toppled to his back on the ground.

I planned this all week. It's all I could think about.

Now, die, Renz—die!

"Oh, no," he repeated. "You can't—" His arms and legs flailed like a pinned insect. "Laura, I love you. I love you, Laura."

He reached up and grabbed her by the shoulders. His bony fingers tightened, digging into her sweater, into her flesh. "I love you. I love you. . . ." He struggled to pull her down to him.

With a surge of strength, Destiny shoved the tent pole all the way through his body, into the ground.

Die, Renz—die!

A gurgling sound escaped from Renz's open mouth.

Destiny stared in horror as Renz's body began to fall apart. His arms and legs crackled and curled. The skin on his face melted away. His chest caved in. His skull disintegrated, leaving only his fangs.

In seconds, his clothing lay on the grass, empty, except for a few flakes of powdery dust that floated into the air.

Gasping for breath, Destiny spun away—and saw her father standing behind her.

"Destiny, I'm here," he whispered. "I saw—"

"Dad . . ." Destiny said, her entire body trembling. "Dad . . . I killed him. I had to. He . . . he came for me!" She pulled down the collar of her sweater and showed him the twin marks on her throat.

"No!" Dr. Weller let out a cry. He stared at her for a long moment, eyes wide with shock.

Then he grabbed the wooden stake from the ground and raised it high above his head.

"No!" Destiny screamed. "Dad, please don't! Don't hurt me!"

"Why didn't you tell me?" her father shouted. He heaved the stake across the field and wrapped Destiny in his arms. She could feel his hot tears on her cheek. "Dee, why didn't you tell me? I would never hurt you. Never!"

"Because . . ." She pulled away from him. "Because I know who you are, Dad. I know you're a hunter."

He shook his head. "Yes. Yes, I'm a hunter. But, Dee—I can help you. I have a cure."

She gazed up at him. "You . . . you're . . ."

He nodded. "Yes. I'm also the Restorer."

Chapter Forty-One

"I Guess I Should Tell You the Truth"

Dr. Weller grabbed Destiny's hand. He pulled her to his tent on the other side of the field. Safely inside, she dropped to her knees and watched him open his medical bag.

"What are you going to do, Dad?"

He bent over the bag. "I have a formula, Dee. It's taken me a long time, but I'm sure I finally have it right."

He held her arm and raised a hypodermic needle in his other hand. He searched for a vein, then plunged the needle into her arm.

The needle stung. "Will it really cure me?" she asked in a tiny voice.

He nodded, his face solemn. "It may not be instantaneous. But you will feel the symptoms begin to fade." Tears rolled down his cheeks. "I never dreamed I'd have to use it on my own daughter." He returned the needle to the bag.

Destiny felt a surge of heat roll through her body. The cure was right in my own house all along, she thought. "But—Dad, how did you find this? How can you do this?"

He squeezed her hand. He let out a long sigh. "Dee, there are so many things I've kept from you. I guess I should tell you the truth."

She stared at him. "The truth?"

"The truth about your mother . . ."

Destiny's throat tightened. "What about Mom?"

He took a deep breath. "You're not going to like what I have to say. I hoped never to have to tell you. You see . . . your mother was attacked by a vampire. It happened last year, at the end of the winter."

Destiny gaped at her father. "But . . . you said she committed suicide."

"Yes, she did. She couldn't bear the horror. After she was bitten, she started to change. We told you kids she was sick. There was no way we could tell you the truth."

"Oh my God," Destiny whispered. "Oh my God."

"I went to work in my lab," her father continued, holding her hand tightly. "I worked night and day. I knew I could find a cure with the research I'd been doing. But . . . I failed. I didn't find the cure in time. I failed, Dee. I felt so helpless, so miserable."

Destiny's head spun. "Mom? Attacked by a vampire? But, Dad, I can't believe it. I—"

"At first, she wasn't too bad. But her hunger grew. I tried to help. I brought lab animals home for her to feed on. But then the next full moon was approaching. She wasn't herself at all. She needed more and more blood. Her thirst for blood became so intense, she prowled at night. She didn't know what she was doing. She . . . she took more than one human victim."

Destiny gasped and shut her eyes. Not Mom . . . oh, no. Not Mom . . .

"This is so hard for me." Dr. Weller's voice broke. "How can I tell you all this? I—I can't live with it myself."

Destiny opened her eyes. "Go on, Dad. Please. I want to know the truth."

He took another breath. "Well . . . Coach Bauer's wife—poor Marjory—your mother's best friend, she was one of your mother's victims.

"After that, when your mother realized

what she had done to Marjory, she was over-come with horror and grief. She couldn't bear the guilt. She . . . she killed herself. She—"

He turned away from Destiny. She could see his shoulders trembling.

She stared at him, trying to digest all that he was telling her. "And that's why you became a vampire hunter?"

He turned back to her. "Yes. I tried to learn all that I could. I learned how to find vampires, how to hunt them, how to kill them. And all the while I worked in my lab—worked until I couldn't see straight—until I found a formula that could cure vampires who weren't entirely lost."

Destiny squeezed his arm. "But Mrs. Bauer—?"

"I tried, but I failed. Too much time had passed. I couldn't restore her. Poor Coach. He begged me to end her misery. He couldn't do it himself. So I came with my helpers and I did it."

A sob escaped his throat. "I've lived with such horror. I didn't want you to know any of it. I—"

"Oh my God! Livvy!" Destiny cried, jumping to her feet. "Dad—Livvy too! Livvy was bitten too. I can't believe I forgot her. We have to find her—fast!"

He shoved a flashlight into Destiny's hand. Then he latched his medical bag and picked it up. "My poor girls. My poor girls. Hurry. Let's go."

They searched the campground, then the lakefront.

Please let her be okay, Destiny thought. Please let us be in time to save her.

They stepped into the woods, following the circle of light from the flashlight. The full moon shone brightly overhead, making the tree leaves glimmer like silver. Somewhere, a night dove cooed, sweetly, calmly.

Livvy, where are you?

Livvy, don't hide from us.

They cleared their own path through the trees and the brambled weeds. The flashlight flickered, threatened to die, then revived.

Destiny gasped when she saw Livvy and Ross at the edge of a narrow, grassy clearing. They were both on their knees, bent over a fallen deer.

Dr. Weller's light swept over them.

Livvy and Ross slowly raised their heads from the deer. Their faces dripped with bright blood.

"Go away!" Livvy rasped. "Can't you see we're hungry?"

Chapter Forty-Two
Vanished

Destiny froze. "Livvy—no," she choked out. "You don't have to do this. Dad is the Restorer. Dad can cure you both."

Ross blinked several times as if dazed. Then he lowered his face into the torn belly of the deer. He began to drink, making loud sucking sounds.

Livvy stared at Destiny and her father defiantly. "We don't *want* to be cured," she shouted. "Ross and I—we made our choice. We want to be together—forever."

"Livvy, don't do this!" Dr. Weller shouted. "There might still be time. If you let me—"

Destiny strode up to the deer. "Let Dad try," she told her sister. "Maybe he can cure you. You have to let him try!"

"We're a family!" Dr. Weller cried, tears staining his cheeks. "Livvy, we're a family. We need you. We need you with us."

"It's too late!" Livvy screamed. "I've been an immortal *since camp!*"

"No!" Destiny gasped.

"Renz drank my blood and I drank his," Livvy rasped, blood dripping down her chin. "I didn't want to die like Mom. I couldn't stand the idea of death, of lying under the ground forever like Mom. I wanted to live forever—and Renz gave me the chance."

Destiny shook her head, trying to think clearly. "But you and I, Liv, we—"

"I'm sorry, Destiny. I'm so sorry. I didn't want to be his Laura. But I didn't know he would go after you. When we returned home, I only pretended to be a neophyte," Livvy said, her eyes wild, locked on her sister. "I only pretended to be frightened about what was happening, Dee. Didn't you wonder why I never helped you search for the Restorer? I already had my new life—my *immortal* life, and I was happy. And I thought you could learn to be happy too."

"No, Livvy. No!"

"And tonight Ross and I exchanged blood," Livvy said, grabbing Ross's hand. "Our blood mingled under the full moon. We did it, Dee.

Because we want to be together—forever!"

"No! No! I can't let you do this," Destiny cried, staggering up to the fallen deer. "You're my sister. My twin!"

A strange smile played over Livvy's blood-stained face. "Maybe you won't want me for a sister when I tell you the rest. I was the one who killed Bree and Courtney. I didn't want to. They were my friends. But what could I do? I couldn't fight my hunger. I had to feed. I had no choice. I killed them both."

"No!" Destiny screamed. "No. Please—no! You're lying. Please—tell me you're lying!"

Behind her she glimpsed her dad, fumbling in his medical bag. He pulled out a hypodermic needle. "Maybe there's still time," he shouted. "We're a family, Livvy. We're a family. Think of Mikey, how much he needs you. Please—I need you too."

Destiny took a deep breath. Then she dove over the side of the dead deer, sliding on the blood-soaked fur. She reached for Livvy with both hands. "I won't let you get away. I won't!"

Livvy jerked back—and Destiny toppled into the wet, pulpy open stomach of the deer.

She looked up in time to see Livvy and Ross

begin to change. Their bodies folded in on themselves. Their bones crackled. Their faces disappeared.

They rose over the fallen deer as blackbirds, wings spread, flapping gently, catching the wind.

Dr. Weller sank to his knees. The needle fell from his hand. *"Noooooooo."* He buried his face in his hands.

Destiny watched the birds take off, two winged shadows over the full moon. Then they were gone . . . vanished into the black sky.

"Destiny?"

She heard a voice behind her. She turned to find Ari running into the clearing. "Destiny? Are you okay? I checked your tent, and you weren't there."

"Oh, Ari," she uttered. She threw her arms around his neck and began to sob.

Epilogue

Destiny slept uncomfortably, rolling over, bunching up her pillow, tossing off the covers. Six weeks after Livvy had left—and Destiny couldn't sleep without dreaming about her.

I don't want to sleep because then I have the nightmares.

But I'm so exhausted. I need to sleep.

"Dee?" A tiny voice at her ear.

She raised her head and realized that Mikey had climbed into bed with her. "Dee? Are you awake?"

"Uh-huh." She squinted at him.

"I can't sleep." He snuggled against her. "I keep dreaming about Livvy."

"Me too," she whispered.

He was silent for a moment. Then, "Is it true? She's never coming back?"

Destiny sighed. "I don't know, Mikey. I really don't. All we can do is hope. . . ."

She sat up when she heard a tapping sound. At the window?

Yes. Tapping and fluttering.

Mikey stood up. Destiny climbed out of bed after him. They hurried to the window.

A clear, moonlit night. Everything so still.

And then a bird flew up against the window glass. "A blackbird," Destiny whispered.

Mikey trembled beside her. She slipped her arm around his shoulders.

The bird hovered outside the window. Wings spread high, it floated on the other side of the glass, peering in . . .

. . . peering in longingly . . .

. . . with Livvy's green eyes.

"It . . . wants to come in," Mikey whispered.

Destiny hesitated. A chill ran down her back.

She stared into the bird's green eyes.

"Open it," Mikey whispered. "Let it in, Dee."

Destiny reached for the window.

But the blackbird turned and flew off into the night.

Dangerous Girls

The Taste of Night

A novel by
R.L. STINE

HARPER
TEEN
An Imprint of HarperCollins*Publishers*
Parachute

Contents

Part One

July

Chapter One

My Sister Is a Vampire

As Destiny Weller made the turn onto Collins Drive, a light rain started to fall. She squinted through the windshield, through the tiny, shimmering droplets of water, and pressed her cell phone to her ear.

"I think it's going to get really stormy," she said, glancing up at the lowering, black clouds. "I really don't feel like going out tonight, Ana-Li."

Her friend Ana-Li May made disappointed sounds at the other end. "I know it's hard for you, Dee. But the summer is going fast, you know. You should try to have at least a *little* fun."

Fun? How could she be talking about fun?

Destiny clicked on the headlights. The wipers left a smear on the windshield glass. She kept forgetting to replace the blades.

Hard to think about things like that.

"You've been really great," she told Ana-Li. "I mean, all summer. You're the only one who knows the truth about Livvy. I mean, except for Dad and Mikey. And Ari, of course. And you've been—OH!"

Destiny let out a cry. The cell phone fell from her hand as she hit the brakes hard. Her tiny, silver-gray Civic skidded on the wet pavement.

Startled by the sound, the girl on the sidewalk whipped her head around. Her face came into view.

Destiny gasped. No. Wrong again.

A car honked behind her. Heart pounding, she lowered her foot on the gas pedal and fumbled for the phone.

She could hear Ana-Li on the other end. "What's wrong? Dee? Are you okay?"

"Sorry." She leaned forward to squint through the smeared windshield. The rain pattered down harder. "I keep losing it. Every time I see a girl with long blond hair, I think it's Livvy."

"That's why you've got to get out of yourself," Ana-Li said. "You know. Go out. We'll go to a club or something. Dance our asses off.

Maybe meet some hot guys. It'll take your mind off . . . everything."

"*How can I take my mind off it?*"

She didn't mean to scream, but the words burst out of her in a shrill, trembling voice. "Ana-Li, my twin sister is a *vampire*! She's out flying around, prowling at night, hungry for warm blood, killing—killing things. I . . . I don't know what she's doing. I haven't seen her in two months. Do you know what that's done to my family? To my dad? My poor little brother?"

"Yes, of course I know, Dee. You don't have to scream at me. I—"

"There's *no way* I can take my mind off it," Destiny continued. She made a sharp right, tires skidding again. She'd almost missed her turn. "I think about Livvy all the time. And Ross too. I still can't believe he went with her. Ana-Li, I . . . I want to see Livvy. I just want to hug her. I know it's impossible, but I want to tell her to come back to us."

There was silence at Ana-Li's end.

"Ana-Li? Are you still there?"

"Yeah. I just don't know what to say. You know, I'll be leaving for orientation. Yale is a long way from here. I thought maybe in the short time we have . . ."

Destiny pulled into a parking spot at the curb in front of the familiar, low redbrick building. The rain had slowed. The wipers left a thick, gray smudge as they scraped over the glass.

That's the way I see everything these days, Destiny thought bitterly. Through a dark blur.

"Listen, Ana-Li. I have to go. I'm here, at my dad's office. I have to pick him up because his SUV broke down again. He never takes care of it." She sighed. "He can't seem to take care of anything these days. Just stays in his lab twenty hours a day. Then he comes home too wrecked to talk or do anything."

"Sorry," Ana-Li murmured on the other end.

"No, *I'm* sorry," Destiny said. "Here I am, laying all this on you again for the hundredth time. I'm really sorry. Can I call you later?"

"Yeah. Sure."

She clicked the phone shut and dropped it into her bag. Then she took a deep breath while checking her short, blond hair in the mirror.

Ana-Li has been terrific, she thought. She's always been a great friend. After that horrible night Livvy and Ross decided they wanted to live forever as vampires . . . Ana-Li has always been there for me.

She slid out of the car and gazed up at the sign above the glass door: WELLER VETERINARY CLINIC. Yes, her dad still treated sick cats and dogs, spayed and neutered them, gave them their shots, washed away their fleas, and mended their broken bones. But he spent most of his time in his lab at the back of the building, reading, studying old books, mixing chemicals, working out endless equations, searching for a cure for vampirism.

Destiny made her way through the brightly lit waiting room, empty now, quiet except for the gurgling sounds from the fish tank in the wall. "Hey, Dad—are you ready?" Her voice echoed down the hall as she passed the empty examining rooms.

"Dad?"

She found him hunched over the worktable in the lab, surrounded by darkness, standing under a cone of light from the single ceiling lamp. His eyeglasses reflected the light. He didn't seem to hear her at first.

"Dad? I'm here."

To her surprise, he had tears running down his cheeks. He crumpled the papers in his hand, then furiously ripped them in half and sent them flying to the floor.

"Dad—?"

Dr. Weller turned to Destiny, his face flushed, his eyes hidden behind the shiny glasses. "I'm afraid I have very bad news," he said.

Chapter Two

"Can You Kill Your Own Daughter?"

Destiny's breath caught in her throat. "Dad—what is it?" she finally choked out. She hurried across the room and stood across the table from him, under the bright, white light.

He shook his head. "It's my work. It's going nowhere. I'm no closer to finding a cure than I was two months ago."

Destiny grabbed the edge of the metal table with both hands. "But you'll keep trying, right, Dad? I mean, you're not giving up, are you?"

His pale blue eyes stared at her from behind his glasses, thick gray eyebrows arching high on his balding head. "I don't know how much time I have." His voice came out in a whisper. His eyes didn't move from Destiny's. "I'm under a lot of pressure."

"Pressure? I don't understand, Dad."

He stepped around the table and put an arm around her shoulders. "A lot of pressure." He hugged her briefly, then guided her to his small office at the side of the lab.

He dropped heavily into his desk chair, brushing back the tuft of gray hair on top of his head. Destiny stood, tense, in front of the desk, arms crossed over the front of her blue T-shirt.

"You know I have chosen two roles," Dr. Weller said, gazing up at her. "I'm the Restorer, the one who can restore neophyte vampires to their normal lives, if they're not already complete vampires."

I know very well, Destiny thought with a shiver. You don't have to explain, Dad. You restored *me*, remember? I was bitten too, just like Livvy. But you restored me, and now I'm fine, perfectly normal. But Livvy . . .

"And I'm also the Hunter," her dad continued, breaking into her thoughts. "Ever since your mother died . . . killed herself because of a vampire . . . I . . . I . . . I've vowed to kill as many vampires as I can. To rid Dark Springs of this . . . this filthy plague."

He rubbed his chin. Destiny saw that he hadn't shaved for at least a day or two. "My two roles . . . curing and hunting . . . they don't always go together."

"What do you mean, Dad? Destiny lowered herself into the wooden armchair across from the desk. "What's going on?"

"I've been working so hard to find a cure," he said. "You know. A cure for Livvy. And for Ross too. And any other vampire who wants it. And I've been neglecting my duties as a hunter."

Destiny leaned forward, her hands tightly clasped. All her muscles tensed as her father went on.

"The vampires in this town . . . they've become an even bigger danger. There are too many of them. People are starting to become aware . . ."

Destiny swallowed. "You mean, that couple that was murdered in Millerton Woods last weekend?"

Dr. Weller nodded. "The police have been able to keep everything quiet. People in Dark Springs don't know about the vampires. Like your friends, Dee. Your friends all think that Livvy and Ross ran away together. They . . . they don't know the truth."

Destiny nodded. "Just Ana-Li knows. And Ari, because he was there that night. No one else."

Dr. Weller frowned, deep lines creasing his forehead. "Well, people are starting to guess. The police have been getting calls. Mayor Hambrick has been getting frightened calls. He wants to get the governor to call in the National Guard. I can't let that happen. Too many innocent people will be killed."

"What are you going to do?" Destiny asked.

"I have no choice. I have to get my hunters together. I have to hunt them down—and kill as many vampires as I can."

Destiny let out a sharp cry. "Kill them?"

She suddenly pictured Livvy . . . Livvy before this all happened . . . when their mother was still alive. Livvy in that sexy red halter dress she wore to the spring dance their junior year. Her hair all shimmering, cascading down her bare back. The bright red lipstick . . . her sparkly earrings . . . her smile . . .

Destiny shook herself to chase the picture away.

"You can't just go out and kill vampires," she told her father. "How will you find them?"

Dr. Weller leaned forward over the desk. He grabbed Destiny's hands and held them between his. "There's an abandoned apartment building across the river from the campus. It was supposed to be student housing, a dorm for the community college. But the construction company went bankrupt and the building was never finished."

Destiny narrowed her eyes at him. "And—?"

"We think several vampires are using that building. Sleeping there during the day. Living in the apartments. I have my hunters organized. We're going there. Going into those apartments and killing as many of them as we can."

Destiny pulled her hands free. She jumped to her feet. "When? When are you doing this?"

"In two weeks—the next full moon."

Destiny swallowed, her throat suddenly dry. "Two weeks!"

He nodded. "Yes. We'll go in at sunrise when they're all asleep. I wanted to warn you. I mean, if something happens to me . . ." His voice trailed off.

"But, Dad—" Destiny realized she was shaking. "What about Livvy? What if Livvy is in one of those apartments? You . . . you can't kill your own daughter. You can't!"

A sob escaped Dr. Weller's throat. "My daughter is already dead."

Destiny moved around the desk and grabbed her father's sleeve. "But she's not! She's still alive. You know she's not dead. You can't do it. You can't kill her—*can* you?"

"I don't know!" Dr. Weller hugged Destiny again and held her tight. "I don't know. I don't know! If I find Livvy in there . . . I don't know what I'll do."

Chapter Three
The Vampire Hunt

*D*r. Weller pulled the dark baseball cap down over his head and gazed up at the moon, full and low in the sky, pale white as the sun began to rise. Dressed in black, hats down over their foreheads, the hunters—twenty volunteers—gathered in a silent circle around him at the open entrance to the tall apartment building.

Dr. Weller heard the flap of wings high in the sky. He glanced up the side of the redbrick building, at the window openings, glassless and dark. A tall pile of concrete blocks stood near the front of the entrance. Boards of Sheetrock in varying sizes, wire, and rolls of cable were strewn across the ground. Signs that the construction had stopped abruptly, long before the building had been completed.

A thin arc of red sunlight rose in the distance. The hunters leaned on their wooden stakes, waiting for their orders.

Dr. Weller took a deep breath. "The vampires should be sleeping by now," he said, eyes raised to the window holes. "But this may not be easy. If they somehow got word that we were coming . . ."

"We can handle them," a young man said, raising his stake in front of him like a knight's lance.

"They might have set a trap for us," Dr. Weller said. "We need to take all precautions. As we spread out in there, we need to be in constant communication. Did you check your walkie-talkies?"

Some of them muttered yes. Some nodded. Some reached for the phones clipped to their belts.

"Make sure they're all set on the same frequency," he continued. "If you're in any trouble, just press the button and shout your location. We'll all hear you."

They nodded again. One man at the edge of the circle made a striking motion with his pointed stake, as if he were killing a vampire.

"Let's go," Dr. Weller said. He hoped they didn't see the shudder that ran down his body. He spun to the building and began jogging toward the entrance, raising his stake as he ran.

Livvy? Ross? Are you in here?

The thought of his daughter lying white and pale, asleep in this vacant building, made his stomach churn. He could feel the muscles tightening in his throat. A wave of nausea swept over him, and for a moment, he thought he was going to vomit.

Livvy?

Oh, Livvy.

Then he was inside the dark lobby, cooler in here, the smell of plywood and pine and plaster dust, and his stomach settled. Through his glasses, his vision grew sharp as he focused his mind. In the dim light, he could see the half-tiled walls, the opening of the elevator shaft.

He suddenly could hear every footstep of his hunters, hear their shallow breaths, even hear their *thoughts*! At least, he imagined he could.

Every sense alive now.

Alive. Yes, I want to stay alive. I don't want to die tonight in a nest of vampires.

A nest of the *undead*.

Undead. My own daughter . . .

A shaft of red sunlight poured through the open lobby windows. The day was pushing out the night. He felt as if he were moving through a dream, colors changing, darkness giving way to bright light.

Trying to force away all thoughts, he led the hunters to the stairs. And as they climbed, single file up the concrete stairway, shoes thudding and scraping the dust, Dr. Weller heard the moans. Soft at first, then louder as they stepped out onto the first floor.

A shrill animal howl somewhere down the long hallway. Open doorways to the left.

Stakes gripped against their sides, the hunters trotted toward the open doorways. Dr. Weller clicked on his flashlight and sent a beam ahead of them on the floor. He saw piles of trash, rattling and blowing from the gusts of wind through the glassless windows.

Sudden movement. An animal scampered out from under the trash. Dr. Weller stopped and motioned for his hunters to stay back, and then lowered the beam of yellow light to the creature. A fat raccoon.

The animal waddled away from the light, down the trash-cluttered hall, followed by four small raccoons, running hard to keep up.

Dr. Weller motioned for his posse to move

again. Stepping over the garbage and stacks of newspaper, they walked silently toward the dark apartments.

No doors on the apartments. They heard hoarse coughs. Loud snoring. Eerie moans and groans . . .

Yes, they're here.

Yes, they're asleep.

Yes, it's time.

Dr. Weller raised his wooden stake and pointed it down the hall. "Let's kill vampires!" he cried.

Chapter Four

"Good-bye, Livvy"

He stepped into the first apartment, wooden stake raised in his right hand, flashlight gripped in his left. He swept the light around the floor. It stopped on a figure sprawled on his back, arms dangling over a nearly flat mattress on the floor.

Heart pounding, Dr. Weller moved closer. A young man, asleep, his mouth open. And the dark stain on his chin . . . the dark stain . . . caked blood. Running down his chin onto his bare chest.

He must die. I have no choice. I have accepted this responsibility.

But yet Dr. Weller hesitated. Am I taking a human life?

No.

Not human. Not human any longer.

A scream of agony ended his thought, followed by another shrill scream from down the hall. The hunters had found their prey. Vampires were being slaughtered.

He set down the flashlight. He raised the pointed stake high in both hands.

Another scream of horror from another apartment.

The young man stirred in his sleep. Closed his mouth. Eyes still shut, he licked at the caked blood on his chin.

With a loud grunt, Dr. Weller arched the stake high, then brought it down with all his force. The point pierced the young man's chest, then sank deep into his body.

His arms shot up and his legs kicked. He opened his eyes wide and a scream of pain shattered the silence of the room.

Dr. Weller buried the stake deeper, pushing hard, gripping it with both hands. The vampire's eyes sank into their sockets. The arms and legs, still now, began to shrink. A rush of air escaped the vampire's mouth, and then he didn't move again.

Dr. Weller freed the stake with a sharp tug. It pulled out easily, no blood on the tip.

He grabbed the flashlight and lurched back out into the hall. Screams echoed off the plaster walls. Screams and howls of pain and shock, and the hard-running footsteps of the hunters as they invaded the open apartments to kill their deadly prey.

Dr. Weller stopped for a moment to catch his breath. Then he dove into the next apartment, the wooden stake trembling in his hand.

The light danced over the apartment floor. A small, square rug in one corner. A suitcase against the wall. A wooden table cluttered with bottles and tubes and jars of cosmetics.

Dr. Weller swallowed. A female vampire lived here. His legs suddenly felt weak as he moved toward the bedroom in back. The flashlight grew heavy in his hand. He took a deep breath. Held it. Burst into the room.

And saw her sleeping on a low cot.

He recognized her with his first glance. Livvy.

Oh, no. Livvy.

She had cut her hair as short as Destiny's. She wore a long, black nightshirt down over her knees. Her hands were crossed over her chest. In the trembling glow of the flashlight, her short, blond hair shimmered around her pale, sleeping face.

I can't do this, he thought.

I brought her into the world. How can I kill her now? I despise all vampires. A vampire murdered my wife, took away the person most precious to me.

I hate them. Hate them all.

But to drive a stake through my own daughter? That's asking too much of any man.

Images flashed through his mind, bright and clear as photographs. Livvy as a baby. Livvy and Destiny in their snowsuits building their first snowman. Livvy and her mom giving each other makeovers, bright purple lipstick shining on his wife's lips, sparkles in her hair.

Livvy . . .

I can't.

With a sob, he turned to leave. He stopped when she stirred, groaning in her sleep.

She's not my daughter, he realized.

It's not Livvy anymore. It's a deadly creature in Livvy's body. And I have no choice.

He moved back to the cot. Raised the stake high in both hands. Changed his mind.

One last kiss for my daughter. A good-bye kiss.

Good-bye, Livvy.

He lowered his face to her cheek.

And he let out a startled cry as her hands shot up. Her eyes opened wide. She grabbed him by the neck and tightened her fingers around his throat.

"Ohh—" he gasped.

She stared up at him, and the fingers squeezed tighter, tighter . . .

"NO!" he choked out, struggling to free himself from her grip. "NO! LIVVY—PLEASE! NO!"

Part Two

One Month Earlier

Chapter Five

Livvy's Graduation Party

"I love the blue eye shadow. It's so retro," Livvy said. She turned to her two new friends, Suzie and Monica. "How does it look?"

"Awesome," Suzie said. "But wait. You have lipstick on your chin." She dabbed a tissue over the dark spot on Livvy's chin. "There."

"Is that the cinnamon lipstick or the grape?" Monica asked. She shoved Suzie aside to get a better look at Livvy. "It's so hard to tell in this light."

A single sixty-watt bulb hung on a long cord from the ceiling.

Livvy took the tissue from Suzie and dabbed at her lips. "It's black. For nighttime. My favorite time."

Monica grinned at Livvy. "My favorite time too. Party time." She licked her full, dark lips. Then she picked up her hairbrush and began running it through her long, straight black hair.

"Hey, it's date night," Suzie said.

"Every night is date night," Monica said, "when you're hungry."

Livvy turned to Suzie. "Are you coming with us?"

"I think we should go out on our own," Suzie replied. "See what's out there. Check out the fresh meat. You know. And then we can meet later."

Livvy studied Suzie's face, so pale, nearly white as snow. Suzie had been an immortal for a long time, for so long Suzie didn't remember when she made the change.

One night when the moon was still high in the sky, and the three girls had fed well and were feeling comfortable and full, Suzie told Livvy and Monica her story. She'd had a tough time, chased from town to town, nearly caught by vampire hunters in a city near Dark Springs.

Her troubles showed on her face, Livvy thought. Suzie's pale, papery skin was pulled tight against her skull, so tight her cheekbones nearly poked out. Her hair was patchy and thin. Her arms were as skinny as broom handles, her fingers bony, almost skeletal. Her eyes had started to sink back into their sockets.

She tried to cover it up with loads of

makeup and by wearing trendy clothes, young people's clothes. And she stayed in the darkest corners of the night, swooping out only when prey was near. But Suzie was too far gone to hide the fact that she was an immortal.

That won't happen to me, Livvy thought. I won't let that happen to me.

Livvy tossed back her blond hair with a shake of her head. She had cut it short—short as her sister's—and she loved the way it felt now, light as a breeze. "Wish we had a mirror," she murmured.

Suzie laughed. "What good would that do? We don't have reflections, remember?"

The lightbulb over their heads flickered and went out. Livvy sighed. "The generator must have conked out again."

Some clever immortals had hooked up a power generator to the building across the street. The stolen electricity provided light for the whole building. But the generator was too small and kept blowing out.

"Wish we lived in a fancy hotel," Monica said, still brushing her hair. "Instead of this empty apartment building. We could send down for room service. You know. Dial the phone and say, 'Just send the waiter up. We don't need any food.'"

Livvy laughed. "Forget room service. I just want to live in a place where the lights stay on."

"Lights hurt my eyes," Suzie complained, furiously powdering her face.

"I don't mean *bright* lights," Livvy said. "None of us can stand *bright* lights. I just mean lights that don't flicker on and off every few minutes."

The three new friends had built their dressing table out of plywood and concrete blocks left by the builders of the unfinished building. They had set it up in front of the glassless window where they could sit and watch the sunset.

Livvy had found a cot in one of the downstairs rooms and dragged it up to her bedroom. Suzie and Monica shared an apartment downstairs but came to Livvy's room in the evening to do their makeup and get ready to go out.

Livvy liked them both. Monica was big and dark and sexy and had no trouble getting the guys. And Suzie had the experience. She knew everything they needed to know to survive.

"When's the full moon?" Monica asked, adjusting the top of her tank top.

"I think it's in a few weeks," Suzie said, gazing up at the darkening sky. A faint smile crossed her pale lips. "Warm blood under a bright full moon. Poetry, right? Does it get any better than that? I don't think so."

Livvy turned to her. "What about tonight? They'll be some hot guys out tonight. Why wait?"

Monica brushed her arm. "Hey, didn't they have graduation at your school this morning? I thought I saw some cute guys walking around in blue robes."

Livvy glared at her. "Why bring that up?"

Monica backed away. "Whoa. I didn't mean anything. I was just asking."

"Do I give a damn about high school graduation?" Livvy snapped. She surprised herself at how angry she felt. Was she angry at Monica— or at something else? "I don't give a damn. Trust me."

"Okay, okay." Monica raised both hands as if asking for a truce.

"I've already graduated," Livvy said, still feeling upset. "I've graduated to what I want to be." She stood up. "Hey, maybe tonight I'll celebrate my graduation. Maybe I'll have a little graduation party of my own."

"We'll all party tonight!" Monica said, licking her lips.

Suzie gazed out the window. She seemed to be in her own world. "You know," she said, finally turning back to them, "the better looking the boy, the richer the blood."

"No way," Monica insisted. "That's superstition."

"It's a proven fact," Suzie said, toying with a strand of her long hair.

"Who proved it?" Livvy asked.

"I did." Suzie grinned. "Listen to me. The hot guys have the hottest blood."

Monica stared at her. "No lie?"

"No lie."

Livvy sighed. "I get so high when the blood is fresh and warm. I mean . . . the way it feels on my lips and then on my tongue. I can feel it all the way down my throat. And afterwards, it's so wild. I always feel like I'm flying . . . just flying out of my body, into outer space."

"I always feel so warm," Suzie said, her eyes dreamy. She sighed. "Like a happy, contented baby. But then the hunger starts again. So soon . . . it starts again, that gnawing . . . that needy feeling."

"Let's keep it light," Livvy scolded. "It's my

graduation party tonight, remember?" She stood up. "How do I look?"

She had her short, shimmery hair combed straight back, pale lip gloss, light blue eye shadow covering her eyelids, a pink midriff top over low-riding, white jeans, lots of bare skin showing, three earrings in each ear, a glittery rhinestone in her right nostril.

She walked up and down the bare room, doing the model strut. Monica and Suzie made admiring sounds. "Whoa. I love the nighttime!" Livvy exclaimed. "I feel lucky tonight!"

She realized that Suzie was staring past her. "Hey, what's up?"

She turned—and saw a fat brown field mouse hunched near the open doorway, gazing up at them with its shiny black marble eyes.

Suzie spun off her chair and lowered her lean body into a crouch, eyes unblinking, locked on the mouse.

"Oh, no. You wouldn't," Livvy said. "It's so cute."

With a sudden lightning movement, Suzie pounced. The mouse let out a squeak as Suzie grabbed it, wrapped her fingers around its stubby brown fur.

Its last squeak.

Suzie tore off its head and tossed it out into the hall. Then she tilted the body over her mouth and squeezed out the juice.

When she had finished, dark blood trickling down her chin, she heaved the drained corpse into the hall. Then she turned to Livvy and Monica with a grin. "Appetizer," she whispered.

Chapter Six
Night Birds

Livvy transformed into a slender blackbird. She perched on the windowsill, gazing out at the purple night sky.

Her feathers felt stiff and scratchy, and it took a while to get used to the rapid pattering of her heart. Once she adjusted to seeing two views at once, her eyesight was sharp.

She raised her wings and lifted off the window. The cool air ruffled her chest feathers. She swooped higher, pale white stars blinking so close above her. What a thrill!

To fly. To be free of the ground. To swoop and soar like a wild creature.

I'll never get tired of this, Livvy thought.

And then she felt the hunger, a sharp pang that tightened her belly. She opened her beak and let the onrushing air cool her throat. The gnawing hunger was insistent, wave after wave, until she felt dizzy from the need.

I have to feed.

What will I find tonight? Who will help me quench my thirst?

The yellow moon loomed above her, wisps of gray cloud snaking across it. Livvy lifted her wings and floated, gazing up at the moonlight.

No one else can see the moon like this. I am so lucky.

But then she felt a ripple in the wind at her side and heard the flutter of wings. Livvy turned and saw another blackbird, more plump with a streak of white in its wings, soar beside her.

The two blackbirds flew together, side by side, wings touching. They lifted high toward the stars, then shot low above the shimmering trees.

Livvy landed softly in tall grass and felt the dew tickle her feathers. The other bird shook its wings hard as it bounced to a landing a few feet beside her.

They both transformed quickly into their human forms.

Straightening her pink top, Livvy gazed at Ross Starr. The moonlight gave his short, blond hair a glow. He wore straight-legged jeans and a sleeveless T-shirt that showed off his muscular arms. He flashed her his Hollywood smile—the smile that had convinced her she needed Ross, needed to bring him with her to the other side.

"Hey, Ross," she murmured. "What's up? That was nice, wasn't it."

He stepped forward and kissed her. "You and me. Flying together. Yeah. That's what it's about, right?"

He tried to hug her, but Livvy pulled away. "I'm hungry. I mean, I'm starving." She held her stomach. "I . . . can't even think straight."

He smiled again. "Oh, yeah. Fresh nectar. I want mine super-sized!"

She kissed him on the cheek. "Get lost, okay?"

He grabbed her around the waist and pulled her to him. "Come on, Liv. I need more than a kiss. You look so hot tonight."

"Ross, please—" She squeezed his hands, then pushed them off her. "I told you I need to feed."

He shrugged. "Okay. I'll come with you."

"Oh, sure. That'll be helpful. You're gonna help me pick up a guy?"

He frowned at her. "I don't like you with other guys."

"What's your problem? He's not a guy. He's a meal."

She didn't hear what he said next. She transformed quickly, stretching her wings, ruffling the stiff tail feathers, a blackbird again.

She bent her thin bird legs, pushed up from the dew-wet grass, letting her wings lift her . . . lift her . . . over the treetops. She saw Ross swoop ahead of her, then fall back, teasing her, following her despite her pleas.

He bumped her playfully, swiped his beak against her side, lowered his head and bumped her again.

They flew side by side, gliding over Millerton Woods, light and shadows over the thick tangle of trees, shivering under the golden moonlight.

Livvy made a wide turn, wings straight out at her sides, and realized she was flying over Collins Drive now. Her father's office came into view. The light glowed from the front window. Was he still at work this late at night?

She swooped higher, away from the little, brick building. I don't want to see him. He's not part of my life anymore.

Flying low, the two blackbirds turned onto Main Street. Livvy landed behind a maple tree and gazed at the people in line at the movie theater. Ross dropped beside her.

They transformed into their human shapes, hidden by the thick tree trunk.

"You know, graduation was this morning," Ross said.

"Shut up," Livvy replied sharply.

"How are we going to get jobs?" Ross said. "We're not high school graduates."

"You're so funny," Livvy replied. "Not."

Ross turned to the movie theater. "What's playing? A vampire movie?"

Livvy's stomach growled. She ignored Ross and his jokes. I've never fed in a movie theater, she thought. It's dark enough—and the sound is loud enough to muffle the scream.

Livvy's victims only screamed once. They always screamed at the first bite, then gave in to the pleasure.

"Oh, no. Oh, wow." A moan escaped Ross's throat.

Livvy turned from the faces in the movie line. "What's wrong?"

He leaned forward, peering around the tree trunk. "My family is there. See them? Mom and Dad and Emily."

Livvy saw Ross's sister first, then his parents. "Don't worry. They can't see us."

"I . . . I want to see them," Ross said. "Livvy, I'd just like to talk to them for a little while. You know. See how Emily is doing and everything. They think I ran away with you. I want to tell them I'm okay."

"Ross, you can't," Livvy said. "You know you can't do that. You'll only upset them. You'll mess them up even worse."

"But—I just want to say hi," Ross said. "I guess I'm homesick."

"It won't work. Trust me." Livvy stared hard at him. She could see how excited and upset he was.

"Maybe I feel homesick too. But listen to me. I made a vow," Livvy told him. "I vowed I'd never go back home. You need to make the same vow. It's not our world anymore. We've chosen a different world. You know. A more exciting life. I . . . I'm not going to torture myself by trying to drop in on Destiny and Dad and . . . and . . ."

She couldn't say Mikey's name. Thinking about Mikey always made her cry.

"I guess you're right," Ross said. "But look.

My family—they're going inside the theater. I could just walk over, say hi, and leave."

"No. Go away, Ross. Fly away—now. You know I'm right."

Sighing, he watched until his family disappeared inside. Then he kissed Livvy on the cheek. "Later."

He changed quickly. Raised his wings and fluttered off the ground. She watched him hover over the sidewalk. Then she changed into a blackbird too, turned and flew away.

I don't want to hear about how homesick Ross is, she thought. A shudder ran down her body. The air suddenly felt cold. The moonlight sent down no warmth.

I shouldn't have brought Ross to this new life. I care about him. I still do. Maybe not like before. But I care about him.

But he's too sentimental. He's too soft.

I thought he was strong, but he isn't. He always seemed so confident. I can still see him with that strutting walk of his, moving down the halls at school, flashing that great smile. I used to wait for him to come by. I had such a major crush on him.

But now . . . he's weak. His attitude is

wrong. He's not thinking right.

He'll get himself killed. I know he will.

Hunger gnawed at her, interrupting her thoughts. She glanced down and saw flashing lights on a big, square building.

Where am I?

Sliding on a wind current, she let herself down and recognized the dance club: Rip.

Oh, yes. Lots of fresh talent here. Kids hanging out in the dimly lit parking lot. Lined up at the entrance. Lots of dark corners, and the woods close behind the parking lot.

Lots of older guys getting trashed at the bar and looking to hook up.

How perfect is that for a hungry vampire?

And there below her she saw Suzie and Monica at the entrance, chatting with two guys, about to go in.

Excellent.

Livvy dropped to the gravel path at the side of the building. She could hear the throbbing beats from inside, hear laughing voices, the roar of a crowd.

Yes, yes, yes. I'm so hungry.

I'm sure some lucky guy will be happy to come to the woods with me.

She transformed into her human body, brushed a few feathers off the front of her jeans, tugged down the top of her top to look sexier—and hurried to meet her friends.

Part Three
Earlier That Day

Chapter Seven
The Evil at Home

"As you leave this high school where you have spent four wonderful years of growth and learning . . . As you go forth into the world—no longer students—you must realize that the world belongs to you now. Your generation will decide where we all go next. You will be the ones to shape the future. You will be the ones . . ."

Destiny tuned out as the graduation speaker droned on. She wiped her sweaty hands in the folds of her blue robe.

"It's so hot in here," she whispered to the girl next to her. "When can we take these things off?"

The flat blue cap, tilted over her head, felt as if it weighed a hundred pounds. Destiny knew it was going to leave a permanent dent in her hair. Sweat streamed down her forehead. Would the cap leave a blue stain on her skin?

She glanced at the rows of robed kids on the stage. As they all gathered in the auditorium this morning, her friends had been bursting with excitement about graduation. Ana-Li May was practically *flying*, swirling around in circles, making her graduation robe whirl around her.

Fletch Green, Ross's best friend, gave Destiny such a big hug, he accidentally knocked her cap off her head. "Do you believe I graduated in only four years?" he exclaimed. "My parents predicted six!"

Ari Stark seemed excited too. He greeted her with a kiss. "Freedom!" he shouted. "A few more hours, and we're *outta* here! Freedom! Freedom!" He started a chant, and a few other kids joined in.

A sad smile crossed Destiny's face. She knew why her friends were so happy and excited. They really were getting out of here, out of Dark Springs. They were going away to college. In a few months Ari would be at Princeton in New Jersey. And Ana-Li would be off at Yale being brilliant the way she always was.

And I'll be here, Destiny thought, unable to fight away her sadness. I was accepted at four schools, including Dartmouth, where I really wanted to go. But no. I'll be here, living at home, going to the dinky Community College.

But what choice did I have? How could I leave Mikey, my poor, troubled little brother? How could I leave Dad? They both need me so much now . . . now that Livvy . . .

She wanted to be excited and happy. Graduating from high school was a major thing in your life. It was supposed to be a day you'd never forget.

And it *was* kind of thrilling to march slowly down the auditorium aisle in time to "Pomp and Circumstance," the music played at every graduation. And to hear your name called, and walk up to receive your diploma.

Destiny smiled and waved the diploma at her dad. She could see him wave back to her from the fourth row.

Kind of exciting.

But then the kids in her class settled into their folding chairs, sweating under their robes, shifting the caps on their heads. And the balding, scratchy-voiced speaker in his tight-fitting gray suit—an assistant mayor, she thought—began to speak.

". . . The future isn't only a promise, it's a responsibility. How will you find your role in the future? By looking to the past. Because the past is where our future springs from . . ."

Yawn.

As he rambled on, his voice faded from Destiny's ears. And she felt the sadness rise over her, like a powerful ocean wave.

There should be an empty seat next to me, she thought. A chair for Livvy. Livvy would have been here with me this morning, and we would have been so happy.

Destiny gazed down the rows of blue-robed kids. And there should be a chair for Ross. Destiny felt a flash of anger. Yes, I had a crush on Ross—and Livvy knew it. And she took him away . . . where no one will ever see him again. So selfish . . . so stupid and selfish . . .

There should be a chair here for Ross. He should be graduating today. And there should be two more empty chairs, Destiny thought. Chairs for our friends, Courtney and Bree, both murdered by vampires.

Four empty chairs. Four kids who will not graduate this morning.

The sadness was overwhelming. Destiny felt hot tears streaming down her cheeks. She turned her head away. She didn't want her father to see.

Poor Dad. He must be thinking the same things, she told herself. Somehow he's managing to keep it together. I have to try hard to keep it together too. She glanced down at the red leather cover on her diploma and saw that it was stained by her tears.

Loud cheers startled Destiny from her thoughts. All around her, kids leaped up and tossed their caps in the air. Blinking away her sadness, Destiny climbed to her feet and tossed her cap too.

The ceremony had ended. I'm a high school graduate, she thought. I've spent twelve years with most of these kids. And now we're all going to scatter and start new lives.

New lives . . .

She couldn't stop thinking about Livvy. No way to shut her out of her mind, even for a few minutes.

"Return your robes to the gym, people," Mr. Farrow, the principal, boomed over the loudspeaker. "Don't forget to return your robes to the gym."

All around her, kids were hugging, laughing, talking excitedly. Some jumped off the stage and ran up the auditorium aisles to meet their parents.

She waved to Ari, hurried to return her robe, then found her dad outside in front of the school talking to some other parents.

It was a warm June morning, the sun already high in a clear blue sky. Yellow lilies circling the flagpole waved gently in a warm breeze. Families filled the front lawn of the school, snapping photos, chatting, and laughing.

Dr. Weller turned when he saw Destiny and wrapped her in a big hug. "Congratulations," he said. She saw the tears in his eyes. She hugged him again.

"We have to make this a happy day," he said. "We really have to try, don't we?"

Destiny nodded. Her chin trembled. She fought off the urge to cry.

"I have to get to my office," Dr. Weller said. "But I'll take you and Mikey out for dinner tonight—our own private celebration. Good?"

"Good," she replied. She saw Ari and Ana-Li come out of the building.

"If Ari would like to come with us tonight . . ." her dad started. He had grown used to seeing Ari around the house at all hours. The two of them got along pretty well.

"I think he's going out with his family," Destiny said.

Dr. Weller nodded. "The three of us. We'll have a nice dinner." She walked him to his SUV. It took him four tries to start it up.

"Dad, you've really got to get this car serviced," Destiny said.

He smiled at her. "It's on my list."

"Dad, you know you don't *have* a list."

"It's on my list to make a list." Tires squealing, he pulled away.

Destiny felt a tap on her shoulder. She turned and Ari kissed her. "Hey, we're graduates. I'm totally psyched. Do you believe it? No more gym class. No more Coach Green telling me what a loser I am."

Ana-Li laughed. "Just because you have a diploma doesn't mean you're not a loser."

Ari pretended to be hurt. "What's up with that? You're dissing me on graduation day?"

Ana-Li opened her diploma and held it up. "Check it out. They misspelled my name. Two n's."

"That's terrible," Destiny said, studying the diploma. "How could they do that?"

"It means you didn't really graduate," Ari told Ana-Li. "No one will believe that's your diploma. Your whole life is going to be messed up now."

Ana-Li shook her tiny fist at Ari. "I'm going to mess *you* up!"

Laughing, Ari raised both fists and began dancing from side to side. "You want a piece of me? Huh? You want a piece of me?"

Ana-Li ignored him. She turned to Destiny. "How you doing?"

"Tough morning," Destiny replied. "You know."

Ari lowered his fists. His smile faded.

"What are you two doing now?" Destiny asked. "Want to come back with me? We can sit around and reminisce or something."

"Is lunch included in this invitation?" Ari asked.

Destiny nodded.

"Count me in."

"Just let me say good-bye to my parents, and I'll meet you at your house," Ana-Li said. She trotted back toward the school.

Ari slid an arm over Destiny's shoulders, and they walked the few blocks to her house.

Cars filled with their friends rolled by, horns honking, music blaring from open windows.

"Did you hear about Fletch's party last night?" Ari asked. "His parents were in L.A. So Fletch had two kegs. Everyone got trashed. And his brother's garage band played all night."

Destiny sighed. "I'm sorry. I know you wanted to go. But I just didn't feel like partying."

They stepped onto her front stoop. Destiny fumbled in her bag for her key. She found it, turned the key in the lock, pushed open the front door—and screamed.

"OH, NO!"

Ari grabbed her and they both stared in disbelief at the living room walls.

Fanged creatures with curled horns on their heads . . . A winged, two-headed demon, both heads spewing black blood . . . A grinning devil . . .

Ugly, black demons painted all over the walls.

Chapter Eight

"The Monster Did It"

"Oh, no! oh, no!" Destiny held onto Ari and pressed her head against his shoulder. Staring at the crude, childish paintings, she led the way into the house.

"This is too weird," Ari muttered.

Destiny opened her mouth to speak. But a shrill cry interrupted her—and Mikey came leaping off the stairs onto Ari's shoulders. He curled his hands around Ari's throat and screamed, "I'm a MONSTER! I'll kill you! I'll KILL you!"

Ari dropped to the floor under the eight-year-old boy's weight. He sprawled on his back and pried Mikey's fingers from around his neck. "Whoa. Easy, man. Mikey, you're choking me."

"I'm not Mikey. I'm a *monster*!"

Destiny reached down to help pull Mikey off.

"Hey, what's up?" Ana-Li burst into the

room. She let out a cry when she saw the crude creatures smeared over the walls. "Ohmigod."

Destiny pulled Mikey to his feet, then tugged him away from Ari. "Calm down. Don't move. Just take a deep breath, okay?"

Mikey tossed back his head and let out a hoarse, demonic laugh.

Destiny kept a hand on his thick, coppery hair, holding him in place. Mikey was slender and light, small for eight, with arms and legs like sticks. He had dark, serious eyes that looked as if they belonged on an adult. His front teeth were crooked because he refused to wear his retainer.

Groaning, Ari climbed to his feet. Ana-Li couldn't take her eyes off the walls.

"I can't believe you did this," Destiny said, shaking her head.

"I *told* you I didn't do it. The monster did it," Mikey insisted, finally back in his normal, high-pitched voice.

Destiny and Ana-Li exchanged glances. Ana-Li knew the problems they'd been having with Mikey. The poor kid had been acting out, severely troubled by the loss of his sister.

He had nightmares that made him scream.

He was afraid to stand near an open window. He'd been getting into fights at school. Sometimes he was afraid of the dark. But he kept his room dark as a cave and spent hour after hour in there with the door locked.

Destiny never knew what to expect. Sometimes Mikey acted like a terrified victim, trembling, crying. And other times, he acted like a monster, striking out, screaming in a rage.

She felt so bad for the little guy . . . and so totally helpless.

Ari stepped up to the wall and examined the paintings. "I think the monster is in trouble big-time," he said to Mikey. "How do you think the monster should be punished?"

"His head should be cut off with a machete," Mikey answered. "And then they should turn him upside down and let all his blood drain out on the floor."

Ari turned to Destiny. "Big trouble," he whispered.

"Wasn't anyone here watching Mikey?" Ana-Li asked.

Destiny sighed. She turned to Mikey. "Where is Mrs. Miller? She was supposed to watch you."

"She had to go home to check something," Mikey said. "She didn't come back. I guess she got busy."

"Mikey's the one who got busy," Ari said, gesturing to the wall.

Mikey let out a roar. His eyes grew wide. "*The monster is coming back,*" he whispered.

"We should get him out in the sunshine for a while," Ana-Li whispered to Destiny. "You know. Take his mind off this stuff."

Destiny nodded. "Hey, how about a soccer game?" she asked Mikey. "You and me against Ari and Ana-Li."

Mikey reluctantly agreed. Destiny grabbed a soccer ball in the garage and led the way to the backyard, and the four of them started a game.

The Wellers' backyard was deep and wide, covered by a carpet of low grass and interrupted by only a few sycamore and birch trees. Almost perfect for soccer.

The wind had picked up, but the sun blazed high in the sky, making the air warm as summer. Destiny passed the ball to Mikey, and they drove down the field toward Ana-Li and Ari. Mikey brought the ball close to the two slender saplings that formed the goal. Ari made an attempt to block his shot. But Mikey sent the ball flying through the trees. *Goal!*

It was obvious to Destiny that her two friends were letting Mikey be a star. But Mikey didn't notice. He jumped up and down cheering for himself.

This was a good idea, Destiny thought. His mood has changed completely. A little sunshine and some physical exercise, and he's acting like a normal kid again.

The game went well for another ten minutes. Destiny loved the intense expression on her brother's face as he moved the ball forward, dodged Ana-Li and Ari and their feeble attempts to block him, and kicked two more goals.

Destiny began to feel hungry. Maybe it was time to stop the game and make lunch. She looked up in time to see Ari give the ball a hard kick that sent it flying toward the trees at the edge of the yard.

Mikey and Ari both took off after the ball. It hit the trunk of an old sycamore tree hard and bounced off. Mikey slid under the tree, chasing the ball.

Destiny heard a cracking sound. She raised her eyes in time to see a high branch of the tree come crashing down.

"Mikey—look out!" she screamed.

Chapter Nine

The Vampire in the Tree

Mikey's eyes went wide.

Destiny heard the crack of branches as the falling limb smashed through them.

Mikey let out a scream, dropped to the ground, and rolled away.

The limb hit the ground a foot or so from Mikey, bounced once, and came to a rest on the grass.

Destiny had her hands pressed to the sides of her face. "Are you okay?" she screamed.

Mikey didn't answer. He jumped to his feet and pointed up to the tree. "Vampire!" he cried. "It's a vampire! In the tree!"

"No, wait—" Ari shouted. He made a grab for Mikey. But Mikey took off, running to the house.

"Mikey, it was just a tree branch," Destiny called. She chased after her brother and caught him at the kitchen door.

"Let go!" he screamed. "It's a vampire. In the tree! Didn't you see it? Didn't you?"

"No. There's nothing up there," Destiny insisted, holding him by the arm. "Listen to me—"

But he jerked his arm free and dove into the house. She heard him sobbing loudly as he scrambled up the stairs to his room.

"Mikey, wait. Please—" Destiny darted up the stairs after him.

He slammed the door in her face. She heard the lock click. She could hear him still sobbing on the other side of the door.

Destiny turned and saw Ari and Ana-Li at the bottom of the stairs. They gazed up at her, their faces tight with concern.

She made her way down the stairs slowly, feeling shaky and upset. "I'd better call Dr. Fishman," she said. "He's Mikey's shrink. He keeps telling us it will just take time. But I've never seen Mikey this bad."

"The poor guy is scared to death," Ari said, shaking his head.

"He sees vampires everywhere," Destiny whispered. "And then sometimes he pretends *he*'s a vampire." She led them into the living room. She motioned to the couches, but no one sat down. They stood tensely near the wall.

"I know the only thing that will help him," Destiny said. "Bring Livvy back. He knows the truth about her. Maybe it was a mistake to tell him. He's so scared now. If I could just bring her back here—"

"Hey, I'm scared too," Ana-Li said, hugging herself tightly. She shuddered. "I mean, Livvy and Ross are out there somewhere, right?"

Destiny nodded.

"And they're full vampires now. I mean, real ones. Needy . . . thirsty." She shuddered again.

Ari raised his eyes toward the ceiling. "Shhh. Not so loud. We don't need to be talking about this in front of Mikey."

"But what if they come back here?" Ana-Li whispered. "What if they're out flying around one night, and they're real thirsty? I mean, so thirsty they can't control themselves. And they fly back here and find us? I mean, they could attack us, right? Aren't we obvious victims here?"

"No way," Destiny replied, shaking her head. "She's still my sister. No way she'd come back here and attack my friends." She frowned at Ana-Li. "Do you honestly think Livvy would come back here and drink your blood?"

378

"I . . . don't know," Ana-Li replied, her voice cracking. "I really don't."

Destiny opened her mouth to reply, but a sudden noise above her head made her stop.

A flapping sound. Like a window shade flapping in a strong wind.

Destiny raised her eyes to the sound and saw a darting, black shadow.

"Hey—!" Ari let out a cry, his mouth open in surprise.

The shadow swooped low.

Destiny felt a cold whoosh of air sweep past the back of her neck.

It took her a while to recognize the sound— the flapping of wings.

And then she saw the bat. Eyes glowing, it soared beneath the dark wood ceiling beams. Then low over their heads, flapping up to the mirror, turning and shooting over them to the other wall. Then flying over them again, lower each time, raising its talons as if preparing to attack.

Ana-Li covered her head. Ari ducked. Destiny opened her mouth in a scream of horror.

Chapter Ten

Is Livvy in the House?

The bat let out a screech and soared up to the ceiling. Destiny watched it cling to a beam, wings flapping hard. Its glowing eyes locked on Destiny.

"How did it get in?" Ana-Li cried, clinging to Ari's arm. "What's it doing in here?"

Trembling, Destiny stared up at it. "Livvy? Is that you?" she called, but she could only manage a whisper. "Livvy—?"

And then without warning, the creature let go of the wooden beam and came swooping down.

Destiny saw the eyes glow brighter. Saw the creature raise its talons and arch its wings high behind its ratlike head.

She tried to duck away, bumping hard into Ari and Ana-Li, sending them tumbling against the couch.

Then with another whistling shriek, the bat

latched onto Destiny. Wings flapping loudly, it dug its talons into her hair. She heard its ugly cry as she struggled to slap it off.

"*Eeeeee eeeeeee!*" Like a car alarm going off in her head.

"No! Get off! Get OFF me!"

The talons dug into her scalp. Sharp, stabbing pain swept through her head.

"NO!"

Her heart pounding, Destiny ducked low again, swung her hand, hit the creature hard. She felt its furry warmth. Felt the breeze from its flapping wings, felt the bat's hot breath prickle the back of her neck.

"Get OFF!"

Another hard slap sent the creature sailing to the floor.

Ari raised his foot to stomp on it.

"No—don't!" Destiny screamed, shoving him back.

The bat recovered quickly. It let out a low buzz, then shot back up into the air. Destiny covered her hair with both arms as it swooped low over her again. Then the creature made a sharp turn and flew into the back hallway.

Holding her head, Destiny lurched after it.

"Livvy—?" she called. "Is that you?"

The bat darted out the open kitchen window, leaving the yellow window curtains fluttering behind it.

"Oh, wow." Destiny sank onto a white bench at the kitchen table. She brushed back her hair, waiting for her heartbeats to slow.

"Are you okay?" Ari put a hand on her shoulder. "Dee, you're shaking."

"It . . . attacked me," she stammered. "Why did it attack me?"

Ana-Li opened the refrigerator and pulled out a bottle of water. She spun off the top and handed it to Destiny. "Here. Drink something. Try to calm down. You're okay, right?"

Destiny nodded. She took a long drink of the cold water.

Then she turned back to her friends. "Why would a bat fly into the house in the middle of the day? And why did it attack me?"

Ari shrugged. Ana-Li stared back at Destiny without an answer.

Destiny took another drink. "How can we live our whole lives scared to death?" she asked. She pounded a fist on the table, making the ceramic fruit bowl shake. An apple rolled onto the floor. "I have to do something. I have to find Livvy. I have to talk to her . . . convince her to come back."

"Maybe she *was* back," Ana-Li said softly. "Maybe she was that bat. Maybe she came back to warn you."

"To warn me of what?"

"To stay away from her. To leave her alone."

Destiny grabbed her friend's arm. "That's crazy, Ana-Li. She's my sister. My twin sister. We belong together. She must know that. Even the way she is now . . . she must know that I'll do anything to bring her back to us."

"I have to go," Ana-Li said, moving quickly to the front door. "I have to get out of here. I mean, out of Dark Springs. It's too terrifying here. Bats and vampires and people dying. I'm so glad I'm going to New Haven in a few weeks."

She turned at the door. Destiny could see tears in her eyes. "I'm sorry, Dee," she said in a voice trembling with emotion. "I didn't mean to sound so cold. I know you've lost your sister. I didn't mean to sound selfish. I just . . . I . . ."

She spun away and disappeared out the door.

Ari stepped over to Destiny and wrapped her in a hug. "That was so horrible," he said softly. "That bat . . . when it attacked you, I—"

She silenced him with a kiss. The kiss lasted a long time. She wrapped her hands around his neck and held onto him, and they pressed together tightly as they kissed.

"You . . . you're going away, too," she whispered, finally pulling her lips away. She pressed her cheek against his. "You're going away too."

"Not until August. We have five weeks," he said.

She sighed. They kissed again. She shut her eyes and tried not to think about Ari leaving.

"About tonight," he said, holding her in his arms. "I know we have dinners with our parents tonight. But we can go out later. It's graduation, Dee. Let's go to that dance club that just opened. You know, Rip. Let's go there tonight, and pretend everything is okay . . . just for one night."

His eyes burned into hers. "Okay? Please say yes."

"Yes," Destiny agreed in a whisper.

"Hey, all right!" Ari pumped his fists in the air in victory.

Destiny started to kiss him again, but they were interrupted by a shout from upstairs.

Mikey, at the top of the stairs.

"Dee—hurry! Livvy's back! She's back! Hurry!"

Chapter Eleven
Rip

Destiny ran up the stairs, pulling herself up two steps at a time. At the top, Mikey grabbed her hand and pulled her to his room.

Destiny blinked in the darkness. Mikey kept the blinds closed, curtains pulled, and the lights off. "Where is she?" Destiny cried. "I can't see anything."

She fumbled for the light switch and clicked on the ceiling light.

"No—don't!" Mikey grabbed her hand and pulled it away from the light switch. "Turn it off. Turn it off."

Destiny obediently shut off the light.

"I was only pretending," Mikey said.

"You mean—?"

"I was pretending Livvy was back. That's all."

Destiny let out a long sigh. "Not again, Mikey." She hugged him tightly. "Not again. You have to stop this. Do you understand?"

Mikey didn't reply.

Rip was a tall, barnlike building on the edge of North Town, the old section of Dark Springs. The club had previously been called Trixx, and before that Wild Weasel. Every year a new owner painted the outside a different color and put up new signs. But the inside was always pretty much the same.

As Destiny followed Ari inside, she saw a tall DJ wearing a white cowboy hat hunched over two turntables on a small stage in the center of the room. Red and blue neon lightning bolts flashed over the high ceiling, the light flickered off the dancers, dozens of them jammed together on the dance floor, moving to the throbbing rhythm, the music so loud the concrete floor vibrated.

A long, mirrored bar curved the length of the back wall. Low couches and fat armchairs formed a lounge on one side. Destiny looked up and saw people gazing down onto the dance floor from the narrow balcony that circled the room.

"I'll get us some beers," Ari said, leading her

through the crowd. He opened his wallet and flashed a driver's license. "I have great fake I.D. A guy sold me this for fifty dollars, and it always works."

Eyes on the dancers, she followed him to the bar. Half the graduating class from Dark Springs High is here tonight, Destiny realized. She waved to some girls she knew. She spotted Ana-Li sitting in a big armchair in the lounge, leaning forward to talk to two guys Destiny had never seen before.

In a corner by the lounge, a girl in a sparkly red mini-dress was lip-locked with a guy in black jeans and a muscle shirt. He had a tattoo of a motorcycle on his bicep. As they kissed, he ran his big hands through her blond hair.

Blond hair . . .

No, Destiny thought. Not tonight. I'm not going to think about Livvy tonight.

But she stared at the girl kissing the big, tattooed guy so passionately, and she couldn't help but picture her sister there.

"Here you go." Ari bumped her shoulder. She turned and reached for the beer bottle in his hand. "The guy carded me," Ari said, grinning. "The Delaware driver's license always works.

Want me to get you one?"

She frowned at him. "Ari, you don't even *like* beer that much. What's the big deal?"

He shrugged. "Come on. We're at a club, right? We gotta drink beer. Besides, I've got a lot of time to make up for. All those years, sitting in my room at the computer, going to dorky UFO websites or watching *Star Trek* reruns. I didn't know what I was missing!"

Ari has changed a lot, Destiny thought. I guess all the terrible things that have happened snapped him out of his fantasy world.

Ari started to raise the beer bottle to his mouth—and Fletch Green grabbed it out of his hand. "Thanks, dawg." Fletch emptied the bottle in less than five seconds and handed it back to Ari, a big smile on his face.

Ari stared at the empty beer bottle.

"Sorry you guys missed my party last night," Fletch said, sliding an arm around Destiny. "Hey, Dee, you look hot tonight."

Destiny wore a short, pleated black skirt, a tight, white midriff top, and her favorite red strappy sandals.

"So do you, Fletch," Destiny shot back. He was wearing baggy cargo pants and a black T-shirt with a martini glass on the front.

"It was a great party," Fletch said. "The cops came out three times. We have totally obnoxious neighbors. They call the cops if I sneeze too loud. But it was awesome. Gil Marx threw up in the fishpond. That was kinda gross. But no one else got too sick."

He took Destiny's beer from her hand and finished that one too. He handed the bottle to Ari. "Thanks again, dawg. You know, you're too young to drink." He gave the back of Destiny's hair a playful tug. Then he spun away and shambled off.

"Is he here with someone?" Ari asked, watching Fletch push his way through the dance floor.

Destiny shrugged. "Beats me. I heard he's been drinking a lot. I mean, a *lot*." She sighed. "The poor guy. He and Ross were like this." She held two fingers together. "I think he's a little lost without him."

"Hey, I thought we weren't going to talk about that tonight," Ari snapped. He clinked the empty bottles together. "I'll get another round."

"Not now." Destiny grabbed his arm. "Let's dance, okay?"

But he was already pushing his way to the bar.

What's he trying to prove? Destiny wondered. I thought we came here to dance.

Ari returned a few minutes later with two more beers. He downed his quickly and went back for another.

Destiny sipped hers slowly. She talked with three girls from her class, shouting over the throbbing dance music. They talked about how boring the graduation speaker was, their summer jobs, and what they planned to do in the fall.

Destiny could see the girls were a little uncomfortable. They were trying hard not to mention Livvy. Finally, one of them said, "Have you heard from your sister?"

"No," Destiny replied. "We don't know where she and Ross went."

She saw Ari at the bar, talking to a short, red-haired girl, tossing back another beer. Was he flirting with her?

Destiny made her way through the crowd and grabbed him by the elbow. "Are we going to dance or what?" She pulled him onto the dance floor.

They danced for a while under the flashing lightning bolts. Destiny shut her eyes and tried to lose herself to the music, the soaring voices, the insistent beat.

When she opened her eyes she saw Ana-Li nearby, dancing with one of the guys from the lounge. Ana-Li looked great in low-riding, black denims and a green tube top that showed a lot of skin. They waved to each other. Ana-Li pointed to Ari. They both laughed.

Yes, he was a terrible dancer. He had no sense of rhythm at all. Thrashing his arms around, bending his knees, Destiny thought he looked like a puppet that had lost his strings.

Destiny put her hands on Ari's shoulders and tried to guide him. He gave her a lopsided smile. His eyes were cloudy. How many beers had he drunk?

They danced for a long while. Destiny loved the feel of the floor vibrating beneath her, the lights pulsing, the constant beat of the dance music shutting out all other sound.

Ari had a good idea, she decided. I'm actually enjoying myself.

Then she saw the blond again, the one who reminded her so much of Livvy. She was dancing with her back to Destiny, swaying to the music with her arms above her head, her blond hair swinging from side to side.

With a sigh, Destiny stopped dancing. She stumbled into Ari. Her eyes were locked on the blond in the red mini-dress.

The kind of sexy outfit Livvy would wear. Her hair swinging like Livvy's.

"I . . . can't do this," she told Ari, holding onto him with both hands.

She pulled him off the dance floor. They found a small, round table near the bar and sat down. "What happened?" Ari asked, holding her hand.

"I can't do this," Destiny repeated. "I can't be here dancing and pretending."

"Hey, we came here to have fun, right?" Ari said, rolling his eyes. "Just for once, can't we forget about what's happening?"

"I tried," Destiny said. She found a tissue in her bag and wiped the sweat off her forehead. "But Livvy is out there somewhere." She pointed to the door. "Out in the night. My sister alone in the night. How can I—"

"It's not your fault," Ari shouted. "She made a stupid choice. She made a totally *selfish* choice. She didn't think about you, Dee. Or your father. Or your brother. She only thought about herself. So why are you thinking about *her* all the time? Why can't you lighten up for just one night?"

"You don't understand—" Destiny started. "Knowing that she's out there somewhere, prowling around, searching for God-knows-what, it's . . . it's worse than if she were dead."

Ari jumped up, a scowl on his face. "Give me a break," he muttered. "Enough already." He turned and stormed away, disappearing into the crowd on the dance floor.

"Ari, no—wait!" Destiny jumped to her feet and started after him. She bumped into a guy on the dance floor, then pushed past another couple. The flashing lights started to hurt her eyes, made her blink. The steady, pulsating beats began to pound in her ears.

"Ari—?"

Where was he?

I tried. I really tried, Destiny thought. I understand why he lost it. He's been so patient. He wants to have a little fun before he goes off to college. And I haven't been able to shake off this sadness.

She edged her way to the other side of the dance floor. No sign of Ari. Ana-Li stood with a Coke in one hand, talking to Fletch Green and two other guys from their class.

Destiny rushed up to her. "Have you seen Ari?"

Ana-Li laughed. "You lost him?"

"Kinda." Destiny didn't feel like telling her what happened.

"Lookin' hot, Dee," Jerry Freed, one of the three guys, said, grinning at her. He flashed her a thumbs-up.

Ana-Li pointed to the dance floor with her Coke can. "Isn't that Ari over there? Who's he dancing with?"

Destiny spun around. Squinting into the blinking lights, she saw Ari dancing with his hands on the bare waist of another girl . . . the red-haired girl he'd been flirting with at the bar. He pulled her close, and they danced cheek-to-cheek even though the music pounded even faster.

"I don't believe it," Destiny groaned.

"Did you two break up or something?" Ana-Li asked.

"Looks like it," Destiny said. She started

toward Ari and his new dancing partner.

What is his problem? Is he just trying to hurt me?

He's been totally understanding the whole time, Destiny thought. Was it all an act?

She grabbed his arm. "Ari?"

He took his hands off the girl's waist, blinking at Destiny. "Oh. Hi." As if he didn't recognize her.

The red-haired girl frowned at Destiny and continued to move to the music.

"Ari, what's up with this?" Destiny couldn't keep her voice from trembling. "I mean—"

Ari shrugged.

"I mean, what's going on?"

"Just dancing."

She realized her hands were balled into tight fists. Working the turntables, the DJ went into a scratching fit, then changed the rhythm, drum machine pounding in her ears.

"Ari, I thought you and I—"

"Give me a break," Ari said.

The second time he said that tonight, Destiny told herself.

Well, okay. I'm not the kind of person who makes a big scene or screams or carries on in front of people. I can't do that.

So . . . I'll give him a break.

"Good night, Ari," she said through gritted teeth.

She spun away and ran along the side of the dance floor, ran without looking back, out the front door, bursting through a couple just arriving. Out into the cool night air, to the edge of the gravel parking lot, where she grabbed onto a wooden fence pole, held onto it, taking breath after breath.

Okay, okay. I'll give him a break, she thought.

Was she angry or hurt, or both?

Have fun, Ari. Have fun without me.

See if I care.

Destiny had no way of knowing that she would never see Ari again.

Part Four

Chapter Twelve
Livvy's New Love

Livvy stood at the end of the bar, tilting a bottle of Rolling Rock to her mouth. The bartender was a fat, old guy; not interesting. Despite the cold beer, Livvy's stomach growled, and the hunger gnawed at her.

She turned and gazed around the dance floor, searching for Monica and Suzie. Squinting into the darting red and blue lights, she spotted them both. Whoa. Who was Suzie dancing with? Ari Stark?

Uh-oh. Looks like Destiny left her boyfriend behind.

Bad mistake, Dee. Look at the stupid grin on Ari's face. He thinks he's gotten lucky tonight.

Monica stood at the edge of the dance floor, her pale arms around a big guy who looked like he could play middle linebacker. She nestled her head against his shoulder and led him toward the lounge.

Way to go, Monica.

Feeling the powerful hunger again, Livvy brushed back her blond hair, straightened her tube top, and gazed down the bar. A dark-haired guy a few stools down seemed to be staring at her.

Livvy flashed him a smile. He had a beer glass in one hand. He raised it as if toasting her.

Livvy didn't hesitate. She strode over to him, a smile on her face. "I'm Livvy," she said. "How ya doin'?"

"Patrick," he replied. He had dimples in his cheeks when he smiled. He was probably a college guy—in his early twenties—cute.

Livvy clicked her bottle against his glass. "What's up, Patrick?"

He shrugged. "Just chillin'. You know."

He had short, wavy brown hair, dark, serious eyes with heavy, brown eyebrows, and a penetrating stare. Livvy felt that he was staring right through her.

Did he like what he saw?

Livvy did. If the good-looking guys have the tastiest blood, I'm in heaven tonight.

Patrick was tall and athletic-looking. He wore black cargo pants and a dark brown leather vest over a soft gray long-sleeved shirt. An interesting look.

He had a silver ring in one ear. And Livvy glimpsed a tattoo of a spider on the back of his hand when he raised his beer glass.

"Like this club?" Livvy asked, squeezing beside him.

Wouldn't you rather go out for a drink, Patrick?

Out to the woods maybe?

"Yeah, it's okay," he said. "I don't like the five-dollar beers. But it's a pretty nice place to hang."

Livvy flashed him her sexiest smile. "I think it just got nicer," she said. Not too subtle, but she felt too hungry to be subtle.

He has a nice long neck, she thought. Easy to get to the vein.

Was she staring at his throat? She quickly raised her eyes to his. "I wouldn't mind dancing," she said. "If someone wanted to ask me."

He was a good dancer, she discovered. He moved easily, gracefully, and never took his eyes off her. When he smiled, those dimples came out, and despite her hunger, Livvy could feel herself melting.

Is this my night or what?

Suzie came into view across the crowded dance floor. Over Ari's shoulder, she flashed Livvy a thumbs-up.

After a while, Patrick took Livvy's hand and led her off the dance floor. She squeezed his hand and leaned against him. Even though they'd been dancing hard, he wasn't sweating. He bought two more Rolling Rocks at the bar and handed one to her.

"I haven't seen you here before," he said.

Livvy grinned. "You're seeing me now." She took a sip of beer. "What do you do, Patrick?"

He snickered. "As little as possible. How about you?"

"I'm in school," she lied. She put a hand on his shoulder. "It's kinda hot in here. And noisy. Want to take a walk or something?"

Say yes, Patrick—or I might attack you right here.

"Yeah, sure," he said, finishing his beer. "But I've gotta tell some guys I came with, okay?"

Livvy nodded. *Tell them you're going out for a quick bite, Patrick.* She felt her heart start to race. Her skin tingled.

I'm finally going to feed.

"Meet you outside," she said. "I'm going to smoke."

She watched him make his way through the dance floor. He had a quick, confident stride. He's hot, she thought. Too hot to die. Maybe I'll bring him along slowly. Then give him a chance to join me, to become an immortal. To live forever with me.

She started toward the exit.

Then what do I do with Ross?

Good question.

I still care for Ross. He was so brave to come with me to the other side. He'd be lost without me . . .

Ross is so sweet. But maybe sweet isn't what I need right now. I need thrills. I need action. I need to live this new life to the fullest.

I need . . . Patrick.

As Livvy passed the lounge, she glimpsed Monica in a dark corner, on a low couch, liplocked with the guy she'd been dancing with. Monica was pressed against him, holding his head as she kissed him, moving her hands through the guy's hair.

He's toast, Livvy thought.

She stepped out into the night. The air felt cool on her hot skin. Clouds covered the moon. A car squealed out of the parking lot, music blaring.

Livvy stepped to the side of the club, leaned against the stucco wall, and pulled a pack of Camel Reds from her bag. She slid a cigarette between her lips. And felt a soft tap on her shoulder.

Patrick?

She spun around—and let out a startled gasp. "*You*? What are *you* doing here? *Get away*!"

Chapter Thirteen

A Surprise Reunion

The cigarette fell from her mouth. Livvy stared at her sister, at her black skirt and white top, her blond hair pulled straight back so neatly, her plastic bracelets on one wrist, everything so neat and perfect.

Except what was that expression on Destiny's face? Eyes so wide and chin quivering. Destiny stared at Livvy as if she'd never seen her before.

And was that fear in her eyes?

"Destiny, go away," Livvy repeated. "I don't want to see you."

"I'm your sister." Destiny's voice trembled. "Why are you saying that?"

Livvy stared at her. "I'm busy right now. I'm waiting for someone. Take a walk, Dee. I mean it."

Destiny swallowed. She didn't move. "You look so different. You cut your hair. You've lost weight, haven't you? And those dark rings around your eyes—"

"Hey, no beauty tips, okay," Livvy snarled. "I don't read *Cosmo Girl* anymore."

"You're so pale, Livvy," Destiny continued. "You look as if you haven't slept in weeks. Listen to me—"

"No, you listen to me, Dee," Livvy said through clenched teeth. "Read my lips: *Go away*." She glanced over Destiny's shoulder. Where was Patrick?

"Was that you this afternoon?" Destiny asked, crossing her arms in front of her. "The bat?"

"Excuse me?" Livvy pulled another cigarette from the pack. Her hand shook as she slid it between her lips. "What bat? I don't know what the hell you're talking about."

"It wasn't you?"

"No way. Were you dreaming or something?"

I don't know why I did that, Livvy thought, remembering the afternoon. I'll never do it again.

"I thought I saw you in the club," Destiny said, motioning to the entrance with her head.

"You didn't see me, did you? I was with Ari. But I think he left. We had a fight. I feel terrible. He's so sweet."

"Tell someone who cares," Livvy said. She yawned.

Destiny startled her by grabbing her arm. "Come home, Liv. Come home with me right now."

Livvy rolled her eyes. "Yeah, sure. Good idea." She tugged her arm free.

"No, really," Destiny insisted. "Dad will find a cure. I know he will. He's working so hard, Liv. He'll find a cure for you, and you can be normal again. You know. Back home."

Livvy let out an angry cry. "You never could stand to see me have fun!" she shouted. "Get a clue, Dee. I don't want to go back to that boring life."

"Yes, you do," Destiny replied, tears in her eyes. "You don't mean what you're saying. You can't like what you're doing. The way you're living. You *can't*." A sob escaped her throat.

Livvy took a deep breath. Her hands were clenched into tight fists at her sides. "Don't you see? I've made my choice. I'm going to live forever. That's my choice. You want to stay home and see your boring friends and that boring geek Ari, and go to school like a nice girl and be a nice, boring person for the rest of your life. And I've made a different choice. That's all. No big deal, right?"

"But, Liv—"

"I'm going to live forever. That's my choice. So get out of my face, Dee. Go away and don't come back."

"I . . . don't believe you." Destiny let the tears roll down her cheeks. "You're my sister. My *twin* sister. And the two of us belong together. We—"

"We belong together? Okay!" Livvy cried. She let her fangs slide down over her lips. "You want to stay together forever? Fine. You stay with *me.*"

She grabbed Destiny around the waist and started to drag her across the parking lot toward the woods.

"Hey—let go!" Destiny screamed, unable to hide her panic. "What are you doing?"

"We'll be together," Livvy growled, saliva running down her fangs. "You and me. Together."

Destiny grabbed Livvy's arms and tried to

pull them off her. But Livvy held onto her tightly and dragged her over the gravel toward the tall trees.

"You and me," Livvy rasped. "Just the way you want it, Dee."

"Let go! Let go!" Destiny pleaded.

Livvy pressed her mouth against the back of Destiny's neck. "You and me—forever," she whispered.

Chapter Fourteen
The Taste of Night

Livvy held on tight as Destiny squirmed and struggled to free herself. Finally, she gave Dee's hair a hard tug—and let her go.

Destiny staggered forward several steps. Then she spun around to face her sister. "Were you . . . were you . . ." She struggled to catch her breath. "What were you doing? Were you just trying to scare me?"

Livvy grinned at her. She made loud sucking noises with her fangs. "Want to stay and find out?"

Trembling, Destiny studied her for a long moment. Then she turned and ran across the parking lot.

Livvy watched her sister run away. Her heart was pounding in her chest. She suddenly felt dizzy.

I'm so confused. My feelings are all mixed up.

I always loved Destiny. Do I really hate her now?

Is it because she's trying to ruin my new life?

I made my choice. Why can't she leave me alone?

Livvy turned and saw Patrick watching her from the club exit. She slid her fangs back into her gums. Then she straightened her hair and forced a sexy smile to her face.

"There you are," he called, taking those long strides toward her. "I thought maybe you split or something."

"No way." She took his arm. "It's nice out, huh?"

He nodded. She liked his serious, dark eyes, the way they seemed to lock on her as if holding her captive.

The clouds floated away from the moon, and pale light washed over them. "I like the moonlight," he said, glancing up at the sky.

"How old are you?" she asked, leaning against him, guiding him to the trees.

"Old enough," he said. "How old did you think I was?"

"I don't know. Inside the club, you looked

sixteen. But now you look older." She let her hand slide down his arm and gripped his hand. "I'm going to be eighteen soon."

"Are you in college?" he asked. Their shoes crunched over the gravel. He didn't wait for her to answer. He turned and kissed her. He held her chin in his hand and kissed her long and deep.

Yes, she thought. And as she kissed him, a strange phrase played through her mind . . .

The taste of night.

The taste of night.

Where did it come from? She didn't know. But she knew she was enjoying it tonight—the taste of night. The taste of the cool, fresh air and the moonlight, the taste of his lips, the taste of an exciting, new adventure. And in a few moments . . . the taste of blood.

It was all part of the taste of night.

I'm totally into him, she thought. I mean I'm really attracted to him. He's so good looking and mysterious and sexy.

We just met, but I already have strong feelings for him, she realized.

Almost as strong as my thirst . . .

He pulled his face away. They were both

breathing hard. He still had his hand on her chin. "Where are you leading me?" he asked.

She grinned. "Astray?"

He laughed. A big laugh that seemed to come from deep inside him.

"I thought we'd take a walk in the woods," Livvy said. "Such a nice night. We can talk. It's so peaceful out here."

"You're an outdoors-type person? You like to camp?"

"Not really," she replied. "But I like to do *other* things in the woods." She pulled him into the trees. The moonlight seemed to follow them. She pulled him farther. She needed darkness.

"Hey, where are we going? I can't see a thing," he said, tugging her to a stop.

"That's the idea," she whispered. She grabbed the sides of his head and pulled his face to hers. They kissed again, moving their tongues together.

I'm so hungry, she thought.

I can't wait another second.

I need to drink. He's driving me crazy.

She pulled her lips from his and nuzzled his ear with her mouth. "Now, Patrick, I'm going to give you a kiss to remember," she whispered.

"But here's the sad part. After I give it to you, I'm going to cloud your mind so you won't remember it."

"Huh? I don't understand." He held her by the waist and stared into her eyes. "What are you saying?"

So hungry . . . so hungry . . . Oh, damn—I'm so hungry . . .

Livvy lowered her fangs and dug them into his throat. Deep, deep into the soft flesh.

And then she pulled away—and opened her mouth in a scream of horror.

Chapter Fifteen

"I'm Not Just a Vampire"

Livvy staggered back, stumbling over an upraised tree root and landing hard against the fat trunk of a maple tree. Patrick didn't move. He stood still as a statue, a shadow against shadows.

"You . . . you're a vampire too," she whispered finally. She struggled to catch her breath. Her body still tingled from the excitement of nearly finding blood.

But Patrick's blood wouldn't nourish her.

He stepped closer, and she could see the smile on his face. "I'm sorry," he said. "I wanted to see how far you'd go."

Her surprise quickly turned to anger. "You were just playing a game? Having a little joke at my expense?"

He took her hand. "No. It wasn't just a joke. I really like you."

"What were you doing in the club?" Livvy asked.

"Same as you. Looking to hook up."

"But I wasn't looking to hook up with a vampire. I'm so hungry," Livvy moaned. "You've wasted my time."

He laughed. "Hey, don't hurt my feelings. I said I really like you."

"But I don't need a vampire. I need—" Livvy started.

He put a finger over her lips. "I'm not just a vampire, Livvy. Things are going to change now that I'm here."

"Excuse me?" She let go of his hand. "What are you talking about?"

"I'm going to take care of everyone. Make it a lot more exciting for all of us."

Moonlight filtered through the trees, and Livvy could see his smile and his eyes, crazy eyes, intense and unblinking. He seemed to be aiming all his power at her.

She turned away.

"Where do you live?" she asked.

"Same building as you," he replied.

She kept her eyes away from his. "How do you know where I live? You've seen me before?"

"Truth? I've had my eye on you."

"You've been watching me? Why?" she asked.

He didn't answer. He pulled her close, lowered his face to hers, and kissed her. Kissed her hard, so hard she could feel his teeth pressing against her lips . . . so hard it hurt.

When the kiss ended, her lips throbbed with pain. Heart pounding, she pressed her forehead against the front of his shirt.

Livvy realized she was trembling. I'm hot for him—and I'm afraid of him—at the same time.

Patrick took her by the shoulders and moved her away. "It's getting late. I'm thirsty too."

"But I want to know more about you," Livvy said. She flashed him a grin. "You can't just take a girl into the woods and leave her there."

Once again, he brought his face to hers. And he whispered in her ear. "Later."

He whirled away from her—and transformed quickly into a slender red fox. Squinting into the patch of silvery moonlight, Livvy watched the fox scamper away through the thick underbrush.

Yes, later, she thought.

Catch you later, Patrick. I think you and I are going to be seeing a lot of each other.

Chapter Sixteen
Destiny Flies

Destiny searched for Ari in the club but couldn't find him. She wanted to apologize. He was only dancing with that red-haired girl, after all. She shouldn't have embarrassed him by acting so jealous.

This night is a disaster, she thought. No way is it a celebration.

She ended up walking home by herself. The night air felt cool against her hot skin. Crickets chirped. Fireflies danced in front of her, seeming to light her path. The moon appeared and disappeared behind high, gray clouds.

She walked through tall grass along the side of the road. Her shoes became wet from the dew. Cars rolled past without slowing.

She found herself thinking about Ross. She wondered how he was. She couldn't picture Ross as a vampire. He was so good looking and athletic and . . . healthy.

Destiny had a crush on Ross for years, and Livvy knew it. But Livvy went after Ross anyway. And she took him away.

Forever.

The tiny lights of fireflies sparkled in Destiny's eyes, making the world appear unreal. The lights darted and danced around her.

Before she knew it, she arrived at Drake Park, three blocks from her house. As she crossed the street and stepped into the park, she could hear the trickle of water from the narrow creek and the rustle of the trees shaking in the warm breeze.

She followed the dirt path that curved toward her house. A creature scampered over her feet, startling her. A field mouse? A chipmunk?

She thought about Mikey. What did he do tonight? The poor kid. I hope he didn't spend the whole night shut up in his dark cave of a room.

Destiny told herself she should spend more time with Mikey. But it wasn't easy. Tomorrow morning she was starting her summer job at the Four Corners Diner. A waitress behind the lunch counter. Not a very challenging job. But at least the restaurant was across from the Community College campus. Maybe she'd meet some new people . . .

The moon disappeared behind a blanket of clouds. The fireflies had vanished. Destiny felt a chill as the darkness washed over her.

She kicked a stone in the path. The creek trickled behind her now. She knew she was almost home.

And then a figure stepped out from a thick clump of pine trees. A girl. She seemed to float silently onto the path.

"Hello—?" Destiny called in a whisper.

The girl didn't answer. She moved toward Destiny quickly. Startled, Destiny began to move out of the way, but she wasn't quick enough.

"Hey—" Destiny let out a cry—and then recognized her sister. "Livvy? What are you doing here?"

Livvy stared at her for a long moment, her expression intense, eyes locked on Destiny's.

Why did Livvy follow me? To apologize?

Did she change her mind about coming home?

And then to Destiny's shock, Livvy raised

both arms and wrapped her in a tight hug.

The two sisters stood there on the dark path, hugging each other, faces pressed together, tears rolling down their cheeks, tears running together as they sobbed and held each other.

Finally, they backed away from each other. They both wiped away tears with their hands.

"Livvy, I'm so happy," Destiny said in a trembling whisper. "Why did you follow me? Did you change your mind?"

"Yes," Livvy replied. "Yes, I changed my mind. I . . . I'm so lonely, Dee. I need to come home. I need to be with my family again."

"Dad and Mikey . . . they'll be so glad to see you," Destiny said.

And then the two sisters were hugging again, hugging and crying.

Destiny finally released her sister. "Let's go home," she whispered. "It's late, but Dad will still be awake. He doesn't sleep much—ever since . . ." Her voice trailed off.

Livvy clung to her sister. She didn't reply.

"I'm so glad," Destiny said. "I mean, I'm so happy, Liv. I mean . . . I can't really say what I mean."

Livvy's arms remained clamped tightly

around Destiny. Her head was turned so that Destiny couldn't see her face.

"Please let go," Destiny whispered. "I . . . can't breathe."

Livvy didn't move.

"Let go," Destiny repeated. "Come on. Let's go home, okay?"

Livvy didn't reply. Her arms remained clamped around Destiny's waist.

"Livvy—let go!" Destiny cried. "What's wrong? What are you doing? Let go of me. Let go!"

Destiny tried to pull free. And as she squirmed and twisted, she saw Livvy's body begin to transform.

"Livvy—stop! What are you doing? Let go of me—please!"

And now, scratchy brown feathers scraped Destiny's face. She heard a warble from deep inside Livvy's body. And she realized that powerful claws, hard as bone, had replaced her sister's arms.

Livvy had transformed into an enormous, throbbing bird, at least seven feet tall. A giant hawk! And Destiny was pressed tightly against the prickly feathers around its belly, held by the huge, powerful claws clamped around her waist.

"Livvy—NO!"

The bird raised its head, flapped its massive wings, sending a burst of air over Destiny. It dragged Destiny along the grass for a while before it lifted high enough into the air. And then, flapping its wings so slowly, so easily, it floated up into the dark sky, carrying Destiny in its claws like a prize . . . like dinner.

Destiny let out scream after scream as she floated over the treetops of the park, then the houses of her neighborhood.

Is she planning to drop me?

The houses looked like dollhouses now. The car headlights down below looked as tiny as the firefly light that had followed her as she walked.

"Livvy—please!"

She could feel the pattering heartbeat of the huge bird. The oily feathers grazed her cheeks.

And then they were soaring down, swooping with the wind. The onrushing wind blowing so hard in her face, Destiny struggled to breathe.

A hard bounce. The claws let go. Destiny landed on her back. Felt the air knocked out of her. Lay there on hard ground, gasping.

Where are we?

Livvy loomed over her, human once again.

Livvy's hair fell over her face, but Destiny could see her eyes. Wild eyes, bulging with anger . . . with hate?

"Where are we? Where have you taken me?" Destiny cried. She raised herself on two arms and gazed around, blinking in the darkness.

Nothing to see. No trees here. No houses. Flat ground, a black strip against the blacker sky, stretching on forever.

"Where are we?"

"It doesn't matter, Dee." Livvy spoke in a cold whisper. "It really doesn't matter."

"Why? What do you mean?"

Livvy narrowed her eyes at Destiny, and her face hardened to stone. "Because you're never leaving."

"I don't understand, Livvy. What—?"

Livvy's fangs slid quickly from her gums, making a loud *pok* sound. She opened her mouth wide, tongue playing over her teeth, drool running over her chin. Then she sank her fangs deep into Destiny's throat.

Chapter Seventeen

Trouble at Ari's House

Destiny felt sweat run down her forehead. Her nightshirt clung wetly to her back.

She blinked, reached a hand to her throat, and smoothed two fingers across it.

No wound.

She blinked some more, realizing she was gazing into bright sunlight. From the bedroom window.

She jerked herself upright, breathing hard. A dream? Yes.

It had been a dream—all of it. I didn't walk home last night, she remembered. Fletch Green gave me a ride.

But the feeling of walking home through the park . . . the sparkling fireflies . . . her sister stepping out of the darkness . . . transforming into the gigantic hawk . . . All so real.

So real she thought she could still feel those bonelike claws wrapped tightly around her waist. She could still feel the suffocating rush of wind as the giant bird carried her into the sky.

Could still feel Livvy's fangs . . .

Does my twin sister really have fangs?

A soft cry escaped Destiny's throat. Yes, it was a dream. But the rest of my life is real . . .

. . . and it's a nightmare.

"Dee! Dee!" She heard Mikey calling from downstairs. She jumped out of bed, gazing at the clock radio on her bedtable.

Oh, no. Late. I have to give Mikey breakfast and get him off to day camp. She brushed her teeth, pushed back her hair with her hands, and went running down to the kitchen in her night-shirt.

"Where's Dad?" she asked Mikey.

He was dressed in denim shorts that came down past his knees and a blue-and-red Camp Redhawk T-shirt about five sizes too big for him. He gripped a stuffed lion in one hand. He'd had it since he was a baby. These days it looked more like a washcloth than a lion.

He shrugged. "Work. He woke me up. Then he left. I'm hungry. And so is Lester." He waved Lester the Lion in Destiny's face.

She popped two frozen waffles into the

428

toaster. "We're a little late. You'll have to eat your waffles fast."

"Take the crust off," he said, sitting down at the table, plopping Lester in front of him.

Destiny turned to him. "Crust on waffles?"

"Yeah. Take off the crust."

He had become the fussiest eater. He suddenly had rules for everything. And he found something wrong with everything put in front of him. A few nights ago, he had even refused to eat the french fries at Burger King because they were "too curled up."

She poured him a glass of orange juice and handed it to him. "No pulp," she said before he could ask.

He tasted it gingerly, a tiny sip. "Too cold."

"What are you doing at day camp today?" she asked, brushing back his thick mop of hair with one hand.

"I'm not going to day camp," Mikey replied. He pounded Lester on the tabletop for emphasis.

"You have to go," Destiny said, lifting the waffles from the toaster. "Ow. Hot. There's no one here to take care of you."

"You can take care of me," he said.

"No, I can't, Mikey. You know that I'm

starting my summer job today, remember?"

"Well, I can't go to camp. Hey—you forgot to cut off the crusts. And I don't want butter. I want syrup."

Destiny took the plate back and carefully pulled the edges off the waffles. "And why can't you go to camp?"

"Because they're showing a movie at the theater." He took another swallow of orange juice.

"You like movies," Destiny said, handing the plate back to him. "So what's the problem?"

"It . . . it's cold and creepy in the theater," he replied. "There might be vampires in there."

Destiny stopped in front of the diner and checked her hair and lipstick in her reflection in the front window. The name FOUR CORNERS DINER was painted in fancy gold script across the wide window.

Destiny chuckled. It seemed an odd name for the little restaurant since it was located in the middle of the block. Surrounding it on both sides were small, two-story brick and shingle buildings that contained clothing stores, a bank, a CD store—shops that catered to

Community College students.

She turned and glanced at the campus. Four square, granite buildings around a narrow rectangle of patchy grass and trees. Not the most beautiful campus in the world.

Destiny let out a sigh. I made the right decision, she told herself. I couldn't go away to college and leave Dad and Mikey now. I'll go to the Community College for a year or two. When things are more in control at home, I can transfer to a better school.

When things are more in control . . .

She turned and hurried into the diner. The smell of fried grease greeted her. Bright lights made the long lunch counter glow. A ceiling fan squeaked as it slowly turned.

Destiny counted three people seated at one end of the counter. Two guys about her age and an older woman. The four booths in back were empty. Mr. Georgio, the owner, stood behind the counter, setting down plates of hamburgers and french fries for the three customers.

"Mr. Georgio, sorry I'm a little late," Destiny said, glancing up at the round Coca-Cola clock above the coat rack in the corner. "I had trouble getting my brother off to day camp."

"Call me Mr. G., remember?" he said, setting plastic ketchup and mustard dispensers in front of the customers. He walked over to her, wiping sweat off his bald head with a paper napkin.

He was a thin, little man of forty or forty-five. The white apron he wore over black slacks and a white sport shirt hung nearly to the floor. He had big, brown eyes, a thick, brown mustache under his bulby nose, and a split between his front teeth that showed when he smiled.

"Late? No problem," he said. "We're not exactly packing them in today." He motioned with his head to the three customers.

"Summer is slow," he said, wiping a grease spot on the yellow counter. "Most of the students aren't here. There are only a few classes. My business is students. Breakfast and lunch. You'll have a nice, quiet time, Ms. Weller. You can read a book or something."

"Please, call me Dee. Remember?" Destiny said.

He smiled. "Okay, you're Dee and I'm G."

"Could we have more Cokes?" a guy at the end of the counter called, holding up his glass.

"Take care of them," Mr. G. told her, pulling

off his apron. "And clean things up a bit, okay? I've got to go out." He pointed to the kitchen window behind the counter. "You remember Nate? The fry cook? He's back there somewhere. Probably sneaking a smoke. He's a lazy goof-off. But if you have any questions, he'll help you out."

Destiny had worked some weekends at the diner, so she already knew her way around. She waved to Nate through the window, carried three glasses to the soda dispenser, and filled them with Coke.

The bell over the door clanged as two more customers came in. Destiny didn't recognize them at first because of the white sunlight pouring in through the front window. But as they settled into the first booth behind the counter, she saw that she knew them. Rachel Seeger and Bonnie Franz, two girls from her class.

Destiny picked up two menus and carried them over to the booth. Her two friends were talking heatedly, giggling and gesturing with their hands. But they stopped their conversation when they recognized Destiny.

Rachel's cheeks blushed bright pink. She had light blond hair and really fair skin and was an easy blusher, Destiny remembered. "Hey, Dee. What's up?" she asked.

"You waitressing here?" Bonnie asked.

Destiny laughed. "No. Just holding menus. It's like a hobby of mine."

The girls laughed.

"I have a summer job too," Bonnie said. "At the campus. I'm filing stuff in the administration office. Yawn yawn."

"Are you making any money?" Destiny asked.

Bonnie shook her head. "Eight dollars an hour. And my dad said he had to pull strings to get me the job. I mean, like hel-lo. I could make that at McDonald's, right?"

Destiny handed them the menus. "Know what you want?"

"Not really," Bonnie said.

"Are you working this summer?" Destiny asked Rachel.

She made a disgusted face. "I couldn't find anything. So I'm just hanging out this summer. You know. Partying. Getting ready for college. You're going away, right, Dee?"

"Uh . . . no." Destiny hesitated. She didn't want sympathy from her friends. "I decided to stay close to home and go here." She motioned out the window to the campus. "You know. It's kinda tough times at home . . ."

"Have you heard from your sister?" Rachel asked, blushing again. "I mean, she and Ross have been gone so long."

Destiny lowered her eyes to the yellow tabletop. "No. Haven't heard anything yet."

Rachel gripped the big, red menu with both hands. "Do the police still think they ran away together?"

Destiny saw Bonnie motioning for Rachel to shut up.

"The police . . . they don't know *what* to think," Destiny said honestly.

"Sorry," Bonnie muttered.

The two girls stared down at their menus. An awkward silence. The conversation had ended.

Destiny raised her pad to take their orders. Everyone treats me so differently now, she thought. I used to hang with Bonnie and Rachel and goof with them all the time. Once, a sales clerk at the Gap made us leave because we were laughing too loud in the dressing room.

But now, people feel sorry for me. They feel

awkward. They don't know what to say.

"Could we have a check?" a woman called from the counter.

"I'll be right back," Destiny told the two girls. She hurried along the counter to take care of the woman's check.

As soon as she left, her two friends started chattering away again.

After work, Destiny decided to drive over to Ari's house. She'd been thinking about him all afternoon.

I'm going to apologize for last night, she decided. What happened at the club . . . it really was my fault.

Ari wanted to celebrate, to have some fun. And I was a total drag. I should have tried harder to forget my problems, to just go with the flow . . .

She pictured him dancing with that red-haired girl. Thinking about it gave her a heavy feeling in her stomach.

Ari is going off to school soon. And I'm going to miss him terribly. I have to be nicer to him.

Yes, I'm definitely going to apologize.

Thinking about last night, there was no way

to shut out the memory of her meeting with Livvy. Turning onto Ari's block, sunlight burst over the windshield. And through the blinding white light, Destiny saw two blond girls standing on the front stoop of the corner house.

"Oh—!" she let out a cry.

The car moved under the shadow of trees. The two girls disappeared into the house.

Destiny frowned. Every time I see a girl with blond hair, I think it's my sister.

Livvy was so mean to me last night. Has she completely forgotten that we're sisters? It's only been a few weeks, and she has changed so much. She looked so pale and thin and . . . and worn out.

Livvy acted so cold and angry. I hardly recognized her.

Destiny saw the tall hedge in front of Ari's yard, the white-shingled house rising up behind it. She turned and pulled into the drive—and stopped.

"Hey—"

Two police squad cars blocked her way, red lights spinning on their roofs.

"Oh, no." Destiny's heart started to pound. She felt her throat tighten.

Ari's dad had a heart attack last summer. Has he had another one?

Hands trembling, she pulled the car to the curb in front of the neighbors' house. Then she went running up the driveway.

The front door was open. She burst inside. She heard voices in the front room. Someone crying.

"What's wrong?" she shouted breathlessly. "What's happened?"

Chapter Eighteen

Who Is the Next Victim?

Destiny ran into the living room. She saw Ari's mother hunched in the tall, green armchair by the fireplace. Her head was buried in a white handkerchief, and she was sobbing loudly, her shoulders heaving up and down.

Mr. Stark stood beside the chair, one hand on his wife's shoulder. He was very pale and, even from a distance, Destiny could see the tear tracks on his cheeks.

Two grim-faced, young police officers stood with their hands in their pockets, shaking their heads, speaking softly to Ari's parents. They spun around when Destiny entered the room.

"What is it? Where's Ari?" Destiny cried.

But even before anyone answered, she knew. She knew why they were crying. They had bad news about Ari. Maybe the *worst* news . . .

"No—!" Destiny screamed, pressing her hands against her face. "No. Please—"

No one had spoken. But she knew.

Mr. Stark came across the room to greet her, walking stiffly, as if it took all his effort. He was a tall, heavyset man, and now he was walking as if he weighed a thousand pounds.

He put his hands on Destiny's shoulders. "It's Ari," he whispered. "It's horrible, Dee. Ari . . . Ari . . ." He turned away from her.

"What . . . what happened to him?" Destiny stammered.

Mrs. Stark uttered a loud sob across the room.

One of the police officers studied Destiny.

"I'm Lieutenant Macy," he said, keeping his voice low. "Are you Destiny Weller?"

Destiny nodded. Her throat felt so tight, it was hard to breathe. "Yes. How did you know?"

"We've been trying to reach you all day," he said. "The phone at your house . . . it rang and rang."

"I started a new job today," Destiny said. "Is Ari—?"

Macy had bright blue eyes and he kept them trained on Destiny. "I'm sorry. He's . . . dead."

A cry escaped Destiny's throat. Her knees folded. She started to collapse to the floor, but

Macy grabbed her gently by the arm and held her up.

She struggled to catch her breath. It felt as if her chest might burst open.

"Come sit down," Macy said softly. He led her to the green leather couch in front of the window.

Tears flowed down her cheeks. She fumbled in her bag for some tissues. "What happened?" she asked Macy. She gritted her teeth. She didn't really want to hear.

"We were hoping you could help us out with that," Macy said, leaning forward, bringing his face close to hers. "You were with Ari last night, right? You were at the dance club?"

Destiny nodded, dabbing at her tears. She glanced up to see Mr. Stark staring down at her, hunched behind Macy. She glimpsed the pain in his eyes and turned away.

"Well, a young couple found Ari at the edge of the parking lot there," Macy said. "It was about two A.M. Were you still with him then?"

Destiny stared at the officer. His voice sounded muffled, as if he were speaking underwater. Ari dead in the parking lot? Two in the morning? She struggled to make sense of it.

"No. I . . . left early," Destiny said finally.

Macy stared at her, waiting for more of an explanation.

"We had a fight," Destiny said. "Well, no. Not really a fight. An argument, I guess. And I . . . I left early."

"How early?" Macy asked.

"I left around midnight, I think. I got a ride home with a friend. I remember it was a little after twelve-thirty when I got home."

"And was Ari still at the club when you left?"

Destiny nodded. "I . . . think so. Yes. Yes, he was."

"You saw him there before you left?" Macy demanded.

Destiny nodded again, wiping at her tears. "He was dancing. I saw him dancing . . . with another girl."

Across the room, Mrs. Stark uttered a loud sob. Mr. Stark hurried over to comfort her.

Destiny raised her eyes to Macy. "How . . . did Ari die?" she whispered.

Macy's blue eyes burned into hers. "Strangest thing. He had two puncture wounds in his neck. His blood was completely drained."

* * *

"Do you really think Livvy did it?" Ana-Li asked.

Destiny shook her head. "I don't know what to think."

They were sitting on the couch in Destiny's room above the garage, the room she had shared with her twin. The couch divided the long, low room in two. Destiny hadn't touched anything on Livvy's side. She'd left it exactly as Livvy had it.

When Livvy comes back, it will be ready for her.

That's what Destiny had thought. Until now.

"Livvy and I talked outside the club," Destiny told Ana-Li, folding her arms tightly in front of her. "We didn't really talk. We just screamed. I mean, Livvy did the screaming. She was awful to me. She . . . she's changed so much."

Ana-Li took a long sip from her Diet Coke can, her dark eyes on Destiny. "What did you fight about?"

"Nothing, really. I begged her to come home. She told me to leave her alone, to stay out of her life. That's all. But it was the way she said it. So cruel. As if she *hates* me."

Ana-Li squeezed Destiny's hand. Her hand was cold from the soda can. "Livvy wasn't angry enough to murder Ari—was she? I mean, she's known Ari as long as you have. No way she'd murder him out of spite or something."

Destiny sighed. "I don't know. I don't know what to think anymore. I thought I knew her. I mean, she's my *twin* sister. But now . . . I don't know her at all."

"You can't believe she'd murder your boyfriend," Ana-Li said. "It had to be someone else, Dee. It's just too sick."

"Yeah. Sick," Destiny repeated. "That's the word. This whole thing is sick."

"What do the cops say?" Ana-Li asked.

"They've been back to question me three times. They interviewed the red-haired girl. She said she danced with Ari a couple of times, and then she didn't see him again. She thinks he went off with another girl, but she doesn't really know."

"That's a really busy parking lot," Ana-Li said. "Didn't anyone see anything strange going on?"

"So far, no one has called the police," Destiny replied.

"The police know there are vampires in Dark Springs," Ana-Li said, tapping a long, red nail fingernail on the Diet Coke can. "They help your father and his vampire hunters, right? So they must know—"

"They're trying to keep it quiet," Destiny interrupted. "The cops didn't reveal what really happened to Ari to the news people. They don't want to start a panic."

She let out a cry. "I just can't believe my own sister could do something so horrible. But she was there. And she told me how thirsty she was."

Ana-Li shuddered. She set down the soda can. "Dee, there's something I have to tell you."

Destiny blinked at her. "What?"

"I'm leaving for school early," Ana-Li said. "I can't stand it here anymore. I'm leaving on Saturday. It's just too frightening here. I have to get away."

Ana-Li didn't give Destiny time to reply. She hugged her, then turned and, with a sad wave, made her way down the stairs.

Destiny remained on the couch, feeling numb. Unable to stop the upsetting whirl of thoughts that troubled her mind.

Ari is dead.
Ana-Li is leaving.
My friends are all gone.
Will I be next?
Will I be the next victim?

Part Five

Two Weeks Later

Chapter Nineteen

"Maybe He's Just What I Need"

"Two over easy, side of toast," Destiny said, poking her head through the window to the kitchen. Then she let out a startled gasp. "You're not Nate!"

The guy at the stove waved his metal spatula at her. "Hey, you're real sharp."

"Where's Nate?" Destiny asked, glancing around the tiny diner kitchen.

"Fired. Didn't Mr. G. tell you?"

"Guess he forgot. Who are you?" she blurted out.

He grinned at her and adjusted his apron. "You can call me Not Nate. Or maybe the Anti-Nate."

"No. Really," Destiny insisted.

"Harrison," he said, his dark eyes flashing. "Harrison Palmer." He saluted her with the spatula. "And you are . . . wait . . . don't tell me." He studied her, rubbing his chin. "Naomi

Watts? I loved you in *The Ring*."

Destiny rolled her eyes. "Ha ha."

"You look a lot like her," Harrison said.

"Yeah. We're both blond and we both have two eyes, a nose, and a mouth," Destiny said. "You'd better start that egg order." She narrowed her eyes at him. "Have you ever done this before?"

He grinned. "Yeah, sure. No problem. Uh . . . just one thing." He held up an egg. "How do you get the yellow part out of this shell thing?"

Destiny laughed. He's funny, she thought. I haven't really laughed in a long time.

She watched him break the eggs on the grill and move them around with the spatula. He's cute too. Tall and broad-shouldered. A great smile. Those big, dark eyes that crinkle up at the sides. Short, brown hair spiked up in the front.

I can't believe Mr. G. forgot to tell me he was starting today.

After the lunch crowd left, she and Harrison had time to chat. She mopped the counter clean while he came out front to help collect plates.

"Good work," she said. "You've done this before."

He shook his head. "No. I bought that book last night. You know, *Fry Cooking for Dummies.*"

"No. Really—" she said.

"You have to know where to put that sprig of parsley," he said, dropping a stack of dishes into the dirty dish basket. "Parsley placement. I flunked it twice at cook school."

Destiny laughed. "Aren't you ever serious?"

He didn't answer.

Destiny moved to the back booth and started collecting dirty plates.

"You go to school here?" he asked, motioning out the front window to the campus.

"I'm starting in the fall," Destiny told him. "You?"

He nodded. "Yeah. I finished my first year. Now I'm taking some summer courses. Language stuff. I'm studying Russian."

Destiny turned to look at him. "How come?"

"Beats me." He snickered. "It impresses girls. Are you impressed?"

"Totally," Destiny said. Her face suddenly felt hot.

He's really cute.

"Do you live near here?" she asked.

He nodded. "Yeah, I have an apartment near

the campus with a couple of guys. That's why I'm working here, trying to pay the rent. Mr. G. is my stepfather's brother. So he helped me out. Gave me this job."

"Oh. Nepotism," Destiny teased.

"Ooh—big word. You going to be an English major?"

"Probably. Maybe. I don't know."

He laughed. "Luckily, you don't have to decide right away."

"I'm only staying here a year," Destiny told him. "Then I'm transferring out."

"Why didn't you go away to school? Because of the tuition?"

She shrugged. "It's a long story."

You see, my sister became a vampire.

That's a real conversation ender—isn't it?

Harrison picked up the basket of dirty dishes and began lugging it to the kitchen. "Hey, you busy Friday night? My friends and me . . . we're just hanging out at my apartment. Kind of a party. It's my roommate Alby's birthday."

Is he asking me out?

Harrison disappeared into the kitchen. She could hear the dirty plates clattering into the sink.

He's waiting for an answer. Say something, Dee.

I have to get on with my life. Maybe he's just what I need. Someone new. Someone funny and new who doesn't know a thing about me.

She poked her head into the kitchen. "Yeah, sure. Sounds great."

Friday night. As Destiny climbed the narrow staircase to Harrison's apartment, she could hear the party three floors up. Rap music pounded through the stairwell, and she heard laughter and loud voices over the music.

The door to the apartment stood open, and Destiny could see a crowd of young people inside. Two girls sat in the hall with their backs against the wall, smoking and talking. In the corner next to a metal trash can, a tall, blond-haired boy had a girl pressed against the wall, and they were kissing passionately, eyes closed.

Destiny stepped around them and lurched into the doorway. Harrison stood in the middle of the room, talking with a group of guys. He swung around as Destiny entered, and his eyes grew wide, as if he were surprised to see her. He had a Radiohead T-shirt pulled down over faded and torn jeans, a can of Coors in one hand.

"Hey—" he called, pushing his way through the crowd to get to her. "Hi. You made it."

Destiny nodded. "Yeah. Hi. Nice apartment."

Harrison laughed. "You're kidding, right?"

Destiny gazed around the long, L-shaped room. The walls were painted a hideous shade of chartreuse. But a nice, brown leather couch and two La-Z-Boy armchairs were arranged around a big TV screen. A bunch of shouting, cheering guys had jammed onto the couch and chairs and were into an intense PlayStation hockey game.

Two Jimi Hendrix posters were tacked to the wall across from the wide, double windows. Destiny counted five large stereo speakers scattered around the room, all of them booming the new Outkast CD. The speaker tops were cluttered with beer and soda cans and ash trays. A long, aluminum table stood in the alcove of the room. It held two large tubs filled with ice and drinks and open bags of chips.

I've never been in a campus apartment before, Destiny thought. This is totally cool.

Harrison handed her a can of beer. "Hey,

want to meet my roomies?"

"Well, yes. You said it's a birthday celebration, right?"

"Yeah. Alby's birthday. You'll like him. He's kinda serious. Like you."

Harrison's words gave Destiny a start. Is that how he sees me? Kinda serious? Does he think I'm *too* serious?

"That's Mark over there," Harrison said. He pointed to a very tall, black guy with a shaved head. Dressed in gray sweat pants and a sleeveless, blue T-shirt that showed off his big biceps. He had his arm around a girl at least a foot shorter than he was, and they were laughing hard about something.

Harrison called Mark over and introduced him to Destiny. Mark studied Destiny for a long moment. "Where'd you meet her?" he asked Harrison.

"At the diner."

Mark squeezed Harrison's shoulder and grinned at Destiny. "When you get tired of this loser, come see me—okay?"

Destiny laughed. "For sure."

"Hey, who wants to be in the game?" A short, stocky guy wearing a vintage Bob's Big

Boy bowling shirt held up a board game. "We're gonna play Strip Trivial Pursuit. Who wants to play?"

He got a lot of hoots and laughs in reply, but no takers.

Destiny saw some guys watching her from the window. She was wearing a blue-and-white striped top that stopped a couple of inches short of the waist of her jeans. Guess I look okay tonight, she thought.

Harrison placed his hand on her back and guided her through the room, introducing her to people. The touch of his hand gave her a shiver.

"Hey, Alby? Where's Alby?" Harrison called.

A tall, lanky guy in black Buddy Holly glasses stepped out of the kitchen, carrying more bags of chips. He had spiky black hair, a silver ring in one ear, and a short, fuzzy beard.

The bags of chips were grabbed away before Alby could set them down on the table. He came up to Destiny and Harrison. "Maybe we should order some pizzas."

"You're the birthday boy," Harrison said. "Order anything you want."

"Hey, thanks."

"As long as *you* pay."

"Hey—nice guy." Alby turned to Destiny and his eyes went wide behind the big, black-framed glasses.

"This is Destiny," Harrison said. "Destiny, Alby."

"Nice to meet you," Destiny said.

Alby stared at her. "We met last night, remember?"

Destiny squinted at him. "I don't think so."

"Yeah. Sure, we did," Alby insisted. "At Club Sixty-One. Remember?"

"Club Sixty-One?" Destiny's mind spun. "No way. I stayed home with my little brother last night."

Alby turned to Harrison. "She has short-term memory loss," he said. "We studied it in Psych last term."

"I was home—" Destiny started.

"We danced. You and me," Alby said. "We had some Jell-O shooters. Remember? You used that fake I.D.? We laughed about that couple that got totally trashed and had to be kicked out? You wore those low-riding jeans."

"Oh, wow." Destiny began to realize what was going on.

And then Alby raised his head, and she saw the spot on his throat. The two pinprick red wounds on his neck.

"Oh, no. Oh, no."

She stared at the cut on Alby's throat—and ran from the room.

Chapter Twenty

"Now You Think I'm a Psycho Nut"

"I'm sorry. I can't really explain it," Destiny said, shaking her head.

Harrison had followed her out into the hall. A couple was still making out by the garbage cans. Through the open doorway, Destiny glimpsed Alby watching her from the middle of the living room, a puzzled expression on his face.

"You . . . don't know why you freaked?" Harrison asked. He squeezed her hand. "Your hand is ice cold. Are you okay? Do you need a doctor or something?"

"No. I'm fine now," Destiny said, heart still pounding like crazy. "I'd better go. I'm really sorry I ran out like that."

He studied her. "You sure you're okay?"

"Yeah. Totally. I just . . . uh . . . I can't explain it."

Actually, I *can* explain it. But you wouldn't

believe me, Harrison. If I told you that Alby ran into my vampire twin sister at the club last night, and she drank his blood, that wouldn't exactly go over, would it?

"You're shaking," Harrison said. "Can I drive you home?"

"No. I . . . brought my car," she replied. "I'll be fine." She forced a smile. "Now you think I'm some kind of psycho nut, don't you?"

He smiled back at her. "Yes, I do. Definitely."

"Great," she muttered, rolling her eyes.

"But I kinda like psycho nuts," Harrison said.

That made her feel a tiny bit better. She leaned forward and gave him a quick peck on the cheek. "See you at work tomorrow." Then she ran down the stairs and out to her car without looking back.

It was a hot, damp night. The steamy air made her cool skin tingle. She fumbled in her bag for her car key. "Where is it? Where is it?"

A wave of panic swept over her.

What did Livvy think she was doing? Except for her family and Ana-Li, everyone thought she had run off to another town with

Ross. But now, here she was parading around in the clubs that everyone went to.

Why was she showing herself like that? What were people supposed to think?

Livvy must not care what people think, Destiny decided. She must be so hungry, so desperate for blood she doesn't care if she comes out in the open.

Ari flashed into Destiny's mind. He had been dead for two weeks now, and Destiny thought about him every minute. Such a good, sweet person. He didn't deserve to die that way. Destiny missed him so much.

Livvy is desperate . . . so desperate, she murdered Ari. She didn't give a damn that I cared about him.

A tap on Destiny's shoulder made her cry out in surprise.

She turned and saw a flash of blond hair.

"Livvy?" she gasped. "Ohmigod! Livvy?"

The girl took a step back, her hand still in the air. "Sorry. Didn't mean to startle you."

Not Livvy. An attractive platinum-blond girl with green eyes, dark eyebrows, and dark purple lipstick on her lips. "Is the party in there?" she asked, pointing to Harrison's building.

Still shaken, Destiny nodded. "Yeah. Third floor. You can't miss it."

"Hey, thanks." The girl turned and strode to the building, blond hair waving behind her.

I can't keep doing that, Destiny told herself. I've got to stop seeing Livvy wherever I go.

She drove home, gripping the wheel with both hands, leaning forward in the seat, forcing herself not to think about anything but the driving.

Her cell rang. Ana-Li, she saw. She didn't pick up. I'll call her later when I've calmed down.

Entering her neighborhood, she braked at a stop sign. She could see Ari's house across the street, windows dark except for his parents' bedroom in the back. A sad house now.

A few minutes later, she pulled the Civic up the drive and stopped a few feet from the garage door. Dad was still not home, she saw. He's worked late every night this week. Mikey and I never see him.

She entered through the front door and saw Mikey jumping up and down on the living room couch. "Hey—what's up?" she called, pushing the door shut behind her. "Where is Mrs. Gilly?

Isn't she watching you tonight?"

"She's upstairs. In the bathroom," Mikey said.

Destiny could barely understand him. He had plastic fangs hanging from his mouth, and he wore a black cape over his slender shoulders.

Destiny rushed over to him and hugged him. He pulled free with a growl, snapping at her with the plastic fangs.

"Don't you know any other games?" she asked. "Do you have to play vampire all the time?"

"I'm not playing!" he insisted.

"Mikey, listen to me—"

"I'm not playing. I'm a *real* vampire," he shouted. And then he added, "Just like Livvy."

"But, Mikey—"

"Look," he said. "I'll prove it." He held out his hand.

Destiny gasped as she saw the deep red bite marks up and down his skinny arm.

Chapter Twenty-one
Dad Might Kill Livvy

"Dad, Mikey is seriously sick," Destiny said, shaking her head. "And I guess I don't have to tell you it's all Livvy's fault."

Dr. Weller had his elbows on his desk, supporting his chin in his hands. The fluorescent ceiling light reflected in his glasses. "His therapist says he's making progress."

Destiny sighed. She crossed her arms in front of her. "I'm not so sure. You saw his arm. Those bite marks . . ."

"Pretty awful," he agreed. He sat up straight, pulled off the glasses, and rubbed the bridge of his nose. "Mikey has suffered a terrible loss, Dee. We all have. But you and I are a little better equipped to deal with it. He's too young to know how to cope."

A dog howled in the holding pen in the back room, and that set off all the other dogs yipping and barking.

"We have to stop him from pretending to be a vampire all the time," Destiny said. She shuddered. "It's not helping him."

"And in a way, it might be," her dad said softly. "By playing the role, maybe it helps him work out his fears. Maybe it helps him deal with the frightening thoughts he's having."

Destiny stared at the floor. She didn't know what to say. And she hated seeing her father so sad and tired-looking. He's aged twenty years this summer, she thought.

When she finally looked up, he was crumpling the papers on his desk.

"Dad—what are you doing?"

He angrily ripped the papers in half.

"Dad—?"

"I want to bring Livvy home. I want to restore her to a normal life. Ross, too. But my work is going nowhere, Dee. I . . . I can't find the formula. I've missed time and time again. I'm a failure. We have to face the fact."

Destiny wanted to say something to comfort him. But what could she say?

"So many pressures," he muttered. "So many pressures . . ."

And that's when he told her about the

abandoned apartment building near campus. Vampires had been tracked there. Vampires were living there.

"My hunters and I . . . we have to clean the building out," he told her. "The pressure is on to take care of the vampire problem in Dark Springs. I'm the leader of the Hunters. I have no choice. My hunters and I have to go in there and kill as many vampires as we can. In two weeks. Sunday at dawn. After the night of the full moon. That's when we'll strike."

All Destiny could think about was Livvy and Ross.

Were they living in that unfinished apartment building too?

Could her father kill his own daughter?

He couldn't—could he?

"I'm sorry to lay this on you," Destiny told Ana-Li. "But I don't have anyone else I can tell."

Ana-Li sighed. "I just came to say good-bye, Dee. I'm leaving tomorrow morning. I . . . I'm so sorry I won't be here to help you."

She wrapped Destiny in a hug.

"I'll e-mail you as soon as I get moved into the dorm. I promise," Ana-Li said; raising one hand as if swearing an oath. "If I can't get my laptop hooked up, I'll call you."

"Thanks," Destiny said, holding onto her friend.

"What about the new boyfriend?" Ana-Li asked. "Can't you confide in him?"

"Harrison? He's been very sweet. And we've been seeing each other just about every night. But . . . I can't tell him about Livvy yet. I just can't. I don't know him well enough."

Ana-Li grinned at her. "But you'd like to know him really well—right?"

"Well . . . yeah. But I can't think about that now." Destiny started to pace back and forth along the room above the garage. She kept staring at Livvy's bed. Livvy's *empty* bed.

"I have to find a way to warn Livvy. Livvy and Ross."

"Even after she was so horrible to you?" Ana-Li asked. "Even after she dragged you off in that parking lot and threatened to drink your blood?"

Destiny stopped pacing. She gripped the back of her desk chair as if holding herself up. "She's my sister," she said through gritted teeth. A tear slid down one cheek. "She's my sister, and I want her back. For her sake. For Mikey's sake. For all of us."

She took a breath and let it out slowly. "But if Dad finds her in that apartment building near campus . . . if Dad finds her . . ." The words caught in her throat.

"He wouldn't drive a stake through Livvy's heart," Ana-Li insisted.

A chill ran down Destiny's back. "He might."

Destiny couldn't sleep that night. Her thoughts swirled round and round until the room spun and her head pounded.

"Dad might kill Livvy."

She pictured her mother, tall and blond and pretty, like her twin daughters. And so young. Destiny only remembered her mother young.

Her mother was bitten by a vampire, a vampire who wanted to take her away, to make her his. She killed herself instead. She killed herself to escape the vampire's clutches.

That's why Dad became leader of the Hunters. That's why he is determined to wipe them out. They took away the love of his life.

And that's why he has been searching for a

cure, a formula to restore vampires to a normal life. But he has failed. His daughter is a vampire, and he has failed to find a cure.

And now he will hunt her down. And his hatred for vampires will force him to kill her. If he doesn't do it, one of his hunters will.

Unless I get there first, Destiny thought, rolling onto her side, scrunching the sheet to her chin.

Unless I can warn Livvy.

But how?

After that fight in the club parking lot, I don't think she'll talk to me. If she sees me coming, she'll change into a creature and fly away. If I tell her what Dad and his hunters are planning, she won't believe me. She'll think it's a trick to get her to come home.

So . . . what can I do?

The ceiling spun above Destiny's head. Light and shadows danced crazily, like wild creatures let loose in the room. Somewhere in the distance, a siren wailed.

What can I do?

And then she had an idea.

Chapter Twenty-two
One Evil Dawn

Destiny sat straight up and kicked the covers away.

Yes. Yes.

Ross.

Ross will talk to me. Ross always liked me. And he was always easy to talk to.

I'll find Ross. I'll tell him what's going to happen. Then Ross can talk to Livvy. And maybe . . . maybe they'll both be saved.

I'll go at dawn, Destiny decided. When the vampires have been out all night and are falling asleep.

At least I have a plan. I'll go into that building. I'll find Ross. I'll tell him . . . I'll tell him . . .

She settled back down and shut her eyes. But she knew she'd never fall asleep this night.

At a few minutes before six, she crept silently down the stairs, into the dark kitchen, dishwasher light blinking, and out the back door. Her old

470

Civic refused to start until the third try. She looked to the house to make sure the grinding sounds hadn't awakened her father.

Then she slid the gearshift into drive and headed off, into a gray world, high clouds blocking the rising sun, bare black trees shivering in the cool, morning breeze.

Not many cars on the road. A few sleepy-eyed people on their way to early morning jobs.

Destiny realized she was gritting her teeth so hard, her jaw ached. This is the best time to look for Ross, she assured herself for the hundredth time. The vampires will all be heading in to sleep, weary after a night of prowling.

Will I be able to wake him? Will he recognize me?

Of course he will. He's still Ross.

She drove her car around the campus square. Squirrels scampered over the lawn. The sun still hadn't burned through the clouds.

A few moments later, Destiny pulled the car up to the side of the unfinished apartment building. She climbed out, legs rubbery, heart suddenly pounding. And gazed up the side of the redbrick wall at the rows of open, unglassed windows.

Two large crows stared back at her from a

third-floor window ledge. She heard a fluttering sound and saw a bat shoot into a window near the top.

"Oh, wow."

So many apartments, she thought. How will I ever find Ross?

I'll just have to be lucky, she decided. I have to save him and my sister.

Taking a deep breath, she made her way through the front entrance, into the dark lobby. She stepped past rolls of wire and cable and a stack of Sheetrock squares, past the open elevator shaft, and started up the concrete stairs.

Her shoes echoed hollowly in the stairwell. The only sound until she reached the first floor—and heard the moans and sighs and groans of the sleeping vampires. Squinting into the gray light, she gazed in horror at the row of open apartment doorways.

I'll start here, she decided, gripping the railing. I can't call out his name. It would wake everyone up. I'll have to peek into every apartment until I find him.

Her whole body trembling now, she forced herself to move away from the stairs, into the trash-cluttered hall, up to the first door.

I should have brought a flashlight. I thought there would be some sun. The pale, gray light from the hall windows seemed to lengthen the shadows and make everything appear darker.

Sticking her head through the doorless opening, Destiny peered into the dark apartment. She couldn't see anything, but she heard low, steady breathing. She took a step inside. Then one more step.

And in the soupy gray, she saw two girls asleep on their backs on low cots against the wall, dark hair spread over their pillows, mouths open revealing curled fangs that slid up and down with each breath they took.

Destiny backed into the hall. The next two apartments appeared empty. No furniture. No sounds of sleep.

A long, mournful sigh echoed down the hallway. It sent a shiver down Destiny's back.

She peered into the third apartment. And saw a scrawny, little man asleep on the floor, a pillow under his bald head, his sunken eyes wide open. Destiny gasped and backed away, thinking he could see her. But he was sound asleep.

Moans and harsh snoring followed her to the next apartment. A man and woman, sleeping on a bare mattress, holding hands, their fangs dripping with saliva.

Back into the hall. Nearly at the end now, and no sign of Ross. She stepped around a pile of trash, mostly newspapers and magazines, tossed carelessly against the wall.

The papers rustled. Destiny stopped. What made them move? There was no wind here.

She stared as the papers crinkled. She heard scratching sounds from underneath the pile. "Oh." She uttered a soft cry as two fat rats slithered out.

They turned and gazed up at her, staring for the longest while, as if challenging her.

Her whole body tensed, Destiny backed away. Are these really rats? she wondered. Or are they vampires in rat bodies?

The swooping bat in her living room flashed into her mind. Livvy? Had it been Livvy?

The two rats raised up on their hind legs and took a step toward Destiny. One of them bared its teeth and uttered a shrill hiss.

Destiny wanted to turn and run. But she knew she shouldn't turn her back on the advancing rats.

They stood still now, on their back legs,

long, pink tails whipping back and forth, scraping the concrete floor. Their eyes glowed dully like black pearls. They both opened their mouths and uttered warning screeches, furiously waving their front paws up and down in slashing motions.

I have to get away.

Destiny spun away from them, tried to run—and collided full force with a figure standing behind her.

"Hey—!" She stumbled and fell into him, and they both staggered back. Her cheek brushed the rough fabric of his sweater.

"Ross—?" She grabbed his shoulders to pull herself back on her feet, shoulders hard as bone. Not Ross.

"S—sorry," she choked out. "I didn't see you. I was—"

She stared at him. He was good looking. Young. About Destiny's age. Short, dark hair, dark eyes, a thin, straight nose.

Then he turned—and Destiny opened her mouth in a horrified gasp.

The other half of his face—*missing*! The flesh ended in the middle, a line right down the center of his face, giving way to solid skull.

Destiny stared open-mouthed, too horrified to breathe. No eye in the gaping, empty socket, no flesh over the toothless jaw.

Half a face, Destiny saw. Normal looking on one side, even handsome. An eyeless skull on the other half.

Trembling, Destiny tried to back away.

"What's wrong?" he whispered. His teeth clicked as he talked, and his single eye rolled around in its socket. "Don't be frightened. Don't worry. I'll save my *good* side for you, babe."

He grabbed her. Circled his arms tightly around her. Arms like bones—and powerful, clamping her to him.

"No, please—"

She couldn't breathe.

He held her so tightly, her ribs ached. Her chest felt about to burst.

He lowered his face to her. She could see both sides at once now, the skeleton and the good-looking face. Both grinning at her coldly, half-lips pulled back so she could see his teeth.

He pressed his lips to hers.

Ohh. She felt soft flesh and bone.

Her stomach heaved.

He pulled his mouth away quickly, single eye flashing.

And then she saw the fangs, yellow and curled, slide down from his open mouth.

"So sweet, so sweet," he whispered, sour breath washing over her, making her choke. And then he sank the disgusting fangs into her throat.

Chapter Twenty-three

"I Want to Go Back to my Old Life"

She felt a stab of pain.

Then heard a loud shout.

"GET AWAY FROM HER!"

The vampire seemed to spin to the voice. But then Destiny realized someone had pulled him off her. Another vampire, face hidden in shadow, had grabbed him by the shoulders.

"First come, first served," the half-faceless one said softly, teeth clicking. He tensed his body as if preparing for a fight.

"I don't think so," the other replied.

And then they flung themselves at each other. Growling, cursing, they wrestled from one side of the hall to the other, smashing each other against the concrete walls.

Gasping for breath, Destiny felt the pin-prick wounds in her neck as she tried to back away to safety.

They're fighting over which one gets me,

she realized. Frozen in horror, she watched the battle.

Their cries and shouts had awakened others, who stood in the dark doorways all down the hall, staring in silence as the two vampires slashed at each other, shoving and biting.

I'm pinned here, Destiny thought. I can't run. If I do, the others will get me.

She backed into a corner, hands pressed against the sides of her face, still gasping for breath.

Fighting over me . . .

Fighting to see who gets to drink my blood . . .

With his back to Destiny, the new arrival hoisted up the half-faced vampire by the waist, lifted him high over his head and, with a powerful heave, tossed him out an open window.

Destiny heard the vampire's scream as he fell down the side of the building. Down . . . down . . . And then the scream was replaced by an angry bird cry, which rose up until Destiny could see a hawk, wings spread wide, through the window, sailing up, turning and taking one last glance at her, then floating away.

And now the winner of the battle, panting

noisily, brushing his wet hair off his face, turned to claim his prize. He lurched toward Destiny arms outstretched . . .

. . . And Destiny recognized him. "Ross—!" she screamed. "Ross—it's me!"

His mouth dropped open. He wiped sweat from his eyes—and squinted at her in the inky light. "Destiny—?"

"Yes. Yes, it's me!"

"Whoa." He was still breathing hard, chest heaving up and down. He had deep scratch marks on one side of his neck, and a red welt had formed under one eye.

"I don't believe it," he said, shaking his head hard. Then he lurched forward and wrapped her in a hug. "Dee, I'm so glad to see you."

Destiny let out a sigh of relief. It *is* the same Ross, she thought.

She gazed over his shoulder and saw eyes staring at them in doorways all down the hall, cold faces, angry and frightening.

"Can we . . . go somewhere?" she whispered.

Ross took her by the hand and led her to the stairway. He helped her up the steep, concrete steps to the second floor. Then he led the way to a small apartment halfway down the hall.

The clouds had finally started to burn away, and morning sunlight peeked into the open window. Destiny hugged herself. The room still had the chill of night.

She glanced around quickly. A pile of clothes, mostly jeans and T-shirts, in one corner. A couch with one cushion missing. A metal folding chair. A clock radio on the floor. The only furnishings.

Ross led her over to the couch. "Dee, I can't believe you're here. I'm so happy to see you," he said. He motioned for her to sit down. Then he dropped down beside her, sweeping his hair back with both hands.

He's changed, Destiny thought, studying him. He used to have that spark in his eyes, that flash of fire. But it's gone. He looks so tired . . . exhausted. And not because of the fight with the other vampire.

"How are you?" he asked. "How's Mikey? And your dad?"

"Not great," Destiny replied. "It's been really hard with Livvy gone. I mean, it's hard to explain to yourself why—"

"Livvy," Ross interrupted, shaking his head.

"Livvy. Livvy. She's hard to figure, you know?"

"I . . . saw her the other night," Destiny continued, the words catching in her throat. "She was so horrible to me, Ross. Like she *hated* me. And what did I do to her? Nothing. I only wanted to talk with her."

"She's gotten weird," Ross said, lowering his head. "This was supposed to be so exciting. You know. Livvy and me. Living forever and everything. She promised. She promised me it would be awesome. But now . . ." He glanced to the window. "Now she usually doesn't want to hang with me. She's got new friends that she cares about."

Destiny nodded. She didn't know what to say. "Ross—?"

He kept his eyes down at the floor. "I'm so unhappy," he said finally. "I mean, this life is so hard. I wish . . . I wish I'd never followed Livvy."

"I'm sorry too," Destiny murmured.

"She likes it. I really think she does," he continued, finally turning to face her. "I don't understand it. But I think Livvy enjoys the excitement. You know, the adventure. She likes the . . . *badness* of it. And the idea that she never has to grow old."

Destiny nodded. "When she was little, her favorite cartoon was *Peter Pan*. You know. The Disney one. Now I guess she liked it because Peter and the Lost Boys never grew up, either.

"I don't know why I went with her," Ross said. He climbed to his feet and moved to the window. He leaned on the sill, keeping his back to the rising sunlight as he spoke. "It was crazy. I guess I went a little nuts or something. But now . . ."

He swallowed. "Now I'd give anything to have my old life back. I mean it, Dee. Anything. I'm so unhappy. I just want to see my sister again . . . and Mom and Dad. I just want—"

"Maybe it can happen," Destiny interrupted.

He squinted at her. "Why? Has your dad—?"

"No. He hasn't found anything. Not yet. But he's working on it, Ross. He won't quit till he finds a cure."

"That's great," Ross said. "I don't know how much more I can take. Really."

Destiny climbed to her feet and hugged herself tightly. "Listen, Ross, I came here for a reason. I came to warn you. The Hunters are going to come. They know about this place.

They're going to kill as many vampires as they can."

Ross nodded. He didn't seem surprised. "We knew they'd come after us sooner or later."

"You and Livvy have got to get out," Destiny said. "You've got to talk to her, Ross. She won't talk to me."

He scratched his head. "I . . . I'll try."

Destiny could feel her emotions tightening her throat. "You've got to tell her," she said. "You've got to tell her to get away from here. Maybe you can convince her, Ross. Have you told her you want to give up the vampire life? Maybe you can convince her too."

Ross hesitated. "I don't think so. Whenever I start to talk about it . . ." His voice trailed off in a sigh.

Destiny felt tears rolling down her cheeks. She didn't make any attempt to stop them. "Tell her. Tell her, Ross."

Ross nodded. "I'll see what I can do. Really. I'll try, Dee."

A sob escaped Destiny's throat. Tears blurred her vision. "Tell her I still love her," she choked out. "Tell her I'll do anything to have her back."

And then she ran, out the door of the shabby apartment and down the long hallway . . . ran away from this world of darkness . . . back to her own life.

Chapter Twenty-four

A Death in the Vampire Family

Is that Destiny?

Yes, of course it is.

Livvy hid behind a trash Dumpster and watched her sister run from the apartment building. Destiny dropped her bag, picked it up, then fumbled inside it for her car key.

What is she doing here so early? Livvy wondered. The sun is just coming up. Did she come to see me? Does she still think if she begs hard enough, I'll come home?

She watched Destiny stumble over a pile of broken bricks, then run to the side of the building. Destiny had such a distressed look on her face, Livvy felt a pang of guilt.

I didn't want to cause you so much sadness, Dee. What I did wasn't about you at all. It was about me. But you can't accept that, can you?

Because everything—*everything*—always had to be about you.

Destiny pulled open her car door and plunged inside.

You must have sneaked out of the house before dawn, Livvy thought. Now why would you pay me a visit at this hour? Do you think I know something about Ari? Is that it?

Think I know something about how poor Ari died? Well, Dee, you've got that right.

I do know about Ari. It was my stupid friend Monica. I warned her to be careful, to go slowly, a few sips at a time. But Monica never knows when to stop. She always wants more more more.

Suzie and I both got on her case when she told us she'd killed Ari. "I couldn't help it," Monica said. "I was so hungry, and I lost track. It was an accident. Really."

Accidents happen, right?

No way.

Not when it gets the whole town excited and upset. And the police. Monica should know better. She risked all of us for one night of pleasure. She's my friend, but she's also a stupid cow.

And yes, I felt bad about Ari. I mean, he was a geeky guy, totally clueless. Spending all his time on horror movies and *Star Trek* websites. But he was smart and funny too. And I know you really liked him.

Whatever.

It's done, okay. He's history.

So why did you come to see me this morning? To hear about how Ari died? How would that help you? It won't bring the poor guy back.

Livvy watched Destiny's car pull away, tires squealing. Again, she pictured the distressed look on her sister's face.

Sorry, Dee. I really am. But get over it.

Don't come here begging me to give up my new life.

Livvy licked her lips. Mmmm. A trace of the sweet blood lingered there.

That Alby is a good guy, she thought, shutting her eyes for a moment. Such sweet blood, almost like dessert. I'm going to bring him along slowly, so slowly he won't even notice.

The morning sun spread an orange glow around the apartment building. Livvy squinted at the brightening light.

I'd better get inside. The sun burns my eyes.

I don't have my shades.

She started toward the front door—then stopped.

Whoa. Hold on. Maybe Dee didn't come to see me.

Livvy bit her bottom lip, new thoughts flashing through her mind.

Maybe Dee came to see Ross.

Maybe she came at dawn hoping to find him without me around.

Has she been seeing Ross all along? Destiny always had a thing for him. I think she was really jealous when Ross decided he liked me better.

When Ross decided he loved me . . .

But Ross is so eager to connect to his old life. He begged me to let him see his family in line at the movie theater. Has he also been trying to get together with my sister?

Livvy darted into the darkness of the building. As she climbed the stairs, she could hear the groans and sighs of the sleeping vampires.

But she didn't feel the least bit sleepy. She had to get to the bottom of this.

Her shoes thudded the concrete floor as she ran down the long, narrow hallway toward

Ross's apartment. She edged past a stack of Sheetrock, then a pile of old newspapers.

Ross, please don't tell me you've been seeing Destiny. Please tell me she came to see *me*.

She stopped at the open doorway to Ross's apartment to catch her breath. Then she burst inside.

"Ross—?"

It took her eyes a few moments to adjust to the bright light that washed into the room from the window. Then Livvy spotted Ross—and she opened her mouth and screamed in horror.

"Ross? Noooooo! Oh, no! Please—NOOOOOOOO!"

Chapter Twenty-five
"It Won't Be Pretty"

Livvy staggered over to Ross's body. sprawled on his back on the floor. Legs spread. Hands raised, still gripping the wooden stake pushed through his chest.

Wooden stake . . .

Livvy gaped at the stake, a plank of light wood. The kind of wood scattered all over this unfinished building.

The stake had been driven through Ross's T-shirt, through the center of his chest. Through his heart.

And now he lay with his eyes wide open, blank, glassy . . . wide open . . . wide open as if still staring up at his attacker.

His head tilted to one side. His mouth hung open in a silent scream. Hands still gripping the stake.

"Ross—" Livvy uttered his name as she dropped down beside his lifeless body. "Oh, no, Ross. Oh, no."

Murdered.

She cradled his head in her arms.

Murdered. His body still warm.

And yes, she knew . . .

Holding onto the boy who had cared enough about her to follow her . . . the boy who had loved her so much, he became a vampire just to be with her. Holding onto Ross's lifeless head, Livvy knew who had murdered him.

Destiny.

She had seen Destiny running from the building. In such a hurry to get away.

Destiny came at dawn, sneaked into the building to kill Ross.

And why?

Cradling Ross's head, Livvy shut her eyes and thought hard.

Why?

To pay me back for deserting the family.

No.

Oh, wait. I get it. I totally get it. That was Destiny's way of paying me back for Ari.

Destiny thinks I killed Ari. So she paid me back by killing Ross.

Poor, sweet, innocent Ross.

Could Destiny really do this? Is she angry

enough? Desperate enough? Crazy enough?

Yes. I saw her face as she ran from the building.

I saw the tears running down her cheeks. Saw the wild look in her eyes. The fear mixed with anger. Mixed with hatred.

She hates me so much, she murdered the boy who loved me.

With a long howl of sorrow, Livvy hugged Ross's lifeless head, pressed it to her, ran her hands through his hair one last time.

"You can't get away with this, Destiny," she said out loud in a cold, hard voice. "I'll find a way to pay you back. Yes, I will. And it won't be pretty."

Chapter Twenty-six
"I'd Like to Tear Destiny to Bits"

Sobbing now, Livvy gently lowered Ross's head to the floor. She climbed unsteadily to her feet, pulled a blanket off his narrow cot, and covered his body with it, tugging the ends of the blanket around the wooden stake.

Livvy's whole body shuddered.

What must that feel like? To have a sharpened wooden stake shoved through your chest into your heart?

She couldn't imagine the agony Ross must have felt. The pain from the puncture. Waves of pain shooting through his body like electric currents . . . as he realized . . . realized he was about to lose his life.

She grabbed her own chest. She suddenly felt as if she couldn't take another breath.

I have to get out of here.

Still holding her chest, she turned away from Ross and stumbled to the door. She started to breathe again out in the hall. And then she climbed the stairs and ran to her room, shoes thudding noisily . . . How wonderful to be able to make a noise, to be alive, to run . . . Ross will never run again . . . never.

Sunshine poured in through the open window. She fumbled on her dresser top until she found her sunglasses. Slipped them on, blinking, heart thudding, two pictures remaining in her mind.

Two pictures refusing to fade . . .

Ross dead on the floor, his hands—his beautiful hands—gripping the wooden stake that killed him.

And Destiny running from the apartment building, tears running down her cheeks, her expression so angry, so upset.

Livvy paced back and forth in the small, nearly bare living room, her hands balled into tight fists. The anger boiled up in her until she felt ready to explode.

I'd like to follow Dee home right now, she thought. Burst in at breakfast and drag her away. Slash her, tear her to bits with my own hands.

Oh, wow. Could I do that? Could I do that to Dad and Mikey?

Maybe. It's not like I was ever appreciated at home. Or like anyone tried to understand me. Destiny was always the princess. And I was always . . . trouble.

Well, I tried to escape all that. I tried to escape my family. I tried to do them a favor. Go away so I wouldn't be trouble anymore.

So why couldn't my sister leave things alone?

Stay home and be the good twin, Dee. Stay with Dad and Mikey and be the princess.

Don't come here and kill someone I really care about.

She could feel the anger rising again, feel all her muscles tensing. And then suddenly, she felt as if she weighed a thousand pounds.

So weary.

Out all night, and then come home to such horror.

She yawned. I need to sleep. Sleep will help me think more clearly. I can make a plan. I can—

She heard a scraping sound from the other room. Footsteps.

"Monica? Suzie? Are you in here?"

No answer.

Livvy stared at the doorway to the bedroom.

She took a few steps. "Who's in there?"

And as she stared, a figure stepped out of the shadows. He smiled at her.

"You?" Livvy cried. "What are *you* doing in here?"

Chapter Twenty-seven
Blood on Her Lips

*P*atrick came toward her slowly, hands in the pockets of his black denim jeans. His dark eyes locked on hers. As his grin widened, she saw the dimples in his cheeks—and remembered the way he smiled at her at the dance club.

"How long have you been here? What are you doing here?" she asked.

He shrugged. "Just waiting for you."

Livvy rushed to him. "Oh, Patrick. I'm so glad to see you. Something . . . something *terrible* has happened."

His smile faded quickly. "What is it? Are you okay?"

"No. No, I'm not. I . . . I . . ." She grabbed his arm and pulled him out of the apartment. "You've got to see. I . . . I'm so upset."

She pulled him through the hall, then down the stairs to Ross's apartment. They stepped through a square of bright sunlight on the floor, to the back of the apartment, to the body covered by a purple blanket, wooden stake poking straight up into the air.

"Here," Livvy said, trembling. She tugged away the blanket.

Patrick gasped and bent to examine Ross's body closer. "Oh, no," he murmured. "I don't believe this."

Angrily, he grabbed the stake in both hands and ripped it from Ross's chest. Then he flung it against the bedroom wall, where it hit and clattered to the bare floor.

He turned to Livvy, his features tight with anger. "Who did this? We can't let them get away with this."

"He . . . was my friend," Livvy said in a whisper. "He was a good guy. He . . ."

Patrick leaned his back against the wall and brushed a hand through his long, brown hair. "Murdered in his own apartment," he murmured. "He was your friend?"

Livvy nodded, tears running down her cheeks.

He raised his eyes to her and studied her. "When did this happen? Do you have any idea who did it?"

Livvy hesitated.

Yes, I have an idea who did it.

But I can't tell him.

I can't turn my sister over to him so easily. I want to handle her myself. I want to make Destiny pay for what she did. I don't want someone else to get the revenge *for* me.

"No. I don't have a clue," Livvy said, lowering her eyes to the floor. "It probably happened this morning. I'm sure Ross was out all night. His body . . . his face . . . it was still warm when I came in here."

Patrick narrowed his eyes at her. "Do you always come in to see him early in the morning?"

"Uh . . . no," Livvy replied. "Not usually."

"Well then, why did you come to his apartment this morning?" Patrick asked.

He sounded suspicious. Livvy didn't like the question.

"I wanted to ask him something. I wanted to ask Ross if he knew a guy I met last night." A total lie. Was Patrick buying it?

He seemed to. He scratched his head. "And you can't think of anyone who had a grudge against Ross? Who might've wanted revenge or something? No enemies? You were his friend, Livvy. No one comes to mind?"

She shook her head. "No. No one." She glanced down at the body and let out a sob. "I . . . I'm really going to miss him."

Patrick crossed the room quickly and wrapped Livvy in a hug. She pressed her hot, damp cheek against his. He tightened his arms around her waist.

It felt good to be held by someone, someone solid and strong.

Livvy raised her face to his and kissed him. She wrapped her hands around the back of his neck and held his head as they kissed.

"Mm." She let out a sound as she felt his teeth bite into her lips. He pressed his mouth against hers, and she felt a shock of pain.

Suddenly, he ended the kiss. He pulled his face away, then lowered it to hers again—and licked the blood off her lips.

Livvy realized she was breathing hard, her heart racing. For the first time in her life, she felt dizzy from a kiss.

Patrick held her tightly, licking the top lip clean, then the bottom. When he backed away, he had her blood on his lips.

"I'll see you later," he said, and vanished from the room.

"Yeah. Later," she repeated. She stood unsteadily, eyes clamped shut, waiting for her heart to stop racing. And then . . . she thought about Destiny.

Destiny, who had murdered Ross.

Chapter Twenty-eight
Livvy's Revenge

A few days later, unable to forgive Destiny, unable to control her rage, Livvy found the Four Corners Diner. Peering through the front window, she saw Destiny behind the counter.

Seeing her sister working so calmly, so normally, as if nothing had happened . . . as if she hadn't murdered someone who'd been close to them both . . . made Livvy boil with anger.

What can I do? How can I pay her back for this?

What could she have been thinking? How could Destiny hate me *so much* that she would murder Ross?

Heart pounding, Livvy made her way to the back of the restaurant. Then she used her powers to transform into a tiny, white mouse.

Down on all fours, she found a crack in the back wall. She squeezed through it, into the kitchen. Creeping along the molding, Livvy moved silently toward the front. The aroma of frying eggs and bacon made her stand up and sniff the air with her pink nose.

As she stood up, the young man behind the fry grill came into view. Very nice looking, Livvy thought. Check out those big, brown eyes. And he looks like he works out.

He turned away from the grill. Livvy ducked under a cabinet.

"Tuna salad on whole wheat," Destiny called from the front. "And Harrison, are you working on that cheeseburger rare?"

So his name is Harrison, Livvy told herself.

She started to feel hungry. Not from the smell of the food frying on the grill—but from the look of Harrison's broad shoulders, those eyes that crinkled at the corners, that long neck, the perfect throat . . .

She let out a soft squeak.

Oh, wow. Control yourself, Livvy. Did he hear you? She pressed tighter under the cabinet.

Why did I come here? She wondered, staring up at Harrison.

To spy on Destiny, of course. To see her face, the face of a murderer. Why? Well . . .

Because . . . Because . . .

I'm not sure.

I'm so confused and upset, I can't think straight.

Destiny appeared in the kitchen, carrying a stack of dirty dishes. She dropped them into a basket on the sink counter.

"Whew." She wiped her forehead with the back of her hand, then washed her hands in the sink. Livvy watched her walk over to Harrison.

"How's it going?" Destiny put a hand on Harrison's shoulder.

"Not bad," he replied, scraping the grill. "Want some eggs or something? A little lunch break?"

"No, thanks. Check this out." She held up a coin. "A quarter. That table of four—they tipped me a quarter."

Harrison stared at it. "You and I split that, right? When do I get my share?"

They both laughed. The quarter fell from Destiny's hand and rolled onto the floor.

Then Livvy watched them kiss, a long, tender kiss.

And she knew what she wanted to do.

Harrison is my guy. This is going to be so *sweet*.

Destiny, dear, let's see how eager you are to kiss your lovely Harrison after I turn him into a vampire!

Part Six

Chapter Twenty-nine
The Party Crasher

"I think you're definitely helping Mikey," Destiny said.

Harrison shrugged. "I didn't do anything."

"He responds to you," she replied. "He likes you. I mean, you got him to come out of the Bat Cave—his room—and actually throw a Frisbee around in the backyard. That was an amazing accomplishment."

"Yeah, true," Harrison agreed. "That poor guy seemed so stressed out when he got outside. Until I made him chase after the Frisbee a few times, he was shaking like a leaf. He kept gazing up at the sky, checking out the tree limbs. I don't know what he expected to find up there."

He expected to find Livvy, Destiny thought. But Harrison doesn't know that.

She told Harrison that Mikey had a lot of problems because their mother had died so suddenly. She hadn't told Harrison anything about

Livvy. He didn't even know she had a twin sister.

Destiny felt her throat tighten. She had been thinking about Livvy. Did Ross talk to her? Did he pass on my message to her?

It had been three days, and she hadn't heard from Ross or her sister.

Destiny chewed her bottom lip. Should I go back there and talk to Ross again? Was sneaking over there at dawn a waste of time? Is Livvy just going to ignore my visit?

Harrison pulled the car to the curb. Destiny slid down the visor and checked her lipstick in the mirror. She gazed out at the row of townhouses, aging three-story buildings—paint peeling and shingles missing—that had been turned into apartments for community college students.

Lights blazed in the front windows of the house on the right. And Destiny could hear rap music blaring without even opening the car door.

"Do I look okay?" she asked. She wore a light blue tank top, baggy, white shorts, and flip-flops. It was a steamy hot July night and she wanted to be comfortable.

Harrison smiled and nodded. "Awesome."

He started to open his door, then stopped. "Are you getting tired of these crowded, noisy parties?"

"No way," Destiny said without having to think about it. "I'm meeting some nice people. And it kinda makes me feel like I'm already part of the scene. You know. Like I'm already in college."

She climbed out of the car and straightened her shirt. She saw groups of young people on the grass in front of the building. Several sat on the stoop, cans of beer in their hands. Two large golden Labs with red bandannas around their necks chased each other across the street and back.

Harrison took her hand and they walked up the stoop, stepping around two girls on the steps who were smoking—both talking heatedly at once—and into Harrison's friend's apartment.

Destiny stepped into the big, smoky front room, filled with people her age in shorts and jeans, sprawled over the furniture, standing in clumps, shouting over the deafening music. She recognized some girls she met at Alby's birthday party and hurried over to say hi to them.

Livvy was always the party person, she thought. But I'm starting to enjoy them more. Maybe because I'm older now—and being out of high school makes *everyone* more relaxed.

Harrison introduced her to Danny, his best friend from high school. He was a short, stocky guy, kind of funny-looking with tiny, round eyes on top of a bulby nose, and thick, steel wool hair standing up on his head.

He and Harrison walked off talking, and Destiny crossed the room to get a Coke. She ran into Alby at the food table, and they hung out for a while.

Destiny tried not to stare at the bandage on Alby's neck. But it made her very uncomfortable. She made an excuse and hurried away.

People were scattered all over the town-house, and Destiny gave herself a tour. Wish I could live away from home, she thought. The fun of college is being away from home, living on your own for the first time.

But why even think about it? No way she could leave Dad and Mikey now.

She returned to the front room and talked to some people she'd met at the diner. A couple of guys hit on her, and she brushed them off easily.

After a while, she realized she hadn't seen Harrison for a long time. She glanced at her watch. She hadn't seen him for at least half an hour.

Weird.

Destiny gazed around the room. Harrison, where are you?

She saw Alby in the corner with a skinny, red-haired girl a foot taller than him, and made her way through the crowd to him. "Have you seen Harrison?" She had to shout over the loud voices and the booming rap music.

Alby shook his head. "No. Not for a while. Do you know Lily?"

No. Destiny didn't know Lily. She stayed and talked to her for a while. She kept expecting Harrison to appear at her side, but—no sign of him.

She searched the back rooms and the kitchen, piled high with garbage and empty beer and soda cans. He's got to be here somewhere, she thought.

Doesn't he wonder where I am?

Destiny returned to her spot in front of the fireplace in the living room. A few minutes later, Harrison turned from the drinks table, spotted her, and his eyes went wide, as if he was surprised to see her there.

He carried two cans of Coors and hurried over to her. "Here's the beer you wanted," he said. "How'd you get back here so fast?"

Destiny stared at him. "Excuse me? I didn't ask you for a beer."

He crinkled up his face, confused. "Of course, you did. Outside on the stoop, you—"

"Huh? Outside?"

Destiny's heart leaped up to her throat. She narrowed her eyes at Harrison, her mind spinning.

Outside.

He was talking to me outside on the stoop.

But no. No. It wasn't me.

Livvy!

Chapter Thirty
Livvy and Harrison

*D*estiny handed the beer back to Harrison and took off. She heard him shouting to her, but she didn't turn around.

Livvy is here. On the front stoop.

Did Ross talk to her? Did he convince her to come see me?

She bumped into a couple leaning on the wall by the door who had their arms around each other, cheeks pressed together. They both let out startled cries as Destiny pushed past them.

"Sorry," she called.

She pushed the screen door open and burst out onto the stoop. "Livvy? Are you here?" she called.

A blond girl in a red halter top and jeans spun toward Destiny.

"Livvy—?"

No.

Destiny ran down the steps onto the grass. The sun had gone down. The moon floated low in a clear, purple sky dotted with stars.

The people on the lawn were all shadows. A few couples were lying in the grass, wrapped up in each other. A circle of guys down near the sidewalk were singing a Beatles song at the top of their lungs.

"Livvy? Are you here?"

Destiny cupped her hands around her mouth and shouted. "Livvy? Livvy?"

No. No answer. Gone.

But she had been here. Harrison had talked to her. And thought he was talking to Destiny.

Did she do that deliberately? Did Livvy come here to trick Harrison? Was it some kind of joke she was playing on Destiny?

Destiny gazed around the front lawn. Music boomed from the open windows. "Livvy? Livvy? Please?"

Then Destiny saw the bat. It fluttered off a slender tree near the curb and flapped slowly toward her. Eyes glowing, the bat swooped low over her head, then spun away and floated toward the street.

Heart pounding, Destiny turned and chased after it.

The bat floated slowly, low to the ground, its wings spread wide, gliding easily. Destiny ran under it, reaching for it with both hands, calling her sister's name breathlessly.

"Livvy, stop! Please—!"

The bat swooped away, just out of her reach.

Running hard, Destiny made another grab for the bat—and missed.

"Ohh—!" Destiny let out a cry as she ran full force into the side mirror of a parked car. The mirror hit her chest. Pain shot through her ribs. She staggered back.

She raised her eyes in time to see the bat vanish into the inky night sky.

Livvy, why did you come? she wondered. If you didn't want to talk to me, what were you doing here?

Chapter Thirty-one

"You're Still Connected to Your Sister"

Livvy swooped to the side of the abandoned apartment building, fluttered high against the wall, then dropped gently onto the sill of a glassless window. The night air felt cool on her wings. For a moment, she thought she might turn around and fly out again, fly away from her troubled thoughts, cover herself in the darkness above the trees.

But no. She changed her mind and scuttled inside, shutting her eyes and willing herself to change back to the body that was familiar to her—and unfamiliar at the same time.

Here I am, Livvy Weller once again. Only I'm not really Livvy Weller. I'm someone else, someone new.

She took a deep breath. It always took a while for her heartbeats to slow from the racing rhythm of a bat's heart. And it took a minute or two for her eyes to adjust to normal, for the night vision to fade, for her hearing to return.

Livvy reached for the floor lamp she had found on the street. Would it work? The electrical generator downstairs was usually broken. She clicked it, and a triangle of pale, yellow light washed over the floor.

"Oh." She blinked as Patrick climbed up from the floor, dusted off the seat of his faded jeans, torn at both knees, and slowly ambled over to her.

She laughed. "Don't you ever knock?"

He grinned, showing those dimples, and pointed behind him. "No door."

She kissed him on the cheek. His skin felt cool and smooth.

"Where've you been?" he asked.

She gave him a sexy smile. "Like it's *your* business?"

"Yes, it is my business," he said, smile fading. He swept a hand back through his dark hair. It had been brushed straight back, but now he'd messed it up. "I . . . I'm interested in you, Liv. I like you, okay? So I want to make sure you don't mess up."

She narrowed her eyes at him. "Mess up? Mess up what?"

He shrugged. "Everything."

Livvy ran her finger down the side of his cheek. "What are you talking about?"

"Where were you tonight?" he asked again.

"Out flying around," she said. "You know. The usual."

He turned those dark, deep eyes on her, and she could feel their power. "You're lying, Liv. Why would you lie to me unless you knew you were out looking for trouble tonight?"

Livvy stared back at him. Was he hypnotizing her or something? Using his powers to invade her mind?

She turned away, but she could still feel the strange power of his stare.

"You went to your sister's party," Patrick said. "You pretended to be your sister, and you fooled her boyfriend, that guy Harrison."

Livvy let out a groan. "I don't believe this. So you're *spying* on me?"

He nodded. "Yes. Why did you do it, Liv? Explain that to me."

Livvy shrugged. "I don't know. I . . . I just don't know. For fun, maybe."

Patrick shook his head. He crossed the room to her. "You didn't do it for fun. You did it because you're still connected to your sister."

"Connected? What the hell is that supposed to mean?" Livvy snapped.

"You've chosen a new life, right?" Patrick asked. "You're one of us now. But you're not really here yet, Liv. You're not whole."

"Not whole?"

"You won't be whole as long as you have a soft spot in your heart."

Livvy stared at him, hands on her waist. "You mean for Destiny? Listen—"

"Your heart still beats for your sister," Patrick said. "You still care about her."

He's wrong, Livvy told herself. I hate Destiny. Hate her! She killed Ross.

"You're crazy," she snapped at Patrick. "I just went to that party to mess with Destiny's mind."

"But, why?" Patrick demanded. "See? You've proven my point, Liv. Why did you go to mess with Destiny's mind? Why did you go to that party? Because you still care about her. You still care what she thinks."

"That is *so* wrong," Livvy insisted.

Patrick softened his tone. "You know I'm right. Admit it. Admit it."

"Stop trying to push me around," Livvy said.

"Listen to me," he said. He wrapped his arms around her. "Listen to me," he repeated, whispering the words now. "You want to be immortal?"

"Of course."

"Then you have to break all ties with the other world."

"I . . . I don't know if I can do that."

"Well then, you have no choice. Don't you see, Livvy? Don't you see the answer? You will never truly be an immortal—*until your sister is one of us!*"

Chapter Thirty-two
A Date with a Vampire

"Destiny a vampire too?" Livvy stared hard at Patrick. "Yes. I like that idea."

The perfect revenge for what Destiny did to Ross, Livvy thought. Why didn't I think of it?

Maybe I do still care too much about her. Maybe that's why I didn't imagine a revenge this good.

"Yes," she told Patrick. "You might be right. Destiny would be much better off as a vampire. And then I wouldn't have to think about her, about my family back home."

"I knew you'd agree," Patrick said, sitting down on the window ledge, gazing up at the nearly full moon. "Most people finally agree with me."

"It's not like you're an egotist or anything," Livvy said.

He laughed. "I like you, Liv. I really do. And I think I'm really going to like your sister too."

Livvy narrowed her eyes at him. "Like Destiny? What do you mean?"

"I'll go after Destiny myself and turn her into an immortal. You take care of the new boyfriend. Harrison Palmer." He grinned. "You'll enjoy that, right?"

Livvy nodded. "It won't be hard work. I already spent time with Harrison at that party tonight. We hit it off really well. And he didn't have a clue I wasn't Destiny."

"Excellent!" Patrick rubbed his hands together. "A little project for the two of us."

He wrapped his arms around her waist in a tight hug. Then he kissed her hard, grinding his teeth against her lips until she cried out in pain—and in pleasure.

Destiny arrived at the diner and found Mr. G. behind the grill. "Where's Harrison?" she asked, sliding behind the counter.

"Some kind of mix-up at school," Mr. G. shouted over the crackling and hissing of the eggs and bacon. "He had to go straighten it all out. Don't look for him today. Once you go in that administration building, they don't let you out."

Destiny went to work, clearing dirty dishes off tables, refilling coffee cups, taking orders. Breakfast was the busiest part of the day. A lot of the professors, instructors, and other college workers stopped here before heading to their offices.

"I asked for rye toast, not white."

"Could you top this cup off for me? No—decaf. Make sure it's decaf."

"I asked for *extra* crisp bacon. Look at these soggy things."

Breakfast was the busiest time—and the most difficult.

Destiny wondered what kind of trouble Harrison was having. He hadn't mentioned anything to her at the party last night.

The party . . .

Luckily, Harrison hadn't seen her chase after the bat. If he had, he'd think she was totally nuts!

And of course she didn't tell him he'd spent half an hour talking with her vampire twin. If Harrison knew the truth, he'd freak.

He's a great guy, Destiny thought. I wish I could confide in him. Tell him everything. But I don't want to lose him . . .

A young man leaned over the counter, staring at her.

She shook her head hard, forcing away her troubled thoughts. "Sorry. I didn't see you there." She wiped her hands off on a towel, picked up a menu, and carried it over to him.

He smiled. He had the cutest dimples in his cheeks. Dark eyes, very round and wide, dark hair brushed straight back over his broad forehead. "You were off on some other planet," he said.

She handed him the menu. "Just daydreaming. How long were you watching me?"

He shrugged. "A little while. You look like someone I know."

She studied him. "Oh, really? Are you from Dark Springs?"

"No. Not really. I mean, I am now. I teach across the street. I'm a teaching assistant. For Professor Clark. Heard of him?"

"No. Sorry. I'm starting there this fall. What do you teach?"

"English. Creative writing, actually." He lowered his eyes to the menu.

"I'm very into creative writing," Destiny said. "Maybe I'll be in your class sometime."

He smiled. Again those dimples. "I'd like that."

How old was he? Maybe twenty? Except his eyes looked older somehow.

He stuck out his hand. "My name is Patrick."

She reached over the counter to shake it. "Destiny Weller. Do you know what you want?"

He eyed her meaningfully. "I'm thinking about it." He held onto her hand for the longest time.

Destiny could feel herself blushing. She wasn't sure why. Something about the way his eyes locked on hers?

"Guess you have a lot of time for daydreaming in this job," Patrick said.

She shrugged. "Once the breakfast crowd leaves, it gets kinda quiet."

His grin grew wider. "And what do you daydream about?"

She grinned back at him. "Things that are none of your business."

"Didn't you daydream this morning that a nice guy was going to come in, order ham and eggs, and ask you out for Friday night?"

"Is that what you want?" Destiny pulled out

her pad. Why was her hand shaking like that? She suddenly felt fluttery. "Ham and eggs?"

She looked up to see his dark eyes trained on hers. "Yes, that's what I want. Ham and eggs. And for you to go out with me Friday night."

"And how do you want the eggs?" Destiny couldn't remove her eyes from his gaze. It was as if he held her there, froze her with those deep, dark-jeweled eyes.

Suddenly, she felt very frightened. This isn't right. Something very wrong is happening here. I feel like . . . a prisoner.

"Scrambled, please," he said. "And could I have a toasted bagel with that? And what time should I pick you up Friday night?"

His eyes . . . the stare was so intense, it made Destiny's head hurt.

Then slowly the pain faded. And she felt comfortable again. No. More than comfortable. She felt as if everything was floating. As if she were floating off the floor. And the whole diner became soft, and shimmering, and bright. Not real . . . not real at all.

And she saw things in Patrick's eyes. She saw clouds and blue sky, and a pale, white moon, fluffy like tissue paper, round and full.

A full moon in Patrick's eyes. And he was saying something to her. But she was floating now, and he was so far away, his voice so distant and muffled.

What was he saying?

Something about Harrison.

No. Harrison and I don't have an exclusive arrangement. No, Patrick, I'm free to go out with anyone I want. Yes, I'd love to see you Friday. Can you pick me up at home?

Yes, that would be great.

And what will we do Friday night?

She struggled to hear his voice, muffled by a strong wind, the wind that blew behind the full moon in his eyes. All that blue sky, so clear and bright, and the full moon trembling in the middle of it.

What did you say? You want to take me into Drake Park, sink your fangs into my throat, and feed on my warm blood?

Oh, yes. Excellent. That sounds awesome.

Yes. I'm definitely up for that.

And then Destiny felt as if she were sinking. Suddenly heavy, she dropped from the clouds. The blue sky faded away, taking the full moon with it. And she stood heavily behind the counter, leaning on the yellow Formica, in the darkness of the diner, the smell of grease and bacon invading her nose, and stared at the young man with the dimples, sitting on the stool across from her.

What was his name? Patrick?

Yes. Patrick and I are going out Friday night after work.

I'll have to be careful not to let Harrison know.

"I'll get those eggs," Destiny said, taking the menu from Patrick. "Anything to drink?"

"Just your blood."

He didn't say that. Destiny, why are you making up these things? Why can't you concentrate this morning?

"Coffee," he said. "Black is fine."

"You got it," she said.

"I'm looking forward to Friday," Patrick called after her.

Chapter Thirty-three
Harrison and Livvy

Livvy met Harrison at the Cineplex at the Dark Springs Mall at eight o'clock. A warm night, the air heavy and wet. She wore a white shirt over a sleeveless green tank top and white shorts. Something Destiny would wear.

She had put on clear lip gloss, a dab of peach-colored eye shadow. Totally boring, Livvy thought. But Destiny likes that clean-cut, all-American-girl look.

Can I fool Harrison into thinking I'm my sister? Livvy watched him climb out of his car and come hurrying toward her. Well, Harrison was totally clueless at that party. No reason to think he'll figure it out tonight.

I'll bet Destiny hasn't even told him about me.

Afraid she'll frighten him away by making her family seem too weird.

Well, guess what, Harrison, my boy? You *should* be frightened. Because an evil vampire is out to get you—namely me.

Tonight I'm going to start getting you ready. No big deal, guy. A few sips of blood from your lovely throat. You'll hardly feel it, a big healthy hunk like you.

So sweet . . . I know you're going to taste so sweet.

Once we get started, we won't want to stop, will we? Sunday night is the full moon. That's your big night, Harrison. Sunday night when the moon is at its height, you and I will hook up in the best way.

We will mix our blood. I'll drink yours and you'll drink mine. It's so sexy and so delicious and so . . . *hot*, Harrison. Wait and see.

I'm getting all tingly just thinking about Sunday night.

Oh, wow. I just want a taste. I'm *dying* for a taste, Harrison. Can you see how much I want you?

He's so cute and nice and . . . sincere. That's why you like him, isn't it, Dee? That's why he's your new guy.

Well, how are you going to like him after Sunday night when he's one of us? A vampire, Dee. Your summer hunk is going to be a vampire.

Will you still go to his house parties? Still

hang out with him on campus?

I don't think so.

Hey, don't blame me, sister. It's all *your* fault. I'm just paying you back. You murdered Ross. You came into my building at dawn and murdered my boyfriend.

Did you really think I would just hang back and not do anything at all?

You're going to pay, Dee. Patrick and I will see to that.

Where are you tonight? Probably home thinking you're safe and sound. Well, Patrick will be there soon. Sunday night the two of you will mix *your* blood under the light of the full moon.

Then you can rejoin Harrison—forever. You can have him forever, Dee, because you'll be an immortal too.

The perfect revenge? I think so.

And then Patrick and I . . .

Patrick and I . . .

Livvy pictured Patrick, tall and strong. A leader. Smart and quick.

But with those dimples. Those adorable dimples and the wavy, brown hair. Is he to die for? Yes.

She thought about the way he held her so tightly, as if she were his prisoner. And she thought about his kisses, tender for only a second, and then so hard, so hard and passionate, they hurt.

Blood on my lips. As if he *wanted* to hurt me.

Cruel kisses. Exciting and frightening at the same time.

Like Patrick.

And now Harrison came trotting up to her, jamming his car keys into his jeans. He flashed her a smile. "Hey, Dee. Am I late?"

"No. Right on time."

"You look great."

"Thanks."

He motioned to the movie theater. "So you want to see something tonight?"

Livvy wrapped her arm in his. She licked her lips. "Wouldn't you rather take a walk?"

Chapter Thirty-four
Destiny and Patrick

Destiny balanced the cordless phone on her shoulder as she used her hands to check the oven. "Dad, I thought you were coming home tonight," she said into the phone.

"I can't, Dee." Dr. Weller sounded tired, his voice hoarse. "We're down to the crunch here."

"The crunch? What do you mean?"

"Sunday night is the full moon. My hunters and I are going into that abandoned apartment building at dawn Monday morning. I've got to get everyone prepared. I—"

"Hold on a sec, Dad," Destiny said. "Mikey's pizza is burning."

She pulled on oven mitts and lifted the pizza tray from the oven. Then she carried it over to the white Formica kitchen counter. "Hey, Mikey—it's almost dinnertime!" she shouted. "It just has to cool."

She lifted the phone back to her ear. "Dad?

Are you still there? I'm terrified about this whole thing. Do you really have to go into that building?"

Destiny never told her father that she'd already been inside it. Never told him how strange and frightening it was with vampires—dozens of them—settled in the empty apartments.

She knew he'd be furious that she took such a risk.

But now *he* was determined to take an even bigger risk. To attack the vampires in the building at dawn as they slept, to kill as many as he could.

"Dad, do you really think these vampires will just keep on sleeping as you wipe them out one by one? Don't you think they might fight back?"

A long silence at the other end.

"We've taken all precautions," he replied finally. "We'll be heavily armed against them. We're going to surprise them, Dee. They won't know what hit them."

"But, Dad—"

"I can't talk about it, Dee. When is Mrs. Gilly supposed to come take care of Mikey?"

"At seven. I hope she comes on time. I'm going out tonight."

"With Harrison?"

"No. A new guy. I met him at the diner."

Why am I going out with a new guy? What about Harrison? What if he finds out? Why did I say yes to Patrick?

Destiny couldn't remember.

"Well, make sure Mikey eats his dinner," Dr. Weller said. "And tell him—"

Destiny's phone beeped.

"Dad, I have another call. Can you hold on one sec?"

She pressed the flash button and waited for the second caller to come on. "Hello?"

"It's Mrs. Gilly, Dee. Hi."

"Oh, hi. I have my dad on the other line, so—"

"I'm terribly sorry. I can't come tonight to take care of Mikey. My cousin Jill is sick, and I have to hurry over there."

"Oh." Destiny's brain raced. That means I can't go out. I have to stay and take care of Mikey. "Sorry about your cousin. Thanks for calling."

Mrs. Gilly hung up after a few more apologies.

Mikey entered the room, stood on tiptoes to sniff the pizza on the counter, and went to the fridge. "Sit down," Destiny told him. "I'll slice your pizza for you."

She realized she'd forgotten about her dad. She clicked the phone. "Are you still there? Mrs. Gilly can't come. I'll stay with Mikey."

"What about your date?" Dr. Weller asked. "Can you call him?"

"Uh . . . no." Why didn't she get Patrick's cell number? "Guess I'll just have to tell him when he gets here. Well . . . bye, Dad. I'd better—HEY!"

She let out a shout as she saw the red liquid puddling over the kitchen floor.

"Mikey—stop it! Are you crazy? Dad—he's pouring a big can of tomato juice on the floor. Mikey—stop! Put it down!"

"It isn't juice!" Mikey screamed. "It's BLOOD! It's BLOOD!"

Patrick arrived a little after seven-thirty. Destiny met him at the door. "Ready to rock?" he asked, flashing her his smile. He wore a black T-shirt under an open white sport shirt, straight-legged black denims.

Destiny shook her head. "I'm really sorry, Patrick. I didn't know how to get in touch with you. I have to stay and take care of my little brother."

Patrick's smile faded. "Oh. Wow. I'm sorry." His dark eyes flashed. "Hey, no problem. I'll stay and take care of the little guy with you."

Destiny could hear Mikey up in his room shouting about something. She had to fight him away to clean up the tomato juice. Then he refused to eat his pizza because he said the pepperonis were bugs.

"I don't think so," she told Patrick. "Mikey's being really difficult tonight. I think he needs *all* my attention."

Patrick sighed. Destiny felt the weight of his eyes on her. And once again she began to feel as if she were floating off the ground.

"How about Sunday night, Destiny?" Patrick asked. His voice seemed so muffled and far away. "Sunday is the night of the full moon. We could have fun Sunday night. Are you free?"

Destiny tried to focus, but everything was a blur. Finally, she turned away, lowered her gaze from his, and started to feel normal again.

"Yes. Sunday night," she repeated. "Okay,

Patrick. Sorry about tonight. See you Sunday."

She started to close the door, but Patrick pulled it open again. He brought his face close to hers, and once again she fell under the spell of his eyes.

"I'm going to drink your blood Sunday night," Patrick whispered. "And you will drink mine. We'll have such a nice night, Destiny."

Then he wiped her mind clean and pulled his face from hers.

"Sounds great," Destiny said. "Can't wait, Patrick. See you Sunday."

Chapter Thirty-five

An Evil Creature of the Night

"Whoa! I feel great!"

Harrison came bursting into the diner. He started dancing in front of Destiny, shaking his booty, hands high above his head.

Destiny stood behind the counter, a stack of dirty plates in her hands.

"I feel great! I feel so great!" Harrison exclaimed.

A few customers laughed. Mr. G. stuck his head out through the window from the kitchen. "You're the fry cook, remember?" he called. "Not the entertainment. Get back here before you scare all my customers away."

Grinning, Harrison ducked under the counter. He took the stack of plates from Destiny and kissed her on the cheek.

"Harrison, are you losing it?" she whispered. "What's your problem?"

"I'm in a totally awesome mood," he said.

"Is that a problem?"

He tried to kiss her again. Destiny saw Mr. G. watching them and slid away.

Harrison handed the dirty plates through the window to Mr. G. Destiny picked up her order pad and went to talk to two customers in the booth near the window.

When she returned, Harrison was still grinning at her. He brought his face close to hers. "That was great last night," he whispered.

She stared at him. "Excuse me?"

"Order?" Mr. G. poked his head out the window.

"Oh, yeah." Destiny lowered her eyes to her pad. "Two All-Americans with ham, hold the potatoes, white toast."

She pulled down two white coffee mugs, moved to the coffee-maker, and filled them with the steaming hot coffee. She put the mugs on a tray with a small milk pitcher and carried it to the two men in the booth.

Harrison grinned at her again. "Didn't you hear me? I just said I had a great time last night. That was really so totally excellent. I mean—"

Destiny narrowed her eyes at him. "Have you lost your mind? Last night?"

Oh, no. She had a sudden feeling of dread. It tightened her stomach and made her head spin for a moment.

Last night?

And then she saw the two tiny red points on Harrison's throat.

And she knew.

Livvy. Again.

Livvy was coming after Harrison. First Ari, now Harrison.

But why?

Didn't Ross tell Livvy how much I still care about her? That I'll do anything to help her and bring her back to us? Didn't Ross tell her?

Why is she going after Harrison?

Destiny spun away from him. She couldn't bear to see the two wounds on his neck.

There's only one reason why Livvy is doing this, she decided. She trembled so hard she had to grab the counter to hold herself up. Only one reason . . .

She is beyond saving. She has truly become one of them . . . an evil creature of the night.

Chapter Thirty-six
An Unexpected Murder

"Does my hair look okay?" Livvy asked. "I never realized I'd miss mirrors so much."

"It looks fine," Monica said, brushing the back of Livvy's hair with her hand. "That purple lipstick looks really hot."

Livvy snickered. "It used to drive my family crazy. One night my dad asked me why I wanted to look like a Halloween witch."

Suzie sighed. "You were lucky. My dad never paid that much attention to me. He'd never comment on my lipstick or . . . anything."

"I miss my mom and dad," Monica said, turning to the window. "They didn't deserve me. They deserved someone better."

Livvy gave her a gentle shove. "Hey, don't get down on yourself. You have your good qualities, you know. You're a really good friend. You're kind. You're generous . . ."

"And I'm a vampire," Monica said. She

shrugged. "I made my choice, right? But sometimes I wonder."

"You're just hungry," Suzie said, adjusting the top of her striped tube top. "We're all hungry."

"Party night!" Livvy exclaimed.

"*Every* night is party night, right?" Monica said, but without much enthusiasm.

"Hey, are you still feeding on that guy, Alby?" Livvy asked.

Suzie grinned. "Yeah. Both of us. Monica and I have been sharing him." She giggled. "He doesn't have a clue."

"Tomorrow night is the full moon," Livvy said, carefully applying purple eye shadow over her lids.

"Duh. Tell us about it," Monica said.

Livvy turned to them. "Are you going to make Alby a vampire?"

Suzie shrugged. "Why not? He's so cute."

Monica turned to Livvy. "What about that mystery guy you've been chasing after?"

"He's toast," Livvy replied. "Tomorrow night, he starts to live the good life."

Monica squinted at her. "Is he really hot? Why are you so into him?"

An evil smile spread slowly over Livvy's pale face. "Because he was my sister's boyfriend." She laughed.

Monica shook her head. "Weird. All three of us still have family problems."

Livvy shook her head. "No problem," she said softly. "No problem at all."

As a bat, Livvy swooped low over her old house. Through the front window, she glimpsed Destiny. Destiny on the couch and beside her . . . yes, Harrison.

Lucky guy.

Harrison with his arm around Destiny, the glow of the television washing over them, bathing them in dull reds and blues.

Ah, look. The two of them cuddling together.

What a sweet scene. Enjoy it, Harrison. Tomorrow night you will be mine. And Destiny will be Patrick's. And it will all change.

Your world will end. And a new one will begin.

Livvy raised her wings and swooped higher. One circle of the house, she thought. A house I'll never enter again.

The light was on in Mikey's room but the curtains covered the window. Livvy circled again and perched on the narrow window ledge outside her old room above the garage. The room Destiny and I shared . . . before the murdering . . . before the blood began to flow . . . before the *hunger*.

She saw her bed, carefully made. Her old stuffed leopard standing on the pillowcase as if on guard. The shelves of CDs against the wall beneath her Radiohead poster.

She felt a sudden pang—of what? Sadness? Loneliness? Longing for her old life?

No way.

No way. I don't feel anything. I'm just hungry, that's all.

But she pictured Ross. Sitting on the edge of her bed, the two of them wrapped up in each other. Her hands in his hair. His arms tight around her. Kissing her . . . kissing her for so long, until they were both breathless, until their lips were dry and chapped. Kissing and then . . .

No!

I don't want to remember any of this. I don't feel anything. Not anything.

She kicked off with her spindly bat legs,

flapped her wings hard, feeling the warm air against her skin, and soared away from the house, high into the charcoal night sky.

She flew low over the trees, breathing the warm air, refreshing herself, sending all thoughts away, except for the thought of feeding. And on the edge of town, where the last tiny cottages stood, a few blocks from the rock quarry, she found a guy just waiting to feed her.

He stood beside his Harley motorcycle at the curb, shiny blue helmet in his hand, the light from the streetlamp revealing his shaved head, the bushy, dark mustache spread over his lips. Black vest over a black T-shirt, tight black jeans. Cowboy boots with big heels.

Livvy landed on the sidewalk in the next block and quickly transformed into her own body. She straightened her short skirt over her bare legs, adjusted her halter, and strolled up to the chopper dude.

"Hey, what's up?" she asked, gazing into his narrow, brown eyes.

He shrugged his broad shoulders.

The guy must work out twenty hours a day, Livvy thought. But he won't be strong enough to fight me off.

He grinned at her and patted the seat of the motorcycle. "Lookin' for a ride?"

"Not really."

She lowered her head and bulled into him and knocked him onto his back before he even realized what was happening. The blue helmet bounced down the sidewalk.

He let out a groan and started to lift himself to his feet. But Livvy was on top of him and sank her fangs into the tender skin under his chin. A howl of pain burst from his open mouth. But it faded to a whisper as Livvy began to drink.

A few seconds later, he was sprawled on his back, whimpering like a frightened dog. Livvy had his arms pressed against the pavement. Her hair spread over his face as she drank, making loud sucking, lip-smacking sounds, grunting softly with pleasure as the thick, warm liquid oozed down her throat.

She stopped before she had her fill. She never could drink enough to be satisfied. That was the curse of it all, she knew. Never to be satisfied. Always to need more.

She climbed to her feet and wiped blood off her chin with the back of her hand. The guy lay sprawled on his back, half on the curb, half in the street. His eyes were shut and he was still whimpering.

Humming to herself, Livvy strode down the sidewalk a few yards, picked up his helmet, carried it back, and placed it on the guy's stomach. She licked her lips. She loved the taste of dried blood, so sharp and sweet at the same time.

"Bye, cutie." She transformed to a bat once again and took off without looking back.

She returned to the apartment building early. Dawn was still a few hours away.

I need my beauty sleep, she decided. Tomorrow night is the full moon—and my night to shine. A big night for Harrison, and for my sister. I want to be ready for it.

She stepped into the building in human form and made her way up the dimly lit staircase. On the first floor, rats scampered through piles of garbage. A tall stack of old newspapers teetered in the late-night breezes.

As Livvy walked past open apartment doors, she heard low moans, groans, and whispers. Orange light flickered in the apartment that Suzie and Monica shared.

Were they back? Were they still awake?

Livvy heard a scuffling sound. A hard *thud* from deep in the apartment.

Curious, she stepped into the doorway and squinted into the flickering light.

Oh, no. She pressed both hands over her mouth to stifle her cry.

Monica lay on her back on the floor, fully dressed, one shoe on, one off. Her hands outstretched, legs apart—a wooden stake standing straight up. A wooden stake through her chest. Monica's head tilted at a harsh angle, eyes still open.

No. Oh, no.

Monica murdered in her own apartment.

Hands still pressed to her mouth, Livvy heard noises in the bedroom.

A scraping sound. A groan. A sharp cry.

A shiver of terror rolled down Livvy's body.

The murderer—he was still in the apartment!

Chapter Thirty-seven
The Real Murderer

*H*er legs rubbery and weak, Livvy staggered forward a few feet. Holding her breath, she stepped over one of Monica's outstretched legs. Fighting off her panic, she moved silently to the bedroom doorway. And peered inside.

Her breath caught in her throat when she saw the struggle in the bedroom. She pressed her back against the wall and watched in silent horror as Patrick and Suzie battled.

"You're weak!" he cried, his face red, eyes bulging with anger. "You're too weak. I can't let the weak ones survive!"

He slammed her into the wall as if she were weightless. Suzie bounced off, let out a painful groan, and fell onto her back on the cot.

Before she could move, Patrick raised a pointed stake high over her body—and with both hands, swung it down hard. Suzie let out a shrill scream as the stake penetrated her chest, drove through her heart, and poked out of her back with a loud sucking sound.

No! Livvy thought, frozen in terror, unable to move, unable to take her eyes away. *She's my friend . . . my friend!*

Suzie writhed and kicked, her hands and feet thrashing the air like a pinned insect. Patrick held the stake, thrust it deeper through her chest, gripping it with both hands, sliding it through her body.

Another cry from Suzie, weaker this time. She grabbed at the stake, tried to shove it away. But her strength was fading. And her body was beginning to disintegrate.

Her skin peeled off quickly. Large chunks fell off her arms, her face. Her eyeballs dropped from their sockets and rolled across the room. The flesh of her cheeks and forehead melted away, revealing bone underneath.

Her skeletal arms still grabbed for the stake, thrashed and swiped at it—until the bone began to disintegrate.

Livvy gaped in horror as Suzie's skull crumbled into powder. Her arms—just gray bone now—fell motionless to the floor and crumbled to chunks, then powder. In a few seconds, her crumpled clothing lay spread on the floor, no body inside, a few ashes blowing in the breeze from the window.

She was older than I thought, Livvy realized. So old she crumbled to ashes. She . . . she didn't deserve to die like this.

"Too weak," Patrick muttered, heaving the stake angrily against the wall. "I can't allow the weak ones to stay. I can't!"

A soft cry escaped Livvy's lips.

Did he hear it?

She didn't wait to see. She spun away and started to run. Stumbling over Monica's body in the living room, she caught her balance, and kept running.

She darted frantically down the long hall, tripping over garbage and piles of newspaper. Breathing hard by the time she reached the stairs, she grabbed the metal rail and pulled herself up, forced her legs to carry her higher.

Gasping for breath, she reached the second floor, and ran blindly to her apartment halfway down the hall. Into the warm darkness, a hot breeze from the open window area.

Into the darkness and safety of the bedroom where she stood shivering, hugging herself tightly. She shut her eyes and gritted her teeth, forcing her body to stop its trembling.

But she couldn't shut out the picture of Patrick, shoving the stake through Suzie's chest, the fury that twisted his face, the sick sound the stake made as it poked through Suzie's body. Her bony hands in the air as if begging . . . begging for mercy.

Livvy's stomach lurched. She felt sick. She stumbled to the glassless window hole, leaned out, and vomited up some of the blood she had drunk—her dinner. It had tasted so sweet going down. Now it sickened her, sour and acid.

Still gagging, she heard a sound behind her. Wiping her mouth with the back of her hand, she turned to the door.

Patrick?

No. The footsteps passed. Some other vampire returning home after a night of feeding.

Livvy kicked off her shoes and climbed into bed. She pulled the blanket over her head and tried to stop shaking. But how could she stop thinking about her two dead friends?

Patrick. Patrick murdered them.

He's weeding out the weak.

And that means . . . *Patrick killed Ross*.

Buried under her blanket as if in a dark, warm cocoon, Livvy's mind whirred. It was becoming clear to her. The horror of her situation. The danger she was in.

It all began to come clear.

Destiny didn't murder Ross. Patrick murdered Ross because he was weak. Because he wanted to see his parents, because he was homesick.

Patrick is the murderer. He is killing his own.

Destiny is innocent. She probably came here to warn me. Or just to plead with me to give up this life and come home so Dad can cure me.

And now I've agreed to let Patrick go after Destiny, to let him turn my sister into a vampire, too. And I agreed to trick her boyfriend into exchanging blood and becoming an immortal.

Livvy gasped. It's all a test. Patrick is testing me.

And do I have a choice? I have to go through with it.

If I try to stop Patrick from attacking Destiny, then he will know that I am weak.

And he will kill me too.

Part Seven

Night of the Full Moon

Chapter Thirty-eight
Harrison's Big Date

*H*arrison gazed up at the full moon as he pulled his car to a stop. The moon floated low in the blue-black evening sky. It had rained earlier in the day. And now the moonlight was reflected in dozens of puddles and tiny pools all along the road, making the whole earth seem to sparkle.

Unreal.

Harrison slapped his hands on the steering wheel in rhythm to the dance music beat on the car stereo. He sang along, waiting for the light to change to green.

He thought about Destiny. Also unreal.

Picturing her made his heartbeats drum, almost as fast as the music. She had been different lately. So much needier. So much sexier.

Harrison flashed back to the other night. Destiny kissing him, kissing him so passionately, pressing herself against him, moving her hands through his hair.

And making those little sighs, the soft moans. Kissing his face . . . his neck. Yes. Kissing his neck.

It was all so unreal.

Harrison touched the little bite marks on his throat. Destiny had really gotten carried away.

Man, she was suddenly so *hot*!

The light changed. Harrison lowered his foot to the gas pedal. He couldn't wait to see her tonight. She had promised him something special.

Something special . . .

He knew what that meant. And now, his heartbeats were drumming *faster* than the music on the radio!

He turned onto Union Street. He could see the entrance to the mall up ahead. They planned to meet where they met last time in front of the Cineplex.

Harrison brought the car around to the front of the movie theater and ducked his head to search for Destiny through the passenger window.

No. Not here. Where was she?

He checked the dashboard clock. Eight-thirty-six.

Destiny said she'd be here at eight-thirty.

Yes. Eight-thirty. She said she had a nice surprise for him. But she wanted to give it to him when the full moon was high in the sky.

Unreal.

What did the full moon have to do with anything? Why was Destiny being so mysterious?

He glanced up at the moon. Higher in the sky now, more golden than orange, with a single wisp of black cloud cutting it off in the middle.

"Dee, where are you?"

He drove past the theater, turned and pulled into a parking place between two SUVs. He drummed his fingers on the wheel. Checked his wallet to make sure he'd remembered to bring some money. Gazed up at the full moon again, hazy behind a thin film of cloud. Then back at the clock—eight-forty-five.

Destiny was always on time. This was not like her.

Leaving the car running, Harrison climbed out and stood in front of it, searching under the bright lights at the front of the Cineplex. He saw a short line of people in front of the box office. Two teenage girls waiting for someone at the side of the theater.

No one else. No Destiny.

I want my special surprise, Destiny. I want you to keep your promise. Where are you? You don't want to keep me here in suspense, do you?

He took a few steps away from the car. "Hey—!" He saw a couple of guys he knew going into the theater. He waved to them and called out, but they didn't see him. They vanished inside.

Harrison strode back to the car and dropped behind the wheel. Almost nine o'clock. Maybe she got hung up. Maybe she couldn't make it for some reason. No. She'd call. Maybe she was in an accident or something.

Harrison sighed. He hated to wait for people. It always made him very tense. Most of his friends showed up half an hour late to everything, and it drove him crazy. He was always on time. That probably drove his friends crazy!

He picked up his cell phone. He stared at it for a few moments. Nine-oh-seven on the clock. He punched in Destiny's cell number. And listened to four rings. Then her voicemail message: "This is Destiny. Leave a message, okay?" The long beep.

He clicked off the phone.

Where is she?

He tried her cell number again. Maybe the phone was buried in her bag, and she didn't hear it. Again, he listened to four rings. When her message came on, he clicked off the phone and tossed it onto the seat.

He climbed out of the car, slamming the door behind him. He paced back and forth in front of the movie theater for a while.

At nine-thirty, he climbed back into the car. He gazed up at the full moon, high in the sky now, a bright, silvery circle. Then he backed out of the parking place.

Where are you, Destiny? Did you stand me up?

That's so not like you.

Harrison felt his muscles tighten, felt a weight in the pit of his stomach. This wasn't like Destiny at all.

Something must be wrong. Something must be terribly wrong.

He sped out of the mall and turned left on Union Street.

He decided to drive to Destiny's house. He had to find out what was going on.

Chapter Thirty-nine

Destiny Surprises Patrick

Patrick couldn't take his eyes off Destiny's throat.

The skin pale and smooth, like velvet. Her neck long and straight. He could taste it. He could taste that spot just under her chin, that soft spot without muscle where the veins ran free and close to the skin.

As they danced, he watched the veins throb, a subtle blue against the smooth, soft skin. She said something to him, shouting over the loud music. But he didn't hear her. He was concentrating so hard on the tiny, throbbing veins, on her delicious throat.

Soon, Destiny, you and I will be together forever, he thought, returning her smile.

The beat changed as the DJ worked his mix. Destiny changed her rhythm and Patrick changed with her, moving his body slowly now, bumping against her. Any excuse to touch her. Eyes on her throat. If only he could sink his teeth into that soft skin right this minute and drink . . . drink until she moaned and sighed.

He knew the full moon was high in the sky by now. The dance club had no windows. But Patrick could *feel* the moon above him. His excitement rose with the moon. And so did his hunger.

Destiny's face held its smile as she danced under the flashing lights over the dance floor. She's gentler than her sister, Patrick decided. She has a sweetness about her—an innocence?—that Livvy doesn't have.

He wondered how Livvy was doing with Destiny's boyfriend, Harrison. She seemed so eager to go after him, so eager to take him under the moonlight and turn him into a vampire.

Did she hate her sister *that* much?

Patrick wondered why. He wondered why one twin chose the vampire life—and the other had to be forced into it.

Tonight . . .

I will force her tonight. She won't know what is happening until it is too late.

What drove the sisters apart? Why does

Livvy carry such anger against her twin?

And then as he danced, his thoughts changed, and he thought about the group of vampires he had joined. So many weaklings and fools who were endangering the whole group. Patrick knew the Hunters were organizing. He knew the Hunters would soon find their hiding place and try to drive them out.

He had to weed out the weaklings before the battle began.

He intended to win this battle. For nearly a hundred years, he had been driven from town to town. Forced to flee, to hide.

No more.

He intended to take a stand here. If the Hunters think they can chase us away so easily, bring them on. We'll be ready.

But first, he had to make sure everyone was strong.

Will you come through for me tonight, Livvy? Will you complete the job on Harrison? Or will you let him go, and prove that you are also one of the weaklings?

Patrick knew he didn't want to kill Livvy. He was attracted to her, drawn to her—to her sister too. But if he had to, he would kill Livvy the same way he had killed her friends.

We're going to be strong, strong enough to kill any Hunters that invade our homes.

He turned to Destiny. He realized she was squeezing his arm. "Patrick, what's wrong? You have such an unhappy look on your face."

"I . . . was thinking about something," he said. He took her hand and led her off the dance floor. "Enough dancing? I've worked up a real sweat." He picked up a cocktail napkin from the bar and mopped his forehead.

"That DJ is great," Destiny said. "That's why I like this club."

"Let's get some fresh air," Patrick said. He guided her through the crowd and out the front door. He heard shouts and saw a group of people in the parking lot. "What's going on?"

They followed the path to the parking lot. "An accident," Destiny said. "Someone backed an SUV into that Mini."

"Ooh." Patrick made a face. "The Mini is wrecked. Why didn't the SUV pick on someone his own size?"

A tall man in a wrinkled suit was screaming at the parking valet and shaking his fist in the air. Two women were screaming at him.

"Let's get out of here," Patrick said. He glanced up at the full moon. "It's such a nice night. Would you like to take a walk?"

Destiny smiled and took his arm. "Nice. Do you know Drake Park?"

He shook his head. "Not really."

"There's a path I like to walk. It's real pretty at night, especially under a full moon." Destiny glanced up at the moon too. "It leads to a pretty little creek."

"Let's go," Patrick said. He suddenly felt so hungry, he wiped a gob of drool off his chin and hoped Destiny didn't see.

They drove to Drake Park. Patrick kept a hand gently on her shoulder as they made their way along the twisting, dirt path, through thickets of tangled trees and low shrubs, to the creek.

As they walked, Destiny talked about her job at the diner, about her father, a veterinarian, and about her little brother, Mikey. Patrick didn't listen. His hunger had become a roar in his ears, like a pounding ocean wave crashing again and again.

He couldn't hear her. He could think only of

his thirst, of the gnawing in his stomach, the ache . . . the ache . . .

The moon had risen high in the sky. It filled the creek with silver light that made the narrow, trickling stream shimmer and glow.

Destiny took his hand. She gazed at the sparkling water. "Isn't it beautiful?"

"Yes," he managed. He knew he couldn't hold back much longer. "Yes, it is."

She squeezed his hand. "With the moon lighting the water, it's almost as bright as day."

"Yes," he agreed again. His fangs slid down over his lips.

Destiny was staring at the creek. "I've done all the talking," she said. "You haven't told me a thing about yourself."

"Well . . ." His brain was spinning now. All dazzling bright lights and wild, throbbing music. The hunger so strong he wanted to toss back his head and howl.

Instead, he grabbed Destiny by the shoulders. Lowered his face to her throat. Dug his fangs deep into the soft flesh of her throat.

He dug deeper, making loud sucking sounds, holding her tightly, pressing his forehead into her chin.

And then with a cry of disgust, he staggered back. Dizzy, his stomach heaving. "Noooooo." A sick moan escaped his throat. He lurched away from her, bent over, and started to retch.

"You're . . . not . . . Destiny," he whispered when he could finally talk. He stood up straight and shook himself.

She hadn't moved the whole while. Moonlight washed over her, making her blond hair gleam, making it appear that she was standing in a spotlight.

"You're Livvy, aren't you," he accused.

"Patrick, you're such an ace," she replied. "Really sharp. You just pick up on things so fast, don't you?"

He stared at her in disgust, holding his hands in front of him as if shielding himself from her. "What are you doing here, Livvy?"

"My sister decided she didn't want to go out with you. She said you're just not her type. But I didn't want you to be lonely."

Patrick narrowed his eyes at her. "Are you crazy?" He pointed to the moon. "You know you have an assignment tonight."

Livvy shrugged.

His anger grew quickly. "Don't you realize how dangerous it is to play this trick on me? To disobey me? What about Harrison, Livvy? What about your assignment?"

"Oh, I stood him up. I gave myself a new assignment," she said. Her body tensed. Her smile faded.

Patrick scowled. "What the hell are you talking about?"

"I brought something from home," Livvy said. "I brought it out here to the woods earlier . . . just for you. A surprise."

She bent behind a tree, grabbed something in both hands, and swung to face him.

"It's the stake," Livvy said, her voice trembling now, her face tight with fury. "The stake you used to kill my friends."

Patrick's hands flew up. His eyes bulged in shock.

She raised the stake high—and, with a loud cry, thrust it into his chest.

But he moved quickly, stumbling back. He grabbed the stake before it could penetrate his skin. Grabbed it in both hands and struggled to wrench it away from Livvy.

He caught her off-balance, still moving forward in her attempt to stab him. Now she gripped one end of the stake, and he gripped the other.

Patrick swung the stake hard and sent her spinning against a tree.

Livvy let out a cry as the stake flew out of her hands.

She shoved herself off the tree trunk and spun to face Patrick.

"Nice try," he said breathlessly. "But not nice enough."

He raised the stake in both hands—and cracked it in half over his thigh. Then he kept the pointed end and tossed away the other half.

"I've given *myself* a new assignment," he said, moving in on Livvy. He raised the pointed stake in one fist. "Can you guess what it is?"

Chapter Forty-one
A Vampire Must Die

He brought the stake down hard and fast, aimed at Livvy's heart.

She transformed into a bat, and the point sailed past her, barely grazing a wing. With a loud screech, she brought her wings up and sailed over Patrick's head. Then she stuck out her talons—and swooped down.

Hissing and shrieking, she scratched at his eyes.

He let out a cry of pain and stumbled back.

She scraped his cheeks with her talons. Blood streamed down his face.

With a groan, he swiped her hard with the back of his hand. His hand caught her in the belly, knocking her air out.

Stunned, Livvy toppled to the ground.

She gazed up in time to see Patrick raise a shoe to trample her. She scuttled out just as the heel slammed the ground.

Flapping her wings hard, she shot back into the air. He had dropped the stake and was bent, searching for it.

Livvy swooped to the ground behind him, transformed back into her own body, and grabbed up the stake as Patrick spun around.

"No—" he uttered as she slammed the stake with all her strength into his throat.

A sick cry burst from his open mouth as the stake poked through the skin, deep into his neck. His eyes bulged, and he grabbed for the stake with both hands.

But Livvy was too fast for him this time. She tugged the stake out, staring at the gaping hole in his neck. Then she slammed it into his body again, thrusting the point into his chest, into his heart.

He fell back, cracking his head on a tree trunk.

He didn't utter a sound. He stared up at Livvy as he collapsed onto his back. His legs folded, and his arms dropped limply to his sides, and didn't move.

A shaft of silver moonlight washed over the stake, tilted up in the air now as Patrick lay on his back, not moving. And then his skin started to melt and crumble away. Big chunks dissolving quickly, revealing the bones underneath.

Struggling to catch her breath, her chest heaving up and down, Livvy turned her back on him.

I don't want to see what happens to him.

I killed him.

I killed him because he killed my friends. And I killed him to save my sister.

Livvy felt upset now, confused. She didn't feel as if she'd scored any kind of victory.

What will happen next?

Her thoughts turned to Destiny.

Have I saved you tonight, Dee?

Or have I killed you too?

Chapter Forty-two
"One Last Kiss . . . Before I Kill You"

Dr. Weller stood trembling in the abandoned apartment building, listening to the screams of agony all around him.

Vampires were dying. His hunters were working fast, catching them while they slept in their open apartments, piercing their hearts with wooden stakes, and quickly moving to the next apartment.

Dr. Weller had trouble moving as quickly. He had killed one vampire in his bed, a young man with dried blood caked down his chin. He had thrust his pointed stake between the young man's ribs, watched him come awake, eyes bulging in disbelief. Listened to his scream of pain as he realized what had happened to him. Then watched him die.

He's not really a human, Dr. Weller told himself. He's a creature now, an evil creature in a human body. He preyed on living humans, innocent humans. He ruined lives. He deserves to die.

But now as the sun began to rise in the glassless windows of the unfinished building, Dr. Weller stood trembling in front of a low cot, unable to act, unable to move or think straight.

This is not a human, he told himself, staring at the sleeping girl in the long, black nightshirt. This is an evil creature now.

He gripped the stake tightly in his right hand. His left hand was raised to his feverish forehead.

This is an evil, inhuman creature now.

But she is my daughter.

He gazed down at Livvy, gazed through the tears that blurred his eyes, that ran down his cheeks. This is my daughter, and I have no choice—I have to kill her.

I am the leader of the Hunters, and I have vowed to rid Dark Springs of these blood-sucking killers.

A vampire murdered my wife, their mother.

And now I'm about to lose another precious family member to the evil ones.

Dr. Weller raised his eyes and cursed the sky.

His stomach tightened. For the second time that night he felt he might retch.

How can I kill my own daughter?

Could I ever face Destiny again? Mikey?

Could I ever tell them the truth: *I killed your sister. I killed Livvy with my own hands.*

I . . . I can't, Dr. Weller thought. He staggered back from the cot, his eyes on his sleeping daughter. Her blond hair flowed over the pillow. Her fair skin caught the glow of the red morning sun from the window.

I can't do this. It's asking too much of any man.

I'm not a coward. I'm a brave man. Here I am in this apartment building, risking my life, attacking vampires where they live. No, I'm not a coward.

But . . .

He heard a high, shrill scream from down the hall. A girl's scream. Another vampire murdered by one of his hunters.

A high wail of pain floated down the hall. Another victim of the hunters.

Dr. Weller gripped the walkie-talkie attached to his belt. So far, no calls for help. The operation seemed to be going flawlessly.

He sighed, staring down at his daughter's sleeping face.

I'm the one who should call for help.

I should call for one of my hunters. I should leave the room, whisper good-bye to Livvy, and leave the room. And let my hunter do the job we came here to do.

Can I do that?

Livvy stirred. She let out a soft sigh.

She turned toward him, eyes still closed.

It isn't really Livvy anymore, he decided. His heart began to thud in his chest. It isn't my daughter.

He took a deep breath. Raised the stake high.

Changed his mind.

I just want to kiss her good-bye.

Kiss her good-bye . . . before I kill her.

And as he leaned his tear-stained face down to kiss her cheek, Livvy's hands shot up—and grasped him tightly around the neck.

"LIVVY—NO!" he shouted. "LET GO!"

She opened her eyes. "Don't do anything, Dad!" she cried, holding onto his neck, wrapping her arms around his neck. "Don't, Dad! It isn't Livvy. It's me."

He blinked. Stared hard at her. "Destiny—?"

She nodded. She kissed his cheek, then let

go of his neck. "I'm sorry, Dad. I didn't want to scare you. But I had no choice. I—"

"Destiny?" he repeated. "Destiny?"

She nodded. "Yes, it's me. I traded places with Livvy. I had to save her life."

Chapter Forty-three
Thicker Than Blood

Later, Destiny explained to her father. "Livvy and I planned it all last night. She risked her life by taking my place with a vampire named Patrick."

"But why did you take her place in the apartment?" Dr. Weller asked.

"I had to," Destiny replied. "Livvy risked her life for me. I had to risk my life for her. It was the only way to prove to her how much I want to save her."

"You took a terrible risk," Dr. Weller said. He poured milk into his coffee mug, then slid the milk carton across the table to Destiny.

"We couldn't really say it out loud. But we showed how much we cared by risking our lives for each other," Destiny said. "Crazy, huh?" She poured milk into her mug and took a sip of coffee.

Dr. Weller stared at her across the kitchen

table, thinking hard. He raised his hands from around his coffee mug. "Look at me. I'm still shaking. We've been home for half an hour, and I can't stop shaking."

Destiny lowered her head. "I'm sorry, Dad."

He grabbed her hand. "No. Don't say that. You did a very brave thing tonight."

"So did Livvy," Destiny replied.

Dr. Weller nodded. Behind his glasses, his eyes teared over. "Twins," he murmured. "Twins stick together, right?"

Destiny took a long sip of coffee. "Yes. Being sisters meant a lot more to both of us than . . . than anything else."

"And you hatched this plan last night?" he asked.

"Last night," Destiny said. "Livvy flew into my window. She explained that she was furious at me. She told me about Ross. She—"

Destiny stopped. Her voice broke. She raised her eyes to her father. "Ross is dead, Dad. Killed by another vampire."

"Oh, no," Dr. Weller whispered. "No . . ."

Destiny nodded. "Yes, he's dead. I suppose we have to tell his family. Livvy thought I murdered him. That's why she was so angry."

Dr. Weller shook his head. "Ross dead," he murmured. "He was a good guy. And Livvy could be dead too. If only—"

"She may be okay, Dad. I'm sure I'll hear from her again."

"Tell her to come home," Dr. Weller said. "Tell her if she comes home, I'll work even harder on finding a cure. I'll do everything I can."

"I'll try, Dad. I'll try." She squeezed his hand. "But don't get your hopes up."

Destiny left out one part of the story. She didn't tell her father that she and Livvy planned to meet the next night in their room above the garage.

"Don't tell him," Livvy had insisted. "I'll come see you, but I just can't see Dad. Not yet."

Destiny had agreed. And now it was the next night. The night after the full moon and all the horror it brought.

Destiny paced back and forth in her room, clasping and unclasping her hands, feeling so tense she could barely think straight.

Did Livvy survive last night? Did she kill Patrick? Is she okay? Will she come? Will she

584

keep her promise?

Dr. Weller was working late at his lab. Mikey was closed up in his room watching Nickelodeon.

A warm breeze ruffled the curtains in the open window. Destiny heard a car horn honking far down the block. White moonlight washed into the room and slanted across the carpet.

Hugging herself, Destiny stepped into the square of moonlight. Cold moonlight, she thought. Moonlight is always so silvery hard and cold.

The curtains fluttered again. A blackbird landed gently on the sill. It shook itself, raising its wings, then hopped onto the bedroom floor.

Destiny jumped back. The bird tilted its head, gazing up at her with its shiny black bead of an eye.

"Livvy—?" Destiny whispered.

The blackbird transformed quickly, its body rising, arms poking out where the wings had been . . . a head . . . blond hair. All so quick and silent.

In seconds, Livvy stood across from Destiny. She brushed back her hair and glanced around the long, narrow room they had shared. "You . . . haven't changed a thing," Livvy said. She picked up her stuffed leopard and pressed it against her cheek. "Everything is the same."

Destiny stared at her sister. Livvy wore a tight white midriff blouse over a black miniskirt. Long, red plastic earrings dangled from her ears. She had a tiny rhinestone stud in the side of her nose.

A laugh escaped Destiny's throat. "You haven't changed, either," she said. "I mean, you look exactly the same."

Livvy frowned. "I've changed a lot, Dee. Don't think I'm the same old Livvy." She tossed the leopard onto the bed.

"You . . . you're okay?" Destiny asked. "I mean, last night—"

"I killed him. I killed Patrick," Livvy said. "See? I'm not the same. I've *killed*, Dee. Do you believe it? I've killed."

Destiny let out a sob. "I'm just so glad you're okay." She rushed to her sister. They hugged, hugged each other tightly, pressing their cheeks against each other. Destiny's cheek was damp from her tears. Livvy didn't cry.

A voice from downstairs made them jump apart.

"Hey, who you talking to?" Mikey called up.

Livvy's eyes grew wide. She took a step toward the window. Destiny could see she was thinking of escape.

"No," she whispered to Livvy. "Let Mikey see you. He needs to see you and talk to you. You can help him, Liv."

Livvy looked doubtful, but she stayed.

"Come here, Mikey." Destiny went down and guided Mikey up the steps. "Livvy is here. She came back because she wants to see you."

As she and Mikey walked up the stairs, a feeling of panic swept over Destiny. Maybe this isn't such a good idea. Maybe Mikey will totally freak.

He stepped into the room. His eyes went from Destiny to Livvy. He froze.

"Mikey—" Destiny started.

Mikey took a few steps toward the two girls. He stared suspiciously at Livvy. He stopped a few feet away and studied her.

"Are you real?" he asked finally.

Livvy laughed. "Huh? Am I *what*?"

Mikey narrowed his eyes at her. "Are you real?" he repeated.

Livvy's expression softened. "Yes, Mikey, it's really me."

She hurried to him and wrapped him in a hug. Mikey burst into tears and began to sob at the top of his lungs.

"It's okay. It's okay," Livvy whispered, holding him. "It's okay, Mikey. Really. I love you. I still love you."

Destiny bit her bottom lip to keep from crying too. Would this help the poor little guy? Would it help him to know that Livvy was still around, still his sister, still loved him? Or would it make him even more sad and crazy?

Livvy held him until he stopped crying. Then he backed away from her, rubbing his eyes.

He studied her again. "Can you really fly?"

"No," she lied. "I'm just me. Really."

"But don't you fly and bite people in the neck?"

"No. I don't do that. That's *sick*," Livvy told him. "I . . . I just had to move out for a while. That's all."

He thought about what she said. Destiny couldn't tell if he believed Livvy or not.

"Are you coming back? Will you take me swimming?" he asked.

"Someday soon maybe. Not today," Livvy said.

They talked a while longer, with Livvy reassuring Mikey that she was normal and that someday she'd return. Livvy hugged Mikey again. Then Destiny took him to his room and put him to bed.

When she returned, Livvy stood staring out the window. "I have to go," she said. She shuddered. "Seeing Mikey . . . that was really hard."

"He seemed very happy," Destiny said. "I think maybe you helped him." She grabbed her sister's hand. "Don't go, Liv. I won't let you go again."

"Don't be stupid, Dee. I can't come back here. I've gone too far into the dark world. I can't return—even if I wanted to."

"Yes, you can," Destiny insisted. "Dad will find a cure. You *can* come back."

Livvy pushed Destiny's hand away. "Bye, Dee."

Her body began to shrink, so fast Destiny could hardly see the transformation. The wings sprouted . . . the black feathers . . . the spindly legs hopping on the carpet.

Livvy, a blackbird once again, jumped into the pool of silvery moonlight on the windowsill.

"Don't go! Please don't go!" Destiny shouted. She made a grab for the bird.

But Livvy took off, raised her wings high, and soared into the moonlight. Then she swerved sharply, and vanished into the darkness of the night.

"Don't go. Don't go. Don't go," Destiny whispered.

So close. I was so close to reaching Livvy, to convincing her to stay. So close . . .

She spun away from the window when she heard the doorbell downstairs.

She's back. She changed her mind. I *did* reach her!

Destiny raced down the stairs, taking them two at a time. She bolted through the kitchen, into the front hall.

The doorbell rang again.

"I'm coming. I'm coming, Liv."

Breathlessly, she pulled open the front door.

And stared at Harrison.

"Dee? Are you okay?"

She nodded. Struggled to catch her breath. "I ran the whole way from upstairs," she explained.

He squinted at her. "Where were you last

night? You were supposed to meet me, remember? How come you didn't show?"

"Last night?" Destiny sighed. She pulled him into the house. "Harrison, that's a very long story . . ."

Robert Lawrence Stine

is one of the best-selling children's authors in history. He began his writing career at the age of nine, writing short stories, joke books, and comic books for his friends—and has been at it ever since!

After graduating from Ohio State University, R.L. moved to New York to become a writer. He wrote joke books and humor books and created *Bananas*, a zany humor magazine, before he turned to the scary. He wrote Fear Street and then Goosebumps, the phenomenal series that made him an international celebrity and the number-one best-selling children's author of all time *(Guinness Book of World Records)*.

He recently published two original collections of scary stories—the *New York Times* best-seller NIGHTMARE HOUR and THE HAUNTING HOUR—and his book series The Nightmare Room, also published by HarperCollins, was adapted into a popular TV series.

R.L. lives in Manhattan with his wife, Jane. You can visit him online at www.rlstine.com.